the XANAROCK

Published in the UK in 2022 by Padica Publishing

Paperback ISBN 978-1-7396693-0-0
eBook ISBN 978-1-7396693-1-7

Cover design and typeset by SpiffingCovers

the
XANAROCK

PATRICK COLLINS

BOOK ONE OF THE *ASTRAL REVELATIONS* SERIES

About me

Ever since I can remember I have always had a fascination with books. I always remember being really young and writing short stories for my parents which they always said were brilliant but were probably completely rubbish (as parents do). Life got in the way, and I've never really thought about it growing up.

When I was 30 I remember listening to an audiobook on a long car journey to South Wales and thinking 'this isn't hard, I could do this,' so the next day I started jotting down a few notes. A few notes turned into a story, and a story turned into a fascinating universe of fun and wonderment. After 3 ½ years of juggling my family life, work, and trying to write a novel, I finally finished The Xanarock.

I love stretching my imagination and thinking outside of our metaphorical box of human understanding, but I love making people laugh too, so why not combine the two?

With a long series ahead in Astral Revelations, I know I'm going to be writing this for a long time into the future, but I couldn't think of anything more I'd want to be doing.

Dedications

This novel is dedicated to my wonderful wife and three amazing children, although if she divorces me at any point, feel free to omit her from this dedication. I received more support from them than I ever could have imagined as I know it must be hard when I lock myself away for hours on end to write.

I'd also like to thank everyone who has helped me along the way in getting this project completed, down to editing, cover design, and everything else I was clueless about.

CHAPTER ONE

Disappearance

I'm struggling to recall a time throughout my entire life when I've felt more content than I do at this particular moment. To say that these last few days have been perfect would be the understatement of the year. Compared to my previous twenty-eight years on this planet, I could honestly say that these last three years, since I met Lara, have been better than all the others combined, without a shadow of a doubt. I know a statement like that can be considered somewhat hyperbolic, but in this case, it's undeniably true. Okay, I can't remember a single thing before the age of eleven, but I'll blame the amnesia for that. The extent of what I recall, is waking in a hospital bed beside my mum and dad with an ear-splitting pain searing through my cranium. Apparently, my neighbour found me unconscious in a park near my house and called an ambulance because I'd been involved in some sort of accident. I can't recall a thing before that point in time, including how I ended up in that state. My parents have told me that I was on my way home from school, which was three streets away, and I never arrived. The amnesia was strange for the first few years, but eventually it became normality.

'Ow!' Lara exclaims, her head whacking against the door frame as we cross over the threshold. 'This is supposed to be romantic,' she whines, with her hand rubbing against her now injured head.

'Sorry, it's harder than you think trying to carry someone through a single door while they're lying sideways,' I retort.

Lara sends a glance my way, which resembles the look she gave me yesterday as we made eye contact when she appeared at the end of the aisle. A wayward smile, which sends goosebumps down my spine and lets me know she finds it funny, in turn, making me laugh out loud. I walk inside and plonk her onto the settee playfully. She's always had a knack of making me smile, whether it's voluntarily or involuntarily. I question every day what she sees in me as she's way out of my league; I'd probably put her in an adults' team and put me in the under twelves, but I'd be a fool to challenge her over it. She's almost six-feet tall, with long caramel-coloured hair that she's always tied back into a ponytail. Her physique could rival that of any gold medallist Olympian, and her piercing sky-blue eyes could light up even the darkest room. I, on the other hand, am slightly shorter than her, have dark brown hair that I sweep over to one side, and the most average, mundane, blue eyes that you could ever expect to see.

The decision to get married yesterday, on the day before Christmas Eve, was ultimately Lara's. She's always loved Christmas time, but I'm pretty sure the deciding factor was being able to have two Christmas dinners in the same week, as they gave us the option to serve it for our main course; she's always loved Christmas dinner.

The illumination from Lara's mobile phone screen lights her face with an enriching, heavenly aura in our cosy, yet small, living room. We don't live in a massive house by any means, but it's cosy enough for just the two of us. Once we have kids in a few years it might be worth trying to upsize, but it's good enough for now.

'Have you seen what one of the girls just sent me?' Lara asks, sounding utterly perplexed.

'Care to narrow that down a bit?' I reply in a derisive tone.

'Look at this picture from the wedding, do you remember seeing those people there?' Lara queries, almost forcing the device into my hand, pointing an elongated white-coloured fingernail at a particular spot on the screen.

Examining the screen with as much precision and concentration as I can, almost squinting to make out the figures in the background of the photograph, I use my fingers to zoom in and out on the screen. 'Are they pyjamas?' I ask in utter bewilderment at the three men huddled near the bar. 'I don't remember seeing them, but then again, as the night got later, I don't remember much if I'm completely honest. Probably just a bunch of students on a night out to one of those weird pyjama parties that decided to crash the wedding on the way.'

'I guess so, but the weird thing is, nobody else remembers seeing them either and they've turned up on a number of photographs,' Lara adds.

'Dunno, maybe they're vampires and they only show up through the lens of a camera,' I say in my spookiest of voices and using my fingers to imitate a creepy gesture. 'I'm going upstairs to get my Christmas pyjamas on, be back in five.'

The moonlight's shine illuminates the room iridescently as I draw the curtains in our bedroom. Out on the street, a courier is delivering a parcel to our neighbour's opposite. No doubt that would have been me if I hadn't booked the week off work for the wedding. My boss, John Weinzierl, Head of Distribution, was not one bit happy that I was taking a week off work over the busiest time of year, but there was no way I would have been able to work; Lara would have killed me. Being a courier is demanding work these days. I've been in this line of work now for almost five years, and I'm sure every Christmas time it gets twice as busy as the last. It doesn't make things easier when John demands that we have a ninety-nine per cent first-time delivery success rate so that customers receive their packages as quickly and efficiently as possible. I was so under pressure a few weeks back, that I left a parcel in a customer's wheelie bin as neither them nor their neighbours were home, but in my defence, how was I supposed to know it was refuse collection day? John wasn't happy one bit when they received the customer complaint. He did that thing he does where it looks as if steam if going to come out of his ears and his head is going to explode, but it never does, unfortunately. His face just turned into a huge tomato-coloured ball of fury. He informed me that there's an ongoing investigation due to me not following the correct delivery process, but they'd support me as much as they can throughout as head office may want to take the complaint further.

Fetching my pyjamas from the wooden chest of drawers at the end of our bed, I begin getting dressed into my pyjamas and nightgown, but midway through, the sound of our doorbell interrupts me. Who on earth could be visiting us at this time on Christmas Eve? I didn't notice anybody walking down the path through the window a moment ago.

Reaching the bottom step of our cream-coloured carpeted staircase, it doesn't surprise me one bit to see the glow still lighting up Lara's features. I'll bet any money that she's messaging her friends gossiping about the wedding, discussing who was wearing the worst dress, and who made the biggest idiot of themselves because they'd had one too many.

'I'll get it, don't bother getting up,' I comment to Lara jeeringly.

'Thanks love, you're a star,' she replies in a deadpan tone, the noise of her prodding fingers on the screen still audible. She's not even listening, is she?

'Ho-Ho-Ho!' I call jovially as the cold air enters the house like a mid-winter blizzard. Our next-door neighbour, Gregory, stares back at me with a smile that runs from ear to ear.

'Congratulations young whippersnappers!' he bellows happily, forcing a small bunch of flowers into my hand. 'How did it all go? Not killed each other yet I see?' he chuckles. Gregory is a rather small, balding man, no taller than around five foot three, and he always seems to wear one of those trendy caps that old men wear that I've only ever seen in old movies. It's obvious he always tries to look smart, and today he's chosen to adorn a grey cardigan accompanied by brown cord trousers and a dashing black bow tie. 'I remember the day I got married, you've never saw love like it, I couldn't take my eyes off the lass all day. But still, I think the happiest day of my life was when she left, ha-ha!' he snorts, making me laugh out loud.

Gregory is a sweet old man, although I was shocked when he said he was only sixty-five as he has the traits of an eighty-year-old. He's that kind of old man that you'd love as a grandad due to his inappropriate jokes and infectious cheeriness. He's cornered me a few times with his quirky stories of when he used to be an astronaut, but it's hard to tell if he's winding me up or telling the truth. No doubt this would certainly be a contributing factor as to why I always catch him sitting outside on the front lawn staring at the sky in deep concentration. One day last week, I came home from work and he was lying on his car bonnet engrossed with the night sky above, not even noticing me as I arrived in the driveway and passed him to enter our house.

'Thanks Gregory, they're lovely,' Lara says thankfully, making her way over to the door from the settee. The splashing of running water fills the room as Lara places the flowers into the kitchen sink.

'I was just wondering whether you would take me up on the offer of joining me for a cup of tea or coffee? Wouldn't want to leave an old man alone on Christmas Eve, would you? One of my nephews bought me some fancy coffee called *Kopi Luwak* or something or other. Apparently, they make it from monkey poo, but it's supposed to be absolutely divine,' he says informatively, still smiling. My first answer would have been no, but he had to give us the guilt trip and throw in that bit about leaving him alone on Christmas Eve, didn't he?

'Yeah sure,' I answer meekly. 'We'll have to be quick though. I've still got presents to wrap before we go to bed, but I think I'll pass on the poo coffee if you don't mind.'

'Let me just go and get my pyjamas on, can you give me five?' Lara asks, to which we both nod in agreement and she clip-clops up the stairs noisily. Still standing in the doorway, Gregory's focus now becomes the night sky outside, and he stares surreptitiously. After observing him for the next few seconds, I decide to join him in his assessment of the starry night. The winter air begins to swirl around my body and attack me from all angles now I'm dressed in pyjamas; I didn't notice how cold it was earlier when I was fully dressed. The muted silence is eerie on our housing estate, to the point where I sometimes wish there were families of nutters instead of respectful families because we could all use a bit of drama in our lives and nothing out of the ordinary happens.

'Isn't it amazing?' Gregory remarks, holding out his arms to the sky as if to embrace it like an old friend.

'Sure is,' I reply, mostly to be polite, but I can't help being transfixed at the flickering lights and impossible twinkles that envelop the ceiling above us in the ominous sky. A blanket of grey is making its way slowly towards us to block out part of the view.

'You see that one there?' He points a finger towards a cluster of small white sparkling stars. 'That's Neplio, and that one there,' he moves his finger to the right slightly, 'that's Macro. And that one just to the right is Szera.'

'Impressive. You really know your stars, don't you? I bet you miss being up there,' I reply, genuinely impressed with his knowledge of the night sky. For all I know though, he could be making the whole lot up and I'd be oblivious to whether it was correct or not. The view would probably be even more amazing if the residents of our street weren't obsessed with buying every Christmas light they can get hold of and battling it out like one of those cheesy festive movies and filling the atmosphere around us with light pollution.

We're interrupted by Lara appearing at the bottom of the stairs with a thick, bright pink, woolly dressing gown wrapped around her. 'I'll meet you over there in two minutes Gregory, I'll just put the heating on and get locked up, then we'll make our way over,' I add.

Gregory's mouth widens amiably to show every one of his teeth. The crunch of ice-covered grass beneath his feet makes me feel even colder as he heads towards his front door over the adjoining lawn.

Before I can process what's happening, I'm smothered by a pair of warm hands that grip around my midriff. The familiar scent of lime and cucumber fills my nostrils as caramel-coloured hair wraps around my cold face unintentionally. I hated this smell when she first started using it, but over time it's grown on me massively. Sometimes I find myself sniffing the bottles furtively in the supermarket like some kind of creepy stalker because it reminds me of her so much.

'I love you so much you know,' she whispers, her warm breath causing every hair on my neck to stand to attention. My mouth convulses into a beaming grin as a wave of happiness involuntarily washes over me.

'I love you too babe,' I reply with a hushed whisper, almost silently under bated breath. 'Promise you won't ever leave me. The thought of spending one day not by your side is unbearable. You are without doubt the best thing that's ever happened to me.' Lara's soft, silken fingers brush through mine as our hands intertwine, merging together like jigsaw pieces. Turning to face her, she does what she always does, and her free hand brushes my hair over to one side romantically. A supernova of radiance reflects back into my eyes as her focus mirrors my own and our eyes meet in a forceful grapple. The sides of my mouth almost make contact with my ears as they rise up my cheeks, and I know that this woman is going to spend every living day with me until one of us ceases to be. Her hand running through my hair is one of those small, meaningful things that I think I'd always miss if she wasn't around.

'Not in a million years,' she replies genuinely. All this romanticism transports me mentally back to the day we met. Hobbling up her unweeded, paved pathway with my final delivery of the day, I could never have guessed what was waiting for me behind the tattered, navy-blue door. My blank, awe-filled stare must have given the game away that I thought she was the most beautiful thing I'd ever laid eyes on. The clattering of my handheld scanner hitting the floor as my body went into spasm was enough to make her giggle resoundingly at me; I felt a right idiot.

Thinking that the intense chilliness is causing me to quiver, I'm soon to realise that it is in fact my phone vibrating in my pyjama trouser pocket. With the uncomfortable juddering irritating my leg muscles, I retrieve the device to raise hell with the individual who has ruined such a perfect moment. The illuminated screen informs me that my boss, John, is the culprit. Why would work be calling me on Christmas Eve of all days? I'm hoping it's just to wish me happy holidays.

'Mind if I take this babe? It could be urgent,' I ask Lara apologetically.

'It's fine, I'll meet you over at Gregory's, it's bloody freezing out here. Besides, he's probably got a cup of poo coffee waiting in there with my name on it,' she utters to me, her hair blowing in the breeze like live snakes, tightening her dressing gown as she dances across the frost-encrusted grass towards Gregory's house.

Making my way back towards our front door, I answer the phone cheerfully. 'Hey John, happy Christmas!'

'Happy Christmas,' he replies rather mundanely. There appears to be an edge in his greeting which I don't like much, but that could be down to the fact that's he's been forced to work on Christmas Eve.

'Please don't say you need me to work over Christmas, I've booked the week off,' I state sternly.

'No, it's not about that, it's more of a pressing issue I need to discuss with you before the office closes for the next two days.' The pounding of my heart increases twofold as I dread the bad news, but how bad is it going to be? As if the weather knew the conversation we were having and tried to match the severity of the situation, my nose twitches at the feeling of a lone glacial snowflake tickling my nose as it falls from the heavens above. The chattering of my teeth fills the moment of otherwise silence between both parties, and I dread hearing the words 'you're fired' like in that TV show I've seen advertised many times.

'Unfortunately, we've received an email from head office regarding the package that you left in the customer's bin. I know you've worked with us for quite a few years now and you've been doing an amazing job, but the customer has posted it all over social media. The higher-ups have regrettably informed us that we have to cancel your contract with immediate effect.'

'What?!' I shout, unsurprised by the news but being angered all the same. 'Why would you choose to tell me this on Christmas Eve? Surely this could have waited a few days. Not only have you ruined one of the best times of my life, but now Christmas is ruined as well. Thanks a bunch, after all I've done for you lot!' I yell vehemently down the receiver to cut through the otherwise silent street.

'I'm sorry Tristan, you do have the right to appeal, I'm just not sure whether head office would rescind the decision considering the nature of what's happened,' he says sheepishly.

'Screw head office, and you know what, screw you too John!' I shout venomously before ending the call. What am I supposed to do now without a job? It's difficult getting a courier job at this time of year with any company because they all take on extra staff over peak times and then filter out the rubbish ones once peak is over. How am I supposed to tell Lara? What if she doesn't want to be with me anymore because I've no longer got a job?

Suddenly, a scintillating, blasting flash of thunder attempts to escape from every one of the windows in Gregory's house simultaneously and a strange ethereal noise resounds through the atmosphere. I couldn't even begin to explain what the sound was, as it was unlike anything I've ever heard before; maybe a cross between a siren and an angel singing blissfully. My first instinct is to run inside to see what's happened, but my second instinct is to not go near the house in case something has happened inside. From where I'm standing it looks as if it was thundering indoors. Another resounding flash fills the house mere seconds after the earlier one, except this time the windows shatter tumultuously beyond repair, spewing shards of glass out at every angle. A shard of glass, around the size of a tennis ball, propels past my face and misses me by what must be millimetres. My conscious mind springs to life, and the sudden rush of blood to my head lurches me forward towards the house. A familiar aroma enters my almost-numb nostrils as the smell of bubblegum floating through the air puzzles me.

The silence in the pitch-black hallway is eerie and causes a shiver to course through my body, causing me to physically tremble. An icy breeze from the now vacant windows flows suspiciously through the corridor, which has caused a shroud of condensation to land mysteriously on the glass panes of the hanging photographs mounted on either wall. The sound of commotion and concerned bickering make their way in through the open front door from the neighbour's outside, who must be wondering what happened in this house and all gathered in the street outside.

My anxious yells throughout the house don't bring me an answer, and my deep, rhythmic respiration seems to be louder than anything I've ever heard. Heading towards the ajar door of the kitchen, which seems to be the most obvious place to look as she was going to have a cup of tea with Gregory, the first glimpses of something being amiss become visible.

Various appliances seem to be strewn across the kitchen, which indicate signs of a possible struggle. The toaster lies on its side on the floor, the table is skewed at an odd angle, and the rear bi-folding doors are wide open. I yell once again urgently, praying with all my heart that a voice answers, but once again there's nothing. The moonlight shines extravagantly to partially illuminate the small, grassed garden area outside, but apart from that, the exterior appears unoccupied.

She definitely came in here, but where could they have gone? That strange scent of bubblegum no longer seems to linger in the blizzard-like air. More doubts and questions fill every corner of my mind, but I can't seem to think of a possible answer to what may have occurred. I feel like a lost puppy who's been separated from the rest of the pack. With probably my first rational thought in the last few minutes, I realise that the first thing I probably thought of should have been to call her. I retrieve my phone and dial, but it goes straight to her answerphone as if her phone isn't even turned on.

As my hand rubs the back of my neck instinctively (as it usually does when I'm searching for a logical thought), the sound of a slamming door resounds around the house. With a hopeful dash, I burst back into the hallway, only to be greeted by an unfamiliar male figure who stands in the blackness with his hands on his knees panting heavily as if he's just run a marathon.

'Did you see anything?' I ask him hurriedly.

He continues in his desperate quest to regain his breath and tries to force out his words. 'I saw… someone came… through the back… he shot them… then… disappeared.'

'How could someone have shot them? There's no blood or bodies or anything, what are you talking about?' I blurt out frustratedly, urging him to start making sense.

'I mean it,' he claims, panting like a thirsty dog. 'Somebody came in… through the back door… shot them both… but they disappeared instead of… being wounded… then they disappeared themself,' he repeats. 'I live behind… saw it all out of my… bedroom window.'

Whatever this guy is talking about doesn't appear to make sense. How can somebody burst into a house and make everyone disappear? 'What did the person look like?' I ask.

'They were small, maybe the size of an eight-year-old,' he says, hardly believing it himself.

'Eh? Sorry, but have you been taking something you shouldn't be? You haven't been at a Christmas party today by any chance, have you?' I ask, not believing a word he's saying.

'I'm telling you what happened, believe me or not, I saw it with my own eyes,' he replies matter-of-factly, finally gaining the ability to stand upright.

The familiar sounds of police sirens penetrate the frosty air, causing both me, and the neighbour, to head outside. The blue and red flashes rebound from every surface in the street as if we're in a disco, and the kerbsides are abused by the revolving tyres that mount them with a deafening screech. Swathes of figures unload from the cars, running towards the house we've just vacated, armed to the teeth with various firearms. The officers exchange tactical words that I can barely even recognise as English as they advance forward in formation.

'Where are you going?!' I call into the crowd. 'There's nobody in there, she's gone!' I bellow frustratedly. I approach one of the officers in an attempt to let them know it's all clear, but all I receive is an offensive obscenity and get warned to back away. A handful of figures stay near the vehicles, taking cover from the open doors, one of them barking orders into a small handheld radio. He's quite a tall man, with dark hair and a bushy moustache. If I approach him, I may be able to let him know what's happened, but instead, and for reasons unbeknownst to me, I decide to run desperately in the opposite direction. If she's been taken, she could still be close. A theory comes to mind about what could have happened here. Maybe Gregory has kidnapped her, and this neighbour is in on the whole thing to act as a witness and give some cock-and-bull story about them disappearing. I was at the front door, so they must have left out the back. If I can get around to the back of the houses, I may be able to find some clues of where they've gone.

Running frantically through the busy roads to reach the houses behind, my heart seems to be attempting an escape, as if it's trying to break out of my ribcage and do a runner. Tasting the saltiness from the tears now running down my face, it wouldn't surprise me one bit if they turned to icicles in this severely cold weather. The powder-white deposit from the heavens above throws constant reminders at me that I have to cease what I'm doing and head home, but I must find out where she is. Arriving at the houses to the rear of Gregory's, I can't see evidence of anything untoward, and with the snow starting to make an icing-like layer on the ground, it's hard to even make out where I'm stepping. It's too cold to be running around in pyjamas, and the police may have found something that can point them in the right direction.

After a few moments of contemplation and uncontrollable weeping at the thought of never seeing Lara again, my common sense and logic decide that it would probably be best to head back and speak to the police officers. The man with the moustache looked friendly enough, maybe he can shine some light on what's happened.

There are still numerous police officers stationed at the scene, and yellow tape cordons off both mine and Gregory's house. 'Are you Tristan?' the moustached officer enquires politely with a delicate approach.

'Yeah,' I reply, with the soft dressing gown sleeve now rubbing at my face.

'Would you mind telling me why you fled from the scene earlier?' he asks bluntly.

'I was trying to find my wife. I'm not sure if you noticed, but she's disappeared into thin air,' I reply anxiously. 'Have you found anything yet?'

'Why don't you leave that to the professionals,' he states proudly, pointing a hand towards the officers stationed outside Gregory's house.

'Yeah, of course, and when are they getting here?' I ask mockingly. A part of me knows I shouldn't be mocking a police officer, but here and now, I'm not in the mood for niceties with anyone, I just want to see Lara.

'Funny bugger, aren't you? Get yourself inside, we need to have a nice little chat,' he says, with more of a command than a request.

Slowly but surely, the feeling in my numb digits begin to return. The moustached police officer stares at me solemnly from across the small coffee table which holds our steaming beverages. An overpowering aroma of scented Christmas candles fill the air from the diffuser which I bought for Lara last Christmas.

The officer introduces himself as *Sergeant Wainwright* in a hoarse voice. A small, black, leather wallet is almost thrust into my face showing me a photograph of him with his credentials alongside. A numbness inside causes me to barely take any notice as I claw unintentionally at the arm of the settee.

'I know this is a difficult time for you, and I don't mean to be intrusive, but could you explain to me what happened to your wife?' the Sergeant asks calmly, readying a small notepad and pen to take notes.

'Sure,' I mutter, while trying to muster the concentration to make words expel from my mouth. 'She went next door to Gregory's house. I was going over with her, but I had to take a phone call. When I got off the phone, the house lit up and all the windows shattered, this happened twice in just a few seconds. I went inside and there was nobody there, just a ransacked kitchen with the rear doors open. The neighbour from the houses behind came over when I was in the house, and he tried to explain what had happened.'

'And what did he say had happened exactly?' he asks next.

'He said a man entered through the back of the house and shot both of them, and then he disappeared.'

He glares at me worryingly in obvious disbelief. 'Can you make any sense of these accusations?' he asks.

'Not at all,' I reply disconcertedly, looking up from the steam rising like a well-lit fire from my mug, feeling almost shell-shocked.

'Does she have any enemies that you may be aware of?'

'I don't think so,' I lie, knowing that in her illicit line of work she must have more enemies than I have friends, but she doesn't do that anymore. It's just a shame I can't inform the Sergeant of what her job entailed.

'I'm not sure what your neighbour saw exactly, and I know the dark may have played tricks with his mind, but one thing is for certain, people don't just poof into nothingness.'

After more questions and queries which I don't have an answer to, the Sergeant seems to reach the conclusion that I have nothing more to offer and makes his way towards the door, plunking a white-coloured contact card on the side table. 'If anything else comes to mind, or you recall any details that you may have omitted, please let me know.' He sighs disappointedly and offers me a wayward glance from the door. 'We'll enquire to see if any of the neighbours have CCTV that may be able to aid us in our investigation, and we also need to find out why your neighbour has claimed that they "disappeared". We'll be in touch as our investigation progresses.'

I look up at him once again, despair seeping from my voice as I say, 'Maybe it was magic or something,' but even I know that I'm clutching at impossible straws.

CHAPTER 2

What a Difference a Year Makes

The clatter of children playing loudly is enough to rouse me from my peaceful slumber. As my eyes open, they carry out the usual routine of blinking numerous times to adjust to the light, except the brightness seems to be duller than I'm expecting. The rock-hard, cold terra firma underneath me gives the impression that I'm lying on stone. The sky above enthrals my senses, and I'm flabbergasted by what is visible in my line of sight. A yellow veil is splayed across the entire sky, but the most bizarre thing I can make out is the array of planets and stars that cover the heavens beyond. Have they always been there? I'm finding it difficult to recall anything about who I am, or why I'm here. The rays of sunlight from the sky penetrate my skin with a fierce warmth making me feel as though I'm lying on a beach in Spain.

Trying to assemble an ounce of focus to turn my head to the right is a challenge, but it's one I can manage to complete with the aid of mental strength and will.

The children lunge, and duck, and weave, and parry, as they strike one another with wooden sticks. I vaguely recall playing this game at some point in my life, but I can't seem to think clearly enough to remember what it's called. There are two boys, and one girl, from their sizes and actions I can tell that they're marginally pre-adolescent. The dark-haired boy is quite chubby, and the other boy doesn't have a trace of fat on him. The buildings in the distance that cast shadows on one another are all different shapes and sizes; triangles, parallelograms, spheres, and even more shapes

I'm unfamiliar with. For reasons unknown to me, in the back of my mind there's something telling me that all buildings are supposed to be big, boring, huge squares and rectangles, but maybe I'm just not remembering things correctly.

I try to call out, 'Hey, where are we?' But the words seem to get lodged in my throat; my mouth doesn't even open. In my extraneous efforts to stand up and approach the children, it becomes clear that the only mobile functions still under the control of my mind are my neck and eyes. The inability to move causes the transmitters in my brain to activate panic mode, and the sole thing that shows any signs of making this subside is the distraction of the conversation which the children begin having.

'Wanna see something cool?' the skinnier boy asks the girl after they decide to take a break from playing. They're all panting and sweating profusely.

'Sure, what is it?' she asks, a peculiar interest evident in her tone.

With a movement of his arm, giving me a full view of his bare armpit, the boy reaches into the hood of his clothing. A smug grin covers his face, and as his hand comes back into view, he's now grasping an immaculately white, foot-long stick, which he begins waving about slowly in front of his face.

'Are you sure you're allowed to have that?' the chubby boy asks with a nervous, flailing quiver in his voice.

The girl looks instilled with a concoction of excitedness and impressiveness as she eyes what the boy now has gripped in his hand. She looks genuinely fascinated and doesn't make any attempt to conceal her fascination. 'Wow, that's amazing! Can I have a go?' she asks, her mouth hanging open in incredulity.

'Let me have a go first,' he proclaims to the girl with a protesting hand. 'What can I test it out on though?'

Why are the children all so impressed by a stick? From what I can make out there's nothing special about it, but then again, I'm not even sure who I am, or where I am, so what can I say?

'You shouldn't have that Salamander, I'm gonna have to tell someone!' the chubby boy shouts. The thinner boy turns his attention to the other and raises the stick to point directly at him threateningly. With his legs trying to carry him away as fast as they can, one foot clips the back of the other, causing him to clumsily fall flat on his face as he turns. The sound of bone on solid ground causes a cringeworthy thud. Tears fill the boy's eyes and wails escape from his mouth. A red treacly substance drips down his leg, visibly pouring toward his shin.

'Salamander, don't do it, you'll end up in serious trouble!' the girl pleads desperately in his direction, holding out both hands in protest.

'Why not?' he replies, disinterested at the girl's pleas. 'He's a fat waste of space anyway, is anyone really going to miss him? See ya Theo,' Salamander says without a vestige of sympathy. He calls out the words, 'Diruo Eternal,' while pointing the stick in his direction with immense concentration. A blue, semi-transparent, bubble surrounds Theo as he attempts to clamber awkwardly back to his feet. He becomes motionless, but his eyes continue to stare, fixed in one meaningless direction. A few seconds later, no more than five, a blinding white flash fills the vicinity, and the smell of bubblegum enters my nostrils. The blinding flash instinctively causes my eyes to close with the intense brightness, and when they open again, I don't appear to be in the same place.

'No!' I scream at the top of my lungs, the words expelling from my mouth like a round from a pistol. Relief courses through my entire body from head to toe as the fact that I've just woken from a peculiar dream comes to fruition. Momentarily, I felt I was caught in limbo between dream and reality where I wasn't quite sure what was real. My eyes sting from the vigorous rubbing as I try to remove sleep's side effects from my eyes. That must be one of the most bizarre dreams I've ever had. It's probably one of the most bizarre dreams anyone's ever had, come to think of it; surely it can't be anything meaningful though, it's just a dream.

The sight of the dull, mundane, hellish room transitions me instantly back to reality.

It's been twelve months today since Lara disappeared right in front of my eyes. At this exact time last year, we would have been waking up in our hotel room the morning after our wedding and not having a care in the world. It was an amazing day, it was an amazing life, it's just a shame I could only experience it for one day. The musky smell of the room would be enough to wake anyone from sleep, and I'm aware of that, but do I care enough to clean it? Not really.

My eyes sweep the room as they do every morning, and I ask myself that same question I do daily; do I get up and try to move on with my life, or do I wallow in self-pity until the day arrives when death reunites me with Lara? I don't need to ask myself that question to know what the correct answer is.

It's still a mystery what happened that night, and I'm still not sure if she's alive or dead. The only thing I know is that my hope is starting to dwindle more and more with each day that passes. The police investigated Lara's disappearance, rummaging through hundreds of hours of CCTV from the surrounding houses, and questioning hundreds of people, but it just seemed pointless. At first, the idea of her disappearing sounded like complete and total rubbish, but looking at the evidence, it does seem the only plausible explanation; even at the risk of me sounding like a complete nut-job.

Since she disappeared, my life's gone from bad, to worse, to even worse, to total rock bottom, to whatever is below rock bottom. I lost my wife, my job, my home, and I don't have two pennies to rub together. This is how businessmen must feel when they've got a thriving company and loads of money, then it all goes under, and they end up with nothing.

I've tried working a few jobs over the last year, but since Lara's disappearance, I have the concentration levels of a glass of water, and no desire to get up and actually go to work. I never used to have a speck of sympathy for people who were depressed, and I was naïve enough to think you could pick yourself up from any situation with willpower and the right attitude, but this is relentless; I totally get it now.

One of the specialists I frequented earlier this year told me I need closure, but how do I get closure when I don't even know what happened to her? Something inside tells me I'll never see her again, but without that closure, it's torturous. I'm not ashamed to say that when it's been at its most desperate, I've pondered suicide, and not just once either. Every time I question it, I immediately dismiss the notion because knowing my luck, I'd end it all and she'd turn up the next day.

I've spoken to my mother recently, and she's suggested possibly moving back home to live with the family as I'm struggling to look after myself and they're all worried about me. Apparently, I've changed, and I'm no longer fit to take care of myself, but who wouldn't change after the ordeal that I've been through? Okay, I haven't showered for a few days, and all I eat is processed food, but it's not that bad… is it?

I've decided to have a bit of a social gathering at my flat today in commemoration of Lara's disappearance. I'm completely regretting the decision now, and the last thing I want is a bunch of people visiting and talking about how amazing she was. They said I need closure, not exposure. Something inside me wants them to visit so I can ask questions and maybe pick up some clues to what happened to her, but there is another part of me that just wants to cancel it all and stay in bed.

Since I couldn't afford to pay the rent for our previous house, I was evicted and placed in council accommodation, which is this dismal one-bedroomed flat. The council pay the bills for me, and I still get money from benefits so I can afford basic food, drink and cleaning products. When I first moved in here and had no income, I used to have food delivered from a food bank. Pride got the better of me and I couldn't find the dignity to use it more than a couple of times. The lady who used to deliver the food to me, Sarah, was really nice, but I could tell she hated delivering to me as all I used to talk about was how pathetic my life was and how much I missed Lara; I must have sounded pathetic. There are a lot of unusually weird people who live in this building so chances are she thought I was just another crazy person.

The flat consists of only three rooms; a living space barely big enough to house my TV and sofa, a bedroom which doesn't have any windows for some strange reason, and a small kitchen/living room that I can't fit a dining table in. This place is like a student's idea of a dream. The most appealing aspect of this flat is the small balcony which leads out from the living room, but I can't say I use it much due to the constant drone of traffic and pedestrians below. On a Saturday night it's like a parade outside. A rather busy nightclub stands opposite the building called *Chillies*, and I can't afford the pay-per-view boxing channels on TV, so sometimes I just chill on the balcony, crack open a beer, and watch the drunk partygoers fight over the road once it's chucking out time.

Due to my restricting financial issues, I've had to rely on money from my parents to pay for the drinks for today because I'm completely brassic, even though they decided not to come because they're away for Christmas as usual. It's thanks to my dad that I still have access to a car as he had an old one spare to give to me. It may the worst car I've ever laid my eyes on, but it still gets me from A to B so I can't complain.

I've asked everyone to get here by six o'clock and the place looks like a bomb's hit it, so I'm going to have to get a move on.

With the flat now completely tidy, and drinks filling almost every inch of the small kitchen area, I conclude that I deserve a chill on the settee after all my hard work. It's been a while since I had a workout that intense, and I even managed to pick up the mound of dirty, smelly washing that's been piled up in the corner for the last week. As I do multiple times each day, I scroll through the news channels in the hope that there's something, anything, that points me to Lara in the latest headlines.

'*A mysterious character has escaped arrest after a government building was broken into at around 11 pm last night. The authorities were alerted to their presence when the sirens on the building began to ring out. CCTV footage shows a man fleeing from the scene in the darkness,*' the newscaster reads out as an image of an official-looking building is shown beside him on the screen. An unkempt male member of the public appears on the screen with a microphone held in front of him, telling the interviewer that he saw people jumping onto the roof from an adjacent building.

'*Next up, in local news, a pizza delivery driver has been left cheesed off after he was mugged on the streets of Barscough today in broad daylight. The delivery driver fell from his moped after hearing a bang, and the next thing he remembers is waking up in only his underwear with no moped or pizzas.*'

The power button on the remote control brings the screen back to its ordinary state of blackness. Do they not realise that there's real crime going on out there, why are they covering all this garbage when my wife could be out there somewhere?

Three rhythmic taps from a knuckle alert me to the first guests arriving. As the creaking door opens unenthusiastically, I'm greeted cordially by Lara's parents, Gina and Paul. They both retired two years ago and now spend their days pretty much the same as mine; trying to figure out what happened to their daughter. We met up quite a few times after the incident to discuss possible hypotheses and theories, but as time progressed, the contact became less and less; it became a tad daunting when every conversation and conclusion arrived at a dead end. They're still convinced Gregory had something to do with it, that's obvious though isn't it? I'm not sure who this other small man was who apparently entered through the back door, but surely he was an accomplice of Gregory's. What's strange is that after the police continued their investigation, it came to light that Gregory was never registered as living at that address and they had no record of who the guy even was. The house was still in the name of the previous tenants, a Mr and Mrs Jackson; it was like he never even existed. After questioning the neighbours, the police found out that the Jacksons also disappeared; they went out one night to a local restaurant to celebrate their wedding anniversary and vanished from the face of the earth, never to be seen again.

Paul's vice-like grip squeezes my hand hard, almost causing me to yelp out in pain. His free hand taps me on the back as he pulls me in to receive tickles from his bushy beard. 'How are you son?' he asks gently.

Not wanting to risk any in-depth conversations and have them worrying, I reply meekly with my usual response. 'Same old, same old.'

Gina hands me a bottle of wine and removes her coat made from some form of animal pelt. She's massively overweight but doesn't really seem too bothered by it. She's always strutting around in fancy, yet baggy, dresses. Red lipstick has been smothered all over her lips as if she's auditioning to be a clown, which adds to the fact that she regards herself as upper class with an exaggerated accent and quaint actions.

Paul, on the other hand, couldn't be more different. A bald head which reflects any remnants of light in the room and a bushy beard are the extent of his facial composition. He always seems to follow Gina around like a lapdog and comply with every request she gives him. I know it's all about keeping up appearances, but if I were him, I'm not sure how I could cope. He should be able to live his own life and do what he wants, but there is a part of me that thinks he enjoys it.

'Isn't this place… interesting?' Gina says scornfully, crossing the threshold and moving her head around in obvious revulsion. Alright, I know it's not exactly the Ritz, but give a guy a break. 'I used to visit places like this when I was a social worker.'

'Come on, it's not that bad love, we've all fallen on hard times at some point in our lives,' Paul adds, in an obvious attempt to defend me in his deep northern-English accent.

'Very well, but have you not even bothered to decorate? It's Christmas Eve you know. We've got a lovely set of Christmas lights up this year, Paul put them up last week,' Gina explains.

'Yeah, I know I did, while you were sitting on your backside and I was out in the freezing cold,' he replies with a blatant dig at her, pointing out that she doesn't really help him with anything.

I look between the two of them, trying to figure out the best way to move on from this line of conversation as they send scowls across at each other. 'So, who else is coming from Lara's family?' I enquire hastily before one of them speaks again.

'It's just us two dear,' she adds. Then I hear her mutter under her breath. 'If they were, I'd call them to cancel after seeing this place,' which just annoys me more than anything else.

'Ignore her son,' Paul says in a friendly tone and nudges me amiably with a bony elbow. 'I learned how to master it years ago,' he chuckles heartily. 'Oh, I found this outside on your doorstep; where's your bin?' he asks and begins folding up a pizza leaflet for a restaurant called *Tony's Pepperonis and Macroroni*.

'I'll take that, I'll have to order food in anyway; I might as well order it from here.' Browsing through the menu, I'm astonished at how cheap everything is; it seems to be half the price of the usual place I deliver from. As my eyes reach the bottom of the page, a peculiar telephone number catches my eye – 739-15-2665. That must be a foreign number that the owners still use if they've moved over from abroad because it doesn't appear to be in the correct format.

I've received confirmation of attendance from everyone, except for all of Lara's ex-colleagues. I call them colleagues, but I'm not sure if that's the right word for a bunch of thieves. Don't get me wrong, even though the people she worked with were criminals, their intentions were always good. They were akin to modern-day *Robin Hoods* and called themselves *The Do-gooders*. Basically, they were hired to steal things back from crooks and return them to their original owners for a fee. She decided to call it a day when one of her colleagues was killed during a mission and she deemed it too risky.

With every guest accounted for, the pizza ordered, and my small, pathetic flat way too overcrowded, I can finally relax. Watching the people gathered around chatting about Lara gets the cogs in my head turning and ponder my own life, mentally debating whether anyone would miss me if I died as I don't exactly have a massive number of friends. No doubt, I'd be buried alone with nobody to celebrate my existence except for mine and Lara's parents. I've often wondered what it would be like if I faked my own death and set up a camera so I could see who attended and find out what they really thought of me.

As I'm refilling Lara's hairdresser, Mary's, glass with prosecco, a knock rat-tat-tats on the front door as if the tax man had just arrived to pay a visit.

'Pizza's here!' one of the guests calls, as if that wasn't already obvious.

'Oh, pizza, lovely,' Gina remarks snobbishly from the settee.

'We had pizza on our first date love,' Paul replies to her. In the corner of my eye, I notice Gina quietly scolding Paul for his outburst that implies she likes the taste of pizza, and not just caviar on toast for every meal.

'Pizza guy!' a broad American accent calls from the other side of the door. A waft of greasy melted cheese instantly hits my nostrils. 'Hey man, is this the right place?' the pizza man asks. 'Are you Tristan?' Without a reply, I stare in confusion, sniggering under my breath at his outlandish appearance and obviously staged accent. The pizza delivery man sweeps his hand through his silky, dark hair that hangs down onto his shiny, leather jacket.

'I got pizzas for you, that'll be £52.20 please,' the pizza man says. Is this guy serious? That's got to be probably the worst attempt at an American accent I've ever heard, but why would you fake an accent? Maybe he's an undercover cop and he's trying to take down a gangster who orders pizza from the pizza place.

He hands me four pizza boxes, and three small, brown, grease-ridden bags. 'Tell you what,' he says. 'If you let me use your bathroom, you can have all this on the house. I'm bursting, and the guys at the pizza place barely let you stop to take a leak; I haven't been once since I started my shift.' Is he allowed to do that? Wouldn't the owner wonder where all the money is for the food?

'I think you've got the order wrong,' I inform him, still utterly confused at the current events. 'I ordered six pizzas, two garlic bread, and three fries.'

'Thanks man, is the bathroom just through here?' He barges past me without invitation. The strange man strolls humbly towards the bathroom without a hint of shame or acknowledgement. What just happened? Well, we got free food and I'm broke, so do I have a right to moan? What harm can he really do anyway? He's only using the toilet.

'Right weirdo him, wasn't he?' Mary says as I take a seat beside her on the armrest of the settee. The amazing aroma from her perfume hits me hard in the face.

'Not half,' I reply. 'There was something really odd about him, and not just the rudeness. There was something else that I couldn't quite fathom out.'

'So, how are you doing anyway?' Mary asks courteously.

'Pretty bad to be honest,' I inform her truthfully. 'Life's just not the same without her. She was, without a doubt, the best thing that ever happened to me. After such an awful upbringing, it was nice that there was someone there to rescue me, even if it wasn't for that long.' I sigh heavily and twist off the cap of an ice-cold beer.

'Why was your upbringing bad?' Mary asks intriguingly, reaching over to grab a slice of pizza from the table.

'I woke up one day in hospital when I was eleven with no memory of who I was,' I inform the listeners with my head down, as I begin subconsciously peeling the label from the beer bottle.

'And you can't remember anything, anything at all?' Mary asks.

'Nothing, it was like being born at age eleven and starting

anew. Apparently, I had been to school, and on my way home, passed out, then somebody found me in the street.'

'Wow, that must have been really tough for you,' Mary says, and puts a sympathetic hand on my leg, squeezing it gently to offer commiserations.

'I read this story once in the papers,' a voice says. Stopping what they're doing, every pair of eyes around the table all move simultaneously to look at an extremely obese lady who is sitting on the opposite settee. Her obviously Botox-filled lips look as if they're about to burst to the point where I have to fight an urge to run to the kitchen and fetch myself a pin to test it out.

She speaks like a true chav and churns out words quicker than anybody I've ever held a conversation with. 'Alright fine, it wasn't the papers, it was *OK* magazine. There was this kid, and he was adopted, yeah, by this couple, and he couldn't remember anything from his past either, yeah. They said the people who were adopting the kid, wiped its brain, so it couldn't remember it was adopted, and it thought they were his biological mum and dad, yeah. Anyway, years later, the kid found out they weren't his mum and dad, and he was well gutted,' she fires off like a machine gun without taking so much as a slight intake of breath. The room of people, including myself, all continue to stare at the woman in fascination while she tells this ridiculous story. It seems rather obvious that she must receive some sort of mental help.

'Don't talk rubbish Natasha,' Mary retorts.

The entire room move their gaze in unison to the other side of the room as a flushing noise is followed by the pizza man exiting through the bathroom door. 'Wouldn't go in there for a while,' he says, wafting his hand in front of him. 'Must have eaten something dodgy, let's hope it's not that pizza you've all been eating,' he chuckles, then makes his way to the door and exits.

'Sweet Lord!' one of the guests nearest to the bathroom exclaims, waving their hand in front of them to try and diminish the smell. It's amazing that the wallpaper isn't peeling from the walls with the horrendous smell that now wafts through the flat. Collars are put in front of noses, perfume bottles are sprayed, and windows are opened to try and diminish the smell, but nothing succeeds.

The topic of conversation between the guests seems to make

a shift from talking about Lara and everyday life, to who on earth that pizza man was, and how I can make a complaint to the pizza place. The smell is putrid, and it doesn't seem natural, somehow reminding me of when students used to detonate stink bombs in school and the hallways would clear rapidly.

One by one, the guests leave, and I can't blame them for leaving; it's 9 pm on Christmas Eve after all.

The first thing to do is call the pizza company from my recently called contacts, but it appears to be out of service. Repeating the action, I'm met with the same outcome. Concluding that the number is no longer in use, I access the web browser on my phone and type the name of the pizza place into the search engine. To my utter surprise, the search engine returns no results for what I've searched for. There's the possibility that it could be a brand-new company, but surely there would be something on the government records. Checking my spelling for Tony's Pepperonis and Macroroni, it seems to be correct. Hold on, have they misspelt macaroni?

A wave of confusion and paranoia flow through me as I question what has occurred tonight. Why would there be a pizza menu for a company on my doorstep belonging to a place that clearly doesn't exist? Why did the pizza man turn up at my door with an obviously staged accent, brought the wrong order, given me the food for free, and done god knows what in the bathroom? Call me highly suspicious, but none of this makes any sense. Perhaps I'm on a hidden camera show and Ant and Dec are going to jump out at any minute. The throbbing in my head causes an audible drone to seer deafeningly throughout every neurological synapse to the point where I have to sit down.

Dawdling aimlessly in my metaphorical cage of loneliness and despair, I spy a maroon-coloured photo album on one of the side tables, presumably left by one of the guests. My trembling hands turn the pages in trepidation on the centre of my lap. Small beads of water begin splashing on the pages like an Olympic diver crashing ineptly into a pool. Sniffling noises emanate from me, and a melancholic sadness begins to transcend. Before I'm aware I'm doing it, the glossy material on the page provides comfort for my finger as it rubs against Lara's face.

My sniffles transform into cries, and before I know it, my lungs are struggling to deal with the hysteria that overcomes me. In surrender, my mind waves a white flag in my direction and concedes to pure emotion as it gives up the fight and commands me to stop acting as if everything's fine. Everything is not fine. Everything is bad, everything is sh... sure to be over soon. The pulse within is pounding at my head like a drum, and with each pulsation, the urge to no longer exist and endure this pain is becoming more extreme. I'm submitting, I'm giving in, I'd rather be dead than be without her. This pain is too unbearable, too unmanageable, and I can't stand the thought of lasting one more day on this planet without seeing her face. I love you Lara, and I always will.

The balcony door swings open as my brain shakes hands with my body and they agree that it's been a good game, but the game's now coming to an end. My confident steps backward towards the opposite side of the room become real and I offer an agreeing nod towards the balcony before I make my charge towards death. A waving farewell from the blowing curtains provide with an acknowledgement that this will be my doorway to whatever follows life.

After being brought up a Catholic, there's only one thing I can think of that may give me sanctity during this unforgiveable crime I'm about to commit. 'Our Father, who art in heaven, hallowed be thy name.' I step forward confidently. 'Thy kingdom come; thy will be done...' My legs work faster to end this hastily and relieve me from my pain.

As if fate has stepped in, as it usually does at the times you least expect it, a sound from my left causes my legs to halt, and my head to turn curiously. One of the most random things I would ever expect to have happened, happens. The crinkling of a paper envelope sliding itself underneath my door causes a distraction that my curiosity seems to be compelled by. Part of me wants to ignore this sudden distraction and turn my gaze back towards the balcony doors, but there's another part of me that is curious enough to check what's in this envelope.

Letting curiosity get the better of me and admitting that the moment is now ruined, I hold the letter with shaking hands and gaze at its impossibility with a combination of confusion, puzzlement, relief and guilt. My name is scrawled across the front of the letter accompanied by a kiss in a child-like handwriting which I know only too well.

'Lara?' I mutter out loud with a sob and put my hand to my mouth, which is shaking like a leaf in a summer breeze. The rhythmic thumps from the music in the bar across the street, and the constant swooshing of traffic, make it increasingly difficult to focus. 'Will you just shut up for one minute?!' I scream at the top of my lungs towards the open balcony doors. Jerking the front door open to see if the mystery postman is still outside, I see nothing except for the dim lighting in the corridor.

Instinctively, and animal-like, I begin tearing at the paper ferociously to find out what the contents are. A small, neatly folded-up piece of piece stares back up at me. It vibrates in my hand, teasing me, flirting with me, as if its sole purpose in this world is for me to discover its contents. With a deep breath, and a rapidly beating heart, I unfold the paper to read the message inside:

Hey Tris,

   I'm hoping this reaches you in time before you do something stupid. I hope things haven't been too difficult for you while I've been gone. I've tried as hard as I can to find a way back to you, but it's been impossible, literally impossible. I've tried to contact you in many ways, but it just can't be done. I've missed you so much, and I'm safe and well, I just hope you are. I'll explain everything when you get here. The rest is up to you…

   Here's the tricky bit.

   I need you to get to Macro Meadow in a place called West Findel. We've been there before if you recall, we rented a pedalo once and circled the lake, then we lay on the grass for hours and chatted until the sun was going down. Next to the lake there's a small wooden hut. If you go around to the back of the hut, you'll see a collection of gravestones. One of the gravestones has a gargoyle on top of it and the name James Martin Macro inscribed on it. You'll need to get to this gravestone by 10 am on Christmas morning and not a minute later. You should see it change and you need to touch it, then it'll take you to me. I can't stress the importance of time, and if you don't make it, there may be no other way of getting to each other.

I know this probably all sounds a bit far-fetched, but I'm sure it'll be worth it when we're reunited. You should have received this letter the night before on Christmas Eve, and hopefully you'll have more than enough time to get there.

Love ya loads and can't wait to see you again.

Your number one girl,

Lara,

Xxx

A burning sensation arrives in my cheeks to the point where it feels like I'm sitting in a sauna. My bodily functions seem to have abandoned me and time ceases to be. I feel like I'm standing in a void of nothingness.

Can this be legit? This could have been left by one of the guests to try and instil a fraction of faith, but why would they put all this rubbish about meeting somewhere? And why is it in her handwriting? I've mocked her handwriting since the day we met and it's definitely hers; I've always said she writes like a T-Rex would have. There's no point questioning this is there? In my eyes, the only option I've got is to follow the mysterious instructions and hope for the best.

I remember going to Macro Meadow together not long after we met and it's not that far away. According to the maps on my phone, it's one hour and three minutes away. Currently it's 10 pm, so that gives me twelve hours to get there. I can either sleep now, and travel there in the morning, or I could go there now, and sleep in my car until I need to arrive. What if I get stuck in traffic in the morning though? My primary route would be down the M62, and it can get busy in the mornings. I think the best thing to do would be to travel now and hang around until 10 am. Besides, after the letter I just opened, I don't think I'll be sleeping anytime soon.

With jubilation coursing through me and excitement taking over every thought, I bounce into the kitchen area with a newly found spring in my step. My blood is pumping fiercely through every artery, and I don't need to look at them to know that my hands are shaking uncontrollably. I'm going to see her again; I can't believe what's happening. Grabbing my car keys from the hook above the kitchen counter, I canter hastily towards the front door. Due to having an emotional meltdown, and considering suicide, tidying up wasn't exactly top of my priority list after the guests left; it's thanks to this that there are empty pizza boxes stacked at the side of the settee. My right foot catches on the stack of pizza boxes as I navigate my way around, my body involuntarily lurching forward. Everything feels like it's moving in slow motion as I'm thrown haphazardly forward towards the coffee table. Before the sound of glass shattering makes its way into my ears, I'm plunged into darkness without any hope of getting to her.

CHAPTER 3

Merry Christmas and a Crappy New Year

I feel completely dazed. A concoction of differing emotions ignites inside my mind to inform me that I'm waking up. However, a mental alarm is telling me that there's issues and I'm not just waking up on any average day.

A beam of sunlight from millions of miles away prods at me forcefully with its celestial fingertips, rousing me back to consciousness. Where am I? The dark descends upon me once more as my corneas don't approve of the onslaught and decide to take cover behind their protective shields. One of my hands joins in the fight and my outstretched arm attempts to make a wall between my eyes and the gigantic clear glass window. Once my eyes have adjusted to the daylight, I'm returned to full consciousness by a grey-haired, middle-aged lady holding a clipboard like it's a newborn baby.

'Good morning, happy Christmas,' she announces cheerfully.

'Where am I?' I mutter, almost silently with a croaked edge to my voice.

'You're at Sacred Heart Hospital. Not to worry, you're in good hands. *Your lobotomy is our priority* we always say, although I never did like that motto much. Can you remember much of last night?' she queries, almost certainly knowing that I do not remember much from last night.

'No, what happened?' I ask.

Her hair droops down over her face as she examines the clipboard in her hand. 'You had a bit of a fall and injured your head. One of your neighbours contacted the police to say that they'd heard a loud crash coming from your flat above. When the police arrived, your door was unlocked. You were splayed out on the floor with blood streaming from your head. Your balcony doors were wide open, so you're lucky you didn't catch your death of cold. I do have one question though, if you'd be kind enough to answer.'

'Yeah, what's that?' I ask, my hand reaching for a glass of water on the side table, presumably left by the nursing staff for when I wake.

'Who won in the fight, you or the table?' she chuckles.

Her joking and lack of seriousness are annoying me, but the pain is doing an adequate job of distracting me from becoming irate. 'I'm not sure what you're talking about,' I reply dully.

'Get some rest, you've had quite a bit of medication,' she advises. 'You're lucky you've woken up; it's gone quarter past eight and it's almost breakfast time. Anything you fancy?'

Without answering, my head hits the fluffy pillow and I stare at the ceiling blankly.

'I'll tell them you're not hungry then,' she adds, turning to walk out of the swinging doors of the room.

Memories of what happened last night are beginning to take form inside my mind. I remember people coming round to my house, and that weird pizza man that came, the desperate crying, and the thoughts of ending my life were stronger than ever. Wasn't there something else though? How did I fall and hurt my head? I know there's more, but the memories are fuzzy, and I can't seem to access the information.

A specific memory makes an appearance in my mind's eye, causing me to sit up straight as zombies do in horror movies. I received a letter! It was a letter in Lara's handwriting, but how is that possible? There was something else in the letter, what was it? I recall rushing out of my flat to get somewhere, and that's how I fell and hit my head.

'Macro Meadow!' I blurt out, in what is almost a shout.

A glance at the circular clock above the ward doors informs me that it's almost 8:30 am. 'Oh god!' I bellow, the reality of the predicament becoming clearer. She told me to get there for 10 am.

It's almost 8:30 am, what am I supposed to do? I'm stuck in here. Instinctively, and without any need for rationality, my teeth clench together as I rip the drip connection from my hand to silence any yelps from the sharp pain. Whatever painkillers they've given me must be working a treat as that didn't hurt half as much as I was expecting.

With legs that now feel like jelly, my bare feet make contact with the shiny, cold floor. My reflection that looks up at me confirms that I do, in fact, look as if I've been dragged through a hedge multiple times. A pair of slippers are peeking their way out from the curtain separating the next bed from mine. Not hearing a peep from behind the curtain, it's as if they look at me and say, 'it's fine, he's asleep, I'm coming with you.'

Donning my new oversized slippers and swaying my way over to the double doors, I glance once again at the clock. An hour and a half to get to my destination without a phone, a vehicle, and no directions isn't going to be easy. I'd go as far as saying this reckless expedition won't even be hard, I'd probably be more in favour of saying it's quite high on the impossibility scale.

A sudden doubt inside flares up, causing me to turn my head back to the bed. This feels like the point of no return. I suddenly feel like Macbeth after he murdered Duncan and once the deed was done, he couldn't turn back. These doors are my Duncan, and I can either conquer them, or turn back and get into that bed. Once I cross the threshold of these doors, my decision's made and I'm going on a pursuit to find Lara if it kills me. For a slight millisecond, I do consider the option due to being extremely tired, worn down, and sick to death of never having a normal day. I want Lara, there's no two ways about it; I love her, and I want to spend every waking second with her as life isn't worth living without her.

The door creaks open into a large corridor, which stretches out in front of me. The clearly labelled signs hanging from the ceiling give me a clear route to which way I should be going. When I've visited hospitals before, there are usually nurses and doctors roaming the halls and checking on patients. Not having to pay staff to work on Christmas Day must mean that there's skeleton staff on shift.

Just as I get a gust of that unique hospital smell, a noise rouses me. 'And where do you think you're going?' the less-than-ecstatic voice queries. The nurse from earlier has exited a store cupboard behind me and stands with an unimpressed glare and arms folded across her chest holding a mop. 'I can't let you leave without being discharged. I'm surprised you can even walk with the medication you've been administered. Get yourself back to bed this instant you fool. What happened to your drip?' she asks, switching to a high-pitched squeal. Her foot taps away impatiently, as if she's speaking down to me like a misbehaving pupil in a classroom.

Knowing that this lady is the first obstacle between me and my chance of ever seeing Lara again, I instinctively push her back into the store cupboard. The mop handle she was holding gets thrust into the door to prevent her from escaping. Almost immediately, repetitive banging resounds from inside, but luckily, the thick wooden door prevents any of her audible rants from being heard outside. If it exists, I am definitely going to hell after this. From what I can tell, only I can hear her wails and bangs on the opposite side of the door. 'I'll call for security if you don't let me out of here this instant! We can't hold you against your will, but you'll have to be discharged, and I highly recommend in your state that you stay in bed to recover!' she thunders furiously as I stumble away down the corridor towards the exit.

Great. That wasted a few minutes of time which I don't have; nice of her to understand though. No doubt she must have a mobile phone though to alert security, so I'll have to hurry; but then again, I know how rubbish the mobile signal in hospitals can be so I might be fine.

Exiting the ward by hitting the circular green button mounted on the wall, I arrive in the main hospital corridor. Coloured lines illuminate the path along the shiny hospital floors leading from ward to ward and department to department, but the only things I take any notice of are the green signs which are labelled *exit* hanging from the ceiling with a symbol of a stickman coloured in white, running. Meandering through the snaking corridors, I head towards the glass double doors at the front of the building. Approaching reception, a large clock peers down at me which reads 8:50 am which causes my heart to sink. One hour and ten minutes doesn't seem enough time to get there unless there's no cars on the road, no traffic lights, and I can travel at top speed the whole way. I don't have access to a vehicle so is there even a point trying? I'll have to find transport asap. Suddenly, as if by magic – or more likely, sheer coincidence – a perfect opportunity arises out of the blue; talk about luck.

A thud, followed by a shrill squeal near the elevator to the left of the reception causes everyone in the vicinity to turn their heads in that direction. In the shadow of a gigantic Christmas tree near the window, an old lady is sprawled on the ground with a horde of concerned bystanders huddling around her like a rugby scrum.

The first thing I notice, which sounds awful, is that her grey handbag has travelled a few metres from where she's fallen. If she has car keys, maybe this could be the perfect opportunity to get my ride which I need. Being the helpful citizen that I am, and while the crowd are occupied with the old lady, I scoop up all her belongings into her handbag; except for the car keys of course, they get slipped into my gown instead. Amazingly, nobody notices my thievery as I hand one of the bystanders the bag and continue hobbling towards the exit.

I know how hospitals work, and I know that anybody who is anybody can go outside for a cigarette without a soul questioning even the sickest man why he's going outside. The sight of a gigantic, brightly lit Christmas tree makes the guilt build up inside and I feel ashamed about what I have just done. Not only have I stolen an old lady's car keys, but I've also locked a nurse inside a store cupboard. These aren't exactly the most Catholic of things I've ever done, and I've only been awake half an hour.

The bitterly cold English weather bites through my paper-thin hospital gown, causing the hairs on my arms and legs to stand to attention as if to applaud the freezing temperature. I try to pick up my pace to a steady jog, but I'm already swaying from side to side as if I've just been ejected from a merry-go-round, so the walk will have to do.

Inside the multistorey car park on the opposite side of the road, it doesn't take long for the orange lights on the red Nissan Micra to reflect from the pillars when I press the button on the black key fob. Perfect; this thing's probably got a top speed of about sixty. I couldn't have exactly expected a Range Rover though from a granny, could I?

I thank the heavens as the spluttering engine bursts to life with a single turn of the key and I notice that the car has a satnav embedded into her dashboard. Luckily, Macro Meadow is in the satnav's database, and it should take me straight to the entrance. The clock in the car now reads 9:10 am on the dashboard, which makes my heart sink down to my stomach. What's the point of even bothering now? I've got no chance; I'll never make it. The car smells as expected; that smell that you can only get from a granny. I'm not even sure what it smells of, it's just a granny smell. A photograph of a small ginger cat stares back at me, hanging from the rear-view mirror, so I tear it off to chuck onto the rear seats behind in an attempt to make the guilt subside.

Reaching the exit barrier of the car park by following the white lines on the tarmacked ground and going around those spiral ramps they have on the sides to go up or down a level, I completely ignore the one-way system and kick myself as I remember that I haven't paid for the parking at one of those pay and display machines. I haven't got time for all this; I've just stolen a granny's car and ran away from hospital while locking an old lady in a broom cupboard. No way am I paying £3 for parking as well!

Approaching the barriers, and almost certain that they won't be opening for me, I know I'll probably have to drive through them like I'm in an action movie or have an argument with the voice over the intercom to let me through because I don't have the funds to pay. An informative sign on the wall informs me that the first thirty minutes are free of charge, but anything over that goes up in increments of one pound per hour. Hoping that my tremendous luck today will still be on my side, I cross my fingers and begin to pray silently to the almighty barrier god. As the car rolls slowly forwards, the barrier rises automatically, and the feeling of relief which courses through my body is heavenly. This has got to be another dream; nobody gets this lucky. My wishes are granted, and with the barrier up, that just leaves a mountain of congested roads and about fifty miles of roadworks and traffic lights between me and Lara.

CHAPTER 4

The Race to Macro Meadow

The small red car drives better than any Nissan Micra I could have hoped for, it's just a shame my head feels like it's splitting in two and I can barely focus on the road ahead. If any police see my driving, they're sure to know something isn't right, but still, it doesn't stop me from weaving in and out of traffic or doing over seventy miles per hour in a thirty zone. Speeding my way through every set of traffic lights, and probably getting more stares than if I was dressed as a chicken, roller-skating down the street, doing the floss, I continue my journey. That's probably the most useful thing about being a courier, you spend that much time on the road and you're so restricted for time, it's inevitable that you drive like a speed demon. Flying down a tree-lined main road, I'm forced to swerve to the side to avoid smashing into two girls that are about to cross the street. After they jump back onto the kerbside, it's impossible to hear the obscenities they bellow at me.

A motorway slip road approaches, and the impending destination time coupled with 10:10 am showing on the satnav informs me that I'm gaining time. A surge of confidence lets me think I can do this, and I will do this, and nothing will stop my momentum.

Around halfway there, with 9:35 am showing on the clock, a sea of red brake lights in front of me causes my hope to dwindle as the reality hits that there must be miles of stationary traffic piled up beyond. Luckily for me, I'm not playing by the rules today. The tyres screech horrifically as the car jerks violently onto the motorway emergency lane, hitting almost ninety miles per hour. The unimpressed retorts of a multitude of car horns make it known that this behaviour is not approved by the traffic jam attendees.

The car screams out in agonising rage, and for probably the first time in its life, exceeds fifty miles per hour. I can physically feel the vibrations and the intense amount of energy the car excretes, shuddering up the pedals and into my body. It's as if we've fused together and are working hand in hand to get to our final destination.

Passing the myriad of stationary cars on the motorway that have collided with one another to cause the backlog of traffic, I continue my mission to see the woman I love and find out what the hell is now going on in my messed up weird life. Why couldn't I have just had a normal life where I meet a woman, spend the rest of my life with her, have kids, and live happily ever after? Doesn't really suit me that, it's as if God thought that was too boring for me. I just don't think settling down was meant for me, although I was so close. The thought of her makes me tingle inside once again. 'I can do this, I will do this, nothing can…'

The whirring of helicopter blades hovering above snaps me from my positive train of thought. My rear-view mirror now displays a convoy of black and white police cars zooming down the motorway towards me like a lion hunting down a gazelle in the wild. The clock now reads 9:40 am. Macro Meadow must only be five minutes away now and my foot firmly against the floor doesn't attempt to lift even an inch, even during the sound of a megaphone speaker calling from the cars behind me.

'Stop right now! We will do all in our power to stop you. You cannot escape. We have aerial and ground services pursuing you and we will capture you. The longer this goes on, the worse your punishment will be!'

The voice from the megaphone booms out loudly. Not an instruction, a command. They will capture me, and I will be punished. He sounds very professional and keeps his voice calm under the circumstances, whoever he is, although knowing what it's like in the north-west of England, this is probably a daily occurrence for them. The way he lets me know *he will capture me* I suppose is part of the mind games to waver my confidence, but not today. This is my day, and I will get to where she told me to go or die trying.

All that's left to do is pull off this motorway and enter the park, but something tells me that under the current circumstances, it will be easier said than done. I recall from last time, that if you want to go through the main entrance, you must exit the motorway via the slip road, and continue down a country lane to get there. I also know, thanks to the car's satnav, that the rear of the park is on my left, alongside the motorway a little further up, as I can see the sea of green on the LCD screen labelled *Macro Meadow* up ahead. When I get to the park, I still need to find this hut with the gravestone, but hopefully I can remember where it is once I get there.

Another few hundred metres further, and I reach down to the dial just above the handbrake to scroll through the radio stations until I find a fast-paced metal track. The purpose of the music isn't just to drown out the noise, it also fills me with an aggression-fuelled rage which spurs me on furiously. The metal track booms out of the speakers and I'm pretty sure it's *Metallica*, but I couldn't be certain.

In the distance, I can make out a roadblock of police cars resembling a dazzle of zebras up ahead. Surely, they'll be using stingers on the ground to puncture the tyres and slow me down. The helicopter above whirrs so loudly now, that I can barely hear myself think, never mind hear the blaring, fast-paced music.

My left hand changes the gear to neutral and my foot slams down on the brake and clutch in unison, causing the car to lose control and swerve all over the road. The car veers left and slams into the side barrier of the motorway, screeching loudly as the metals collide to sing a symphony of hope. The smell of burnt rubber is intoxicating, and the amount of smoke which leave the tyres is like that of a bonfire. Expertly, the car comes to a stop against the side barrier where a gap is visible in the hedges on the side of the road. Before exiting the car, a glance at the clock tells me that it's now 9:52 am.

The crescendo of helicopter rotors still reverberates through my ear drums with a deafening thud, thud, thud, and it makes the trees dance a fandango caused by the powerful whirring of the blades. My clothes and hair blow violently in the powerful gust as if I'm travelling through the eye of a tornado. The persistent branches and foliage knock me back as my arms flail about wildly trying to pass. A concoction of hospital drugs and searing pain from the injury to my head make this as painstaking as it sounds. The terrifying resonations of Alsatian barks add to the death toll pursuing me from behind, and the megaphone still calls faint warnings to me in the distance, but I can't make out a word with the noises of shrubbery and branches attacking me as I try to run. I feel as if I'm going to pass out any second.

The side entrance to the park looms in my line of sight and gives me a shower of hope. Seeing the sign, *Welcome to Macro Meadow*, which is almost fully hidden within hedges, makes me feel lucky that I've made it this far before ten o'clock. Surely it must be ten by now.

The lake which the letter mentioned comes into view, and the hut beyond where I was instructed to go is also visible to the right. The taste of salty sweat in my mouth is revolting but I can't stop, even attempting to wipe my face could slow me down. My legs carry me faster than I thought was possible with sheer brain power and desire, and I'm carried through a painstaking hellish aching that screams at me to stop. Fatigue starts adding to the equation and as soon as I stop – whether I'm taken down or escape – I'll probably sleep for days.

Turning my head back as far as I can while trying to maintain a steady speed, it becomes apparent that they're gaining on me, and somehow I gain even more speed through perseverance and desperation.

The usual dog walkers, joggers and OAPs are enjoying their leisure time in the park, even on Christmas Day, and slowly but surely they begin to turn their attention towards my direction. Around the hut I run. Whatever happens, I can't stop, even for a second, because they'll catch me and throw me in prison for god knows how long. I must have broken most of the laws in the book today.

As my destination comes into sight, my body stops me suddenly and, as if in a daze, I stare in amazement to study the gravestone from a few feet away. My eyes become transfixed on the shining, purple aura surrounding the grey, dank epitaph with the gargoyle perched on top of it. I can somehow sense an ethereal, impossible power radiating from the gravestone, but I'm not sure what it is. I've never even heard of anything like this before, never mind seen it. What can it be? I know I must move forward before they catch me, but my eyes inform my body that something so wondrous must be observed. I'm frozen to the spot, my gaze mesmerised by the complete and total wonderment of this phenomenon. It's beautiful, and the ethereal glow hypnotises me until I can feel the goosebumps cover me once again.

Snapping back to reality with a spark, my legs attempt to carry me like a wounded soldier towards the gravestone, when my hand reaches forward to touch it as instructed by the letter.

A tremendous force pummels me instantly, almost knocking every brain cell out of my head. I felt like death earlier, but I have just been given a true representation of what it must be like to experience real agony. My body is thrown to the side as the huge figure rugby tackles me to the ground mere inches from the gravestone in mid-air. A scream escapes from me, louder than I've ever heard anybody scream before, and it doesn't seem possible to move one bone in my entire body.

'Nice one Jenkins,' I hear a familiar voice retort through deep breaths and my ear-piercing screams. 'Can you not get him to stop screaming though? It's doing my head in.'

'No boss, I'm afraid that's just reactions. I can put my foot over his mouth if you want me to,' the other man replies, which initiates chuckles from the other officers. With my head down on the ground covered in mud and pain taking up every thought, I can't make out who is speaking, but I do recognise the voice.

The man who rugby tackled me turns me over with his giant, booted foot.

'Well, if it isn't my good friend Tristan. Happy Christmas,' the familiar voice says. The police officer from the night Lara disappeared, Wainwright, looks down over me, but what surprises me, is that he looks happy. His silhouette is clear, blocking the sunlight from shining directly onto my face.

He still dons a bushy moustache, and his straight, short haircut looks pristine. 'Seen any more disappearing people or magic tricks in the past year, have we?' he asks mockingly, and the watching officers snigger at this remark. Surprisingly, the sight of Wainwright makes my merciful screams subside due to obvious distraction.

His expression changes from smugness to confusion as he takes note of the look that's etched on my face. 'What is it this time?' he asks, unimpressed.

'The gravestone... it's not glowing anymore,' I plea to him with the small amount of breath I can gather.

'What do you mean it's not glowing anymore? More hocus pocus nonsense, is it?' he replies.

'It was glowing... did you not see it?' I whisper meekly.

'Still a nut-job then, eh? Never mind, I'll make sure I book you in with a nice doctor first thing tomorrow morning.'

The man who tackled me to the ground binds my hands together with handcuffs to almost breaking point and raises me to a standing position with a single hand. The thought that I'm going to be spending the next however many years in prison hasn't even started to sink in yet. Being forced into a shabby, leather seat in the rear of the police vehicle, I stare shamefully down at the floor. Through the gaps in the mesh windows, glimpses of pedestrians in the distance watch the episode as it plays out with phones in their hands; no doubt they're recording videos and taking photographs of the debacle.

What was that glowing on the gravestone? It was definitely some kind of magic, but there's no such thing as magic, is there? Lara must know what it was. Was it only visible to me?

Lara wrote on the letter that it took her months to come up with a plan to meet me, and maybe that was her only chance. I couldn't be more confused or helpless than I am right now. I suppose I'll have to just hope and pray that she can do something else to get me out of this mess, but how is she supposed to do that when I'm trapped inside a prison?

CHAPTER 5

Arrested Development

The pleasant heat inside the deserted police station reception area rebounds off me like a solar wind. I'm flabbergasted by the building's internal appearance as it's not what I expected, but I've never been in an actual police station before. My abysmal reflection glares back at me in the plastic screen which surrounds the reception area.

The handcuffs are cutting their way through my wrists in front of me. The force of the officers holding my arms to my side seems unnecessary as I couldn't exactly go anywhere if I tried; my legs are almost paralytic from running what must have been close to a marathon.

Remorse drowns me and I feel as though I've been humiliated and shamed. Being arrested in a public place wearing nothing but a hospital dressing gown on Christmas Day isn't exactly top of the list of my proud moments. Mud is smothering my face, I'm shivering with cold, and the pain is unbearable. If I were to add the fact that I'm pretty sure I did all this for nothing, it's enough to make me want to be standing opposite the balcony again as I did last night.

A female police officer chewing the top of her pen mans the desk. She looks around twenty-five years old, her face hidden behind what must be a fascinating book as they don't raise when we enter. Her blonde hair droops graciously down either side of her face, and her eyes look magnified through her pink-rimmed glasses. The girl is stunningly pretty.

42

My eyes keep constant contact with the tiled floor, intentionally hiding my face from the pretty girl. Finally noticing that she's in the company of other officers, she lays down her copy of *A partygoer's guide to the best bars in Huytree.*

'Can I check this one in please?' Wainwright asks the receptionist.

'Is this the one from this morning in the car chase?' she asks precariously, her eyes widening as she leans towards the plastic screen for closer examination. She must be expecting some kind of monstrosity, but the way I look at the minute, she's probably right in her assumption. 'He doesn't look like I would have expected him to, he's actually kind of cute, expect for all the mud on his face,' she remarks without a hint of sarcasm, offering me a courteous smile. Without replying, my eyes close with the hope of waking up somewhere else.

'Well take a good look now Cybil, because he isn't going to see anyone for a long, long time,' Wainwright replies. The saliva from Jenkins' laugh smothers my neck, making me feel almost nauseous.

Wainwright takes a clipboard from Cybil and inserts it under his arm. In unison, Wainwright and Jenkins walk me through several corridors into the depths of the police station, snaking through the hallways in complete quietude as I dreadingly await my destination. Eventually, a birch-coloured wooden door with a silver plaque reading *Interrogation Room 1* stares back at me, which Jenkins opens with his free hand.

'Take a seat, we'll be back shortly,' Wainwright commands, but I can't help sensing the smugness in his voice when he speaks. He's definitely up to something.

The room has exactly what I would have envisioned; a glass pane, which obviously can be viewed from the other side, a single door to enter or exit the room, and a small CCTV camera in the corner of the ceiling. I sit in silence for the next few minutes pondering my current predicament and reliving the last few hours. I can honestly say that it's the first time in my life that I haven't actually moved an inch because my head is too busy with thoughts to distribute any commands to the rest of my body.

The next time I hear anything, is when the silver door handle creaks downward. Jenkins is now absent, and instead Wainwright is accompanied by somebody else; a doctor if ever I've seen one. His tan-coloured trousers and white jacket give this away without even mentioning the nerdy black specs. The doctor is an older dark-skinned man with white hair sprouting out of each side of his head like one of those photographs you'd see of a mad scientist from years ago.

'Hello Tristan, seasons greetings. My name is Doctor Bob. I've been called here today to assess you on behalf of...'

'I don't need assessing!' I rudely interrupt the doctor, slamming my cuffed hands on the tabletop and causing a pen to roll off on to the ground. Something snaps inside me, and I know they'll use everything in their power to bring me down. It feels wrong shouting at the doctor because he comes across as quite gentle and timid, but how am I supposed to act towards somebody who is probably here to tell me I'm nuts and put me in a padded room? I'm going to spend the rest of eternity surrounded by cushioned walls for the rest of my life if I let them win. A notice on the wall drops to the ground as the doctor jumps back at my rebuke. With his middle finger, he pushes his glasses back to eye level after they'd jumped down to his nostrils in alarm.

'So, I just have a few questions for you, would you mind answering them for me please?' he asks, visibly shaking.

'Go on then,' I reply rather childishly, rolling my eyes. I'm not even going to lie so I don't sound crazy, I know there's something funny going on out there somewhere. First Lara disappeared into thin air, then I received a letter from her after a year, there was that funny pizza man business last night, then the glowing gravestone, and this is all after seeing those strange people on the photographs who were at our wedding last year. I'm just hoping I can make sense of this before I get locked up for the next ten years, or maybe even longer.

'Thank you, Tristan,' he replies gracefully, as if to thank me for being so cooperative. 'Would you mind telling me what happened to your wife?'

'I've told you all a million times, she disappeared last year on Christmas Eve. She went next door to our neighbour's house. There was a flash, and the pair of them disappeared, and it smelled like hot bubblegum. Our neighbour said he saw them both disappear. Yesterday, a pizza man knocked at my house, and he was weird as anything, he took a dump in the bathroom and then left. I then received a letter from Lara, who told me to go to Macro Meadow at ten o'clock this morning and I'd find a glowing gravestone. On my way out of my flat last night, I fell and woke up at half past eight in hospital with minimal time to get there.'

Wainwright and Doctor Bob lock eyes for seconds and it's impossible to tell if they're going to laugh at me or put a bag over my head and bury me in a desert. 'Very good,' the doctor says. 'Do you still have the letter from your wife?'

'Nope, it was in my flat when I smashed my head in. Sorry, I should have been a bit more cautious. Apologies doctor,' I snort, sounding like a spoilt child and sitting back in my chair.

Wainwright's moustache flinches as he steps eagerly towards me, examining my expression sternly, then glances back to the doctor. 'What was that about a glowing gravestone? Me and the other officers didn't see anything,' Wainwright states, his eyes flickering back in my direction.

'Yeah, it was glowing purple, it was surreal, like something you'd never seen in your life,' I exclaim, not holding anything back. The doctor's hand twitches rapidly as he makes notes on his notepad as if he's marking me down for errors on my driving test. Good job it isn't my driving test; after years of speeding and driving like a maniac to finish work on time, I'd fail before we got out of the test centre.

Doctor Bob looks worryingly at Wainwright. 'I think you were right in your presumptions earlier. A classic case of psychosis, I wouldn't put it past him to start murdering his family within the next few weeks at this rate. It sounds as if his intense grief has rendered him delusional.'

'You know I'm still in the room, don't you?' I butt in rudely, but I can't help feeling there may be at least some truth to this accusation. Maybe I am crazy. What if this is all in my head? What if Lara was genuinely kidnapped and everything since then has been a figment of my imagination? There's also the possibility that when I tumbled and hit my head, I fell into a coma, and I'm trapped inside some kind of mental reality that's occurring inside my mind.

Although, by then I'd already seen the letter, so maybe not.

As the conversation continues, that obviously isn't really going anywhere except to make me sound like I'm completely bonkers, a bizarre noise from outside in the corridor stops us all in our tracks. The sound is extremely peculiar, a sort of mix between a whistle and a wolf howling. It comes to my attention after hearing this noise, that while we've been cooped up in this room, the external sounds have become more minimal over time. Maybe all the other officers in the station are having their lunch breaks, or maybe there's been a mass murderer on the loose and they've all left to hunt them down leaving us in the station alone. It could be that it's Christmas Day and there are less staff on shift, but is that how police stations work? When we first arrived in the room, there were other officers wandering around – I could hear them chatting. It seems to be silent outside now, except for this new strange noise. Wainwright's head lifts cautiously, then he proceeds to the door, poking his head around the door frame in a giraffe-like manner.

'What on earth is that?' I hear him allude to himself. 'Doc, come and check this out.' With extreme hesitation, Doctor Bob trudges warily out into the corridor to follow Wainwright, the door swinging back automatically behind him. I can tell the doctor isn't keen on the idea of following, but his professionalism and obeying demeanour seem to make it impossible to decline.

A shout of panic resounds through the corridor, and then another shout, and then a library-esque silence. The indescribable silence causes a spine-tingling sensation to course through my body like wildfire. I'm not sure if it's terror or a primitive curiosity that give me this feeling, but it's genuine without a doubt. What the hell is going on?

The handcuffs connecting my hands in front of me on the desk give me a terrified, helpless, panicked feeling as if I'm trapped in a room with an axe-wielding maniac with no means of escape. I won't be able to defend myself with these things restricting me. Standing up with trembling knees, I approach the door with a struggle, still in heaps of pain from earlier. I'll half-heartedly admit that I was kind of looking forward to being thrown in a cell so I could have a good night's sleep after all this palaver. I was in bad enough pain after falling, but that Jenkins guy rugby tackling me multiplied it massively. The cold door presses against my ear as I listen for an oncoming crazy person, with sweat beginning to soak my forehead.

There it is. A footstep towards the door, the squeak you get from a new pair of trainers on a shiny gym floor, and again, nearer this time.

I back away from the door cautiously, holding my tied hands together down to my right side so I can attempt to prepare a swing at whoever enters. What could Wainwright have seen outside the room to make him investigate? And why did Wainwright and the doctor shout panickily, then not return to the room?

The shiny, chrome door handle moves down, distorting my reflection as it drops. Hyperventilation has caused my breathing to increase drastically, almost making me drop to the floor. As soon as the handle reaches the bottom, they'll be in here. After what feels like three years, it hits its unlocked position, and the door begins to make its way inwards towards me. A shadow in the doorway stretches onto the ground near me feet.

A hesitation triggers somewhere inside my mind telling me that this person may not even be the person who did… I'm not sure what they did. All I know is that those two men exited the room into the corridor extremely concerned, and now they've gone completely silent after what sounded like a struggle. Do I attack this person or not? What if it's another police officer checking up to see who is in here? But wouldn't they announce themselves before entering?

My hands shoot up from my side simultaneously in the metal handcuffs to swing out into the face of the person who has entered the room. The figure is launched backwards to slam loudly into the corridor wall, and I can make out the sound of plastic hitting the floor as they go hurtling away from me.

'Ow! What the hell was that for?!' The stranger's voice shouts out as he – definitely a he – cups his hands against his face. 'I swear to the Almighty One, I'll kick your nerdy ass if you so much as touch me again!'

As I pass the figure to run for my life through the corridors towards the exit, I halt instantaneously as realisation crosses paths with logic. What the hell? The man who stands opposite the interrogation room door, holds his nose and stares back at me with vengeance in his eyes. He is dressed in a snazzy black suit, accompanied by a pair of white trainers which decorate his feet. His dark hair, which is longer in the middle than it is on the sides, hangs over his now more visible face as his hands begin to drop down. As he flicks his hair back behind the top of his head, the thing that shocks me most is that I recognise him.

'You?!' I gasp, in a tone which implies that I don't know if I'm shocked, angry or relieved. With his suit and trainers, he also wears a red tie, which droops down and ties around his waist like a belt. A pair of sunglasses sit on the ground near his feet, and the pizza man from the night before looks back at me.

'What the heck are you doing here? Who are you?' I ask him, pointing a threatening finger towards him.

'Saving your ass, you ungrateful little…' He stops mid-sentence to bend down and retrieve his sunglasses from the ground, put them on his face, and take a deep breath in an obvious attempt to calm himself down. While he does this, I take the opportunity to glance to the side toward my two earlier acquaintances lying unconscious on the deck. The man speaks with the same quirky American accent that he used last night, except it's slightly less exaggerated.

'What happened to those two?' I ask. 'Are they dead?'

'We'll deal with them in a minute,' he replies, more calmly this time.

'Tell me who you are!' I shout irately, demanding an answer.

'Lara sent me,' he says nonchalantly with a shrug and a raise of his eyebrows.

'What?' I ask, trying my best to process the sentence he just said. 'Lara sent you? Where is she? Is she okay?' I fire the questions at him in quick succession.

'We'll get to that in a minute, I need to teach someone a lesson about manners in the meantime,' he says, then takes a threatening step towards me. It looks like that deep breath he took to calm himself down didn't do much good.

He pulls a cigar out of his pocket, which just confuses me more than anything else. Then he points it at me and says, 'Voodoo nausea.'

Instantly, a surge of vomit rushes up through my throat like lava spewing from a volcano and ejects out of my mouth vigorously. My hands instinctively reach for my knees, but being strapped together, they pass through the gap between my legs, and I drop to the floor, retching past myself like a drunk on a Saturday night.

'Should be about even now,' the man says down to me in a now cheerful tone as if I've had my just desserts, fixing his jacket with both hands.

Once the excessive puking ceases, I dry my mouth with my right shoulder due to the restrictions on my hands, then look up angrily to stare threatening daggers at him. This fighting won't get me anywhere, I need to drop this now and find out who he is and what he's doing. This guy obviously has issues and bickering won't aid me.

'Is Lara okay?' I ask him swiftly, attempting to dry my mouth once again.

'Well, if she sent me, what do you think?'

'Fair enough. So, who are you?' I query.

'Rexton, please don't call me Rexton though, it's Rex to everyone but my mother,' he replies coolly, not explaining as much as I'd hoped for but with a hint of impatience.

'You were at my flat last night. What was all that about? Aren't you a pizza delivery guy?' I ask.

'As if! I'll be honest, I only found out what pizza was a few weeks ago because Lara made me watch every episode of *Friends* and Joey loves pizza. Two hundred and thirty-six episodes she made me watch back-to-back. I had one week to learn this appalling language and she thought the best way around this was to watch every episode of *Friends*! I wouldn't have minded, because I secretly enjoyed it, but I'm still confused why Phoebe didn't end up with David. Seemed a bit odd if you ask me.'

'Wait a second. You didn't previously speak English? And you learnt English by watching every episode of an American TV show in a week?' I ask.

'Pretty much,' he replies. 'It was a bit confusing at first because I didn't know what they were saying, but the more I got through it, the more I understood.'

'So where is Lara now?' I ask, trying my hardest to steer the questions in a saner direction.

'I'm going to take you to her. Don't worry she's fine, still don't know what she sees in you though if you ask me,' he replies with a smile. He didn't have to say it, but I know more than anyone that she could do so much better than me.

'What did you do to those two?' I ask him next. 'Are they dead?'

'Oh yeah, I forgot about those. One of them's dead, accidentally of course, he took me by surprise. Lara is gonna kill me,' he replies, as if somebody's death is the most casual thing in the world. He puts his magic sick-inducing cigar to his mouth and inhales, causing a number of small, round particles to leave his mouth upon exhaling and pop in the air like minute colourful fireworks. 'Let me think what to do here,' he asks himself as he takes another pull on his cigar and clicks his fingers.

Coming to a conclusion of some sort he says, 'Yep, that's probably for the best. Sorry, desperate times call for desperate measures.'

Rex leans over to me and quickly rips a hair from my arm causing me to squeal at the unexpected assault. He attaches my hair to the end of the cigar, which is held firmly in his grip, and points it towards Wainwright's body on the ground. 'Voodoo Avatar,' he bellows with ultimate concentration.

The body of Wainwright seems to transform. His height and build, and even his hair colour changes, as if he's morphing into another person. To my surprise, his clothing even changes. The police uniform is now replaced by the same hospital gown that I'm wearing, including the black slippers to match.

'What did you just do?!' I shout at him in sheer panic, my mouth gaping wide.

'Have a look. Just keep in mind that this wasn't supposed to happen,' he replies, leaning back against the corridor wall, folding his arms and still grinning. His flamboyant and bodacious manner makes me want to hit him again for his lack of information and vague annoying answers.

Approaching the face-down and unconscious form of the police officer, who now has the same hair colour as me, I know exactly what to expect already. 'You've turned him into me?' I whisper silently under my breath in amazement as I nudge him with my foot to turn him over. Seeing yourself, but not in a reflection or photograph feels a lot more bizarre than it sounds. The sight of myself also makes me realise how much of a mess I look currently.

The voice from behind me now comes across as more forgiving and even slightly serious. 'It was an accident; I wasn't supposed to kill him. Just look at this as me cleaning up my own mess. Besides, you don't want to finally leave this hellhole and they're all on the hunt for you, do you? At least this way, nobody will ever suspect that you've done anything wrong and they'll all just think you're dead. It'll now look as if this Wainwright fellow has killed you both and done a runner,' he tells me informatively. 'Why would you want to come back here anyway? It's the pits. I've seen more respectable places near HQ, and that's saying something.'

'HQ? What are you talking about?' This strange man doesn't seem to be speaking in a language I understand. He's using words and phrases which don't sound normal. Why can't he just tell me where Lara is, who he is, and what he's doing here?

'So, let me get this straight; you're taking me away from here and every single person on Earth is going to be thinking I'm dead? Surely somebody will learn of my whereabouts and realise that I'm not dead at some point,' I snap, sounding more confused than confident. 'Besides, won't they just check the DNA, and it won't match or something, you see it all the time in crime shows,' I add matter-of-factly. 'Can you at least tell me where we're going? Surely someone will recognise me no matter where we go, they do have global news these days you know.'

Rex smiles at me conservatively and puts his cigar back in his jacket pocket. 'He's got your DNA. That is technically you lying on the floor down to every exact cell in your body. Also, don't worry about anyone coming to look for you, we're going to Macro.'

'What's a Macro?' I ask.

'It's the planet where Lara is.'

'Another… planet?' An obstruction in my throat causes me to struggle with the words.

'Yep, you ready to go or what? These questions are starting to bug me.'

'Not really. This is all a little bit of a shock if you don't mind me saying so.' I stare with a convoluted gaze, momentarily trying to decode all the information he's just relayed at me. Can all of this be true? It'd have to be one hell of a prank if he were pulling my leg after doing a magic trick in front of my eyes. Finally, I ask him, 'So what's that cigar thing you've got?'

'This thing?' he says and fetches it, once again, from his pocket. 'It's my wand, don't say you don't know what a wand is.'

'A wand?' I reply, totally awestruck. 'Is this gonna be like Harry Potter and you've come to take me away to some wizarding school?'

'Who's Barry Potter? You're a bit old for school, aren't you? Why would I be taking you to school?' he chuckles merrily.

This is becoming really hard work. It's like having a conversation with a two-year-old.

'Was it you who left that note for me outside my door?' I ask him.

He starts counting his fingers as he gives me a list of last night's events. 'Yeah. Your guests really know how to overstay their welcome. So, first, I took the pizza guy's clothes, then I left you a fake menu so you'd call me, and then I delivered the pizza to your place, then I went into that disgusting place you inhabit and cast a smell spell...'

'A what?' I interrupt him.

'A smell spell. That's not what they're actually called, but that's what I call them, it's just a more fun name; it's better than saying *nova aroma* anyway. I had to find some way of getting everyone to leave. It's hard work waiting around for people to bugger off just so I can leave you a letter.'

'But why even bother with leaving me a note at all, couldn't you have just met up with me and told me Lara was okay and she wanted you to get me?'

'Because I didn't realise you were a total dumbass, that's why. All you had to do was go to the portal in Macro Meadow for 10 am on Christmas Day, which would have transferred you to Earth's station, and I could have retrieved you when you got there. Don't make life easy for yourself, do you?'

'So why not just tell me?' I repeat frustratedly as he didn't answer my question and decided to criticise me blatantly instead.

'And you would have believed somebody who you've never met before knocking at your door, claiming that he had a magic wand, knew where your supposedly dead wife was, and that you have to get to a magic portal to go and meet her?' he asks.

'Good point, I probably would have thought I'd gone mad,' I reply in defeat. 'Well can you get these handcuffs off me at least? They're killing my wrists.'

'Sure,' he replies casually. He taps his cigar on the handcuffs, and they pop open like a padlock. 'We done now?'

'Erm, yeah, sure, whatever,' I reply, completely dumbfounded.

'Well let's go then!' he says eccentrically, lifting his two hands in the air and pointing them out in front of him. I follow behind closely, not wanting to lose him around any of the snaking corridors until we reach a fire exit which leads out to the side of the building.

'Where is everybody?' I ask. 'The place seemed to quieten around the time I heard those noises in the corridor.'

'Distracted,' he informs me, keeping his gaze forward. He pushes on the metal bar which lies across the centre of the door that covers the whole width of the frame. A contrasting light bursts in from outside like an angel coming down from the heavens. I'm not sure who this guy is, I'm not sure if he's good or bad, I'm not even sure if he's sane; definitely not sane, but I don't have a choice in whether or not to follow him.

Out in the courtyard at the side of the building, Rex wanders around as if he's trying to find something specific. 'What are you looking for?' I enquire apprehensively.

'Somewhere we won't be seen,' he replies. 'Okay, here we are.' He steps between two SWAT vans parked up beside one another, shielding himself from view. 'Before we do this, there's a few basics you need to know.'

'I think there's quite a lot I need to know actually,' I reply.

He points his cigar-type-wand-thing at the side of one of the vans, then says 'Nova shift,' which causes a swirling maelstrom of black to appear resembling some kind of portal. 'What you need to know, is that our solar system is in danger, and you, my friend, are going to be the one to save it. Assistant Commander Lara has requested your presence, and hopefully, you will be the one to help save us all.'

My mouth opens widely causing slobber to drop onto my gown, and I cannot help but stare into the portal he's just created. My gaze then shifts to him in awe of what he just said. Surely, he's got the wrong guy. 'Right... those basics then,' I gulp, licking my dry lips.

As I begin to feel the force of the portal pulling me in, something catches my eye from behind in the courtyard. A small, tanned, female figure, possibly in their early teens, is staring in our direction with an awestruck expression. The two buns on top of her head are an indication to her approximate age. How did she get into the police station courtyard, who is she? The pull of the portal pulls against me violently to suck me in and an uncomfortable jerk in space and time swallows me whole.

CHAPTER 6

Out Of This World

Lying down on my back feels more relaxing than it should. These last few days have taken their toll on my body, and it's nice to finally be lying down in peace and quiet; it ain't half hot though. In my attempts to move, I'm once again seeded to the spot.

At first glance, I appear to be in the middle of a field somewhere, large stones are scattered around resembling *Stonehenge*, except they're dotted randomly rather than in an organised pattern. The blurred outline of a sun in the sky behind a faint, yellow veil glares down at me from above, hitting my face like a volcanic torchlight. From what I can make out, the sky looks completely cloudless.

Memories of another recent dream I've had begin to arrive at the forefront of my mind. I recall having another dream where the scene was almost replicated, but I wasn't aware of who I was last time. I'm fully aware of who I am this time. Maybe it's not a dream though; it's possible that I went through the portal with Rex and now I've ended up here. I'm so confused.

A mob of people are huddled together in funny looking clothes to my right. Two parents and a young, dark-haired girl are all hugging and crying desperately on each other's shoulders. Everybody else is standing in silence as if they're attending a funeral.

A young boy, who I recognise from the earlier dream I had, stands beside a rather strange-looking, smartly dressed and official bearded man. The man is wearing a suit, but his tie is similar to that of Rex's; it droops down to his navel, but then wraps around his waist to act as a belt.

The man's glasses sit at the end of his nose, almost making contact with his dark, greasy fringe that hangs down to cover his forehead. He begins to speak in a formal tone, like that of a barrister, or a president addressing the nation during his inauguration.

'I am afraid it's time, ladies and gentlemen who are gathered here today. I bear witness to this tragic and unlawful event, which has occurred under our very noses. As you are all aware, rules are rules, and if broken, the offender must pay the ultimate price of exoneration and must be exiled by all accounts to the planet Earth. Salamander Peruvius, you are not the first, and you will certainly not be the last Macronian to be banished, but we must begin this ceremony in haste as we have rather pressing governmental issues to deal with.'

What's going on here? And what do they mean by banished? Is this Salamander kid being punished for what he did to Theo in the previous dream? Surely he can't be sentenced to death no matter what he's done considering his age. Can this even be a dream? Me and Rex went into the portal, and I've started dreaming for some reason; I'm so confused right now.

The official bearded man, who seems to be in charge of the whole fiasco, pulls out a white stick. It looks almost identical to the one I saw Salamander use when he cast the spell on Theo, except the white isn't as immaculately chromatic. Hold on a second, is this one of those *wands* that Rex had? Where am I? I know this isn't real, but I also get the sense that it is. My head hurts.

As the man takes a hold of Salamander's shoulders gently, the mother writhes in the hands of the men who hold her back as she tries to lunge forward kicking and screaming. The sheer desperation in her actions and tone touch the hearts of everyone present, and except for the mother, nobody else whispers so much as a word. Suddenly, the mother breaks free and lurches at the man, knocking down many of the entourage who accompany him. It's like a game of ten-pin bowling, the way they're knocked aside toppling each other down to the ground. As I jump up and attempt to stop this madness, I'm instantly reminded that I'm immobilised, the same way I felt the last time I was in this situation. The woman is restrained before she can reach the boy and held back tightly so that she can't get within a few metres of him. Without sounding like a helpless frail child, tears begin running down my face as the scene is too much to bear. How can any living being have their children taken away from them, it's just sickening having to witness this debacle.

The penitence in the man's face is evident as he leers guiltily at the mother and father, and then back to the boy. He bellows *'Diruo Eternal'*. From what I can recall, that's the same spell I witnessed between the two children. The boy is absorbed into a bubble, causing the crowd of people to howl out in abject retaliation at the act performed. The bubble stands present for a few seconds entrapping the boy, and then it is absorbed into the air like an overinflated balloon popping. *Poof.* The mother's screams are intolerable. An ear-piercing, desperate screech that you couldn't believe unless you were present. It's as if she were in so much pain, her mind and body had been shredded into a thousand pieces. The father cries similarly as he holds the young girl, except you can tell that his masculinity hides the vulnerability in his weeps to act brave. The mother's uncontrolled desperation at losing her son brings a tear to every being in the vicinity. I say being, because some of them don't look like they're human. Strange physical features and qualities make it quite evident that they're not human. Multiple limbs and bedraggled characteristics give a massive hint towards this definitely being the case.

This scene is something I never wish to witness again as long as I live. Watching somebody going through such an ordeal is enough to make even the toughest soldier break down and weep.

I feel the wet moisture flowing down my cheeks like a waterfall as I continue to cry uncontrollably, and the familiar smell of bubblegum hits me once again.

'Why did you have to?!' the mother screams angrily at the top of her voice after finally retrieving her ability to speak. She pants like a dog, and my heart beats crazily as I glance over at the father still standing there crouched over the young girl. Out of everybody who is at this horrifying scene, the daughter is the only one who has a completely dry face and the most emotionless expression that I have ever laid my eyes on. I wonder why she's not upset like everyone else; I'm assuming she must be his sister.

With the droplets still tumbling down my burning cheeks, the scene gets even darker as if a cloud is descending. Like something from a bible extract, the skies fill with an evil, almost sinister darkness which doesn't seem possible, and the sky turns ominously black.

In limbo between this horrifying scene and reality, I struggle to get my mind to focus on what is real. Every time I try to think, it gets swept away and intertwines with my other innocuous thoughts. With my eyes still closed and showing me nothing but extreme blankness, I reach my hand to my face and get a feel of the wet, sticky substance strewn across my features. It doesn't feel like tears, it's somehow more viscous. The wet, disgusting slime drips down the side of my face as my eyes eventually open to a... troll?

My body activates panic mode, and I propel myself from the metal bench I was laid on to turn around and stare at something that resembles an ogre. It has tusks which are too big for its mouth, so they hang out. It has a flat, pig-like nose, and green scaly reptilian skin. Instinctively, I start to back away, horrified of this thing that sits before me, when I notice that there's a whole family of them asleep on the bench next to it. In shock, I turn and begin to run, but upon turning around to face the other direction away from the trolls, the sight before me almost stops my heart from beating.

What is going on? Where am I?

I'm in what I can only describe as an airport lounge; a gigantic out-of-this-world airport with a humongous glass dome roof welcoming me to another universe. Millions of stars fill the glass dome above and it's almost impossible not to be captivated by the truly fascinating scene. What is this place?

It's like some kind of space station, either on Earth or somewhere else. An insurmountable range of different species and beings walk idly past as if they're walking through a terminal in Manchester Airport. The peculiar thing is, they're even dragging suitcases and pushing trolleys around. Families of parents and children, even singular beings, walk (some even waddle and slither) around as if it's usual behaviour being here. Men and women, children, and their friends, they chat and play and shout and scream, but they look strange. Multiple features, fewer features, strange features, an awesome array of beings roam around the place; I can even spot a man with a small monkey-type creature mounted on top of his head.

As I raise my head up towards the amazing display of stars, the current environment captivates my senses, and I can longer see or hear what should be normal.

I stagger forwards open-mouthed, not looking down for even a second, which causes me to trip over clumsily. On my way down to a clear faceplant, I'm stopped in mid-air, caught by something, or someone. As I look toward my saviour, the blue skin and huge ears which hang down to the shoulders make me shriek and back up like a man-eating spider just landed on my arm. The creature replies in an alien dialect, which to me sounds like it is slapping its lips together and flapping its tongue; it definitely doesn't sound impressed. The creature struts off, giving me daggers as it keeps its head pointed in my direction; they should be careful in case they bump into somebody.

It's like something from TV. Like every creature from every sci-fi show ever created gathered in one gigantic room. One species notices me gawping at it in immense awe with my tongue half out, while it feeds its toddler something that resembles worms; and she thinks she has a right to give me funny looks? If looks could kill, then that would have been me done for. I quickly turn away, as you do, to continue observing this fascinating place.

The memories of Rex and our previous conversations begin to make their way back into my train of thought, and it starts to slightly make more sense. The signs dotted around the place start to catch my eye as the more important things have already begun processing in my head. Earth, Macro, Neplio, Jambre. Is this what Rex was talking about? He did say we were going to another planet. I remember before he sucked me into that portal at the police station that my final thought was waking up somewhere else, but I never would have imagined this in a million years.

'Tristan!' I hear the familiar American accent shout from across the room and turn to see Rex pacing quickly towards me holding two paper coffee cups. 'I'm so, so sorry, I thought you were going to be out longer than that. I didn't want you waking up not knowing where you were, I only went over to get us both a coffee.

Asked the Tororu to keep an eye on you and gave him a biscuit in return, they love a good biscuit them Tororus. It's always the way though isn't it; I've sat with you for around two hours, and you haven't so much as flinched, I leave for five minutes, and you wake up. First-time travellers always take a while to wake up, you'll get used to it after a few times. I had to carry you all the way from the departures lounge. Have you ever thought about going on a diet?'

I decide to put the comment about my weight to one side for now, mostly because I know it's probably true that I could do with losing a few pounds. 'You didn't want me not knowing where I was? And where is that exactly? Who are all these freaks walking around?!' I rasp in total desperation and confusion while grabbing his collar with both hands as if I'm about to raise him up from the ground. The sudden jerk as I grab him causes him to fumble the two coffee cups out of his hands and they splash over the floor beneath us. The smell of strong coffee rises and hits my nose instantly. What a waste, I would have loved a coffee around about now to wake me up properly.

'Chill out Tristan, please, I'm sorry, let me fill you in. You're causing a bit of a scene,' he states, visibly shaking as he looks around at all the people staring. Well, if you can call them people that is.

'How can I be causing a scene when there is literally a man walking past behind you who has what can only be described as a penis on the top of his head?!' I half shout and half whisper in panic, trying to keep the volume as minimal as I possibly can given the current circumstances. My grip loosens as I'm alerted to the hundreds of sets of eyes looking at the pair of us. I let go of Rex's collar, patting it back down for no other reason than I've seen it hundreds of times in movies.

'Forget those coffees on the floor,' he says, glancing down at the pool of brown liquid below us. 'Follow me and I will explain all. Oh, and one more thing,' he says, turning back to me. 'You ever lay a finger on me again and I will personally see to it that you don't live another day, you got that?' he retorts, pointing his finger in my face a few inches from poking my eye out. Rex then changes his expression completely and it's like a switch from night to day. He smiles a hearty grin, gyrates on the spot, and points his two hands in front of him as he begins to skip forward jollily.

'Whatever,' I retort, trying to show him that I'm not intimidated, when the fact is that I'm more intimidated than I've ever been.

Rex continues to prance off towards a row of shops against a far metal-plated wall, completely dismissing me entirely. I have no other choice but to follow him through the massed crowds of *people* and tail him towards the shops. Three rather small stores stand lined up in a row ahead of us; a souvenir shop, which looks like it sells all kinds of tat like clothing and books; a restaurant stands next door to that, which just looks like your typical average restaurant, except for the person sitting down eating food with their elephant's trunk. The final store is a small coffee shop with a sign above which reads *Earth Coffee and Cakes.*

'I would have got you something a bit more interesting, but at that store you can only get boring Earth food,' he says, stopping in front of the row of shops.

'You mind if I just grab some clothes from that shop? I'm still in a hospital gown and the thought of wearing this for one more minute is something I don't even want to think about. It's just a good job I've got underwear on, or you'd see an additional moon to the ones out there,' I say to Rex and point up towards the planets above, giving a chuckle.

'Sure, I'll wait outside,' he replies. 'Here, take this credit ball and just scan it at the checkout, spend what you need, I've just got a few calls to make,' he says, then lingers outside the store with his sunglasses down over his face and a small device in his hand.

'Mind if I have a go of your glasses for a bit? What do they even do?' I ask inquisitively.

'Can't you see I'm making a call here? Go and buy something, just be on your best behaviour,' he commands me.

'Thanks dad, what would I do without you?' I reply cheekily, entering the store through doors that automatically raise into the ceiling.

'And don't forget to buy a hat while you're in there!' he calls before I'm out of earshot.

'Is that so nobody recognises me?'

'No, it's because your hair looks a bloody mess,' he calls back.

It's like a library in the store with the number of books filling the shelves. I make my way across the bookshelves and a few of the names stand out to me. *The history of the Oryx and how he ruled*, *Wand Wars and how to play for beginners*, *The History of the Xanarock*, *Neplio: The Capital*, and many more. A woman on the front cover of *The History of the Xanarock*, looks a bit like Lara, causing butterflies to make their way into my stomach once again at the thought of her. I can't wait to see her again; her hair probably won't smell the same because I doubt you can buy the same shampoo in outer space, but I'm sure I could live without that.

Curiously, I pick up all four of the books and make my way over to the clothing range. I'm unsure why I'm even buying these books, but there's usually a lot of waiting round at airports so it should help pass the time. The next thing which I pick up is a backpack to carry my newly acquired books. The backpack has multiple straps which can be removed or added depending on your number of limbs.

Looking through the array of peculiar items on sale in the clothing section, I'm stumped at how any of this is going to fit me. What would I need four shoes for? And what would I do with a pair of trousers with four legs?

After an extensive search through the range, I decide on a quartet of trainers; two of which I'll discard, some black trousers with four legs, two of which I'll wrap around my waist, and a colourful orange shirt that zips up from the back.

Approaching a screen on the wall because there doesn't appear to be a counter to pay for the items, I try to fathom out what everything on the display means. Some of the signs on the wall are in English, but some of them are completely foreign to me; it doesn't even look like writing, it's all colours and illegible squiggles. A sign with an arrow pointing downwards to a sensor seems to be my best bet so I wave the credit ball which I acquired from Rex at the screen. The screen flashes purple in confirmation and the words *thank you for your custom* appear. The credit ball is strange, and it reminds me of one of those 8-ball toys from when I was a kid where you shake it to ask the future. Lastly, I head into the changing rooms before leaving so I can finally get out of this hospital gown. The clothes fit me perfectly, except for the fact that I can't zip up the shirt from the back. The extra legs which hang down at my side in the trousers get wrapped around my waist like a belt to make myself blend into the innocuous crowd at the space station. Exiting the store, I see, apart from the hundreds of strange species still roaming around, Rex with his sunglasses pulled down over his eyes speaking to somebody in an unfamiliar dialect.

'Hey Rex, you alright?'

'Yeah, all good,' he replies, pushing his sunglasses up from his eyes to the top of his head. 'Looking good. Didn't they have any hats?'

'Shut up,' I reply at his jest.

'Fancy a coffee or something and I can tell you about what's going on, or you happy being clueless?'

'Coffee sounds fantastic,' I reply. 'You got anywhere in mind?'

'Let's go to the Café Éxtraterrestrileé? Lara's paying,' he says, as he takes the credit ball from my hand and waves it in front of him gleefully.

CHAPTER 7

Café Éxtraterrestrileé

I shadow Rex through the space station to what I suspect is some sort of swanky fine-dining restaurant, passing more and more odd creatures as we venture onwards. A weird-looking horde of fish-like people pass us, walking on muscular legs and holding contraptions that look a bit like surfboards. A select few even have those funny whiskers that some types of fish have and shiny, flapping gills.

The thoughts of this being a dream keep flicking on and off in my head like a switch. Is it possible that this may not be real? I have had some strange dreams lately and they were no more bizarre than this, but I couldn't move or speak. What if this is just a lengthy, bizarre dream that I can't seem to wake up from.

We arrive at a platform that has no barriers. It appears to be a circular grid that rises up in the middle of the busy plaza through a gap in the ceiling. As we stand on the platform, waiting for what is presumably an elevator to begin ascending, I realise that this could be an exclusive restaurant, like a first-class lounge. There doesn't appear to be many other species trying to gain access. A sign hovering beside the elevator reads *Café Éxtraterrestrileé*, which is accompanied by an illuminated green arrow pointing skywards towards the ceiling. After a few moments, the elevator activates, and a green light fills the small platform as it begins to levitate to what seems like another world.

Approaching the top of the elevator and now having a view of what's inside, I can see that the beings here are wearing more formal clothing. The bizarre thing is, I don't know the attire here, but I can already tell they look as if they're making more of an effort to look fancy.

Rex and I approach the lady who seems to be showing everyone to their seats. 'How you doin'?' Rex says flirtatiously with a charming façade.

'Really?' I say, completely dumbfounded. 'What do you think you're doing?'

'Shut up, I'm trying to pull here,' he whispers meekly through the side of his mouth.

'I'm good thank you sir, and you?' the lady standing behind the reception desk replies politely. The receptionist has long, brown, floppy ears which hang down beyond her shoulder. 'Would you two gentlemen like a table?'

'Yes please, just the two, unless you'd like to join us of course,' Rex replies with a wink.

The lady with the drooping ears just stares blankly and replies calmly, 'I cannot fraternise with customers, but I finish at 8 if you're interested.'

'Cool, I'll add you to my contacts and get back to you in a few days. Lovely meeting you Miss...' Rex says with a charming smile filled with white teeth.

The woman replies courteously, 'My name is Princess Beulah Chinchilla.'

'Whoa, you're a princess?' Rex enquires with fascination.

'Nope, that's just my name,' she informs him, causing his excited look to subside to disappointment. The lady pulls up one of the long sleeves on her arm to show a flashing red dot beneath the skin on her wrist. Rex carries out a similar action and a red dot is also visible beneath his wrist. Their wrists almost touch and a flash on both wrists, along with a quiet confirming beep, must inform them that they've successfully added each other to their contacts list. I wonder what those lights are underneath their skin. Suppose it's not worth asking yet with all these people around though, I don't want to sound thick so I'll hold off until we sit down.

'How come I can understand her, but I can't understand anyone else? One person who spoke to me earlier was smacking his lips together, but I couldn't understand a word of it,' I ask.

'Because she was speaking English maybe?' he replies smugly.

'Should have come to that conclusion myself really, shouldn't I?' I comment.

'We're not as arrogant as you Earth people,' he says, working his way past the other diners to reach a distant table. 'There are no rules as to what species you can or cannot fraternise with; anyone is fair game,' he tells me as he sits, then presses a button on the table. A hologrammatic screen appears in front of him above the table, around the size of an A4 sheet of paper. Rex begins swiping his fingers left and right to scroll through the extensive menu. The entirety of the text on the screen is made completely of light and it doesn't appear to be in English from what I can see reversed as I'm on the opposite side of it. Copying Rex, I press my corresponding button, and the same menu appears in front of me too, which is also not in English.

'What do you fancy to drink?' Rex asks me.

'Whatever. Anything with alcohol please to calm my nerves,' I reply, not paying much attention as I'm taken aback by someone licking their feet at one of the other tables.

'Sorry, alcohol is prohibited everywhere but Earth. I can get you some macrohol though if you want it,' he replies. Not knowing what macrohol is, I request a coffee.

'Two coffees coming up, I don't do macrohol either,' Rex says. 'Got to keep a cool head at all times.' He presses some buttons on the screen and uses the credit ball to tap against a sensor on the table.

The table we are occupying has an awesome view of the infinitesimal wonders beyond the window and I am so captivated that I forgot where we were for the last few minutes. The view is enchanting, and the barrages of colour and light sweeping through the sky seem almost impossible to translate into words. We're stuck on a tiny little planet, and all this is out here that we're unaware of; but why are humans unaware of all of this? Everybody else seems to be part of it, but not us.

A few moments later, a lady (I assume it's a lady) arrives at our table with fresh, steaming cups, and two bizarre-looking cakes. One cake is in the shape of a bright red sphere with an orange line circling around its centre. The delicacy reminds me of a cricket ball, except this is made entirely of marzipan and icing. The other cake is just a plain chocolate cake with fudge in the centre, how boring! She places the peculiar red and orange coloured cake in front of me and hands me a fork, then sets the coffee down on the table alongside it.

Once the lady is out of earshot, Rex's serious glare reappears. 'Look, we only have thirty minutes until our shuttle leaves, so we'll have to make this brief, but I'll let Lara fill in the gaps once we reach Macro. She told me to inform you of any basics like the solar system and the space stations etcetera, but don't bombard me with questions; I hate questions.' Rex then takes a large bite out of his chocolate cake.

I follow suit and take a nibble of the pretty-looking, spherical, fire-red cake and chew until I savour its flavoursome delights. 'Wow!' I exclaim in awe, holding my hand up to my mouth as the sweet delicacy begins to take over my senses. 'This is the most amazing thing I've ever tasted. What is it?'

'It's a *phoenix ball cake*,' he informs me. 'Probably one of the finest delicacies you can find being so close to Earth, but there's much nicer food the further you venture out.' We take a couple more bites and sip our coffees as if we haven't had food or drink in days. I decide this is probably the most fitting opportunity to begin my interrogation.

'So, Lara is in this Macro place you said. Where's that?'

'Yeah, she arrived there just over a year ago. She's told us all about what happened. How much did you manage to figure out on your own?' he asks curiously.

'Well, she went over to our neighbour's house, and somebody came in through the back door, then all three of them disappeared. Presumably, this person who entered was either working alongside Gregory, or he made him disappear too. How did they make Lara disappear? Was it one of those funny spells that you do with your wand?' I ask.

'Probably. Let me show you something,' he says, and reaches into his jacket pocket to retrieve a neatly folded piece of black paper.

'What's that?' I enquire curiously.

'It's a map of our solar system.' He unfolds the map out onto the tabletop and begins to point at several different planets and stars with names that are completely unbeknownst to me. 'There's Earth, that one is Jambre, next to that we've got Macro; you see that small one right there. That one right there is Neplio.' His finger points at a colossal blueish green planet that is easily one of the largest on the map. 'Neplio is the capital planet of the solar system where the High Council are based.'

I stare at the map in excitement, wondering what all these places must be like; the food to taste, the drinks, the species that live there. It's as if somebody has just opened a door to a brand-new universe; technically they have in a manner of speaking.

'Without pointing out the obvious, why can't we see all this from Earth? How come when our top scientists look up at the sky, everywhere else seems to be completely barren and there's no signs of life. Or better still, why aren't there all sorts of alien people walking around Earth?' I ask inquisitively.

Rex takes a large gulp of his coffee, which gives me a hint to this being a long-winded explanation. 'Okay, so hundreds of years ago, Earth was part of this solar system. People used to travel to and from Earth like they do on any other planet. Being the way your species are, it was inevitable that one day they'd do something stupid enough to get on everyone's nerves. After years of uncivilised etiquette and unforgivable criminal behaviour which I won't delve into, the High Council on Neplio came up with a plan to ostracise it completely.'

'Surely we couldn't have been that bad!' I exclaim to try and defend my fellow planet dwellers, but after I say it, my memories remind me that we probably were in fact, that bad.

'Ha!' he laughs out loud to jeer at my previous comment. 'I was only on Earth for two days and I saw the reckless behaviour and drunken states you lot get yourselves into. I didn't actually believe these rumours myself until I saw it with my own eyes. Believe it or not, the final straw was when they all decided it was a good idea to throw a massive party on a nearby star without authorisation from the High Council.'

'It's only a party, these planets are huge, surely a few humans throwing a party on a star isn't exactly crime of the century.'

'Two million is not a few,' he replies, shaking his head in disgust. 'They left a mountain of alcohol containers the size of Olympus Mons, and that's not even the worst thing. Can you imagine the stench of said star when it does not have a stable atmosphere or the ability to recycle its water through precipitation and there are millions of tonnes of waste lying around?'

I balk at this, imagining being there the morning after.

'Every molecular being on the planet was eradicated, killed off by human waste; not a way I'd want to go if you ask me. The rest of the solar system was sick of human behaviour, and they collectively signed a decree stating that action had to be taken.'

'Each year, on the Earth calendar, a planet is chosen to host the *Intergalactic Games*. Thousands of species from around the solar system travel to the host planet to compete in tests of strength and skill to figure out who is the best of the best at each given task. The High Council chose Earth to host the games deliberately but sent out a warning to every other planet that this was a ruse to gather every human in one place. Any humans who were not present on Earth at the time, travelled back home for the games. Once all the humans were gathered on their home planet and every other species was avoiding it, BOOM! They fired a spell at the planet confining it to its own bubble of existence. Of course, there were probably a few anomalies like humans not being on Earth, or other species being on Earth when it happened, but these would have been rectified over time.'

'Wow, really?! That's one hell of a story. I can't wait to get home and tell my mum,' I reply in jest, but Rex doesn't even throw me a glance, picking up the obvious sarcastic tone.

'Why do you think it's near enough impossible to leave your planet? The spell that was cast placed a belt of radiation around the planet; I think you lot refer to it is the *Van-Allen Belt* from what I can recall.'

'I've heard of that. It was one of the reasons they said the Apollo missions were a hoax; it was because we couldn't travel through this radiation belt.' I look back down to the map to continue my investigation. 'So where are we now on this map?' I ask curiously, scanning the map for a small space station near Earth like I'm trying to find *Where's Wally*.

'You haven't figured that out yet?'

'Should I have?' I ask, confused by the fact that I should have figured out where we were as if it was obvious, and I was a complete thicko.

'Each planet has a space station, and slap bang in the middle of Earth and Jambre, there is a place which we're heading to next called *Centrol Station*. Centrol Station is at the epicentre of the solar system and anyone travelling from one side of the solar system to the other must pass through it.' He points at the small star on the map between Earth, and a small red planet called Jambre. 'We use the moons of each planet as stations to travel, the only exception to this rule is Macro, but you'll see why when we get there.'

'But with so many different species, you're the only one I've seen so far that looks human. Are you originally from Earth?'

'God no, I couldn't think of anything worse. People who are originally from Macro, Macronians, are identical in appearance to humans. No doubt there's a genetic or ancestral similarity there, but who knows?

'I know I'm changing the subject quite diversely, but can I go back to yesterday? What was all that business with the gravestone, and the letter from Lara saying I had to get there for 10 am. How come nobody else could see the glowing gravestone, and why did it have to be that exact time?' I can already tell from his expression that my questions are starting to make him irate and what he said earlier about not liking questions is undeniably factual.

Rex takes the final bite of his chocolate cake and sits back in his chair, arms crossed and looking ultimately fed up. 'There are two ways to get to the station from the planet you're currently on; this is either by one of many portals dotted around the planet, or through an ad-hoc type of portal like the one I summoned to get us here, which is activated through a spell. You can't use the portals indoors, as when we are transported, the doors and walls provide a blockade which our particles cannot penetrate through. When we travel through portals, every particle in our genetic structure is broken down into light particles and transported to the departures lounge located at the station you are going to be travelling from, which is the moon of the current planet you're on. This had better be your last question because we'll have to make a move shortly,'

Rex says and begins his preparation to depart from the table. He lifts his coffee cup, then presses another button, which makes an aperture in his side of the table that he inserts his empty plate into, then closes it again.

'The portals down on the Earth's surface are controlled remotely and opened by the operators up here in this station. Lara managed to pull a few strings to book in a one-minute timeslot for 10 am on Christmas Day. She mentioned something about this being the best Christmas present which money couldn't buy for you. For security purposes, the name of the traveller must be provided, and the relevant security checks must be carried out to ensure the individual is permitted to travel from Earth. Because Lara is Lara and she's good at pulling strings, she somehow tricked them into thinking you were allowed to leave Earth and had the nearest portal to your house activated for 10 am on Christmas Day, then had me leave you the letter. Because you're such a dim-witted, asinine, pointless, imbecilic idiot, you missed the deadline and I had to resort to plan B; find a way to bring Tristan to Macro without fail if he doesn't make it to the portal on time.'

'Alright, alright, no need to get nasty,' I say to him apologetically, holding my hands up guiltily. 'But I'm still confused at why you had to go through the rigmarole of taking the pizza man's clothes and delivering pizzas to me, when slipping the letter under my door earlier would have been easier. Instead of planting the menu and have me call you, I could have just read the letter then and skipped all the weirdness with the toilet.'

'Because I had to get the letter to you while you were alone. I knew you were having people around and I didn't want to risk you finding out before then and running your mouth off to everyone. The reason I had to get into your house and get rid of everyone, was because they could have stayed until morning, and then what? The time slot for the portal was booked for 10 am and I did what was necessary to get you out here. I don't see what your problem is, you're here aren't you?' he explains.

If only I would have not tripped over on my way out of the flat. I could have saved myself a whole heap of trouble. I wouldn't have ended up in hospital, locked the nurse in the cupboard, stole the granny's car, went on a high-speed pursuit, got rugby tackled and arrested, had Rex break me out of the police station, and he wouldn't have transformed Wainwright into me, so they thought I was dead because he killed him by accident. What would have happened if I made it to the portal on time at 10 am? I would have presumably been transported here and Rex would have collected me at the departures lounge. Oops, I feel like a right idiot.

'All passengers heading for Centrol Station, flight CS4372 please head to gate BB71. I repeat, all passengers heading for Centrol Station, flight CS4372 please head to gate BB71, shuttle leaves in ten minutes,' the loudspeaker booms through the entire station. Then repeats itself in a few different languages and dialects to relay the message to any other travellers.

'That's us,' Rex says, standing up from his seat.

'Hold on, I've still got a million questions.'

'Then you'll have to wait. If people hear me explaining the basics of our solar system to you and you're from Earth, they could figure out you're a stowaway and I'll be in big trouble. Under no circumstance should anybody from Earth be knowledgeable about life outside the planet without permission from the High Council.'

'What, so I'm here illegally?!' I whisper loudly, still sitting in my seat and grabbing his arm as he attempts to walk away.

'Yes, but don't worry, just don't act like a tourist and nobody will be any the wiser. This place is full of weirdoes; I'm sure you'll be fine.'

'Did you just call me a weirdo?' I ask, but he ignores me and struts off towards the exit.

We take our leave and descend back to the ground floor, continuing to make our way through the station following the signs for *Gate BB71*. Listening to the uncountable array of species that pass us, it seems impossible to know what language they're speaking or what sound they're making. How do people keep track of all these different languages? There must be thousands.

Rex halts abruptly, yanking me by the arm into a quiet corridor off the beaten track as he seems to suddenly realise something; I just don't know what.

'Almost forgot,' he says, panning his head around the corners suspiciously to make sure nobody is looking. 'Give me your wrist.'

'What for?' I ask quizzically but know that I'm in no position to refuse his request.

'Never mind what for, just pass me your damn wrist.'

I hold my wrist out without hesitation, expecting him to read my palm or check my pulse or something of that nature, but he grips it tightly. 'See that woman over there?' he says, nodding to an obscure-looking creature visible out in the main corridor.

'The one with the three legs?'

'Yeah, that one,' he says calmly with an air of concentration in his voice.

'Wow, I bet she's really good at footb... OW!' I scream as the pain surges through my entire arm, as if somebody's just stabbed me with a sharpened pencil. 'What was that for?!' I exclaim angrily. I peer down at my wrist, expecting to see a waterfall of blood cascading to the ground, but it doesn't seem any different than normal; except for the small red light blinking underneath my skin that is. 'What the hell was that for?! That bloody hurt! What do I need one of these for?'

'Relax, you big baby,' he responds. 'It's just your chip implant, everybody has one, there's no way you'd get through security without it. This chip holds every piece of biometric data of your identity, and seeing as you're a stowaway, I don't think it'd go down well with the authorities if you didn't have one, would it?'

'Suppose not,' I reply defeatedly.

'We've had to break a few rules to get you here. You'll need an implant to bypass security and get to Macro, but unfortunately, there's no other alternative. I've made you a fake one. Just remember, your name's Tranjula Pokkoman. That's the name we've registered into the chip for you.'

Although it's quite nerve-racking, I do get a sense of excitement and adventure from this expedition. I feel like I'm in a spy movie and I'm hiding my identity to travel the stars to see the girl that I love.

As we exit the corridor back onto the main stretch, there isn't a single person looking our way as we continue towards our destination to reach Gate BB71. Finally, we join the rear of a snaking queue of various species waiting to board.

Out of the blue, an announcement booms around the entire place:

'*Service Call 99! I repeat, service call 99! All available security personnel please make your way to security gate 4L7Q.*'

'What's all that about?' I ponder to Rex, wondering what a *service call 99* is.

Rex looks as confused as me. 'Dunno,' he says. 'Could be anything from someone stealing a stick of goopok to someone being murdered.'

Standing in front of us as we join the queue, a family that have similar genetic physicalities to foxes, except that they're standing upright on two legs, chat excitedly in line. One of the children seems to be conversing with her mother about unicorns, and then she changes the subject to *Wand Wars*, chatting away about some tournament or other. The thing that surprises me most about this is not the unusual content of the conversation, but more so that I can understand them.

'How come I can understand them?' I whisper to Rex beside me.

'It's the chip in your wrist. It translates any language to your native tongue.' Impressive. Would this work on Earth so I could now speak every language on our planet like Chinese or Spanish? I always wanted to learn a new language, good job I didn't, what a waste of time that would have been now I've got one of these in my wrist.

We arrive at the front of the queue, and I try to imitate Rex's actions as he reaches the gate. There is a pedestal with a scanner on the base that looks like a barcode scanner which we use on the self-service counters in supermarkets with a red light facing up and flashing away. He places his right wrist onto the scanner and the glass panel in front of him opens outwards, granting access to what must be the boarding section. The whole process and appearance almost mirror a replica of a normal Earth airport. As he scans his wrist, the monitor in front of him flashes profusely for a couple of seconds, showing his picture and name. *Rexton Kewell-Pants.* Surely that can't be a real name. I imitate Rex, copying his actions almost entirely. The gate opens outward, and my image appears on the screen for a couple of seconds with the name *Tranjula Pokkoman* underneath. A portrait of me appears on the screen, it's the photograph which Lara has as the screensaver on her mobile phone. Presumably, she still has her phone and uploaded it to their system.

'Tranjula Pokkoman? Who the hell is Tranjula Pokkoman?' I ask Rex, catching up with him down the narrow tunnel leading towards the shuttle.

'He was an entertainer of some kind years ago. I saw his name in a book the morning I created your profile so just went with that, then I got a photograph of you from Lara and attached it to the ID,' he informs me. 'Can you please stop with the questions though? This is sensitive stuff you're talking about here. If somebody overhears us, then we're both screwed.'

We walk side-by-side through a chrome, cylindrical tunnel, which is probably the shiniest, sparkliest thing I've ever witnessed in my life. The sides of the tunnel make me appear different sizes and shapes depending on where I look, akin to those places at fairgrounds with all the strange mirrors inside. Reaching the far side of the tunnel and passing over the threshold, we enter a gigantic, futuristic-looking carriage lined with beds. The beds don't appear to be placed orderly in the middle of the aisles, instead they're embedded into the walls like pods. It beats being on an aeroplane with some snotty child kicking the back of my seat I suppose. Small circular windows are placed beside each bed to peep out at the millions of stars and planets in the distance, and it feels impossible to not be mesmerised by it all.

'I know we're obviously going to this Macro place, but can you elaborate on that a little bit? How long is the flight? What are we supposed to do on the flight to keep ourselves occupied?' I ask inquisitively, walking in front of Rex as we look for beds 3QR and 3QS. Surprisingly, I feel a jolt and my head lurches forwards as a hand slaps me across the back of the head, accompanied by a low growl from behind. 'I totally deserved that, okay I'll stop with the questions, message received,' I say and hold my hands up in acceptance.

'There is one thing I do need to mention,' he says. 'In Earth time, the journey to Central Station from here is roughly seventeen hours.'

'Seventeen hours! What the hell am I supposed to do for seventeen hours?! I haven't got my phone or anything. Are there any movies I can watch at least because I can't see a screen?' I exclaim to him as the last thing I want to do is be stuck on a flight for two-thirds of a day with nothing to do.

'Don't worry,' he replies, smirking at the shocked expression on my face. 'It's not as bad as it seems. This isn't Earth, we are way more technologically advanced. You notice that they're beds and not seats?'

'Yeah, but what if I'm not tired, what if I can't sleep, or lie there awake all night. It's seventeen hours for god's sake.'

'Please let me finish,' he says, giving me an impatient glare and puts a hand on my shoulder as we reach the two beds which must be allocated to us. 'You can induce your sleep. Stay awake, or go to sleep, that's your choice; I know which one I'll be choosing. You see that tube hanging from the ceiling? Just put that over you face, and you can sleep for the whole journey, just make sure you also fit the groin attachment, don't want to wake up when we get there covered in your own pee do ya? This is the easiest way to travel between planets, especially when you're going to Photon, it takes almost three days to get there from here.'

Why don't we have this on Earth? I remember going to the dentist when I was younger, and they'd put a gas mask over my face. Before I even realised, I'd gone to sleep with no memory of getting my tooth extracted. This is a genius idea really. If I ever get back to Earth, I'm going to suggest this; especially for those long flights. It may be an idea to just do it for the kids to shut them up. Or they could just release it into the cabin and all the passengers could sleep. I suppose it'd be against human rights though for the passengers who didn't want to sleep, and they'd make no money from in-flight sales.

Almost every passenger in my line of view is taking off their shoes and socks, or getting ready for comfort in some way, so I decide to do the same. My new trainers get kicked off, and I undo the extra pant leg which is wrapped around my waist. Reaching up to examine the mask which hangs down attached to a clear tube, I note there's nothing too exciting about it really. It's just your average mask that would hang down on a plane when the oxygen levels drop.

'Would you like any help sir?' a lady flight attendant asks.

She must have noticed me fumbling with the mask and looking completely clueless. 'First time on a shuttle sir? You just need to pull the back of the mask, so it stretches behind your head and attaches to your face. The illuminated buttons above your head can be activated to excrete particular aromas. Each aroma can help induce different types of dreams. Please remember to connect the groin attachment, and before you know it, you'll be at Centrol Station.'

Even though she looks like a fox, it's fascinating how attractive she is; is that just completely wrong to say on another level? Is that like saying a dog looks attractive? Probably not. Dogs walk around on four legs and sniff each other's behinds; these foxes are just like women. The attendant gives me a wink and says, 'Have a nice flight sir,' before making her way up the aisle to the rear of the shuttle.

I decide to choose the mint aroma; not because I like mint, more because I'm not sure what any other smell is on the list. Also, I don't want to risk a rancid stench that gives me dreams of being eaten by that troll creature from earlier. Attaching the groin attachment to my crotch, and fastening the mask over my face, I allow the familiar scent of mint to smother me like a wave of perfume. Before I'm even aware of it, my eyes become heavier, and the slumber greets me. I hope these minty dreams are better than these dreams I've been having recently.

CHAPTER 8

Centrol Station

'Morning!' Rex bellows cheerfully, leaning over me with an elated grin. The sudden sight of him causes me to almost jump out of my skin, in turn forcing me upwards into a sitting position spontaneously and headbutting him in the nose. He stumbles clumsily back onto the wall, his hands cupping his nose as if he's about to sneeze.

'What are you doing you idiot?!' Rex barks furiously as I remove my mask.

'What are you standing over me for while I'm asleep?!' I reply with a rambunctious yell.

The unimpressed glare of his eyes connects with mine containing an ire that I can only describe as malicious. 'You didn't have to headbutt me, I was only waking you up.' Thankfully, as he moves his hands away from his face, I'm relieved to see that it's devoid of blood.

With the groin attachment now disconnected and my backpack mounted on both shoulders, my trainers are slipped back onto my feet. Doing their rounds to visit each of the passengers one at a time, the stewardesses wish everyone a safe journey and thank them for using the service of *The Intergalactic Species Transportation Company*.

'We'll deal with this later; I'm going to make a mental note,' Rex warns me with a waggling finger that points in my direction. He then taps it on the side of his skull as if to gesticulate that he won't forget about me assaulting him even though it was an accident. 'Have a look out there,' Rex gestures, and positions himself in front of a large paned window that looks into the planetary system outside.

Following his instructions, I gaze with utter fascination into the incomprehensible cascades of contrasting colours and complex constellations that look back at me. The agglomerations of glistening stars are probably ten-fold what we could see from Earth, which suggests that we're now deeper into space.

Rex begins to explain in extraneous detail as I examine the exterior further. 'We're at the exact central point of the planetary orbit. There are five planets on one side of us, and four on the other. We've just arrived at Centrol Station. This station is like no other because it's the only one that isn't a moon. CS sits inside the asteroid belt between Earth and Jambre.' Rex examines the map which he had shown me previously, and gestures toward the asteroid belt which we're now currently inhabiting.

'If you're travelling from any planet on one side of CS to get to the opposite side, you must travel through CS for security reasons. The security in here is state of the art; they use proton rays to scan every square inch of the station to find anything untoward. It's almost impossible to smuggle anything dodgy through here.'

'Why is that, do things get smuggled a lot?' I ask with intrigue.

'Dunno,' he replies. 'It's been like that since before I was born.'

'Could you kindly make your way to the exit please gentlemen?' a friendly voice asks us from behind. Looking around, I notice that we're the only ones left on the shuttle and the rest of the passengers have already disembarked.

As expected, Rex flirts with most of the flight attendants as we make our way from the window to the exit of the shuttle, but what surprises me is that they all entertain his flirtations without any hints of offence. He isn't the most attractive of men with his pale skin and strange hairstyle, but I can tell that his quirky and bodacious demeanour are something to be desired.

Following the signs to wherever it is we are going, Rex and I walk side by side through the meandering corridors, and I can tell already that there is a more varied collection of species in here compared to Earth's station. After what feels like miles of trekking, we reach a gigantic, bustling room which must contain thousands of people, all crammed together like a busy high street in December. A large glass dome up above gives an extensive view of the solar system outside, displaying a fabulous range of colours from the planets and stars, which has caused a disco ball effect. Naturally, I would have expected all the stars to be white, but they appear to glisten in an assortment of colours.

Walking while staring up at the sky is something I should have learnt from, but only I could make the same mistake as last time in front of Rex, who already thinks I'm completely useless. The latest victim of my clumsiness is a lady clutching a baby to her chest with gigantic, feathered wings. Her eyes glisten mysteriously with a piercing luminosity that makes me shudder fearfully. She glares down at me, displaying a beak, and a flatter-than-flat nose. The word *owl* seems to be the only word that springs to mind when looking at this avian creature.

'Oh my god, I'm sorry,' I blurt apologetically, holding my hands out in front of me as if I'm pushing an invisible wall.

'Ahhh! What do you think you're doing? You could have hurt my baby you filthy, vile, pestilent creature! It thunders vehemently with a high-pitched, guttural vociferation, and clutches its offspring tighter. The mesmeric stare seems to pull me in like a tractor beam, and its hypnotic effects sap the energy from me. Her eyes shift from a blueish colour to a piercing shade of red, which causes my vision to begin waning. A jelly-like feeling spreads through my legs and my jaw drops like an anchor has been released from it. Without prior warning, my knees crash to the floor with an excruciating twinge. A faint flapping of wings follows the sound of her feet levitating from the ground. Every one of my senses has been sabotaged.

The sound of Rex's voice is muffled and it's almost impossible to make out what he's saying. I try to query what's happened, but when I speak, nothing leaves my mouth.

Every single person in the crowded lobby must have stopped to draw their attention towards me, and given the fact that Rex told me to keep a low profile, I know he's going to be majorly cheesed off at me for this latest clumsy accolade. As an overwhelming feeling passes over me – and I'm certain I'm about to pass out at any moment – a weighty slap connects with my neck, causing me to lurch forwards and almost kiss the stone-cold, metallic floor. Shortly after, my vision begins to return, and the sounds of commotion become comprehensible.

'Trust you to pick a fight with a draqowl,' Rex says scornfully, peering down disappointedly. 'I told you not to draw attention to yourself. You're doing a hell of a job proving me right about the whole "you being an idiot" thing, aren't ya?'

'What are you hitting me on the neck for, what was that thing?' I murmur, confused at the sudden, untimely assault.

'The thing that did the thing to you, or the thing that the thing did? Or the thing that I just did because of the thing that the thing did?' he asks, looking more than baffled and pulling an uncertain expression. It sounds like he just confused not only me with that previous sentence.

'All of it,' I rasp impatiently.

'I thought we agreed that you'd stop asking questions,' he retorts, but decides to start telling me anyway. 'This is a liquin.' He holds up a tiny, flat sticker which must be around an inch in diameter with a postage stamp-like appearance. 'When you place a liquin on your skin, it secretes chemicals and dumps them into your bloodstream. They are capable of changing moods, abilities and characteristics. We usually use them on the neck so it can reach the brain at a more prolific speed, but they can be used anywhere on the body.' Rex pulls a small pile of liquins out of his pocket and begins his explanation of how they work.

'Think about how everybody has a specific blood type,' Rex says, looking hesitant. 'There are thousands of different blood types. There are thousands of species that live out here and all have a range of different blood types. Have you ever heard of anyone having an organ transplant and after it, they start craving things the other person liked, or enjoying hobbies that they had; that's because of the blood. Liquins change your blood temporarily and they are created using the blood of certain species that contain characteristics of it. Once the blood merges, your mind and body will be able to take on said characteristics until the body's natural antibodies fight it off.'

'Coo-ool,' I gasp with genuine intrigue. 'Which one did you just put on me? The effects from that owl thingy wore off pretty quick.'

'Those are mostly used in hospitals; it's called a *stability liquin*. Stability liquins remove any unknown effects which the body or mind may have encountered, and they're created using the blood from a creature called a *jringo*. A jringo will heal itself automatically whenever it gets ill because its blood can create antibodies against any parasites or foreign intruders that enter its body,' Rex explains.

'So, you're saying that if I were to have a liquin loaded with monkey blood, I'd start jumping around the room trying to fondle my armpits and eating bananas?' I ask, slight confused at the notion.

'You could,' he states. 'But probably not all at once. The blood taken will contain different cells from the plasma and each drop of blood could contain different characteristics than another. Whoever creates the liquin will assess the blood and sell it based on whatever characteristics it will excrete. Here's the really interesting part though; laboratories around the solar system found a way to create artificial blood that combined specific elements from different species or animals and mix them together. They can remove certain characteristics which the cells contain, or they could add different ones from cells of other species. It's even rumoured that they once got hold of blood from a creature called a Wuxing and made a liquin from its cells. Wanna know the amazing thing about a Wuxing?'

'I wouldn't even know where to start guessing. Can it remove its head or something?' I ask in jest; although it probably wouldn't surprise me if it was true in all honesty.

'It's invisible,' he states, with a hint of narcissism in his tone.

'Whoa, so they made a liquin that could make you invisible? That is so cool; it'd be like being a superhero. Have you got one?!' I ask him, almost as excited as a small child at a playground.

'Nope, sorry. Wuxings are now extinct; at least we think they are. How are you supposed to know if something's extinct if you can't see it? From what I can remember, the liquins they created have a cloud emblazoned on them, but I couldn't be certain because I've never actually seen one.'

'Yeah, I suppose they must be difficult to get a hold of,' I admit. 'Who makes these "liquins" then?' I ask, using my fingers to quote the newly found word.

'Various companies and manufacturers throughout the solar system. The most popular one is probably *Liquinity Celestia*, which is based on Neplio.' Rex shuffles intriguingly through the liquins in his hand like a deck of playing cards. 'Here you go, have a look through these and let me know if there's any you fancy.'

I take the small collection of liquins in the palm of my hand and begin investigating each one. Each liquin has a different symbol on its face. The first one has an icon of a smiley face, which presumably must mean it'll make me happy. Another has an image of a firearm on it; hopefully for if I want to turn my arm into a machine gun. The most bizarre one I come across is an image of Death. A grim reaper, with its hood up over its head and a sickle gripped tightly in its hand; I wonder what this one does.

My thoughts are dismissed as Rex lifts his sleeve to unveil the red flashing chip embedded inside his wrist and presses it gently. Within seconds, a small white robot with a tea towel placed over its arm comes zigzagging through the crowds to stop mere feet in front of the pair of us. 'What refreshments would I be able to get for you gentlemen?' the robot asks in a generic, mechanical whirring voice.

'Two coffees please, both with messanino sugar and milk,' Rex replies. 'Do you have any jarapamples by any chance?'

'No sir, unfortunately we don't have any of those in stock. Would you like anything else?'

'Have you got any lasagne or anything? I'm bloody starving,' I ask politely.

The small robot stares at me quizzically. 'I don't have *lasagne* in my database unfortunately,' it replies.

Rex nudges me amiably. 'You'll notice that the further we get away from Earth, the more difficult it'll be to find delicacies you'd usually go for. You want me to recommend anything?'

'How about a phoenix ball cake?' I ask, excited at the prospect of tasting the scrumptious delicacy once again.

'Coming right up sir,' the robot answers. It stands stationary but begins to vibrate violently and make continuous whirring sounds like a blender. Abruptly, it ceases its vibrations, then opens a panel in its navel to reveal two steaming mugs of coffee and the small spherical fire-red cake. 'That'll be two cosmo please sir,' it says, stretching its hand out to Rex.

With a fist-bump from Rex, the transaction must be completed. 'Before you ask, cosmo is intergalactic currency. We all use the same currency; there's no euros or dollars out here my friend,' he explains. It's starting to annoy me that every single word that leaves my mouth is a question and I do understand why he's so annoyed about the bombardment of queries about absolutely everything.

'Enjoy. Have a nice day gentleman,' the robot says courteously, then turns away to speed off into the distance.

'I've got to meet my friend, Wesley, here at Central Station,' Rex says. 'He's from Earth too. He moved out here when he was just a kid.'

'I thought you said nobody from Earth could know about the rest of the solar system, never mind move out here.'

'It's a long story,' he says as he stops blowing the top of his coffee to cool it down. 'I'll let him tell you.'

As we navigate our way through the next corridor and I eat my cake like a feral child, Rex randomly runs forward with his arms outstretched towards a tall dark-skinned man dressed in jeans and a white t-shirt. When the man notices Rex's pelt towards him, he holds out his arms to accept the hug. 'Wesley!' Rex shouts excitedly. Their friendly embrace seems to last quite a while longer than I'd expect for a man-hug and it's obvious that they're close friends.

'This is Tristan,' Rex informs Wesley, who stares at me with a convoluted gaze as I offer him a friendly nod. 'He's Lara's boyfriend, I've just been to Earth to collect him. I don't know what you see in that place, it's a dump.'

Wesley chuckles, nodding back at me. 'I'm her husband, not her boyfriend,' I pronounce.

'Tomato, tomato,' Rex replies, making the exact same pronunciation for both words as his face becomes a puzzle of confusion.

'So, how come you're out here?' I ask Wesley. 'Rex says you're originally from Earth.'

'Yeah, I am. I was born on Earth, but through a series of unfortunate events I ended up out here,' Wesley says, then holds his hand to his mouth to cough violently to the point where he looks genuinely in pain.

'You alright buddy?' Rex asks. 'Looks like a nasty cough you got there.'

Once Wesley's coughing resides, he says, 'I've had it for a few days now. I think I must have picked it up on my way back from Szera and it feels like it's getting worse. I've booked an appointment for when I get back to Macro next week.'

'Let me know how you get on,' Rex asks, with concern painted all over his voice. 'Let's hope it's not that COVID thing that's been going around on Earth.'

'Anyway, where was I up to?' Wesley asks rhetorically, and as soon as Rex realises that Wesley is speaking, he begins whistling and walks rudely away toward a row of seats.

'I've heard this story a million times. I'd rather flush my head down a toilet than hear it again, but you carry on,' Rex calls back. Before he reaches the row of seats against the wall, he plops down onto the ground and sits with his legs crossed on the floor, puts his sunglasses on his face, and then starts to wave his hands in different directions.

'I know he can come across as weird, but he's one in a million. You'll get used to his eccentricity,' Wesley says before continuing his story. 'I was only ten years old when I came out here.' Wesley coughs again, but less violently this time. 'My mum and dad could have won a prize for the worst parents on the planet, and they didn't really give me a second thought. My dad was a drinker, a gambler, a womaniser, and everything else you can think of that makes someone a nasty piece of work. When I was ten, my dad brought me along to one of his underground, illegal poker nights where he played in the back room of some dodgy pub. Once my dad had gambled all his money away, he had nothing left to gamble with, so he gambled me.'

'No way!' I retort furiously. 'How could somebody do that to their own son?'

'Because that's the kind of parents they were. Once he lost the bet, he didn't even say goodbye. He told me to go with the man, whose name was Pete, and make sure I do whatever he asks, then turned around and walked out.' A tear appears in the corner of his eye and begins rolling down his cheek, his fists clench in rage. Although he's probably told this story a multitude of times, it must be hard telling such a heart-wrenching tale. 'After a few weeks of cleaning, running errands and basically completing his slave-like duties, he must have realised how useless I was. He beat me and kicked me out on the street with nothing but the clothes on my back. Not knowing how to get back to my original home, I sat on a bench in the street for the whole evening crying uncontrollably. I don't think I've ever felt so lonely.'

'That's awful mate,' I say sympathetically, and put a supporting arm to his shoulder as he sniffles but holds the tears back well.

'It's fine. It all looked up after that because that's when I met Lady Missingno. She approached me on the bench and asked me who I was. I tried to tell her in as much detail as I could what had happened, and she asked me to come with her. Not knowing what to say or do, I followed her. Lady Missingno is an Intergalactic Property Agent and just happened to be down on Earth looking for a property for a client who was searching for a holiday home on our planet. We instantly clicked and she felt more like a mother than my biological mother ever did. The fact that she couldn't have kids, and that I was abandoned by my parents, made her a prime candidate to take me under her wing. Obviously, people aren't allowed to just take people from Earth due to the universal decree, but she stated a case to the High Council on Neplio. After some arguing and pleading, they eventually agreed to let her adopt me and take me from Earth.'

'Wow,' I gasp, open-mouthed. 'That's a hell of a story. I love a good happy ending.'

'Finished yet?!' Rex calls over from behind his sunglasses.

'Yeah, you can come over now!' Wesley calls back, which prompts Rex to stand up and approach us once again.

'Sorry, it always gets to me that story. I can't stomach listening to it anymore,' Rex declares solemnly.

'Where are you going now then?' I ask Wesley.

'Lady Missingno has given me permission to go back to Earth for a few weeks. As much as I've been brought up out here, I've always felt like Earth was my home and love being there. If we're ever back there at the same time, we'll have to meet up for a couple of beers,' Wesley hints politely. 'I'm heading to a town called Huytree; apparently the nightlife is second to none.'

'Definitely, I'll hold you to that,' I reply.

'Sorry, that won't be possible,' Rex butts in. 'He can't go back to Earth.'

Wesley looks confused and asks, 'Why not?'

'Never mind,' Rex says.

We're suddenly interrupted mid-conversation by the loudspeaker announcing that we'll be leaving shortly, and Rex gives me a nod of confirmation.

'Looks like that's your cue guys. It was lovely meeting you Tristan. How about we exchange contact details, and we can arrange meeting up soon?' Wesley asks, and then holds his hand out to me in a fist. Now knowing that fist-pumping somebody is enough to exchange details through the chip, I punch his fist, which causes a pinging to resound inside my ear. 'Thanks, but can you do me one small favour?' he asks seriously.

'Yeah sure, what is it?' I ask.

'Look after this muppet for me.' He looks to his left with a smile directly at Rex, who returns the gesture.

'I don't think it's possible to look after me Wesley. Can I ask a favour now Tristan?' Rex asks. 'Can you just go and wait over there for two minutes while I speak to Wesley privately? It's space stuff, you wouldn't really understand.'

Not feeling like I'm in any position to refuse requests from anyone, I take my leave and sit on a bench out of hearing distance. During their conversation, I can't help but notice that Wesley passes Rex a small object, no larger than the size of a ping-pong ball. I wonder what the object is, am I in a position to ask? The chances are, if I do ask, he'll probably just shoot me down anyway so I'm probably best just ignoring it.

After the two men conclude their conversation and hug, Wesley endures another coughing fit. Rex gives his friend reassurance that he'll be fine and then makes his way towards me with a sceptical sway. Behind Rex, a hand raises respectfully as Wesley gives me his regards.

'Everything alright?' I ask. 'He doesn't look too good.'

'Yeah, all good, he'll be fine. Just a bit of a cough no doubt,' he replies nonchalantly. 'Got an important favour to ask of you though.'

'What is it now?' I ask bitterly.

Rex removes the small object from his jacket pocket and shows it to me secretly, looking around suspiciously to check that nobody's looking. The object shines with a silver reflective glow that glistens immensely. A small green dot blinks slowly on the circumference. 'It belongs to Wesley. It's been in his family for years and he wanted me to keep it safe while he's down on Earth. Can you put it in that backpack of yours?'

'Sure,' I reply, taking the small item from Rex. It's twice as heavy as I was expecting it to be. We walk alongside each other to reach the departure gate. Feeling like it's none of my business, I decide not to question the mysterious item which Rex handed to me and follow him through the terminal to the next boarding section. It does kind of make sense now that the item he slipped him was no doubt valuable and he didn't want anyone seeing him passing it over; there could be all sorts of thieves in places as crowded as this.

This is it, once I board, I'll arrive on Macro, wherever that is, and Lara should be waiting for me with open arms. Her image once again fills my mind and the butterflies attack my stomach just thinking of her. It's amazing to think that this time last week I was probably drowning in pity thinking I'd never see her again.

Queuing for the shuttle behind a family of Draqowls, I try my best to keep a distance for obvious reasons. I don't think Rex would let me survive another mishap. After going through the rigmarole of scanning our chips on the flashing pedestals to gain access, we arrive on the shuttle and are led to our stasis beds by the fox-like shuttle attendants.

'This flight is a lot shorter now. It only takes approximately four hours to get to Macro from here, but I suggest you get some shut-eye. You'll need to reserve your energy, we've got another long, long day ahead.' Not again, I feel like I haven't stopped over the last few days. I am looking forward to seeing Lara though, it has to be said.

I can't help but wonder what the strange object Rex gave to me was. It doesn't look like something that would be passed down through generations, it looks more like a bomb, or a children's toy. I do recall Rex mentioning earlier that nothing illegal can pass through here and it's the most secure place in the solar system, so it can't be anything illegal or dangerous.

'Can I ask one more thing before we depart? And I promise this will be the last question before I speak to Lara. How did it take a whole year to come up with this grand plan to get me out here? Also, am I that important that you had to smuggle me away? Surely you must be breaking all kinds of laws taking someone from Earth?'

'I thought you said one more question; I heard the word *also* in there somewhere. I told you before, I'm just following orders. Lara is the Commander of HQ, and I'm fulfilling her request,' he says defensively.

'Commander of HQ?' I ask instantly without a sliver of hesitancy.

'Enough with the questions!' Rex exclaims impatiently. 'Goodnight Tristan. I'm sure you'll feel better in the morning once we arrive,' he adds, then plugs himself in and lies down in his stasis bed facing away from me.

I take the obvious hint that he's annoyed at me and complete the process of connecting my mask and groin attachment. My final thought before I go to sleep is Lara, and the last thing I see before falling asleep is the shining star that we're heading for in the distance out of the large rectangular window.

CHAPTER 9

Welcome to Macro

I had a dream; but it was interrupted and something changed, but what was it? I'm struggling to focus as consciousness begins to return to me, but something doesn't seem right. My eyes spring open abruptly like a trapdoor, but the uncomfortable darkness lingers. My hands feel as though they're stuck behind my back and they're completely immovable. I'm pretty sure I'm in a seated position, but when I went to sleep on the shuttle I was lying down, so why am I now sitting up? I can almost feel the wooden splinters sticking into my backside and this adds to the uncomfortableness. A sudden panic courses through me, causing my body to spasm as I start to struggle to break free of the binds which restrict my every move. My feet also appear to be bound as I try to stand. Where am I?

My desperate pleas don't get far, as whatever is covering my head prevents noise from being audible. My struggle comes to an end as soon as footsteps appear from the other side of the cover, and I try to listen more intently. 'Who's there?' I whimper in utmost desperation.

A thought sparks in my head that this could be Sergeant Wainwright and I've woken up in the police station interrogation room after an amazing, although slightly weird, dream.

'Wainwright?' I ask elusively, but no reply comes. The only thing I can audibly recognise is a strange, heavy breathing from a few steps away. The heat inside the cover over my head is burning me up intensely, which adds to the agitation and anxiety.

'Hello?!' I cry out in a panicked whimper, pleading for help from absolutely anyone. Attempting to twist my head in every direction, I try to free myself from the cover with convoluted jerks and jolts. The echoes of my voice bounce back to me from every wall, which provides enough evidence that they must be made of concrete due to the dull reverberation. This confirms the reality I've been dreading; I'm in an interrogation room in the police station and everything after that must have been a dream.

'Hello,' a gruff voice booms out. I say gruff, it's as if a pig could speak.

'Who's there?' I cry out in a panicked confusion.

I can sense the figure reaching down and grabbing the cover from my head. As it lifts, I find myself looking directly into the eyes of a huge otherworldly creature that stands above me; it's easily eight-feet tall. A black all-in-one gown hangs down to its feet, and its terrifying, ugly face stares down at me with piercing, evil, black eyes.

I scream frantically, struggling with every ounce of energy to try and break free from the binds which attach me to the wooden chair. My desperate struggling wriggles cause the entire chair, with me attached, to fall backwards and the back of my head to high-five the rock-hard metal floor.

The force of the giant's foot pressing down on the front of the chair between my legs, causes me to spring back up to a seated position like a jack-in-the box.

'Ha-ha-ha!' the gargantuan creature roars, and the echoes of the voice which bounce from the walls are almost as loud as my normal voice. I honestly don't think I've ever been more terrified than I am at this moment in time. I'm helpless, scared, and completely lost on my own in the middle of space. Where the hell is Rex?!

'Where's Rex?!' I scream frantically at the huge figure, with my voice quivering to show obvious signs of terror, and how I don't wet myself is a mystery to me.

'Never mind Rex!' he bellows in fury. 'Tell me where you got *this*!' He retrieves the small silver sphere which Rex handed to me from his pocket and shoves it to within an inch of my face. The small green light blinks slowly like a dying heartbeat. The sphere looks half the size that it did earlier due to his gigantic shovel-sized hands.

'I… I got it from Rex,' I squeal helplessly, and even I know I sound pathetic, but I just want this to end. I'll be the first to admit, it doesn't take a lot to break me, especially seeing as I'm alone in this place. I could handle Wainwright, I could even handle his huge accomplice, but this is a whole new level. Is Rex a good guy or a bad guy? Why has he ditched me and given me this item which was clearly going to get me into trouble?

'Who is Rex?!' he bellows furiously with sputum firing from his mouth.

'I don't know!' I shout, now letting panic control my replies rather than logic.

'Do you know what this is?' he asks.

'No, I've never seen it before. If you can find Rex, you can ask him, he was on the shuttle with me.'

'Where did you come from?' he asks quizzically.

'Earth,' I reply, and then mentally kick myself, knowing I shouldn't have revealed to anyone where I was from.

'Earth, eh?' he replies with a mischievous grin, showing me every one of his brown teeth, as if his interrogation has led him down a road which proves his suspicions that I shouldn't be here correct. He brings his wrist up to his drooling mouth and touches it with his other hand. 'You'd better get yourself in here, we've got us a stowaway,' he says.

'Please, no. What are you going to do to me?' I cry out in desperation. Tears cover my face as if he were standing there shooting me endlessly with a water pistol. 'Please! Let me explain, I haven't done anything wrong!' I plead, knowing one punch from this guy would likely be enough to knock me back to Earth; no shuttles involved.

The hulking, muscular figure stares down at me with his expression reverting back to incandescent fury. 'Are you planning an assassination? Why would you be carrying a destruction sphere if you didn't plan on using it?!' he roars.

'A what? I don't even know what one of them is!' I bellow and continue to cry like a small child who's lost their mum at a fairground.

Through the cries and sobs emanating from me, an unknown maniacal laugh blurts out from behind from somebody who just entered the room. How can they laugh at injustice like this? It's just sick.

'Boo!' A voice booms down my ear loudly from centimetres away. If I wasn't attached to the chair, I'm under no false illusion that I probably would have rocketed up into the ceiling and splatted like a pancake. My head twists to the now laughing figure beside me. 'Sorry dude. I can't resist a good prank,' Rex bawls, laughing like a braying donkey. The relief of realising it was all a prank, mixed with anger and rage at Rex for doing this to me, paired with a mental tiredness from the extreme emotional overload I've just endured, causes my brain to go blank for a brief time.

'What?!' I manage to scream with an ire that I never knew I was capable of. Over the coming minutes, the salty taste of tears begins to become less intense, and my breathing and heart rate slowly return to a normal rhythm after a minute or so of watching Rex holding his stomach and laughing as if he's just seen the funniest thing in the solar system.

'You think this is funny?!' I shout at the top of my lungs furiously. How can he think this is funny? 'You're sick Rex,' I bellow.

'It's a little bit funny,' Rex says, then takes a seat on the ground with crossed legs in front of me as it's hurting him standing up and laughing simultaneously.

'You'd better untie me right now Rex, that wasn't funny!' I shout angrily.

To my surprise, he does exactly as requested. He gets to his feet, pulls his cigar-wand thing out from his pocket, and points it at my binds saying, *'Salvo Flare.'* A plume of fire ejects from the wand and hits my restraints. An intense heat scorches my hands as if they've been scalded in hot bathwater, which causes them to instinctively jump in front of my mouth and receive repetitive blasts of air from my lungs in order to cool them down.

'Couldn't you just untie it with your hands?!' I shout vehemently.

'Nah, where's the fun in that?' he responds, still calm as a cucumber, and then casts the same spell on the binds holding my feet together.

As soon as the restrictions ease, I lurch up and jump at Rex with a vengeance with both hands in front of me, only to be held back by one hand from the interrogator behind me who holds the back of my shirt.

'Well, I've learnt one thing. Never let you get captured or tortured because you'll throw me under the bus at the first chance you get! You didn't even hesitate not selling me out,' Rex states clearly with an air of disappointment in his voice. 'Tristan, this is my good friend Genaci Clandor, he works as head of security at Macro Station. Genaci, this is Tristan.'

'Genaci is a *Doomguard*, they're the *Macro Elite Fighting Force*. I woke up on the shuttle about half an hour before you, I was bored, couldn't think of anything to do, so thought what the hell? I'll get him back for headbutting me earlier, so I cast a sleeping spell on you and got Genaci to carry you through the station. Think of this as an initiation; you failed miserably,' Rex says.

'I'm sorry my friend,' Genaci says in his deep voice, then holds out a gigantic hand in apology. 'When Rex asks you to play a joke on someone it's hard to say no. Life can get pretty boring working security every day of your life when nothing really happens. Us Doomguard are all based on Macro and don't get a choice in the matter.' Genaci ends the handshake and hands me a bottle of water from the table, which I rapidly gulp down in one attempt. I'd have thought the litres of my own tears I'd drunk would quench my thirst in some way.

'Have you seen the size of this guy?' Rex says, reaching a hand up to plant on Genaci's forearm. 'He's part of our team who are trying to save the world and defeat the Sorceress.'

'Sorceress?' I reply.

'We'll talk about that later. Now you've calmed down shall we get out of here? Genaci keeps looking at me and I'm getting a bit freaked out by it,' he laughs. 'I don't think he's too happy with me for pranking you.'

'Sorry Tristan, I feel really bad, I was just going along with what Rex was asking,' Genaci adds, tossing the destruction sphere over to Rex, who catches it with ease and pockets it.

'Alright, was it that bad?' Rex asks. 'You headbutted me when we woke on the shuttle.'

'Yes, it was!' I reply abruptly. 'I almost peed my pants for a moment there. Besides, the headbutting incident was completely accidental!'

Genaci begins rummaging through the drawers in the corner of the room. He takes something out, walks over to me, and holds his hand out to offer me whatever is in his grasp. 'Have this as way of an apology. I confiscated it yesterday from a smuggler who was on his way to Kyraton.'

I take the small liquin from his grip and stare in shock at the pattern emblazoned on the front of it. 'A cloud? Isn't this...'

'An invisibility liquin!' Rex says excitedly and begins jumping up and down in exuberance. 'Who did you say you got that from Genaci? Do you know how rare these are? Can't I have it instead?'

'No. You'd be up to no good with something like this. You're lucky I'm giving it to anyone, this should be handed in to the High Council. I just thought it might come in handy at some point in our fight against the Sorceress; I've got a good feeling about you.' Genaci continues to glare at me apologetically.

'Not fair,' Rex says, clearly jealous that he gave it to me instead of him. 'I thought these were just a myth.'

Pocketing the liquin, I throw Rex a smug grin which says, 'You're not having it.'

'So, what's a destruction sphere anyway? Obviously, it's for blowing the holy hell out of something, but why have you got it, and how did you get it through security? I thought the security in CS was the best around,' I query.

'Wesley had it specially made for me. It's undetectable and capable of removing a twenty-foot radius from existence; it's what we plan to use to defeat the Sorceress. She can't be killed by mortal means so removing her from existence entirely seems the only viable option.'

The light on Genaci's wrist flashes a greenish emerald colour. 'I must go, it was nice to meet you Tristan. I hope we meet again soon,' he says, then exits the room abruptly without any explanation of where he's going.

'Right, okay, so first, we need to make our way to HQ to reunite you with your wife,' Rex utters, brushing the incident aside.

'Hang on, I thought she was going to be here to meet us,' I ask presumptuously.

'Lara's at HQ. There's a lot of important business to attend to which cannot possibly be delayed. Didn't expect her to be at the station with a banner and a load of balloons, did ya?' he retorts.

'More important business than meeting her husband who she hasn't seen for over a year? This doesn't sound like her, she would have been here to meet me,' I protest.

'I'm sure she would have, but please understand that this business is important for the entire solar system, not just one selfish, needy person like yourself. She needs your help, why do you think she's summoned you? It's not so you can get all lovey-dovey I can tell you that much.'

'Summoned me? Is that what this is? So, she hasn't brought me here because she misses me? She's carried out this operation to get me here because she needs my help? And there's no other reason she's brought me here? What if I don't want to go? I could just walk away now, and you couldn't say anything.'

'But you won't though, will you? It's for the good of the universe, never mind just our solar system. Please don't be selfish Tristan, it doesn't suit you,' Rex says sarcastically, then exits the security office into a long hallway.

'Before we go, do you know where he put my backpack? I had some books in there I was planning on reading to get to know the ropes a bit more,' I ask Rex, panning my head around the vicinity of the room to see if they're on display.

'Errr... I dunno,' Rex replies and continues walking.

Deciding to stick to Rex rather than searching for a backpack full of books, I tail him out of the long mundane security hallway to the main area of the station, passing hundreds and hundreds of people wearing onesies. 'What's with the onesies? I keep seeing them everywhere, but they're not always dressed in them,' I ask.

'They're not onesies you dumbass, they're ceremonial garbs. When Katarina took over as High Minister, she made it law that everyone had to wear them on the holy days.'

'Did you just call me a dumbass?' I ask, finding the sudden insult a bit offensive.

'Yes, I did, stop the questions, you're starting to annoy me... again!' he retorts, gesturing frustratedly with both hands as if he's about to tear his own hair out.

Rex's quirkiness is highlighted by every single one of his

actions. The way he dresses, the way he walks with his hands in his pockets, his outrageous hairstyle and the way he speaks with that outlandish American accent all give heed to his bizarre qualities and unorthodox ways of being.

'Isn't it Boxing Day today?' I ask, realising that I've completely lost track of time with all the travelling.

'On Earth, yeah. I think so anyway. Nowhere else celebrates Christmas. If you want a big fat guy to sneak into your house in the middle of the night, I can give you a number to call if that's your thing,' he says, chuckling at his own rubbish quip. 'Whatever floats your boat.'

This station is a lot smaller than Central Station, but still awe-inspiring at the same time. The roof is made entirely of glass and an eye-stinging sunlight fills the whole building like a church on Sunday. Looking up through the glass, it's difficult not to notice the tall jade-green coloured buildings welcoming us into a giant metropolis. Unlike the station we arrived at when we were leaving Earth through the portal, this one is actually located on the planet, and not one of the moons. Rex did mention that the Macro station was unlike any of the others so this must be why. I wonder why though?

Now I have actually arrived at another planet, it's clear that the number of species here is a lot more simplified. Almost all the people are walking around in onesies, and pyjamas, and they do look human. So those people in the onesies at our wedding were definitely from Macro. But why would people from Macro be in my wedding photographs, and why would I be dreaming about people from Macro when I've never even seen them before?

'Can I ask you something Rex?' I ask.

'Nope,' Rex replies coolly and pulls a pair of sunglasses out of his pocket. He breathes on them, wipes them on his jacket, and puts them over his eyes.

'When we got married, there were people from Macro in the photographs; at least I think they were because they were all dressed in these garb things. Do you know why they would be at a normal, standard, human wedding? There's obviously something I don't know and I'm guessing the reason Lara has "summoned me" must have something to do with this.'

'Beats me,' he says, gazing at a fixed point, waving his arms about, and not paying any attention to what I'm asking. 'Maybe they were looking for someone, or maybe they were *watching someone*,' he replies spookily, still not looking at me and being transfixed at something he can see through his lenses.

'But me or Lara aren't from Macro, and neither of us know anyone who could be from Macro. Everyone we knew were just normal people,' I protest, trying to get the message across.

'No, you think everyone you knew was from Earth, chances are that you must have at least known a few that you didn't know about.' Mentally, I start to run through a catalogue of people I knew to question whether they were actually from Earth. It's true that throughout my life I've encountered some complete weirdos, but who hasn't? I wouldn't have suspected any of them to be aliens.

Rex continues staring into his lens and elongates his hands out in front of his face. This is followed by a furious twisting and moving of his fingers as if he is swiping an invisible screen. His hand lifts to his mouth and he says, 'Call Caprice.'

'Who the heck is Caprice?' I ask curiously.

He nudges his glasses to his forehead with his finger in order to answer my question, leans his head back, and looks down the lens toward me. 'Caprice is another one of the Protectors of the Xanarock, but more importantly, our ride to HQ. Whatever you do, and I cannot stress this enough, do not mess with her. She is probably the most bad-ass woman in the whole of Macro, and she doesn't tolerate snotty humans asking her a million questions. She's cool though, as long as you stay on her good side anyway.' Rex puts his glasses back down onto his eyes to continue his other activities. I wonder what he's doing.

'Hey Cap, can you meet us at Macro Station asap? I have secured the package, and we're on our way,' he says to absolutely nobody.

I'm guessing by 'the package' he means me. Rex removes his glasses and gives me a look which lets me know I now have his full attention.

'What else can you do with these chips in your wrist?' I ask curiously, looking down to examine mine. The light is pulsating slowly under my skin. It feels tender and it's a strange feeling knowing I'll always have this in my wrist for the rest of my life.

'They're inserted into our wrists when we're born,' Rex explains. 'We can always be tracked by the authorities. The only way to get rid of it is cut off your own hand, which in my opinion, is way too big a price to pay. Who would want to live without a hand? It has its benefits though; you can contact people, keep updated with the latest news, and it even tells you when it thinks you may be ill based on your heart rate and temperature. As you've seen at the previous stations, it holds biometric data so you can scan onto shuttles like a passport. You can purchase things with it as it's linked to your cosmo account, and it can also monitor your moods and release hormones to balance your mental state without the use of a liquin.'

'So it's a bit like a mobile phone?' I ask curiously, trying to fathom out the unlimited possibilities of this new toy.

'I suppose so,' he replies. 'Look, I need to tell you something now, but you've got to promise me you won't mention it to Caprice because she can get a bit tetchy when you mention it. As brilliant as she is, and annoying as you are, I don't want her to kill you, so I'll have to fill you in.'

'How am I annoying?' I ask Rex, giving him an unimpressed leer.

'From birth she had an illness, and they didn't know how long she was going to survive. She was completely paralysed all over and she kept burning up and freezing at random times. If the doctors weren't there to give her the correct meds, she was sure to be a goner. She was incapable of moving or functioning in any way; just a heartbeat in an empty casing. The family had a pet called Mogson, who you'll meet shortly because he follows her everywhere. Her parents came up with the idea of having a chip created that could be interlinked with another chip. With half of the chip inside Mogson, and the other half inside Caprice, Mogson could portray how she felt to her parents without them being at her bedside day after day. He would be able to mimic her feelings and they'd know if she was in pain. After ten long years of Caprice still being unable to function, her parents decided not to waste the rest of their lives looking out for somebody who was effectively dead, even if it was their own daughter. Being a wealthy couple, they donated enough money to the hospital to look after her for as long as she needed, and they moved away. They left Mogson with her in case there was ever a breakthrough and told him to contact them if she ever woke up. Once she reached age twelve, a doctor visited Caprice and informed Mogson that they had found a cure for her paralysis, but it was risky as they'd never administered it before. Mogson tried profusely to contact Caprice's parents to ask their opinion, but he couldn't get hold of them. The decision was ultimately, Mogson's as her guardian. Thinking that she was technically dead anyway, Mogson approved the administering of the cure.'

'Wow. So how is she now?' I ask. 'Did they ever get hold of her parents?'

'Nobody's ever located them. Up to this day, her parents have never been told about Caprice. I don't think it's a massive deal though because Caprice ain't exactly ecstatic with her parents for ditching her and moving away. Caprice woke up at twelve years old and after a short time, it was evident that something peculiar was happening between her and Mogson,' Rex explains vividly.

'What was peculiar?' I ask, noticing the exit doors come into our line of sight.

'Caprice and Mogson share a bond, no doubt caused by their chip. They can still sense each other's feelings, but for some unknown reason, Caprice could speak, even though she'd been asleep for the first twelve years of her life, and Mogson could too.' Rex offers me a cheeky smile, knowing I'd be impressed by a talking pet. Who wouldn't be though?

'Whoa, her pet talks? What kind of pet is he?' I ask astonishingly.

'It's a bit like a cat,' he replies. 'But better. I saw a cat when I was on Earth. All it was doing was lying around lazily and licking its own genitals. Bit disturbing if you ask me.'

Three-dimensional posters are visible, dangling colourfully around the walls inside the station. 'Vote for your Sorceress and make Macro a better place!' Is written underneath each poster in an immaculately white font. The woman's image isn't what I expected at all. A dark-haired pretty woman with white, flaky skin and fascinating emerald-green eyes stares back at me. 'Is that the Sorceress woman you mentioned earlier?' I ask.

'Yeah, she's the reason you're here so you should probably thank her evil ass when you get the chance. Don't be deceived by how she looks, she doesn't look a thing like that anymore,' Rex chuckles with an absurd laugh.

As we walk past the Saturday night pyjama club in their onesies, the view only gets more amazing. Looking up at the sky through the glass ceiling, I double-take at the sight of a strange yellow barrier bordering the atmosphere all around from above. Two moons are visible through the barrier; one is bright orange like it's afire and the other is a ghostly white which glows immensely similar to our moon on Earth during a summer's night. Other planets fill the distant awesome sky, and they all seem to be different distances from Macro and completely different sizes. No matter how much I look at these planets and phenomenon, I can't get over how spectacularly fascinating they appear.

'Ow!' I exclaim, looking down to notice that a small robot has bumped into my left shin. Am I ever going to stop bumping into things?

'Sorry sir,' it replies in a generic robot voice. 'Apologies for my clumsiness. Is there anything I can help you with today?'

'I wouldn't mind a coffee if you've got one handy,' I reply. The robot stays stationary, makes a whirring sound, and a cup of coffee slowly pops out of its stomach compartment with steam rising from the top like morning mist. Sweet, a nice hot coffee, just what I need. 'You want anything Rex?'

'I'm good thanks. You finished yet? Caprice might be waiting.'

'Do I have to pay for this?' I ask Rex, not knowing what to do because the robot stands still staring at me.

'I'll get this one,' Rex says and bumps hands with the robot. 'It's quite expensive to travel by shuttle but Lara told me not to hold back when it came to you. God knows why, not exactly a king are ya?' he says offensively and looks me up and down.

'Gee thanks, you really know how to make a guy feel special,' I reply with a grimace. Rex is really starting to wind me up with the insults and put-downs every five minutes, I can't wait to meet Lara so I can ditch him.

As we reach the exit of the building and walk out into the daylight, my mouth drops with the mesmerising scene that unfolds in front of me. A faint, yellow veil of light covers the entire sky, vehicles hover metres above the ground passing in every possible direction, people walk around in onesies chatting mundanely, and a taxi rank across the other side of the busy road makes my brain kick into overdrive. 'Are they unicorns?' I spurt out with a delighted squeal, the coffee from my mouth splattering on the floor.

'Yeah. What's so special about unicorns, don't you have them on Earth?' Rex asks calmly.

'Hell no! Can we ride one?'

'No! Calm down you freak. Caprice is collecting us, I told you that already. You need to learn to listen,' Rex exclaims.

'Pretty please. Riding a unicorn would be so cool,' I reply like a child who's wanting to ride a donkey at the beach. He glares at me mockingly, which causes me to calm down as I suddenly realise how immature I'm being. 'Can I have a go at those glasses then? What do they do? Obviously, they're tonnes of fun because you haven't put them down since we met. It's been like travelling on my own the majority of the time.'

'They're our way of communicating with each other. Our *Tech Team* invented them. As far as I'm aware, except for us in HQ, nobody else has any. It allows us to speak to each other without physically speaking, so nobody else can hear.'

'That doesn't make any sense,' I say, confused at the notion. 'How can you speak without speaking?'

'I think they designed something similar on Earth, so when I am speaking to somebody through the glasses, I can speak to them, but not speak, so the people around the room can't hear me. It uses your vocal cords to figure out what you're saying without actually saying it,' he says, obviously struggling to explain this in layman's terms.

'Right, I get it!' Surprisingly, for once. 'A bit like Stephen Hawking? He got motor neuron disease and was paralysed from it. They attached him up to a computer and he could speak, without actually speaking, except that spoke out loud through a computer.'

'Ah yes, I forgot about Mr Hawking. What an amazing mind he had. He was probably the most intelligent person who has ever been born on Earth. He was so close to knowing about the rest of the universe with his theories and knowledge. I've heard that he knew all about the outer solar system, but he didn't say anything in case he came across as a bit crazy.' Rex stares off into the distant traffic whizzing towards us from down the extremely wide road. There must easily be ten lanes on either side of the road.

I can hear Caprice's vehicle before I see it. The vibrations from the vehicle fill the air with a tremor. A spec of baby-blue reflecting from the overhead sunlight creates a sparkling glimmer in the distance at the other end of the road. Behind the vehicle, a cloud of smoke fills the air continuously as the dot gets nearer and larger.

'Here we go. That's our ride,' Rex says, as the noises from the vehicle get louder to fill the vicinity with a deafening roar. 'The vehicles on Macro are completely silent because they use other means than motors and engines, but she's just added that noise to her car to make it sound cool.'

'There's no way I'm getting in that car! She drives like Lewis Hamilton,' I reply.

'Okay, I'll leave it to you to tell her you're not getting in,' he replies with a chuckle. 'Let's see how far you get.'

The car mounts the side of the silver-coloured road and comes to a stop right in front of us and must go from a hundred miles per hour down to zero in half a second. Looking at the mirrored windscreen, which is now only a metre or so away, I can only see a reflection of myself rather than the silhouette of the driver.

'Don't worry, she wouldn't have been able to hit you. She can't crash, that's why she drives so crazily. The Tech Team fitted her car with a device that makes the car stop, no matter what speed, if there is a high risk of collision. If she wants to break her neck when it stops, that's up to her, I won't be the one that has to tell her not to.'

'Who are this *Tech Team*?' I ask.

'They work at HQ. They design all of our technology in our fight against anyone and everyone.'

I couldn't even begin to guess who or what is going to step out of the car in this place. This Caprice woman could have three heads and six arms for all I know. As the car door rises like a sports car, a small creature leaps out and bolts towards Rex. It's elongated tongue flaps about as it bounds forwards, leaping up into Rex's welcoming arms and making him stagger back, causing him to almost lose his footing. It looks a bit like a cat, but it's got a long tongue and much longer, sticky-up ears. I stand stunned, frozen on the spot staring in amazement at this otherworldly creature as it turns its head away from Rex towards me and sits in his arms like a newborn baby.

'Please say that's not Caprice,' I say mockingly.

'What the hell are you looking at mister?' Mogson says to me with a hard-knock attitude, which causes me to instantly look up to the sky like I wasn't staring.

'Err. I'm… I'm Tristan,' I stutter like a starstruck fool.

'Have I got something on my face Rex? He's looking at me weird,' the bizarre cat creature says sarcastically before it begins licking Rex's cheek and knocks his glasses, so they become skewed across his features.

'Can you do a barrel roll?' I ask the small pet. 'When I was younger, we had a dog and I taught it to do a barrel roll. It only took me about two days to teach it. It took a whole lot of treats to teach it that,' I say proudly.

'You compare me to a dog again and I'll eat you,' it replies, snuggling into Rex's body.

'What the hell is a barrel roll?' Rex asks intriguingly.

'It's just where you roll over and over continuously until you get dizzy. Never mind,' I say.

The creature jumps down from Rex's arms and starts to roll about on the floor imitating what I just described. 'Like this?' he says, and pants wildly with his tongue outstretched.

'Ha-ha!' I laugh hysterically out loud at the small creature, who ceases rolling around on the floor and sits at my feet peering up at me.

'Do I get a treat now?' it asks hopefully.

'Sorry buddy, I haven't got any,' I say, crouching down to stroke the top of its head. Just as my hand gets within an inch, it jolts its mouth forwards in an attempt to bite, causing my hand to retreat instinctively.

'What was that for?' I ask, confused as to why he would try and bite me.

'Never offer me a treat and go back on your word. I've killed for less,' he replies with a rasp.

'Good boy,' Rex says, rubbing Mogson on the top of his head. 'Did you try to bite the annoying man? Yes, you did,' he jeers playfully.

Suddenly, the vehicle door opens and a tall, attractive, dark-skinned lady steps out. She's the definition of beautiful. She's tall, voluptuous, with long blonde hair, and the most piercing crystal blue eye I've ever seen. I say eye, because her other eye is covered by an eye-patch. She is bedecked with a stunning, shimmering black dress which makes her look more out of place than nice with all the pyjama wearers around.

'How come you two don't have to wear a ones... ceremonial garbs?' I ask.

'Because we don't adhere to the political views of the leaders of Macro,' Rex responds.

'Sup,' Caprice notions, summoning Mogson to her side with a small flick of her wrist.

'Is it just me or is she the definition of cool?' I whisper to Rex, making sure she can't hear me.

'You got that right. She's amazing. All that aside though, she works with us in HQ, and she looks ready to go, so jump in when you're ready.'

'Hi Caprice, I'm Tristan, it's really nice to meet you.' I hold out my right hand to shake hers.

Caprice brings her wrist up to her mouth. 'Tell HQ we're on our way. Inform Commander Lara that we should be there in the next hour,' she says seriously. Caprice enters the vehicle and signals me and Rex to do the same. Upon entering, she puts her wrist up to the dashboard and the vehicle starts with a huge bang. Instantly, the car jumps from stationary to what seems like lightspeed in a second. Despite everything, rude or not, this woman is spine-tingly cool.

CHAPTER 10

The Zombie Apocalypse

The vehicle navigates itself through the streets stopping at what seem like traffic lights but are in fact slightly transparent veils that cover the crossroads. We bob and weave through traffic, speeding up and slowing down accordingly without getting anywhere near an obstruction. Once we departed, Caprice hit a button on the dashboard making the two front seats rotate around so the four seats were facing each other, followed by a table which rose through the floor.

Rex leans in closely from the seat beside me and whispers loudly into my ear so everyone can hear. 'Wanna see something cool?'

'Always,' I reply. 'What more is there to show me? Don't say this weird cat thing has a wife who is about to jump out and they're going to do a double act?'

'Hey, I ain't weird you moron!' Mogson blurts at me abruptly from Rex's lap. The small cat-like creature makes his remark and then goes back to eating some bizarre green foodstuff which resembles a stick of celery, but the way he tears it looks as though it has the texture of chewy meat.

'What's that thing you're eating?' I ask him, genuinely interested.

'Goopok,' Rex says. 'It's disgusting, but Mogson seems to love it. Anything to keep the little guy's mouth busy to prevent him from speaking.'

'Cheeky git,' Mogson retorts, taking a break from his

animalistic chewing.

The camaraderie between these three is evident. I can tell the way they speak to each other and how they act that they must have known each other for a very long time. All Mogson wants to do is sit on Rex's lap and be mollycoddled, and Caprice... well she just seems quiet and reserved but I can't help but feel she's only being quiet because I'm here.

'What do you think Cap? Would Lara disapprove if we showed him the zombies? It might make things a little easier to explain if he sees them for himself,' Rex says with a hint of splendour.

'Whatever,' Caprice replies in a deadpan tone as she stares down at her brightly coloured yellow fingernails.

I gawp at the three of them with wide open, excited but intrigued eyes. 'Zombies? Like actual real-life zombies? Why are there zombies here? Are they like the flesh-eating, contagious zombies that you see in the movies?' I ask in lightning speed. Honestly, I'm slightly scared, but I make it sound as if I'm more curious than terrified. 'I love zombie movies. Can we shoot them?'

'They are actually, but don't worry though, they can't get you. There's a special barrier in the way so they can't eat your brains.' Rex explains this as Caprice spins her chair back around to the dashboard to begin typing a new destination into the keypad, and I see the screen in the centre of the console flash different colours and change course.

'You got any food Cap? I'm still bloody starving here. I haven't eaten since that *noopkin* I found on the ground this morning,' Mogson says.

'You've literally just finished eating. Stop lying,' Caprice responds with the unexpected longer than usual sentence.

Mogson's nose sniffs at me intrinsically like a dog. 'You smell nice Tristan. You got any food on you?'

'Ha-ha. No, sorry little guy,' I chuckle back and pat him on the head. Thankfully, he doesn't go for me this time.

'Give me one of them *shado* biscuits you had this morning if you've got any left Cap.'

'Sorry buddy, you ate them all. I'll get you something when we stop,' she replies to Mogson patiently.

Mogson jumps over the table to sit next to Caprice in the

passenger seat. He is honestly the most bizarre pet I've ever met; he is kind of cute though. Back on Earth I would have killed for a pet like this, especially one that could speak. What was all that stuff about it being linked to Caprice's chip? Rex said that they share moods and emotions, but I suppose it's way out of my understanding of this crazy upside-down world.

'So, what do you think of Macro?' Rex asks me.

'Whoa, whoa, whoa, we were in the middle of talking about zombies, you can't just start chatting about whether I like this place or not. Let's finish the zombie business first,' I say.

'Enough with the zombies, you'll see them when we get there. So, what do you think of Macro? I'm always intrigued when someone comes here for the first time. It must be weird. I know I found Earth weird when I went there,' Rex explains. 'And when I say weird, I actually mean disgusting. I hope to god I never have to go back there.'

'It's just different,' I surmise. 'It's a bit like stepping into the future, but I suppose that makes sense. When Earth got booted from the solar system, everywhere else would have moved forward together and Earth would have evolved at its own slower pace. What's the deal with all the magic though? I've only saw you use a wand and nobody else seems to have one.'

Rex raises his eyebrows with a perplexed expression as if he wants to explain but cannot be bothered using the brain power to delve into it. 'Not everybody has a wand,' Caprice states quietly.

'We get the power for the wands by extracting magic from unicorn horns. As barbaric as it sounds, I don't know where we'd be without our wands,' Rex adds. 'Unicorns are originally from a planet called Photon. Photon was populated entirely by unicorns and dragons until approximately one hundred years ago. Don't ever make the mistake of thinking they're harmless, innocent-looking creatures, because they have more magic in their horns than the rest of the universe combined. Nobody can get within a hundred miles of Photon without being turned to sparkles. If they blast you with their horns, you'll end up as a million pieces of shiny glitter for the rest of eternity. Once people found a way to extract the magic to put into wands, they started sending out parties to harvest unicorns. Their planet is near enough gone, even the dragons; nobody has seen a dragon for a long, long time. Once the unicorn's horn is removed, they still have the ability to fly so some clever sod decided it was a good idea to enslave them and use them as a taxi service for their own personal gain.'

Trust people to take a harmless and beautiful creature and abuse that to the highest level. We can't say anything as people from Earth though, all those horses being forced to race, and animals locked up in zoos. 'The dragons sound fascinating though, what happened to them?'

'Extinct,' he replies. 'Good job too because they were deadlier than the unicorns. Nobody's sure exactly how the dragons came about. Historians have theorised that they evolved from something, but not over time. It's as if evolution jumped from one species to the next in a matter of months; crazy if you ask me.' Rex sighs audibly to give me a clear indication that he's once again fed up and bored of explaining yet more things to me. 'Anything else?' he adds.

'Just a few million things,' I say, disregarding his obvious perturbed tone. 'What's that weird yellow barrier that's covering the sky? I can see it arching at the top and it looks like a big circus tent covering the planet.'

Rex covers his face with his hands in clear frustration but proceeds to answer my question. 'It's the forcefield. It's what protects us from the zombies outside the city barrier. We'll be there in a few minutes so you can see for yourself.'

For the next ten minutes we make our way through the city in the self-driving car. At one point we pass a gigantic shopping centre labelled *Macro Mall* in gigantic green lettering. I haven't seen one blade of grass since we've been here, but maybe they don't have the atmosphere or climate for grass to grow. There just seems to be a lot of rock and metal around and even the floors seem to be made of stone. A gigantic metal fence comes into view as we get nearer to the edge of the city where the barrier meets the ground from above behind the buildings.

'We're here,' Rex announces cheerfully and gives me an exhilarated glare. In front of us in the middle of the road sits a small sentry hut adjoined to a metal gate which lies across the road in mid-air. A rotund figure stands to attention outside the sentry hut and presumably they're in charge of who passes in or out. Caprice bashes a button on the dashboard which makes the driver's side door disappear entirely. Now that we've got closer, I can see that the sentry is human in appearance but has scaly green skin and a large tooth that hangs out of its mouth.

'Do you have cleawance?' the man asks through the window, holding a tablet made of light.

'I don't need clearance, I'm a member of the POX,' Caprice replies and gives him a death-stare, obviously offended that he's even asked.

'Oh, sowwy Miss Capwice, I didn't wealise it was you. You on official business today?'

'Nope,' she replies, and touches the tablet which he holds in his hand, causing sparks to eject from it.

'Thank you for the signature, you may pwoceed Miss Capwice,' he confirms, pressing a button to make the gate open. The vehicle inches forward until we arrive at a clearing of wide-open stone ground.

My eyes almost pop out of my head as the scene in front of us becomes more visible. The faint barrier projects brightly from the ground up into the sky in what I can make out as a large circle which must encase the entire city. The barrier of light rises into the sky and disappears behind the buildings back towards the city centre, the skyline blocking a more extensive view. Behind the barrier, thousands and thousands of what look like zombies walk aimlessly around bumping into each other and dragging their feet across the rocky floor. The only thing missing seems to be the groaning noises. A wave of terror surges through me from head to toe at the sight of these creatures and I can't seem to find the courage to exit the vehicle.

'Geez!' I gasp in wonderment. 'Why are they all behind that barrier?'

'Amazing, isn't it? This a fundamental part of Macro's history. The golden age of the mages suddenly coming to an end with one incident,' Rex says proudly, exiting the vehicle to approach the barrier. I'm not sure what he's talking about, but it does look captivating.

'You coming or what?' Rex calls back to me after realising I'm still inside.

'Think I'll stay here if you don't mind!' I call back to him.

'Come on you big baby. Lara said she brought you here because she thought you'd be useful in our fight against the Sorceress. Fat load of good you are!' he calls, obviously trying to goad me. 'We've only got a few minutes. Lara will already be wondering where we are.'

The sheer mention of her name and the fact that I'll get to see her once we're done here helps me build up the courage to get out of the vehicle and follow them towards the forcefield barrier. The closer I get, the more disgusting they appear. Their missing limbs and decaying flesh give their own evidence that this isn't some kind of wind up.

'Okay, just a couple of questions if I may,' I say, staring in fasciation as I take small baby-steps forwards toward the forcefield with hesitancy. Not giving them a chance to answer, I quickly blurt out, 'Who are they? How did they get there? How long have they been there? Why don't they need food or drink? Shouldn't they be dead? Why the hell is there a forcefield in the way? And can I go home coz this is too weird?' The barrage of the quick-fire questions catches them off guard in the silence, and all three of them smile back at me intriguingly.

Rex begins explaining almost immediately. 'It's not every day we get to tell people this story but here we go, let me give you a little history lesson. It's so much easier to explain if you can see it for yourself, hence bringing you here. I think I might have mentioned parts of this to you already but here's the scoop. Over five hundred years ago, there was a plague which covered the majority of the planet. Most of the large cities were infected badly and it was spreading at a pace nobody could have predicted. These beings you see in front of you are the result of this infection. The Macronians succeeded in getting the uninfected people out of the cities and into a city called Xana. This forcefield was created by the mages to protect those inside from the infected, and the people inside it survived, infection-free. Those inside the forcefield who were found to be infected were eradicated, and they managed to quell the spread of the infection. Out of a whole planet, only one city remained; fascinating, isn't it? The population of Macro went from over three billion, to eighteen million in the space of a few years. It's the most catastrophic disaster that's ever happened in the entirety of the solar system, ever.'

'Even bigger than Earth getting the boot?' I ask.

'Yep. They deserved it, Macro didn't,' he says sternly, then pulls out his cigar-wand and starts puffing on it to create exhaling fireworks.

My eyes follow the base of the forcefield up to the sky. I can just about make it out cascading down the sides of the city; it looks like a giant dome. The whole thing must be easily ten miles in diameter.

The zombies stumble around aimlessly as if they're completely braindead. I get that they had to get them outside the forcefield so they weren't a threat, but in five hundred years, couldn't they have found a way to put them out of their misery? What if one day the forcefield fails and they get in?

'I know what you're thinking,' Rex utters, snapping me from my deep thoughts. 'Why not put them out of their misery? Impossible. Our magic won't work through the forcefield and if anybody tried to get through it, you're talking instant death, or worse, you could become one of them. Even after five hundred years, we're still unsure where this virus originated and what it is.'

'So why can't they just fly out of the forcefield and kill them all? Surely it's a massive risk having all those on the other side. What if something happens and they get through?' I ask inquisitively.

Rex stares at me sheepishly. 'For someone so annoying, you do tend to ask all the right questions. Maybe I'm starting to see what Lara sees… just maybe. The *Board of Tourism* wouldn't allow that to happen. Apparently, having all these zombies endangering our planet is good for tourism so they decided to do nothing about it. The city is at bursting point already, so I'm not sure why they need more people visiting.'

I stare with the usual gaze that I've given him what feels like hundreds of times over the last few days. 'Not another bloody question,' he retorts and drops his shoulders in defeat. 'Go on then, what is it now?'

'I've heard that word a few times now. What's the Xanarock?' I enquire timidly.

'The Xanarock is a ginormous rock that's floating up in the sky projecting the forcefield down to the ground. It's our job, as Protectors of the Xanarock, to ensure that it stays intact and the forcefield doesn't disappear.' Rex takes another lung full of whatever his wand produces and exhales an exploding array of colours once again.

'Time's up,' Caprice declares unexpectedly as her wrist lights up in a multitude of colours and struts coolly back towards the vehicle.

So now we're on our way to HQ... finally. Apparently, that's where Lara is so I'll finally get to see her. Rex mentioned something about her being a Commander of some sort, but I'm not sure what that even means in this place. I just hope that once we meet up, she's the same person who disappeared. The thought of her once again makes me feel light-headed and my stomach churns, but that could just be from intense hunger.

The drive through the streets is slower this time, and I can't help but think they're deliberately going slow so I can see what's outside and absorb everything. It's not a bit like Earth; everything seems newer, cleaner and shinier. There's not a sign of graffiti, yobs hanging around, or pollution anywhere. Before long, as if I've had these thoughts too soon, the streets change dramatically. It's as if we've crossed a threshold from Beverly Hills to the roughest parts of Harlem. Every tenth vehicle on the road is either decimated or burnt out, and dubious gangs of hoodlums stand huddled on the street corners in belligerent fashion. The residential streets are lined with apartment buildings and terraced houses and if it weren't for the sky above, I'd have thought we were on Earth.

'Why does this particular neighbourhood look as if we're on Earth?' I ask curiously. 'The building designs and road layout, even the signs, look like they've been taken from Earth and dumped here.' I have a million questions, but don't ask one because there's so much being processed inside my head; it's like trying to pick from a food menu and not being able to decide what I want because I'm spoilt for choice. Just get to Lara, that's my primary focus. She will be able to tell me what I need to know, and I can trust her with my life. I don't have a clue who these two – three if you count the talking cat thing – even are.

The vehicle comes to an abrupt halt at the side of the road outside an apartment building. After a quick glance around, the other three exit the vehicle and begin to make their way over to the brown double doors at the entrance of the building. Following suit and exiting the vehicle myself, I continue to process the surrounding locality. A bar stands opposite the building we're bound for, the enormous fluorescent sign reading *Galactica*. Hordes of customers are queued at the side of the building waiting to enter behind the silver stanchions joined together with red rope. The bass from the music shudders through the air like a sonic boom and even the trees appear to be boogying to the repetitive thuds.

'Whoa, whoa, what do you call this?' I ask Rex, pulling his shoulder back as I catch up to the other three just metres from the door. 'Why are we in some ghetto? Where's this HQ place we were going to meet Lara at? I've seen better places on *Channel 4* documentaries about people who can't afford to live properly.'

Rex's mouth twitches condescendingly. 'Good disguise, isn't it? Nobody would ever guess that it's in here. This isn't HQ, it's where the portal is located to get to HQ.'

Inside, sofas and coffee tables are huddled together to form cosy seating areas, and on the other side of the room, there is a reception desk occupied by a solitary figure.

'Good day to you m'lady, welcome to Beverly Plaza. How are you on this fine day?' the man from behind the reception desk enquires politely in a smooth and cultured accent.

'Fine,' Caprice replies rudely. 'Can you let us up to HQ?' she asks, folding her arms across her chest impatiently.

'Can I use the toilet please?' Rex asks.

'Certainly sir,' the man replies with a confirming nod. A section of the wall beside the desk transforms into a pool of iridescent light. A maelstrom of pulsating luminosity, similar to that which Rex summoned back at the police station, except that one was dark in colour, is now visible and glows with a seething spiral of impossible lustrous brilliance.

'You wanna go first?' Rex asks, holding one hand out towards the portal politely.

'You've got to be kidding me. Isn't there another way to get there?' I ask nervously, not wanting to contemplate waking up in another unknown location.

'Please yourself. Just make sure you follow us in. Don't wanna be left outside on your own in this place, you'll end up nailed to the nearest door within minutes. This isn't exactly the grandest of neighbourhoods.'

My trio of companions walk concomitantly towards the white glowing light. One by one, they disappear through the magical doorway. I stand for a few moments in solitude, with only the reception desk guy for company. He keeps his focus on me but doesn't say anything, a blank expression adorning his mundane face. The thought of being left alone in this place does not appeal to me at all. With nowhere else to go, and a desperation to see the woman I love once again, I slowly but surely make my way towards the glimmering light and let it absorb me until my head feels woozy once again.

CHAPTER 11

HQ

My head is pounding greatly as if I've just ate the world's biggest and coldest ice lolly. It's obvious based on the décor of the room we've appeared in that this is a completely different location than the reception area we came from. But where are we exactly? Come to think of it, I'm not even sure where this *HQ* place is. Is it underground, in the sky, or up in space? Stacks of boxes, shelves, crates, and many other forms of storage containers litter the room in a warehousy fashion.

'I hate going through that thing!' Rex complains noisily, rubbing his temples in an attempt to alleviate the searing pain. 'How you feeling?' he asks me with friendly concern in his voice.

'Like I've just put my head in a blender,' I reply weakly.

'It's because of the cell reconfiguration when your body dematerialises through adjoining portals. Just got to hope your body puts itself back together okay and hope you don't dematerialise with your head hanging off your backside or your face inside out. It hardly ever happens!' he booms jokingly.

'So where are we now? Are we at HQ? Is Lara here?' I ask my three companions.

'The Vortex Portal we stepped through is a link to HQ. We're now a mile up in the sky on an airship, just beneath the Xanarock.'

'Whoa!' I exclaim surprisingly. Can we really be a mile up in the air?

'The ship was constructed so we could protect the Xanarock from a more practical location. Believe it or not, there are instances almost every day involving terrorists and thieves who attempt to tamper with it or steal it. Our objective is to protect it from these attacks and keep the forcefield intact. Lara is Assistant Commander of HQ and she's in charge of things since our Commander vanished a few weeks ago,' Rex says.

'She's only been here a year; how can she be Assistant Commander already? What do you have to do to make it to Assistant Commander?' I ask inquisitively, not even knowing what an Assistant Commander is or what it entails.

'Through hard work and perseverance, she's probably the best member of the POX that there's ever been.'

Knowing Lara and how dedicated she is to any task she undertakes, it wouldn't surprise me for one second if she were ruler of the universe by now. Lara's always been physically fit and loves anything challenging so this must have been a walk in the park for her.

'I should have asked the guy downstairs for a biscuit, I'm starving,' Mogson says, completely changing the subject and making us all chuckle merrily.

'Does he only ever think about food?' I ask Caprice.

'Yep, and being cradled like a baby,' she says with a humorous grin.

'You can sod off! I swear down dead, if you ever try to hug me, cuddle me, kiss me, cradle me, or anything soppy that ends in the word "me", you'll be wearing them shoes as a hat... except for *feed me*, I'm good with that one,' Mogson blurts out. This sends Caprice into a howling fit of laughter. It's bizarre seeing her laugh like this due to her quietness. Maybe she's not as obscure as I first thought; she might be one of those types who are shy when they first meet people and over time they emerge from their shell. She may be stunningly pretty, but I bet a lot of people act strange when they first meet her because of her eyepatch and insulting pet; she's probably naturally learned to keep people at a distance. Even now, after only meeting her a few hours ago, she seems to be more comfortable being in my company.

'You two really do get on well, don't you?' I say to Caprice and Mogson collectively.

'Besties,' Caprice replies, and holds out a clenched fist for

Mogson to fist-pump her with an outstretched paw.

'Here, use this. It'll take some of the pain away,' Rex says, pulling his hand out of his pocket and slapping a liquin on my neck from behind. I forgot he was even here for a minute due to being so mesmerised by the camaraderie from the other two.

'Ow! Could you please warn me when you decide to assault me in future?' I reply, my hand reaching up and attempting to nurse my neck. The pain subsides in a heartbeat. I need to get a load of these things; hangovers would never be the same again.

Navigating our way through the warehouse of stacked boxes, we reach a wooden door with a metal strip running through the centre from corner to corner. Caprice's wrist touches the panel beside the door, causing it to ascend and give us a clear path through. There is a sudden shift in appearance from the dank warehouse to the immaculate, gleaming white corridors we're presented with on the other side. People carry glass clipboards resembling tablets, and groups of people idly chit-chat cheerfully as we pass. Doors fill the gaps in the walls every few metres and various labels give me an inkling of what each room's purpose is, Health and Safety Office, Conference Room A, Meeting room, Tech Team. Curious glances shoot towards me from strangers as I follow the others and I can't help but think they've been expecting me, and they're gossiping quietly about who I am. What has Lara told these people about me?

'Is Lara here?' I ask.

'Yep, we deserve a damn medal for this,' Caprice responds.

'We?! How do you think I feel? I've had to drag this guy from one side of the solar system to the other. Do you realise how many questions I've had to answer over the last few days? You can't step in at the last minute and say *we*,' Rex retorts, obviously vexed that he deserves all of the credit for getting me here.

An open door labelled *Matter Transporter Room* catches my eyes as we almost reach the end of the corridor. 'What's a *matter transporter*?' I ask, pushing past Caprice towards the door before she can answer to peak my head around the door frame. A machine stands glorious in the centre of the room and its appearance is astounding. A gigantic green border circles a fraction of the floor, with flashing white lights running through the entirety of it. A cylindrical, translucent outline rises from floor to ceiling, and it seems to be alive. It's as though there's a current running through it or a pulse of some sort giving a life-like aura.

'It's a prototype. We've only tried it a few times, but the results weren't exactly what you'd call "successful",' Rex says, holding up his two fingers on each hand to mime air quotes. We plan on using it to transport the team in an emergency if the Sorceress appears. On our first attempt, we tried to teleport an item down to the surface, but it ended up on a different planet. After a few reconfigurations, it's worked fine, but it still needs quite a bit of testing.'

'Why can't you just use one of your magic portals?' I ask.

'When using a portal, you need one at either end. The portal you're going into, and the portal you're arriving at; this can transport you anywhere in the solar system providing we have the correct coordinates. Professor Tutti even thinks that with enough time, research and the correct parts, we may be able to use it to time travel one day,' Caprice explains.

'Wow! Imagine having a time machine, that'd be amazing,' I reply in astonishment.

Can all of this be real? In the last few days, I've heard things that I could have only dreamt about. Dragons, time machines, magic; it's like every sci-fi movie I've ever seen rolled in to one. All of these musings and curiosities have distracted me from the fact that I'm mere moments from seeing Lara again and I shudder once again. Holding out my arm, goosebumps are covering the entirety of it from elbow to wrist. I can't believe I'll get to see her again, but what will I even say to her? Do I act casually, or just let my emotions do the talking? I'm sure when it comes to the crunch, I'll let the emotion take over and follow what instinct instructs me to do.

I'm pushed rudely aside in the doorway as two men in white coats barge past me from behind. 'Cheers. You could have just asked me to move instead of pushing me aside,' I exclaim in discourteous fashion.

'Ralph!' Rex bellows to one of the two rude men in a friendly tone, pushing me aside to gain access to the room. 'Tristan, this is Ralph. Ralph, Tristan,' Rex introduces us in turn, exchanging glances between me and one of the two men.

Ralph's long blond hair drops down to rest on his shoulders and large, black spectacles cover almost his entire face. He offers me a quick glance and a smile, then looks back down to the control panel he's studying.

'Ralph is a baseball nut, which is a bit strange seeing as he's never actually seen a baseball game, but each to their own,' Rex explains. On the wall beside Ralph's desk, there is an assortment of baseball paraphernalia. Baseballs, bats, photographs of players and baseball cards adorn the wall as if we're inside a teenager's bedroom.

'I have seen baseball actually. There are such things as drones you know,' Ralph replies dorkishly. Just the way he speaks gives the impression that he's a complete swot. 'Now, do you mind, I'm working.'

'Sorry Ralph, we'll let you get back to… whatever the hell it is you're doing,' Rex retorts, then hints to us with a shrug that we should leave the room and not disturb these poindexters from their vital work.

In the corridor, there is a humongous window stretching from floor to ceiling that looks down at the city below. The forcefield which covers the city can be seen eking out from all sides above us and dropping down to the ground in the distance. The forcefield reminds me of a massive lid from a domed cake stand, with Macro being the metaphorical sponge cake.

In the distance, beyond the skyline of the colossal jade-coloured buildings in the city centre, there is another structure which stands out that the others haven't mentioned. The gargantuan, rectangular building glistens lustrously in the dim sunlight, thanks to the barrier in the way weakening the impact of the sun's rays. Unicorns fly splendidly at low altitudes through the city to transport passengers from A to B.

As I'm about to query what the huge building in the distance is, Caprice interrupts me. 'You know what's even more amazing?' she asks quizzically.

'What could be more amazing that this?' I reply, still gawping gormlessly at the view outside.

'Look behind me,' she says.

I about-turn to see the words *Assistant Commander's Office* etched beside the double doors on a gold plate with a cursive black font. My heart activates panic mode, and I can feel it almost stop beating in stupor.

'You sure you're ready for this?' Rex asks me with a huge grin, almost definitely knowing that I'm, in fact, not ready for this.

I impulsively begin patting my clothes down in case they're covered in dirt, lick my fingers to flatten my hair down, and put my nose to each armpit to check if I smell foul. Obviously, my hair is a mess, I stink to high heaven, and my clothes are filthy from days of running around and sweating in fear of almost everything. I'm still not sure what these clothes are, I just grabbed anything that fitted from that shop at Earth's Station. What a perfect time to meet the woman of your dreams again after a year apart.

'Have I got time to change?' I ask hopelessly.

'Nope,' they reply simultaneously, both grinning like Cheshire cats.

'Either of you got a mint then? Mogson, you're bound to have a mint on you,' I presume to the animal which looks up surreptitiously from licking its own backside near my feet without a hint of embarrassment.

'If I did, I wouldn't be giving my food away to no humans. Food's way too good to be handing over to you lot. I'd rather die than give food to you,' he replies.

'Honest answer. Stupid of me to ask really, wasn't it?' I nod at Caprice and exhale to give confirmation that I'm ready to enter the room, to which she responds by knocking on the door with three rhythmic taps.

'Come in,' I hear the most familiar voice in the world call from beyond the door. I feel suddenly nervous, like I don't want to go in, like I'm a teenager at their school prom. The butterflies rollercoaster around my stomach once again and I get that empty feeling inside like I haven't eaten in days. Feelings of doubt and nervousness overwhelm me, but it's then countered by the sudden urge to see her. My love for this woman ignites something powerful in my heart and my desperation makes me burst into the room, not being able to keep the emotion inside any longer. Pure urge and an animalistic instinct take over completely.

Her amazing aura fills the room like an explosion of pure

desirability. The only person who has ever given a damn about me and made me feel like I was worth anything stands before me. A smile beams across her face from ear to ear, and we both instinctively run towards each other like a cheesy romantic moment from a movie where they run in slow motion. The papers which she holds in her hand get tossed aside as she begins pelting towards me with a complete disregard for anything else in the room.

'Tristan!' she screams excitedly. We collide with each other like jousting knights and a battle of hugs and elated sobs begin. I couldn't care less what anyone else in this room think. A whole year has passed since I saw this woman and all I want to do is be with her in this moment forever. After what seems like an eternity, our hug parts and we kiss lustfully like never before, our hands in each other's hair and wrapping around each other like boa constrictors as if we want to never let go. I'm sure we wouldn't have moved from this position for a long time, but the simulated balks and coughs from the others in the room break us from the moment to realise how inappropriate this all is. 'You made it!' she says with tears pouring from her eyes, the relief in her voice overwhelming.

'Of course. Nothing could have stopped me getting back to you,' I reply, with tears dropping from my eyes to cover my face and neck. We hug once again with our soaked faces rubbing against each other's napes. Lara does that thing she always does where she sweeps her fingers gently through my hair. Goosebumps and tingles cover me entirely from head to toe after this one simple action.

'I've missed you so much. I'm so glad you're okay, I've been worried sick. You should have been here hours ago.'

'Sorry Lara, my fault, we hit a few bumps along the way,' Caprice butts in to inform her, knowing that we're late because she wanted to show me the forcefield and the zombies.

'It's fine, as long as you're here now. Can I ask you something Tris?' Lara asks.

'Anything, absolutely anything,' I reply, sniffling relentlessly.

'What the hell are you wearing?' she sniffles as we pull apart from each other once again and giggle with tears dripping everywhere.

I laugh with her, and not even because it was funny, just because utter elation has commandeered my senses. 'Long story. Is there anywhere I can get some new clothes?'

'Yes, sorry. Mattip, can you take Tristan to one of the rooms to get a change of clothes and a shower?' she asks a small dark-haired lady who stands near the door dressed in garb.

'Of course, this way please,' the lady replies to Lara with a bow. I can tell she must be some sort of assistant by the way she acts to her superior.

'Go with her Tristan, we'll catch up in a little while. Now you're here, I think it's time to get our meeting underway.'

'Meeting?' I ask sheepishly, using the backs of my hands to wipe away my tears.

'Yeah, now go get changed and we'll fill you in. I love you loads,' Lara says, smiling wildly and sniffling.

'Love you too,' I reply, and don't take my eyes off her as I retreat as hesitantly as I can from the room.

Mattip walks ahead of me with her garb dragging along the floor behind her. 'So, what do you do here?' I ask her in a vague attempt to make small talk.

'I serve the upper hierarchy. I assist where I can and try to make sure that everybody's needs are fulfilled. Are you in need of anything?' she queries politely.

'Na, just a change of clothes and maybe a beer if you've got any,' I reply earnestly.

'We don't have beer on Macro. To my knowledge that's an Earth thing. You should try some macrohol,' she says. 'It might take your mind off things.'

'So I've heard. I'm not sure what macrohol is, but you bet I'm gonna try some as soon as I get the opportunity.' I'm sure it can't be too different from alcohol, I'll ask Lara when I see her, I'm sure she must have tried it if she's been stuck here for the past year.

'What kind of clothes are you looking to wear?' Mattip asks, holding the door open that leads into a small room containing a bed and a line of wardrobes along the back wall.

'I'll take one of those nightgowns if there's any free. Love a good comfortable nightgown to chillax in on a Saturday night.'

Mattip glares at me strangely as if I've just grown another head, then makes her way over to the wardrobes. She searches through the wardrobe with concentration, and I'm blown away by the array of colours and styles I can see her foraging through. 'Anything colourful is fine, I don't mind looking like a prat. It's not like any of my friends are here to laugh at me,' I inform her jokingly.

'I hear that Earth is amazing,' Mattip says, giving the impression that she's dreamt of going to Earth many times before and it's on her bucket list of things to do.

'Well, it's okay I suppose. Nothing like this though, this place is unbelievable. We only have one moon that comes out at night, and you can't see any other planets except through telescopes. When you look up, all you can see is clouds usually or a blue sky.'

'We don't have clouds here, and even if we did, I suppose it wouldn't really help with the forcefield in the way,' she says in a rather melancholic tone. 'Here we are,' she retorts, pulling out a luminous lime-green nightgown. 'Will this yoti fit?' I hold the yoti (which presumably must be a nightgown on Macro) up against me and kick out my legs as if I'm playing football to estimate the size.

'Excellent. Got anything to put on my feet?' I ask.

'How about these?' She holds out a pair of black slippers and hands them to me.

I take the slippers and say, 'Perfection, I couldn't have chosen better myself.'

'Brilliant, you get washed up and dressed and I'll inform the Assistant Commander that you'll be ready shortly to attend the meeting. The shower is just through that room there.' Mattip bows in farewell and exits the room with a gentle smile.

I wonder what this meeting is going to be about. Obviously, it's something important if they've sent for me to come here. Maybe it's about this Sorceress woman I've heard so much about.

CHAPTER 12

The Most Meaningful Meeting of My Life

The door to the bathroom slides up automatically once I approach it, causing me to jump back unexpectedly in fright. Good job nobody's here, I would have looked a right fool. An enormous, frosted glass window stands in place of one of the walls, letting in so much light that it gives the impression that I'm outside. Through it, I can just about make out the jade colour of the city below, but the tinge of yellow from the forcefield seems to dominate the spectrum on the exterior.

The shower consists of a small cubicle in the corner of the room, entirely silver and sparkling like something from a bathroom cleaner commercial. I can't seem to locate a shower head or any knobs to turn, but I undress and get inside, nevertheless. I'm unsure what I'm supposed to be pressing to begin the flow of water, but I'm hoping it'll just activate by itself, or a bunch of knobs will appear for me to twist. There are thousands of almost microscopic grates covering the walls and ceiling of the shower, but surely these can't be where the water comes from.

Without any prior notification, the sliding glass door slams shut by itself, and I hear a clicking of a latch. A purple water-like liquid begins shooting from the small grates and gradually, their intensity increases. Just as I conclude that the water has reached its maximum velocity and the power can't get any worse, it does. Two large mechanical tentacles rise from the basin and assault me with a torrent of soapy, flowing liquid. My hands touch the glass door to push it open, but it's immovable. I can hear the tentacles whizzing around my body to clean every square inch of me, my eyes staying tightly shut to escape the waterfall that I'm currently enduring. Within a minute or so, the assault begins to subside and a feeling of relief rains down over me.

I reach over and push the glass door once again to exit the shower, but it's still locked. 'Argh, give me a break! Can somebody help?!' I bawl, drawing air into my lungs after the unexpected onslaught. There's got to be someone out there who can rescue me. A loud mechanical whirring sound commences from within the walls of my aquatic prison and with water still dripping from every orifice, I wonder how on earth this could still be going on. Am I not clean enough yet?

A cacophony of force pummels my body from all angles simultaneously. As I'm being pushed in one direction, a gust of powerful wind from the opposite side counterbalances the other to keep me in the centre of the shower and not able to move. I genuinely feel as if my skin is going to be ripped off my skeleton and splatted against the nearest wall. An agonising scream escapes from my lungs, even though I know that nobody can hear me. I wouldn't even say the pain is that bad, but it's the concurrent force from the wind, and the fact that I'm helpless that sends me into a panicked, hysterical meltdown.

The functions of the shower finally cease after what feels like an hour but couldn't have been more than around sixty seconds. A feeling of relief embraces me as the shower door emits a clicking noise, and it opens automatically. The steam trapped inside begins to creep out in clouds to fill the room. Surprisingly, I'm completely bone dry and although that was a horrifying experience, I feel more refreshed than I've ever felt after a shower. If I would have even half-expected what was going to happen in there, at least I could have prepared myself for it, and the uncertainty always adds an element of surprise no matter what you're doing.

Stepping out of the human carwash, I search the room for a towel, but I'm stumped at the thought that I don't actually need one. How can you have a shower and then not put a towel on after it? That just seems odd. It's one of those things we always do, but don't realise until it's absent. What did people do before towels? Probably just dry off naturally I suppose.

I spy a well-lit, red-coloured panel embedded into the wall next to the shower door. The words *super strength* are illuminated across the centre of the panel in red lettering, and I know exactly what's coming next. I press the touch-screen panel to scroll through the menu from *super-strength* to *mild* to *foamy*. 'The idiot could have told me there were different settings, that was like a log flume in there!' I moan to myself aloud.

Looking unexpectedly swell in my new nightgown and slippers, obviously not perfect as there was no hair gel, I make my way back through into the corridor where Mattip is waiting patiently outside.

'Nice shower sir?' she asks in a polite manner, her fingernails tapping on the wall behind her.

'I feel like I've been run over by a bulldozer,' I say. 'You could have at least told me there was a lower setting.' I don't want to make the woman feel bad as she's obviously very obedient, but she must know that visitors have to be made aware that they're stepping into a typhoon.

'Holy mother, I'm so sorry!' Mattip says apologetically, realising her mistake at once and raising her hand to cover her mouth. 'One of the big guys was in it earlier and he must have used it last. It's been left on the highest setting. I didn't realise that you were unaware of the controls sir; I keep forgetting you're not from here. With such a diverse size range of species, we design most things to cater for everyone.'

'Ah right,' I say, now understanding the need for the power levels on the shower. I couldn't have expected less really with so many different shapes and sizes of people out here. I'm just glad I wasn't a *Hobbit* or something; I probably wouldn't have made it out alive. 'Okay, so where are we off to now, some kind of meeting wasn't it?'

'Yes sir, if you would be so kind as to follow me,' Mattip says, turning on her heels to tread speedily down the corridor. Mattip comes to a halt outside a set of brilliantly white double doors. 'This is the meeting room, and everybody is already gathered inside awaiting your arrival. I am not permitted to enter but I'll wait outside in case I can be of any assistance for you.' Mattip offers me a bow and a generous smile.

Pushing the doors inwards, I move my eyes from each curious

figure to the next. At least a dozen pairs of eyes stare curiously as if a ghost just waltzed in. I was expecting no more than around five people, but by the looks of it the entirety of the workforce is in here. Lara is standing in the middle of the room, a huge round table akin to a running track is circling around her so the meeting attendees can take part.

As she is the person holding the meeting, Lara introduces me. 'Everybody, as I'm sure you've gathered by now, this is Tristan. Nice choice of clothes by the way,' she adds, looking over to me with a cheeky wink. It's miniscule things she does or says sometimes that make me realise how much we make each other laugh.

'Good day sir!' An extremely overweight man in some form of military attire stands from his seat, greeting me with a salute to his forehead. 'Pavilion Pasternak, head of security here at HQ, glad to meet you sir.' His beard covers most of his beetroot-coloured face, but what catches my eye is his gigantic gut which hangs down over his waistline.

'Nice to meet you,' I say, saluting back to the man.

The room falls silent again, and a slow, rhythmic clapping starts quietly from the back of the room. Before I know it, the whole room have joined in the clapping, and their stares stay transfixed on me. *What's all this clapping for?* I ponder to myself. Surely, they can't be clapping me, I haven't done anything. Could it just be one of those strange things they do on Macro? They used to do a similar thing to the guys at work if somebody turned up late; the other staff would clap sarcastically as if to say 'you're finally here'.

'Welcome,' an aged, frail-looking lady with white hair says proudly as if she's speaking to royalty. Are these guys serious? What's so special about me?

'Err, you're welcome...' I reply to my unexpectedly overenthusiastic audience.

'What are you thanking him for? I was the one who had to endure what can only be described as a full-scale pilgrimage across the entire universe to get him here!' Rex exclaims from his chair as he strokes Mogson like a villain, who sits comfortably on his lap chewing something.

'That was your job Rex. That's what you're paid for, remember?' Lara says sternly.

'What's so special about me?' I ask the audience, once again confused by the sudden interest in me.

Pavilion takes a large swig of a blueish drink, spilling most of it down his beard, then says, 'Because Assistant Commander Lara has assured us that you will be the one to put an end to the Sorceress' reign and return peace to the solar system.'

For the first time in my life, I'm absolutely fuming at Lara. What's all this crap she's been telling them about me? How can she decide that I'm the one who's going to save everyone? I avert my eyes to glare at Lara in a way that I've never done before. My look is almost sinister, but when I notice the look she returns my way, it's apparent that maybe what she's told them might not be the whole truth. Maybe she's come up with a story to make everyone think I'm someone special so she can summon me or respect me in some way.

Everybody sits back down around the table, leaving me with no other option than to sit next to Rex and Mogson as that's the only available space left. 'Right, let's get down to business then, shall we?' Lara dictates to the room in a commanding tone.

Mogson starts sniffing at me at keenly and whispers, 'Got any snacks on you?'

'No buddy. Have you got any? I'm starving,' I reply quietly like a student in a classroom trying to avoid the teacher's attention. The feline creature just scowls at me disappointedly and goes back to lying in front of Rex on top of the table, who continually strokes his back and head.

'First order of business, can we all thank Rex for pulling off the impossible and getting Tristan here?' Lara addresses to the room. 'Amazing job, and we all thank you entirely.'

'Not a problem, it was a doddle,' Rex replies, his face blushing like a phoenix ball cake.

'It has been a while since we had any hope of defeating the Sorceress, but now that Tristan is here, we should be able to execute our plans and bring down the Sorceress once and for all.'

'What's so special about me?' I ask her timidly. 'I'm no hero. Are you sure you rescued the right Tristan?'

'Are you the man that I've been married to for the last year?' she asks me.

'Yeah but...'

'Then yes, I've got the right Tristan!' she interrupts me. 'I'll explain this in simple terms so Tristan can understand as he's new, no offence.'

'None taken,' I lie childishly, offended by the remark.

'I'll start from the beginning. Shacka, try not to fall asleep this time,' Lara says to the older woman with the snow-white hair. The rest of the room respond with chuckles, all in agreement that she falls asleep in every meeting.

'When Sorceress Katarina took over as Macro's ruler, she was undeniably brilliant. She was friendly, kind and charming to say the least, with everybody's best interest at heart. At the age of twenty-three, she became the youngest ruler of Macro in its history. Two years ago, aged twenty-five, Katarina embarked on a journey to Neplio to attend an annual High Council meeting. She didn't arrive for said meeting, and instead, went missing for three months. When she eventually turned up, she was different, as if she was possessed. Sorceress Katarina reintroduced the death penalty, which had been abolished for hundreds of years, and she turned into an evil, conniving bitch; and that's putting it nicely. As time went on, her excessively wicked behaviour became more severe, and it was pretty obvious that while she away, something had happened to her that changed her. Was she possessed, was she sick, or was she being controlled by something?' Lara takes a huge swig of water from the glass beside her and cracks her knuckles the way she used to when she was the centre of attention at parties and gatherings.

'Macro is in the worst position it's ever been in, and people are genuinely scared for their lives. The only thing that keeps Macro surviving is that forcefield above us, and if she were to sabotage that, we'd all be screwed. I'm talking about planetary extinction from one extraordinary evil act.'

I butt in, hoping that I'm asking the right questions and not looking like a rambling idiot. 'She's only one woman though, how hard can it be to kill one woman? Haven't you all got magic spells and weapons that are capable of killing her?'

'It's slightly more complicated than that Tristan. The Sorceress acquired two followers, *Zero* and *One*. Zero and One are magic casters, and for reasons unknown, they're dressed as court jesters like the type that were around during medieval times. If this isn't enough, she also has the ability to fly, along with her followers, and that's just the start of it. She is also able to summon small devilish creatures called *imps* that can cast magic without the need for a wand. Her unnatural ability to summon imps has only ever been heard of once in the collective history of the solar system. Hundreds of years ago, there was an evil being who wanted to destroy life entirely throughout the universe called the *Oryx*. Nobody is quite sure how the Oryx came to be, but according to history books, he terrorised the entire universe and his main aim was to eradicate every being in existence. Whenever he killed someone, he would absorb their soul, and was able to convert them into the imp creatures I just mentioned. It became obvious pretty quickly that the Oryx could not be killed by normal means and something beyond ordinary means had to be executed to destroy him.'

'This is nuts,' I butt in rudely. 'Are you saying that this Katarina woman has a similar thing, and she can't be destroyed by normal means?'

'You're catching on quickly,' Rex says from beside me, filling me with confidence as I seem to be following the situation well.

'Does anybody know how they got rid of him last time?' Lara asks, teacher-like.

'Yeah. They fired his ass into a magnetar and he's still there to this very day,' a man from the other side of the table answers.

'Excellent,' she says, praising the person's background knowledge. 'A weapon was created. This weapon had the firepower to launch him into a magnetar, which pulled him in and magnetised him, with nothing able to free him. The Oryx has been trapped on this magnetar for the last five hundred years, and nobody has ever ventured near it with the likelihood that he's still alive on there.'

'One question,' I ask, an abundance of confusion filling my voice.

'I'm guessing your question is going to be what a magnetar is, so I'll tell you. A magnetar is a particular type of star that has an impossibly strong magnetic field. We tend to stay clear of them at risk of being pulled in, but we didn't give him a choice. Once he was magnetised, his millions of imps died off or fled with their master no longer being able to lead them.'

'Pretty good idea,' I acclaim respectfully. 'But if he's trapped on this star, then how did the Sorceress end up being like this?'

'We don't know,' Caprice states. 'What we do know, is that her symptoms appear similar to the Oryx's.'

'So how do you plan on killing her?' I ask. 'Where is she now?'

'We don't know,' Lara informs me. 'She keeps turning up randomly, killing a bunch of people, and then fleeing. My guess is, she's trying to kill people so she can convert their souls into imps and grow her army. To answer your other question, I need Rex to take over on this one.' Lara turns her attention to Rex, who shoos Mogson away so he can give the room his attention. 'Rex, did you get it?' Lara asks.

'Yep, got it right here,' Rex says, taking the destruction sphere out of his pocket and juggling it like a clown.

Lara glares at him scornfully and says, 'Please don't juggle it. It's not a toy Rex.' He follows her command and holds the small spherical object in the palm of his hand, showing it off to the room like it's a winning lottery ticket. A mixture of oohs and aahs resound around the room impressively followed by a low murmuring of applause. 'This is what we're going to use to kill the Sorceress, Tristan. This object right here is capable of destroying anything within a twenty-feet range. Once activated, the user will have five seconds to throw it at her, then when it explodes, anything in the blast radius will be removed from existence and sent into a void of nothingness for the rest of eternity.'

'So, it's like catching a Pokémon then?' I query, trying to get my head around how they plan to use this grenade-type item.

Lara snorts a laugh. 'If that's how you want to think of it then yes, I suppose it is a bit like catching a Pokémon.' The rest of the room look baffled by our conversation as none of them probably know what we're referring to.

'So, to sum it all up, we're trying to kill a woman, and we have no idea where she is, armed with magic spells and the ability to summon imps, who has two sidekicks, and all we have is a pokéball?' I bellow in disbelief.

'Yep, and it's up to us to use the tools we have to find a way to bring her down,' she relays back to me. 'We have the matter transporter too, how's that coming along Rex?'

Rex looks at her blankly, and I can tell that he didn't expect that to come up during the meeting. 'Err, it's okay I suppose. It works if that's what you're asking, we just need a bit more time to experiment with what we can transport and what we can't.'

'Can it transport people?' she asks. 'It has to be ready for when the Sorceress turns up so we can transport there immediately.'

'It should be fine transporting people, but it's only capable of sending two at a time. Even Tutti is struggling with the complex configurations and he's the smartest person we've got. It only has a cooldown time of fifteen minutes, so we won't be able to transport as a group if we need to fight her,' Rex says.

A man who has been silent so far throughout the meeting speaks up in a gravelly voice. 'So where do you think she'll turn up next?' he asks Lara.

'Well, from previous patterns, she seems to be appearing when large groups gather. We can't exactly put a stop to large gatherings though and have everyone live the rest of their lives in fear of her turning up. Besides, it could be a massive hint to the public that something's amiss and they could get suspicious.'

I'm immediately reminded of when the COVID-19 pandemic hit a few years back. We had to stop public gatherings, but at least we knew it'd eventually come to an end. If they don't defeat the Sorceress, they could be living cautiously for a long, long time.

'I think Wand Wars is a risk. We may have to look at postponing any tournaments until the Sorceress has been dealt with,' a tall white-haired sallow-looking man says.

'Please tell me you're joking. We can't stop Wand Wars; the people would go berserk. If you cancelled Wand Wars, you'd have more than the Sorceress to deal with. The citizens would go ape, it's their main source of entertainment!' Lara retorts back.

'I don't see the attraction personally. A load of people running around firing spells at each other, where's the fun in that?' he replies condescendingly.

'That's because you're a bore, Miles. You obviously haven't seen me compete,' Lara smugly retorts. 'Wand Wars is without doubt the best sport and entertainment this entire cosmos has ever seen, and you're probably the only person to disagree. Cancelling it would be a major indication that something isn't right.'

I've heard Wand Wars mentioned a few times now in passing conversation and it seems to get people excited. Can it really be that good? Have these people not watched football? I can't imagine any sport being better than football.

'I need everyone to be on their toes and keep a close eye on any news or rumours regarding the Sorceress. The second we hear of anything, we have to be ready to strike. I've doubled the guards on the Xanarock to keep an eye out and report any suspicious activity. Anything else to add before we adjourn?' Lara asks the room collectively.

Pavilion raises his hand and begins to speak after Lara's acknowledging nod. 'Have you heard any news on the Commander?' he asks hopefully.

'The Commander is still missing. He's been gone almost a month now and I literally haven't heard a thing, but hopefully, he's out there somewhere. I'll continue to take charge of HQ in his absence, let's just keep our faith that he turns up unscathed.'

'What happened to him?' I ask curiously.

'He disappeared a few weeks back. We don't know much else really, he was here one minute, and gone the next,' she informs me.

'So where exactly do I come into all this?' I ask.

'You are going to help me in defeating her, and once she's defeated, we'll be able to go home,' she replies.

'Really! Like, actual home? As in Earth?' I blurt out excitedly. 'And we can get back to our life together once we get this done?'

'Err, I'm afraid that won't be possible,' Rex's stutters awkwardly to the room. Lara looks daggers at him with suspicious eyes, as if she knows that whatever he's about to say is not something she'll want to hear.

'I kind of had to sort of cast the *Avatar* spell on some guy to turn him into Tristan,' he informs her, sheepishly looking down at the floor. A disappointed look spreads over her face, gazing sternly back at him with folded arms like a mother does to a misbehaving child.

'And what did you do that for, may I ask?' Lara queries.

'Because... because you told me to use any means necessary to get him here,' he declares defensively. 'I was just thinking on the spot. I accidentally killed the guy who was holding Tristan because he was about to shoot me, and I cast the wrong spell in panic. It was either transform his corpse into Tristan, so they thought he was dead, and the other guy had scarpered, or let them think Tristan had killed them and he'd scarpered. Seemed the better of the two options if you ask me. It all just happened really fast,' he scoffs.

'Your orders were clear Rex. I specifically told you not to kill anyone!' she bellows at the now flushed face of Rex. He hangs his head in shame with no attempt to look up, but I can tell by the way he fought his corner that he thinks he did the right thing.'

'Jesus, Rex, couldn't you have just stunned him?' Lara queries. 'Tristan will never be able to go back now at the risk of being recognised because he's apparently dead. I suppose we could always move to another country, but we might as well stay out here if that's our only option.

'I panicked. I'm sorry okay, it's not my fault he couldn't just drive to Macro Meadow and use the portal. If you ask me, it's his fault,' Rex says, pointing a frustrated finger at me. 'I don't see why you want to go there anyway, it's a complete hole if you ask me.'

As I watch them bickering senselessly about Rex's mistake, I try not to get too involved as it quite clearly was my fault. If I had got to the portal on time none of this would have happened so I won't prod a sleeping lion and try to fight either corner.

A voice which sounds unfamiliar to me attempts to break Rex free of the public scolding. 'Can we get back to the meeting at hand please? I've got fourteen children to get home to if you don't mind,' the voice says impatiently. The lady who spoke is covered in reptilian-type scales and dreadlocks which hang down one side of her head. Fourteen kids? They mustn't have TV on Macro. Besides, she only looks about fourteen herself.

'Okay, meeting adjourned then,' Lara says, followed by the loud screeching of chair legs on the ground. 'I won't be around for a couple of days. I've got to make sure Tristan settles in alright,' Lara announces. 'Also, I'm playing in the Wand Wars tournament tomorrow because it's the grand finals of the Katarina Gem. We're up against *The Tempest Stormbringers*, *The Thunderous Thundercats* and *The Dangerous Diamantes* if anyone's interested who's not already attending.'

'I'd rather eat my own tail, what utter rubbish!' the old man, Miles, exclaims in disgust.

'I'll take that as a no then Miles. Rex should be around if you need anything while I'm not here. Take care everyone,' she says, waving a hand. The attendees all begin making their way towards the double doors which lead out into the corridor. Only me, Lara and Rex remain once everyone has dispersed.

'You need a lift down to the ground? I can show you how the matter transporter works,' Rex says to a still unimpressed Lara. Being able to sense that Lara is still fuming over his previous actions at the police station, he continues to defend what he's done. 'Come on, gimme a break, I got him back here, didn't I?'

'Yes, but in doing so, you also ruined our chances of ever getting home,' she says sternly. 'If you hadn't killed him, you could have just wiped his memory.'

'I still don't get why you wanna go back there, wouldn't you rather be playing Wand Wars and fighting the scum of the universe than sitting on your backside eating lasagne, whatever the hell that is?'

I can sense Lara mulling it over in her mind. 'I suppose you're right, what's done is done; it was still nice to have the option though. It was fine when I'd disappeared, I could just turn up and say I'd lost my memory or something. There's no way Tristan could go back now; if somebody notices him it could be catastrophic. Right, come along then, how do you fancy going for a drink?'

'Yeah, wouldn't mind one,' Rex replies to her invitation.

She glares back at him and says, 'I wasn't talking to you.'

'Only joking,' Rex says. 'You two have a good time. Oh, by the way, I got that other thing you asked me to collect.'

'Brilliant, we'll discuss that later, thanks Rex. And thanks for getting him here in one piece; you know I wouldn't have trusted anyone else with it,' Lara smiles at him appreciatively.

'No biggie,' he replies, blushing red again, but for different reasons this time. 'Once you're all ready to go I'll send you down on the matter transporter and show you how it works,' Rex tells us.

'Tristan, you go get some nicer clothes on; we're going for a few drinks. Just promise me you won't wear anything stupid,' she tells me seriously.

'Promise. I'll meet you back here in ten minutes,' I reply, then strut off back down the corridor towards the changing room.

CHAPTER 13

Galactica

Exiting the changing room in my new attire, I meander with a purposeful swagger through the snaking corridors, eyeing Lara and Rex waiting patiently outside the matter transporter room chatting.

In the wardrobe, I commandeered a pair of dark denim jeans and a blue hooded top. To my surprise, there were also some snazzy trainer-type shoes that tighten themselves up once you put them on your feet. When I first inserted my feet inside, I couldn't help but curiously press the buttons on the side; who wouldn't? I've never worn a pair of self-fastening trainers with buttons on the side and I was intrigued. After pressing one of the buttons, it warmed up the inside of the shoes, and the button on the other side cooled my feet down.

Emptying the pockets of my clothes which I wore on my travels to Macro, I came across the invisibility liquin which Genaci gave to me; this has to come in useful at some point. The jealousy on Rex's face when Genaci handed me it was obvious, and it indicated just how rare these things must be.

'Miles better,' Lara exclaims with relief that I now don't look like a giant cactus in the green yoti. We enter the matter transporter room and follow the instructions given to us by Ralph and his team.

'Please stay within the parameters of the *hyper-beam navigational portal field,* and once activated, you'll be transported to the configured destination within the system. If any part of your body is outside the field, you will be dismembered, and your limbs left behind will be vapourised,' Ralph informs us.

The field which Ralph is speaking about is a barely visible green forcefield which surrounds the circle pattern embedded into the floor and stretches up towards the ceiling. I take a grip of Lara's hand and smile at the team peevishly. 'How does this work again?' I ask Ralph, who stands at a glass control panel embedded in the wall with thousands of colours and digits covering every square inch.

Ralph removes his black-rimmed nerdy glasses and starts to chew on one of the arms; and when I say chew, it's more like he's trying to devour them as a starter before his lunch. 'Keep still and within the parameters, and we'll do the rest.'

'Gotcha!' I say enthusiastically and reply with a generous thumbs-up, trying to make him show even the slightest flicker of emotion, but it doesn't work, he just glares at me and continues chewing on his glasses. He presses a sequence of buttons on the glass wall and a blinding flash permeates through the air.

Once the white, piercing flash has subsided, Lara and I appear to be standing outside on the street below. Darkness is beginning to loom on the planet as it orbits away from the sun, which has an immense effect on the planets and stars which are still visible to us. Their colours seem to have doubled in brightness and the sight of it blows me away.

'Beautiful isn't it?' Lara says, both of us peering up at the breathtaking view. 'It never gets boring you know. I still look up every night in wonder at its beauty.' Lara extends her hand to hold mine as we stare in extreme silence at the sky together. I grip it gently, savouring this extraordinary moment that I want to last forever. As my eyes drop from the amazing sky after a few minutes, I catch sight of the familiar bar which I spotted on our way to HQ earlier. The word *Galactica* printed on the building couldn't be more visible if it tried in bright red lights. The red-brick building stands three storeys high and if I didn't know any better, I'd think it was on Earth.

'The guy who designed this district wanted it to look exactly like Earth. He had the buildings erected in Earth style, the roads, the vehicles, and he even put sewers under the ground, even though they're not functional,' Lara informs me.

Two gigantic figures, who look similar to Genaci, guard the double wooden doors of the building and process each individual with some kind of scanner. The customers hold their wrist up to be scanned, and access to the building is granted once it's done. They must be the same species as Genaci because they could be triplets, these two and him. *Doomguard* was it?

We join the queue, standing directly behind a man with extremely oversized pointy ears and three ginger-coloured wagging tails. The Doomguard at the door appear to be scanning each person's wrist, waiting a few seconds until it flashes green, and then allowing them to step inside. So far, all the scanned wrists have caused the device to light up green so I'm unfamiliar with what the process is if it illuminates in a different colour.

'Rex and Mattip both said they don't sell alcohol anywhere apart from Earth, is that true, or were they winding me up?' I ask pensively, praying that the information was wrong, or they were screwing with me.

'Yeah, unfortunately they're right. On Macro they put something called *macrohol* in the drinks instead. It's just as fun as alcohol, and you can have a right laugh when you drink it. Plus, it's tasteless so you can make any drink *macroholic.*'

'What does it do exactly?' I ask intriguingly.

'It's kinda weird when you first hear it, but it's not as odd as it first sounds. Macrohol is served as the base for every single drink, it's literally the only thing on the menu in the bar. You buy your glass of macrohol, and then you have to buy an accompaniment, which is a straw loaded with flavour called a *flavour reed*. Behind the bar, you'll notice there are thousands of different reeds, each one containing a different flavour, which you can put in your drink and make it taste how you want it to. Macrohol enhances your mental capacity. You become significantly cleverer while the macrohol effects are active inside your body. The drawback is that once the chemical has increased your brain capacity to make you cleverer, as the effects begin to wear off, the opposite happens.'

'So you become dumber?' I ask.

'Yeah, it's funnier than it sounds though. Personally, I think the aftereffects are funnier than the actual drinking part. If you thought hangovers from alcohol were bad, try spending the next day as a complete thicko. I went to a pub quiz a few months back with Tutti and Caprice and one team was trying to load up on macrohol to aid them. As the quiz went on longer and the aftereffects started to kick in, they could barely add two and two together,' she chuckles. 'Oh, and they also have macroholic food, but I'm not sure why you'd choose to eat that; isn't the whole point of sitting down and having a drink because it can last a while?'

'Sounds interesting. Think I might steer clear for now though, I need to keep my head together to take all this in.'

'Oh, stop you bore!' she retorts with a mocking jeer.

As soon as the pointy-eared people enter, we reach the front of the queue, facing two gargantuan, muscular, unsightly Doomguard. The security men guarding the door both grip mine and Lara's wrists, then scan them with a device that whirrs and buzzes like a metal detector with flashing lights. The device which scans Lara's wrist instantly flashes green, but mine doesn't respond. A few moments later, and both of them continue to stare suspiciously at the device, waiting for something to happen. 'This has never happened before!' The large entity roars down at me. 'What have you done to my device!'

'I… haven't done… anything,' I respond with utmost terror. These guys are terrifying; I should have been prepared for this after I met Genaci at the station and he scared the pants off me.

Abruptly, and without warning, the device gleams red and they simultaneously aim their eyesight towards my terrified face. Before one of the Doomguard can grab me by the throat, which I can see he is attempting to do, Lara pulls out a make-up brush and shouts *Voodoo Colossus Erase!'* The two men freeze on the spot looking completely braindead, one of them with his hand inches from my neck. Their completely black eyes gaze into nothingness and their tongues are almost licking their chins as they hang limply out of their mouths.

'Hey, you can't do that!' an interrupting voice calls out from behind us. 'I'm calling the Doomguard, you could get banished for that kind of thing!' it calls once again.

Me and Lara both turn in unison to the creature behind us in the queue. 'You'll do no such thing,' she says threateningly to the extremely skinny tattooed man who appears to be on a date with what I can only describe as a teddy bear. Lara points her make-up brush at his face to threaten him, and the new shocked guise on his face confirms his newfound terror.

'Lara?' the man replies, obviously recognising her from somewhere. 'I'm so sorry, do what you want, I'll keep my mouth shut.'

Lara turns to me once again. 'What shall we say?' she asks.

'What do you mean, what shall we say?' I reply.

'To these guys.' She nods towards the two dunderheaded forms in front of us. 'We can tell them what to remember, and what they've seen, rather than what they've actually seen.'

'No way!' I exclaim excitedly. 'Can you show me how to do it?'

'I'll show you how to do it, and I promise I'll let you do it next time,' Lara says teasingly, as if doing this to people is just a bit of fun. 'You both scanned our wrists and the devices turned green, so you let us in,' she says confidently.

With no attempt to rebel against my inner-child, I can't resist the urge to add something extra. 'You'll then both come inside in around five minutes' time and offer to buy us a drink, to which we will accept,' I add brazenly. Lara finds this hilarious and laughs hysterically out loud, and I even sense a slight snigger from the two people behind. I love making her laugh. Entering the bar, Lara swooshes her make-up brush over her shoulder, and the spell hits the guards, returning them to normal and scanning the next in line.

'How come you've got a wand?' I ask. 'I know this may sound a bit assuming, but I didn't think you'd have one.'

'Believe it or not, I actually got it from a dead person,' she tells me, leading us down the darkened corridor towards the inner entrance. 'When I arrived on Macro, before I met the others, I came across a corpse of a frail old lady. Lying next to her was a walking stick with a glistening diamond handle. With the prospect of handing it in once I found the relevant authorities, I took it with me. It was all very confusing when I first arrived here, but we'll get into that shortly. Let's get a drink first then we can chat.'

As we pass through a drawn set of rippled, bright red curtains, I stop in my tracks, dumbstruck at the sight of the room before me. The silent, magnificent utopia is like something from one of my wildest dreams. A rectangular bar stands conveniently in the centre of the room like a landmark, surrounded by a bustling crowd of hundreds of people. An array of differing species are chatting, cheering, chortling and chuntering through the chillingly silent atmosphere. In the bar area, robots, connected to huge hoses which reach up into the ceiling, are dispensing drinks through the palms of their hands into glasses and other drinking vessels for the customers. A cornucopia of straw-like items fills the shelves behind the robots, consisting of hundreds upon hundreds of different coloured liquids of varying luminescence and brightness.

Tables and chairs fill the room, but the odd thing about this, is the fact that a large quantity of them are airborne, levitated into the air and floating peculiarly like drones. There doesn't appear to be any music playing, unlike the deafening thuds of bass I could hear when we first passed the building. The only sounds that seem to fill the room are the sounds of conversations, but some people do appear to be dancing along to something. Maybe this is similar to those parties they have back home where everyone brings their own headphones and dances to whatever they want to listen to. Personally, I've never seen the novelty.

'Take one of these,' Lara notions, picking up a small black device from the stand beside us and sauntering down towards the bar area. I do as instructed and take one of the devices, following closely behind Lara.

'Now, hold it to the chip on your wrist, and press the button on the side.' Once again, I follow her orders, causing a deafening, rapturous, symphonic, reverberation of sound to pulsate through my ears. Jumping unexpectedly at the sudden sound, I cover my ears with both hands, and wince with an unrelenting crumpled-up face. The music sounds like nothing I've ever heard before; it's beautiful in its own magical way. It's almost impossible to describe the music as it's completely alien to me, but they must be using instruments that I couldn't even begin to imagine. I've never really thought about it before, but as humans, we only really know music as what instruments we have access to like drums, guitar, and bass etcetera.

'Sounds amazing doesn't it!' Lara shouts over the loud music, which I can just about hear.

'Yeah, sure does!' I scream back, then touch the device to my wrist again to silence the music so I can do what I do best and ask some more questions.

We approach the bar between two green beings with perfectly spherical craniums like basketballs, and an ear on the peak of each of their heads, except the ear looks a bit like a *Pringle*; it makes me quite peckish to be honest. Upon closer inspection of the flavour reeds on display behind the bar, I can now make out the unfamiliar labels next to each one.

'What would you recommend?' I ask, prompting Lara to study the holographic menu in her hand and use her finger to scroll through the list.

'I'd probably go for either popping baneberry fizz, hot maelstrom, or jarangalipo supreme. I think I'm going to order a wozzleping, but I'm not sure if it's your thing really.'

I decide to order a popping baneberry fizz as it sounds like something I'd buy as a kid from the convenience store on the walk home from primary school.

'Good choice,' she blurts out excitedly. 'Wait until you see mine, they're amazing.'

'What would you like to drink?' a gruff voice booms down to us from behind, causing us both to spin around in alarm. The two Doomguard from the entrance stare blankly at us to fulfil the promise they're unaware of.

'I forgot about those two,' Lara remarks, causing us both to giggle immaturely. I'm swiftly reminded of why I've missed Lara so much. We have an unnatural rapport and a subliminal connection that most couples could only dream of. We could moan, belittle, rant or scream at each other, but we don't take anything to heart. It's not that we don't take anything seriously, but we seem to be on the exact same frequency.

As our drinks are on the higher shelves, the robots use their legs to extend up to the top and then shrink back down to ground level to serve us. The drink I receive looks like a glass of water, which must be that macrohol stuff. Inside my glass, a straw pokes its head out of the top, which is filled with a lime green, radioactive-coloured substance.

After allowing the two security guards to pay for our rounds of drinks, Lara looks at me scrupulously. 'Wanna sit up there, or down here?'

'Do you even have to ask that question?' I reply with a knowing smile, then once again, follow Lara back across the dancefloor to a table that is accompanied by two chairs. On the table, there is a candlelight, but not just any candlelight, this candlelight consists of a creature that looks like a slug, but it glows with a heart-warming and pleasant phosphorescence.

The tables and chairs collectively levitate supernaturally up towards the ceiling. Laughing uncontrollably and hanging on for dear life, the possessed furniture raises us to its allocated height and stops with a gentle easing, adding to my compelling feelings towards this woman in front of me who I love more than anything. Momentarily, it feels as though we've never been apart.

'Lara?' I ask seriously, after our infectious giggling ceases abruptly. 'What happened to you when you disappeared? You haven't told me yet and I still don't know.'

'Sorry, I didn't want to get into it straight away. I wanted to make sure you settled in a bit first and we could break the ice. You remember I went next door to Gregory's, yeah?'

'Yeah,' I repeat.

'He made a cup of tea for us, and we chatted for a couple of minutes about the wedding. There was nothing unusual going on, except for the fact that he made it perfectly clear that he hoped you would have come over instead of me, which I thought was a bit rude in all honesty. I told him you'd be over a few minutes later because you had to take a call. As we were in mid-conversation, his bi-folding kitchen doors burst open, and a mysterious figure stepped inside.'

'Did you see who it was?'

'Yes. It was a really small man dressed as a court jester. He fired a spell at me. Gregory pounced on me to push me out the way. We both got hit by the spell, then I woke up on Macro.'

I pull a face of uncertainty, attempting to soak in the unexpected information from Lara. 'None of this makes sense though; why would the Sorceress get her minions to go to Earth and start casting spells on humans? Rex said we have to travel through the allocated stations to reach other planets, so wouldn't the spell have taken you to Earth's station rather than Macro? Also, what the heck happened to Gregory?'

'We don't know enough about her magic to be able to answer that question. For all we know, she has the ability to send people directly to Macro, or she could have got someone to meet me there once I materialised and carry my unconscious body to Macro. Regarding the question of why she was on Earth, we don't know; and to answer your other question, I haven't seen Gregory since so I couldn't tell you. When I woke on Macro, I was locked in a cell underground. I assumed I was still on Earth and whoever had broken into Gregory's house had taken me and locked me up. My assumption was that it was somehow connected to my work with the do-gooders, and somebody was after me for stealing from them. Within hours of being trapped in there, crying my eyes out thinking I was about to be tortured or killed, a hooded figure approached the cell, let me out, and informed me how to exit the cavernous maze I found myself locked in.'

'That must have been awful.' I hold my hand out supportively onto the table, allowing her to grip mine as she is clearly traumatised by the event.

Lara sniffles through her account of the events. 'When I finally escaped the hellish labyrinth which I found myself in, I was shocked by what was outside. Planets covering the sky, the yellow forcefield covering the city from above, not to mention all the weird aliens walking around and strange buildings and vehicles. I walked for miles, eventually bumping into the dead lady who had the walking stick that I mentioned earlier. I hid in an old building for a few days, stealing obscure foodstuffs and drinks from stores to keep me going. In due course, I was forced to leave my hiding place, and that's when I met Caprice. She noticed the walking stick, knowing it was a wand, and knew I was either capable of casting spells, or good enough to take it from someone who was capable of casting spells. Caprice put a chip in my wrist so I could understand everyone, then got me some work with HQ preventing baddies from stealing the Xanarock.'

Lara retrieves her wand from her back pocket and places it on the table. 'Caprice then converted the walking stick into a make-up brush for me so it was more convenient.'

'Did you ever find out who let you out of the cell?' I ask, still holding Lara's hand, but more tightly now as I feel irate at the thought of her being locked in a cell alone and terrified.

'No, still don't know now. They were wearing a hood so I couldn't see who it was. I'm not even sure if it was a man or a woman.'

'I still don't get why she'd go after you, you're just a normal person,' I utter.

'I don't think it was me she was after,' she replies, then takes a small sip of her drink. I forgot we even had drinks due to being so engrossed in the conversation, so I take a slurp of the straw hanging out of my drink to test the waters. Within seconds, Lara starts to turn blue. Her skin starts blotching and bright, violet colours, begin spreading across her features.

My mouth feels as if its exploding, like there's a firework exploding on my tongue. Convulsing, I attempt to spit out the remains of the liquid, but it's too late, I can already feel it travelling through my insides towards my stomach. The peculiar feeling in my mouth starts to subside, and my tongue returns to normal. Putting aside the party on my tongue, the taste was phenomenal, and by far the most amazing drink I've ever tasted in my life. Lara laughs insanely as the blue features spread vastly across her face with tremendous speed.

'What the hell was that?' I ask her, still struggling with the peculiar feelings my tongue has just experienced.

'Inside the reed you're drinking from, there's thousands of microscopic creatures, they're really, really tiny,' Lara informs me, holding her finger and thumb very closely together to give me an idea of just how tiny they are. 'Don't worry, they're harmless.' My tongue pokes out as far as it can, and I start clawing at it with my fingernails in a desperate attempt to rid my tongue of the remnants of these apparently microscopic creatures. 'Once they mix with the macrohol as it rises through the reed, they go nuts, literally jump around like crazy trying to get out. Feels weird doesn't it!'

'This whole place is weird,' I reply earnestly. 'Why can't we just ditch this place and go home without telling anyone?'

'We've got a job to do, believe it or not. Besides, could you really go back to Earth knowing all this exists?'

'S'pose not,' I reply, remembering that the last time I was on Earth I was attempting to end my own life. It'd be different with Lara by my side though.

'Besides, you're now technically dead, thanks to Rex, so that's not gonna happen any time soon. Right, down your drink, we'll have to get back to my place to get some sleep; we've got a big day on tomorrow.' Lara slurps her drink greedily like a child sucking out dregs of a milkshake, immediately causing a swarm of indigo to radiate all over her face and make her look like a human blueberry. Trying to suppress the giggles once again, I imitate her and suck ferociously at my straw, which invites my tongue to what feels like a live concert being played inside my mouth. After downing the drink in almost one gulp, the feeling from before is tenfold. This stuff is like popping candy on heat.

Five minutes until showtime folks! I hope you're all ready for the greatest show in the cosmos. The Incredible Crustaceans are ready to rock your world in just a few moments!' an announcer calls over the loudspeaker.

'Brill! I've wanted to see these since I came to Macro, Caprice has told me all about them!' Lara shouts excitedly. She presses something on the small device we collected to descend back to the ground below.

'Shall we have one more?' Lara asks suggestively, now looking giddy at the prospect of seeing this show that's been announced. 'These guys are supposed to be incredible. Caprice said she saw them live once and it was out of this world.'

'Yeah sure, I'll have another drink. What are they, a band?' I ask curiously.

'Well, they do play music. They do loads of other stuff too though as part of their act,' she informs me.

We order the same round of drinks each and wait eagerly for the show to begin. 'What's twenty-seven times four?' Lara asks me.

'One hundred and eight, why?' I reply instantly without a moment's hesitancy, and my brain pauses, recalling that mental arithmetic isn't exactly my strongpoint. Our eyes meet immaturely and we both smirk as I look down at my drink wondering what the hell this stuff is.

'So, the more I drink the cleverer I'll be?' I ask.

'Yeah, but the aftereffects will also work in the opposite direction, so try not to have too much or you'll be lucky if you can add two and two in a few hours' time.'

We both sip our drinks leisurely, but before the effects from the drink hit the inside of my mouth, the lights in the room dim suddenly and hundreds of eyes turn to face the stage located directly above the bar in the centre of the room. A suspenseful atmosphere fills the room as everyone waits eagerly for the show to begin.

Through the ominous, highly anticipating silence, a band walks onto the stage, and I am gobsmacked at the appearance of the three weird-looking fish people. Using the button on the device, I make the noise in the bar audible once again in preparation of the oncoming act.

'Good evening!' the leader of the band calls emphatically into what resembles a seashell, which he holds closely to his mouth in cupped hands. 'We are the Incredible Crustaceans! Some of you may have heard of us, some of you may have seen us, but I will bet my fins that you all know who we are!' he bellows confidently into the microphoned seashell. A rapturous applause fills the room as if they're the most well-known band in the whole solar system.

'Never heard of them,' I say to Lara humorously.

The instruments each of them hold are bizarre but well-themed. As they warm up for the next couple of minutes playing practice notes, one of them appears to be touching parts of a wheel which he spins in front of himself like a pirate sailing his ship. As he touches each section, a range of different notes and sounds emit from the instrument. Another of the band members holds two sticks that play a collection of different sounds when held at different angles or held a certain distance apart. As he moves them, the sounds seem to change massively as if you could get a million different notes out of the contraption.

The third and final fish-man is the singer, who grasps the seashell, but is armed with a stand-up piano in front of him filled with small fish as the keys from what I can see on a TV screen. The humongous screen floats near the bar to give a more extensive and close-up view of the action for those who can't see all the act from below.

'Wait until you see what they do; they do this thing where they...' Lara is cut off mid-sentence when, without any warning, the whole room starts to fill with water, but it's not water, it's just an illusion that gives the impression that the room is being submerged leagues under the sea.

'What the heck is going on?' I ask myself mentally, and gaze around the room in awe as it fills with imaginary water.

The first sound of the band is made and I'm in agreement with Lara when I say that this is the most spectacular, although strange, display that I've ever seen. The instruments sound amazing during the intro to the song, but what impresses me the most, is the aquatic exhibition which occurs around the whole room. Dolphins swimming around in hats, thousands upon thousands of sea creatures of different shapes, colours and sizes swim around the entirety of the room. The crowd cheer rapturously like nothing I've ever heard in my life and throughout the whole performance so far, I haven't even remembered that Lara existed; or that I even existed myself due to being so mesmerised by the display. The instruments play, the aquatic wonderland in front of my eyes continues to dazzle me, and the singer begins his obscure rapping performance:

'*Good evening all, we're the Incredible Crustaceans,*
Whether you're a local or you're on vacation,
We will entertain you thoroughly with our amazing celebrations.'

Time stops momentarily, and everything I can see in this place, right here and now, is all that matters in the whole of reality. It's almost impossible to drag my eyes away from the presentation. They continue to sing spectacularly:

'*We will put on such a show, it's guaranteed you'll never want to go,*
You'll want to spread the word,
Of this amazing and fantastical experience you've witnessed,
Watch as your mesmerised by these fishes,
Putting on a show so spectacular, we'll be fulfilling all of your wishes...'

I miss the next few lines as a mermaid swoops around the top of the bar encircling it like a vulture looking for a carcass to feast on. The mermaid nosedives with lightning speed down towards me, stopping mere inches from my face with a lustful smile as she stares intently into my eyes. A low growl from beside me lets me know that Lara isn't exactly ecstatic by the mermaid's lewd and inappropriate actions. The mermaid continues to lure me in and leers directly into my soul. Even though I know this is an illusion, I'm still captivated by her beauty and fascinating gesticulations. As she looms in closer, attempting to kiss me passionately on the cheek, a Lara-shaped figure flies swiftly past my line of vision angrily, causing her to penetrate through the mirage and land on the floor, splayed out awkwardly. I howl with laughter, louder than I probably ever have before, and the only thing that brings an abrupt end to my deriding roars is the sudden disappearance of the illusion filling the room, the cease of the music, and the noise which reverberates loudly through the vicinity, causing everyone to stop in their tracks.

A tumultuous, ear-splitting bang from the exterior makes us both turn our heads rapidly towards the entrance. 'Don't move!' a loud voice booms, almost shaking the whole building and causing half of the room to drop their drinks in terror. 'Everybody line up against the outer walls so we can scan you all individually! Nobody will enter or exit this building until we find the fugitive!' the loud voice blurts out over the horrified screams. High-pitched shrieks and other unfamiliar sounds of bawling emanate through the atmosphere. 'There is no cause for alarm, but you will all have to be processed, and I repeat, nobody is permitted to leave the building until our search is complete!'

At least a dozen of the *Doomguard* enter the room armed to the teeth with unfamiliar weapons.

CHAPTER 14

Sewer Rat

'Why are they here?!' Lara exclaims, sounding utterly perplexed and panicked. Panning her head all around the interior of the room, it becomes obvious that she's looking for a way to escape.

My body is unwillingly dragged urgently into a small side room, which is no doubt used for storage as crates and containers line the walls from floor to ceiling. 'I don't think anybody saw us through the panic,' Lara whispers loudly. 'We need to get out of here right now. We have about thirty seconds until they start searching the side rooms and then we're done for if they find us; they're already searching around the bar area. How did they know you were here?' she muses to herself. 'Your chip must have alerted them when we came in. I'm not sure what the issue was, but that chip in your wrist shouldn't have shown up with an error. I'll look into it when we get back.'

'If we get back,' I yell, panic-stricken and shaking like a tree in a typhoon. 'Can't you just use magic or something? What will they do if they find me? I haven't done anything wrong. What can they possibly do?' I bellow, the sound of my voice clearly heightening the anxiety of the situation. Sweat soaks my palms and an agitated hysteria begins jumpstarting inside my body.

'It's because we brought you here illegally Tristan!' she blurts out in a hushed whisper. 'Under no circumstance can anybody from Earth come to Macro without permission. If they find you, they'll send you back with no memory of all this, and probably me too! That's the last thing we need. The chip was supposed to give you a false identity and show you up on their systems as being a normal civilian of Macro; I'm not sure what happened. They're on their way over!' Lara exclaims, looking genuinely scared as she peeps out through a small crack in the door out into the bar.

Outside the room, the screams are still audible from the patrons, but I'm still able to make out the sound which comes from behind us. We both turn in confusion away from the door, and towards the rear wall where a hole has magically appeared.

An unfamiliar head pops its way through the recess. 'How many times do I have to save your backside Lara? Seriously, sometimes I feel like without me you'd be either in prison or dead,' a small, aged man who distinctly resembles a mole blurts to the pair of us. With hesitation being the last thing on our minds, we burst hastily towards him in a desperate lunge, then attempt to squeeze our way through to the other side. We drop metres down below to land in a pit of darkness. The mole man points a small umbrella at the gap we just came through and says, '*Fortify Reverse*,' in a hushed whisper. The hole appears to close in on itself, and within a millisecond, it is filled in, once again looking like a normal wall. Loud voices and noises can be heard as they search the room for us on the opposite side, and within a minute or so, the sounds cease with silence once again rearing its head.

'Oh my god Tutti, you're a lifesaver!' Lara replies to the aged man and runs towards him to wrap her arms around him thankfully.

'You're most welcome Lara. I was at home enjoying a cup of Darjeeling and a custard cream, when my monitors started bleeping like crazy. After investigating, I saw that you were in the vicinity of the raised alarm so I thought I'd come along and see if I could be of assistance,' he says.

'Thanks so much Tutti, for a moment there I thought we were done for! Just for a moment though,' Lara says appreciatively. 'This is Tristan,' she informs him as they break the hug. In the darkness, I can just about make out his silhouette peering in my direction. He must have good eyesight being a mole man; it's probably like the middle of the day in here for him.

'Welcome young man, I've heard a lot about you and it's nice to finally put a face to a name. Now, patience and rudeness aside, we must make haste. The creatures down here are enough to make your whiskers curl.'

'Where are we?' I stare around the blackness of the tunnel, searching the floor for any strange creatures that may be lurking in the shadows and brushing my clothes off.

'We're underneath the hospitality sector. A word of caution,' Tutti says clearly with a lone finger raised in the air. 'Make sure you don't stand on any *obbins*, they can be quite deadly. They're vermin, a bit like rats but they've got a lot more eyes and legs. And teeth as well thinking about it. Their eyes are luminous green so you should be able to see them, even in this darkness. Lucky for you, the other end of this tunnel takes us up to the surface right outside my home,' Tutti says as he starts to venture forward cautiously.

Lara pulls her make-up brush out of her pocket, says the words *'Nova Guide,'* and a glowing spectral orb rises from the tip and levitates next to her, following her at shoulder height as she walks. The orb emits a glowing iridescence that lights up the tunnel like the brightest torch I've ever seen.

'Where did you learn all these spells?' I ask. 'I struggled to remember the first four digits of pi and I was doing that for years at school.'

'3.142,' Tutti mutters quietly, walking from the shadows.

'Hard work and commitment.' Lara replies.

A haziness, which has been building up over the last few minutes, becomes worse. Maybe it's something I've eaten or drank, or maybe it's a side effect from that macrohol stuff. I only had two drinks and I'm struggling to string a conscious thought together. I begin questioning my mental arithmetic as Lara did with me earlier. I know two plus two is four, and I know three plus three is six, but I'm stumbling to get the right answer for twelve plus twelve; it's as if there's a mental roadblock in my mind that I just can't get past.

We meander through what must be a mile of underground tunnels, with all sorts of small rodents walking across my feet as we walk cautiously through the corrupted blackness with only Lara's ball of luminance providing us with any light.

I suppose it's a positive thing there isn't much light, because if I could see them properly, I think I'd rather face the Doomguard than have hundreds of rodent creatures slithering and squirming all over me. The idea of them beneath my feet makes me shudder profusely, causing me to pull a cringed expression. After the arduous, terrifying journey through the dark abyss, we eventually reach the end of the tunnel to be greeted by a metal ladder that connects this hellhole to a wooden trapdoor above.

'How come you couldn't just cast a spell and make us reappear somewhere else? I thought you could do anything with those things,' I ask Tutti and Lara collectively.

'And in turn I could try to restore your sense of adventure young man,' Tutti replies.

'What?! Are you saying you made me walk through a tunnel filled with weird, crawly rodents because you have a sense of adventure?' Tutti completely ignores me and climbs the ladder, reaching the top and sliding the wooden grate to the side.

Lara whispers quietly to me so Tutti can't overhear. 'Don't be too hard on him, after all, he's the brain that got you here in the first place. Also, as a side note, that's not how spells work, you can't just transport yourself randomly from any location; we have portals for that.'

'Are you two coming or not?' Tutti calls down with an echoing shout, his face hanging through the circular cavity above. 'There's time for chatting once we get up to my adobe. I'll make us all a fresh cup of herbal tea and we can get warm and have a bit of a chinwag. I do love your Earth tea and coffee; all they serve on Macro is fancy colourful drinks that are full of rubbish. Yuck!' he spits out.

Lara and I climb the ladder hastily. After ascending the cold, metal ladder, we appear to be in an unlit, musky, stale-smelling wine cellar. An interesting array of different coloured bottles cover the walls in racks and a nasty aroma penetrates the air, which makes me balk involuntarily and cover my mouth with my hand. After reaching the top of a set of oaken, damp stairs, we arrive in a hallway on the next floor. We appear to be in an apartment building as the décor and furniture couldn't belong to anywhere else; carpeted floors and wooden dressing tables adorned with flowers see to that.

The other two make their way to a pair of elevator doors further down the corridor, and by the way Lara is walking beside Tutti, and not following him, I can tell that this isn't the first time she's been here. Tutti presses the number 12 button at the very top of the panel, causing it to glow orange. A subtle grin covers my face as I realise that we must be on our way up to a penthouse suite or something of the like as we're on our way to the top floor. During the elevator's ascension, I'm able to conduct a more thorough examination of Tutti's appearance now that there's more light. He is very mole-like, and his nose sticks out with large black, thick-rimmed glasses mounted upon them. His wafer-thin whiskers protrude from his face, making his face look small in comparison; he's got no chance of those big glasses falling off with a nose like that.

As the door opens on the rooftop (yes, the rooftop), we step out into the bitter winter air. The icy wind whips at my face like a slap from a snowman and we make our way towards a dingy wooden hut on the far corner of the roof. Some penthouse suite that is!

'Is that it?' I blurt out, glaring at the squalid hut in front of us, but they completely ignore me and continue to stride hastily towards it to shelter from the cold. 'Why is it so cold suddenly? I ask curiously.

'It just goes like that at night, something to do with the forcefield I think,' Lara answers.

'It's because of the atmospheric imbalance caused through convection and displacement in a highly unstable airspace. Basically, the forcefield is causing an artificial state of weather as there is no wind or rain. Without a proper weather cycle, the weather conditions have become what you young people refer to as "messed up". Before the forcefield came to be, Macro was a tropical haven, a place everybody wanted to visit due to its outstanding beauty and gorgeous weather.'

Tutti unlocks the door and enters inside. An intense heat hits me harshly as it whips out of the doorway and causes me to lunge forward and depart from the bitterness. My mouth drops in awe as we cross over the threshold into the small shack. The room which we find ourselves in is significantly larger than it could have possibly been from the external measurements. I step back outside into the cold again to double-check, and then run back inside in confusion.

'It's bigger on the inside!' I shout, flabbergasted by what I'm perceiving.

Once again ignoring my overactive, childish fascination with everything I see, Tutti shouts a greeting to whoever is currently home. 'Hi Doris, we're back!' he shouts welcomingly.

An old lady sits in the corner of the room silently on a chair beside the stone hearth, which houses a fire that roars with powerful intensity. The white-haired, decrepit old lady holds two knitting needles, and a scarlet ball of wool hangs down the side of the chair. Her head is drooped down, staring at the needles below with extreme focus.

'Who's she?' I ask curiously.

'This is my wife, Doris. She was cursed many years ago, so she doesn't really do much now except sit in that old chair and rock to and fro. I look after her as much as I can, but if I'm honest, it's starting to get to me now,' he replies glumly.

'So, she's your wife?' I ask.

'Forty-two years we've been married, but enough about her, who fancies a cup of tea? We have a lot to talk about,' Tutti exclaims excitedly.

CHAPTER 15

Realisation and Conversation

'Would you like any biscuits to go with the tea?' Tutti asks Lara and I collectively, walking carefully across the room holding three white, ceramic mugs that cover his face with steam.

'We're good thanks,' Lara replies, assuming wrongly that I don't want a biscuit as I'm absolutely starving. Tutti takes a seat on one of the chairs that surround the small coffee table which we're gathered around cosily near the fireplace. The heat feels nice on my skin after the trek through the cold, dark tunnel and the icy winds on top of the building.

Tutti's wife, Doris, remains in the corner of the room knitting equivocally in a deep trance. In truth, it creeps me out massively and all I want to do is either leave the room or pick the chair up with her in it and dump her in another room; I suppose Tutti wouldn't be happy about that though, so I'll leave her be. What did Tutti mean when he said she was cursed?

Apart from the front door, which we entered through when we arrived, there are three other doors in the house; I'm assuming one is a kitchen, one is a bathroom, and the other is a bedroom. One of the walls inside the living room consists entirely of one ginormous set of bookshelves, each shelf filled with numerous editions of varying types of books. There is only one perfectly square shelf in the centre of the wall that has a transparent glass pane with a small flashing light encasing it. Beyond the glass pane is a gold and deep-blue coloured book. The title on front of the book reads: *The Perplexed Findings and Discoveries of the Known*

Universe and Beyond.

'Please be careful with that!' Tutti exclaims unexpectedly from across the room, pointing at the book behind the glass pane as I approach it. His mug gets placed on the table gently and he makes his way over to me with sorrow portrayed in his features. After using his wrist to activate the sensor on the shelf, the door slowly opens. Tutti removes the book and delicately rubs the cover with two fingers.

'My father wrote this book; it was the only thing he ever left me. It was also the only book he ever had published before he died, selling exactly twenty-five copies. His knowledge was brilliant, and all I dreamt of from a young age was following in his footsteps and replicating his success; I'm afraid to admit that I'm a total failure.' His head bows disappointingly.

In a mediocre attempt at lifting his spirits, Lara says, 'Come on Tutti, you're not a failure, you're the cleverest person I've ever known. I couldn't even begin to comprehend half the things you say in normal conversation, never mind when you're talking about boring science stuff.' Tutti attempts a desperate chuckle. 'He even passed through university with flying colours from the Macro Institute for Ethereal and Celestial Wisdom. *Universal Studies* is probably the most difficult subject you can take, and he aced it,' she explains, glaring at me as if she wants me to add something. I've only known the guy five minutes, what am I supposed to say?

'Wow, that's really impressive. You must know a lot,' I add, making something up on the spot to act supportive.

'Yes, that's all well and good, but I did graduate when I was twenty-five, and now I'm sixty-two. Besides, I love working for HQ and it's full of great people, plus I get to put my knowledge to the test every day. Would either of you like another cup of tea?' Tutti asks politely.

'Yes please,' Lara and I say simultaneously, passing him our now cold half-empty mugs. Tutti takes them into the kitchen and the sound of clattering resounds through the house.

'Some place this isn't it?' I whisper to Lara once Tutti is out of earshot.

'It's cute,' she responds with a smile. 'He's lived here since he came to Macro. While he was studying in university, he met Doris and bought this place. He's tried so hard to be like his father and become a scholar, but he's never exactly hit the ground running. People aren't exactly his forte.'

'He seems fine to me.'

'It's more to do with people of authority. He applies for positions that become available, but when he's being interviewed, he goes completely blank and starts to squabble. That's what he's told me anyway.'

Tutti enters the room, a small black tray floating in front of him containing three steaming mugs and an assortment of biscuits. The tray is passed around to each of us in turn, allowing us to take our mugs and any biscuits we desire.

'So, what do you think of the solar system?' Tutti asks me curiously, dunking a custard cream into his tea and biting it before its sogginess causes a frightful mess of the table.

'It's amazing. Can I ask something though?' I ask the pair of them, who now stare at me intently. 'Lara, you said during the meeting that you brought me here to help defeat the Sorceress, Rex said it to me too, but what on Earth could I do to help?' Putting down their mugs and giving me a look which I don't like too much, the same look you get when a doctor has some bad news to give you in hospital, they concede to the elephant in the room and begin our discussion.

'There's something we need to tell you babe,' Lara says to me lovingly, making me cringe at what they could possibly be about to talk to me about. 'Okay, so, how do I say this, hmm…'

'It's alright, take your time, not like we're in a rush or anything,' I add sarcastically at the obvious stalling from Lara and bite into a garibaldi.

'Okay, so you know how on Earth we have prisons and deportation when people break the law?'

'Yeah.'

'Well, in the solar system, when people have broken the law, they're banished to Earth for their crimes after being found guilty. When somebody is "banished", they're sent to Earth with no memory of their former self, and they gain a new appearance so they can't be recognised or tracked down. They wake up unconscious with no memory, they then usually visit a hospital, who diagnose them with amnesia, and they carry on their existence with no recollection of what's going on outside Earth and start a new life.'

'Oh yeah. Rex told me about all this when we first met!' I exclaim, making them aware that I already know at least some of this process.

'Brill, at least it should be a bit easier to understand now then,' she says. 'Thousands of people have been banished over the years, all of different ages and species.'

I contemplate this for a couple of seconds and eventually I work something out, causing my brain to go into a spasm. 'No way!' I shout at the room jumping up from my seat with a startle. 'I'm not from Earth?'

'Ha-ha, she said you were good!' Tutti retorts.

My brain spins around in circles trying to fathom out this newly found information. I woke up at eleven years old with no memory. I was found and rushed into hospital, and nobody knew who I was. 'Hold on though, what crime could an eleven-year-old commit that would warrant him being banished to Earth?' I ask, but as I say it, another switch flicks in my head, causing it to start hurting with the amount of information being passed through it. The effects of macrohol still in my system have a slight drain on my mental ability to decipher each thought.

'Salamander,' I gasp emptily to the pair of them, with eyes of stone that stare into the distance, mental images flying through my mind.

'What?' Lara asks.

'Say that again.' Tutti's face turns to contemplation and it's clear to recognise that what I just said made sense to him.

I try with all the brainpower I can muster to recall the dreams I experienced mere days ago. 'I had these dreams before I came to Macro. There were some kids playing, one of them was called Salamander, he cast a spell on another kid called Theo, and then I woke up after he vanished. Then I had another dream where Salamander was being taken away from his family and they were banishing him. It didn't make sense at the time, but thinking about it now, could I have been remembering things from my previous life?'

'Intriguing, very intriguing,' Tutti says, swivelling his whiskers with his thumb and forefinger. 'So, you're Salamander? We assumed you'd been banished when Lara mentioned your upbringing to me, but we were unsure who you were as hundreds of people are banished each year.'

'There was a child who was famously banished quite a while back; come to think of it he would have been around your age at the time. I swear, you couldn't make this up if you'd tried. Salamander Peruvius was the older brother of Katarina Peruvius,' Tutti remarks with a slightly creepy tone as if he's telling a scary story around a campfire.

'What?!' Lara and I both exclaim simultaneously.

'No way!' Lara adds.

'Yes, I'm afraid it's true. Salamander and Katarina's father was the High Justice Minister of Macro, he oversaw the banishing of criminals once they'd received their sentence and were bound for Earth. The High Justice Minister had a wand aptly called "the Banishing Wand". The Banishing Wand was only to be used for this purpose, and it was his job to ensure the safe storage and use of the Wand at all times. Salamander somehow stole this wand from his father's possession, then used it to banish a boy from his school named Theo, which caused him to face trial and be banished. This was probably more of a punishment towards the mother and father than the child as they didn't usually tend to banish youths.'

'So how come I'm having dreams about it if my mind was supposedly erased?' I ask, slightly confused about how it all works.

'I'm getting to that in a second, just give me a minute to explain,' Tutti states, his head looking as though it's working at hyper speed.

'Well can you hurry up? Tea's getting a bit cold again,' I add in jest and shake my cup of tea at him.

'How can you joke at a time like this? Are you not surprised?' Lara asks me.

'Well yeah, but I think I always knew something about me wasn't right somewhere down the line. I've always been a bit weird, haven't I Lara?'

Tutti gives a cough to interrupt and take the reins on the conversation. 'After Salamander used the Banishing Wand, it went missing and has never been found, even now. The original wand was created by a sorcerer who lived a long time ago, using unknown spells and methods to create the wand; it was one of a kind. He was the same sorcerer that created the pulsar to banish the whole planet of Earth. During Salamander's trial, a new Banishing Wand was created to replace the old one. My guess is that because it wasn't made to the standard of the original wand, the effects are starting to slightly wear off and you're having flashbacks about important times in your life before you were banished. Nobody knows the whereabouts of the original wand, but it's out there somewhere, hidden or discarded by Salamander with no way to find it. Until the day of his banishment, he would not divulge where he hid the wand.'

'Does anyone know what happened to Theo?' I ask sympathetically. 'Gonna have to hunt him down and apologise endlessly, aren't I?'

'The chances are, he's living a normal human life down on Earth with no recollection of the solar system, I suppose,' Tutti explains. 'The only difference with him is that he was banished with the original wand, and you were banished with the new, less effective one that was created. I just hope there's not a surge of people down on Earth who start getting their original memories back, it could have some devastating consequences. I'll report this to HQ.'

'So my name's not even Tristan then? Salamander is a stupid name. Why couldn't I have been called Hulk or Clint or something?' I ask the pair who are both staring into space, obviously trying to figure out this news in their heads. 'And, going back to my earlier question, you brought me here because you wanted to tell me about this?'

'I had a million reasons to bring you here, but it was mostly because I missed you. I told the others that with your help, we could defeat the Sorceress because we make an amazing team. I didn't think, in a million years, that you'd end up being Sorceress Katarina's brother.'

'But how come you ended up here in the first place? You're saying Gregory wasn't behind it, but where is he now?' I ask.

'Well, I'm pretty certain Gregory tried to save me. One of the

Sorceress' minions came in and tried to cast a spell on me, then Gregory attempted to shield me, and we both got hit. I'm still not sure why they came after me because as far as I know, there's no reason she'd want me. Looking at it now, it has to be something to do with you, but what?' Lara adds intriguingly. 'What would she want you for?'

'Without sounding ungrateful or thankful, why couldn't you have brought me here any sooner?' I ask Lara, who sips blankly at her cup of tea. 'Why did you have to leave me for a whole year all alone?'

'Because I didn't know how, and I didn't have the authority to. Why do you think I worked so hard to work my way up the ladder in HQ? I knew after a few weeks that if I got myself to a high enough position, I'd be able to gain the authority to send for you. Only the Commander can carry out a request like that and with him disappearing, it was the perfect time for me to gain the authority to do something. I told Tutti our predicament, so he came up with the plan to send Rex to get you; there was no way you'd have been able to get here yourself without proper guidance. The main issue we had was that we had to have them explain who they were and what the solar system was, as there was very little chance you'd have believed the story.'

To think that all of this was happening while I was wallowing in self-pity helps to puts things into perspective. All these people were working hard for Lara to try and get me here, and I was sobbing my eyes out unaware of all of it.

'I came up with the idea of writing a note and getting Rex to deliver it to you as the only person you'd have listened to given the circumstance, was me. I didn't expect it to go perfectly, but I suppose we can't moan, you're here aren't you?' Lara adds.

'You're here, aren't you?' a croaky voice speaks out from the corner of the room, which causes the three of us to spin our heads towards Doris in frightened alarm. She's stopped knitting and now stares blankly at me, her hands gripping the arms of the chair.

'Doris?' Tutti exclaims, sounding somewhat petrified. 'She… She's never done that before,' he says, rising out of his chair with urgency to approach her.

'What the hell?' Lara stares at the old woman, whose eyes don't blink once as she gives me a death stare.

'I thought she was cursed and couldn't move. She can't move, can she?' I ask.

Tutti begins examining her thoroughly to see what's changed and why she suddenly spoke. Following his examination, it looks as though he can't find anything of note, and a minute or so later, she leans forward, picks up the knitting kit, and carries on as before.

'She hasn't moved so much as an inch in years. I'll have to look into this, it's most peculiar, I'll have to conclude some research as this is most unheard of.' He does that thing again where he swivels his whiskers with his fingers when he's deep in thought and looks almost tranced.

'Look, Tutti, I hope you don't mind, but could we stay here tonight? It's getting late and it'll take us ages to get back to my place,' Lara asks Tutti, who is barely listening at this point.

'Sure, sure, you can stay in there,' he says, pointing to one of the bedrooms. He kneels desperately at Doris' side and holds her hand, but she doesn't acknowledge his presence.

'How does she eat or drink?' I ask. 'Or go to the toilet, or get dressed?'

'She doesn't,' Lara answers. 'The curse has literally blocked everything she does; she's got no needs or feelings anymore, she doesn't even sleep.'

'Geez, do you know who, or what, cursed her?' I ask Tutti.

'No, I was contacted to collect her as she was found sitting on the ground in the middle of the street. I managed to get her back up to our apartment, but she hasn't moved since. I tried my best to look after her at first, changing her clothes and feeding her, but over time, I came to realise that she doesn't require any of this. I'm just living in hope that she snaps out of it one day, or I can find a cure for this wretched curse. I've read almost every book on Macro and there's nothing of note that could have caused this.'

'Bummer,' I reply, which is probably not the most sympathetic term to use, and I can see Lara's agreement with the glance she shoots at me.

Lara yawns with a wide-open mouth and stretches her arms high into the air. 'We'll get to bed then Tutti, if you don't mind. Long day ahead tomorrow.'

'What are we doing now, am I ever gonna get a day off? Am I being trained up to be a super killer to take on my own sister?'

'Nope. First, I'm taking you to the museum. It's only a few minutes' walk from the arena and we can get there beforehand. I'll be able to show you the history of Macro, and there's all sorts of other exhibits in there. Seeing as you've just found out that you're Macronian, it'll give you the opportunity to learn more about your home planet.'

My home planet? That sounds odd when you say it like that. I'm not from Earth, I committed a crime at eleven years old and was banished, forced to live a life on Earth as punishment.

Lara beams excitedly. 'Then, you're coming to watch me play in the *Wand Wars* tournament.'

'You really love this Wand Wars thing, don't you?' I ask, to which she nods her approval.

We're both forced to wear our clothes for bed as Tutti doesn't exactly have wardrobes stocked up of men and women's clothes. I hint to Lara to snuggle with me in the same bed, but she point-blank refuses; I can't blame her with the creepy old lady in the next room though. We leer at each other with wide smiles from beds on opposite sides of the room, and I can't help but stare at her fascinating beauty; she really is the most beautiful woman I've ever seen.

'Will I ever get to have a wand?' I ask randomly, completely out of the blue.

'I'll have to speak to someone; they don't just make them willy-nilly. You need rare materials that are almost impossible to find. They haven't made a wand for about ten years because they can't get any more unicorn horns.'

'They use unicorn horns to make wands? Seems a bit mean, doesn't it?' I ask.

'No meaner than using elephant tusks to get ivory,' she adds.

'Good point,' I reply in defeat.

Thoughts of my life begin to run laps through my head like a merry-go-round. The same thoughts appear repeatedly, all seeming to reach the same conclusion. My parents weren't my parents, my family weren't my family, those baby pictures around my house weren't of me. Why didn't my parents just tell me I wasn't biologically theirs? I suppose they didn't want me hunting around for my real parents and everyone was happy enough that I didn't know. The fact that I've always had a fascination with the night sky is probably the most relatable thing I can think of; I used to sit there for hours and hours, just staring skyward with a piqued interest.

'Lara,' I whisper. 'Lara,' I repeat, but she doesn't answer. I just wanted to tell her about the night she went missing, when me and Gregory were looking up at the sky. He was pointing up, telling me the names of all the planets. I thought the names sounded strange when he was saying them, and I remember it like it was yesterday. Szera, Macro, Neplio. These were the names the rest of the solar system use, so he must not have been from Earth. Before I can even think another thought, my eyelids become heavier, constantly thinking about the woman I saw crying her eyes out when Salamander was banished; she must have been my mother. That man holding the little girl was my dad, and the little girl was the person I was sent here to destroy.

CHAPTER 16

Passing With Flying Colours

It'd be a lie if I said I'd slept right through. The events of the last few days have my head bursting with a mixture of excitedness, fear, terror and palpable wonder. Lara looks as beautiful as ever with her caramel-coloured hair enveloping her face entirely. The faint tinkering of knitting needles from the other room creep their way through the air to remind me of the freaky episode that Doris had last night. There was something unusually spooky about what she did, as if she was listening to us and responded subliminally.

A tinkering sound becomes audible in the distance which I decipher must be Tutti making tea again. A few moments later, the familiar face pops around the door frame to greet us.

'Good morning!' Tutti bellows gleefully. I don't think I've known anyone to be so happy at this time of the day, even though I'm not even sure what time it is. Their time on this planet will be completely different to ours, to the point where I can't even be bothered to ask as I must cease the question-asking at some point and learn as I progress. Two pots of tea are placed on a dressing table near the door and another mountain of biscuits. Lara eventually stirs and lifts her hirsute face from the bed.

'Tutti, what's your obsession with tea and biscuits?' I ask, rubbing the sleep from my eyes.

'I just love them. There are so many different varieties, flavours and textures. My favourite is the custard cream, I've never tasted such a splendid array of flavour on one single foodstuff. My second favourite is the Penguin…

Five minutes later

'…My twelfth favourite is the bourbon cream. That small chocolate wonder lights up every taste receptacle on my tongue. I love the way they're so crunchy, and I…'

'Enough!' Lara calls, finally coming round to full consciousness, raising a hand in front of her as her annoyance limit hits overload. 'We don't need to know the history of biscuits; we've got enough on our plate, no pun intended.' I snigger childishly at the unintended joke.

'Right, I'm going for a shower,' Lara says, exiting the room after pecking me on the cheek. Tutti and I glance at each other in an awkward silence for the next few moments until I finally speak.

'Can I ask you something? You know, man to man, or mole to man, or whatever you are.'

'I'm a Mol actually.'

'Close enough. You know while I haven't been here, has Lara spoken about me much?'

'Of course, she talks about you all the time. Why do you ask?'

'She just seems a bit… I don't know, distant maybe? Am I just being paranoid?'

'She's had a lot going on lately. She has a lot of responsibilities and sometimes the stress becomes unmanageable. I think with you now being here it should calm her down a bit at least as I know she's worried a lot about that lately. The things I've seen her do since she arrived could be taking their toll on her also.'

'What do you mean? The things she's done, as in what?'

'She is one of the Protectors of the Xanarock, it's physically and mentally draining. They have to devote their lives to keeping any potential threats away from the Xanarock. If it were to be removed, then the forcefield would fade and the city would be overrun by those things on the outside. Don't forget, she was all alone in a foreign world and that must have been tough in itself, you can't be surprised that she's a tad different.'

Thinking about everything Lara must have gone through makes me realise I've had it easy compared to her. I know I lost her, but I still had everybody else around me, and she was all alone in a place that she didn't even know existed. She wouldn't have even known where she was for the first part.

Tutti begins twisting his whiskers in contemplation once again as if he's pondering something that requires a lot of thought.

'What's up?' I ask, detecting that there's something on his mind. 'You're not still thinking about what Doris did last night are you?'

'No, not at all. I've concluded that whatever curse she's under is making her do odd things, and until I can find out what it is, I'll never be able to figure it out. There's something else.'

'What is it?'

'I've been up all night thinking, but nothing new there, I do that most nights. Do you think that Gregory fellow may have known something about what was going to happen? Was he from Earth?' Tutti questions intriguingly.

'I remembered something last night, but by the time I was going to mention it to Lara, she was already asleep. I recall, the night it happened, Gregory was talking to me about the stars that were out, and he used the names you lot use. I didn't think much of it at the time as I'm not exactly clued up on the names of all the constellations and individual stars, but we don't use names like Neplio or Macro on Earth. My intuitive guess is that he's an alien. What I found out, after the police had conducted their investigation, was that he was never registered as living at the address and he moved in once the previous residents had disappeared from the face of the earth and it was still registered in their name. Also, he wasn't on the database of people who have ever been born or existed on Earth.'

'So my instincts were right. He must have had something to do with this. If we can track down Gregory, he may be able to help us realise why they visited his house in the first place, in turn, giving us vital information on what the Sorceress was scheming, along with her evil intentions.' Tutti clears his throat and his stare turns to a deep, concentrated observance. 'I've possibly come up with a way to find Gregory.'

'How? I'll do anything. If it means finding the person responsible for losing Lara for a full year of my life, then I'll do whatever it takes.'

'Were you close to him?' he asks furtively.

'I suppose so. We used to chat a lot and we always had a

good relationship, but what's that go to do with anything?' I ask, wondering where he's going with this line of questioning.

'Now what I'm going to suggest may take you by surprise, but if you're as willing as you say you are then it may be our only way. Do you think he was close enough to you that he'd attend your funeral if you'd died?'

'I suppose so, but my funeral's back on Earth. Even if we wanted to, we wouldn't be able... hold on a second!' I exclaim. 'Have you got a way to send us back to Earth to see if he turns up at my funeral?'

'What's with the raised voices?' Lara's voice calls from behind us in the doorway, drying her soaked hair with a luminous orange towel.

'Well, Tutti seems to think we could go to my funeral and see if Gregory attends so we can question him. Seems a bit farfetched if you ask me though, don't you think it'd be a bit creepy going to my own funeral? Surely someone there would recognise me.'

'Of course!' Lara exclaims. 'We could use a drone!'

'Anybody fancy filling me in on what a drone is?' I ask. 'Isn't that one of those things that you fly around your garden?'

'Not that type of drone you melon. A drone in Macronian terms is an empty human body with only basic functions which we can use to inhabit. There are thousands of drones on Earth, all over the planet. The owner can control them, see through their eyes, decide what they do, and they can even step into a booth and plug in a headset to have direct control of them if they fancy. You may have noticed them throughout your life on Earth, the way some people seem disconnected from their senses and wander around aimlessly without goals, emotions or needs. They can carry out basic tasks like feed themselves, work mundane jobs and hold conversations, but they truly are just a shell which we use for monitoring and pleasure really,' Lara explains.

'I was a courier, I used to meet hundreds of people like that every day. Don't you think that's a little inhumane though?' I ask the two of them, who no doubt think that this plan will work.

'How can it be inhumane? They're not people, it's not like we've taken somebody and turned them into our own personal toys; they've been created for this purpose. How would we be able to monitor what's happening on Earth without them? I have seventy drones on Earth in total and thirty of them are in the UK. I won ten of them from a scientist I met once in a card game called *Double Down*. I'll show you how to play one day, it's tonnes of fun. Anyway, I have headsets which you can wear that can connect to the drone and you can effectively be that person,' Tutti explains.

'Like virtual reality?' I ask, startled at this notion.

'If that's what you'd call it, then yes. You can walk around and live a normal life or do whatever you want using the drone's body, but in reality, you'll be standing in my house inside a drone-chamber. Lara's been watching you for the last year using drones.'

I can't help but feel a tad violated at the fact that these people have been watching me like an episode of *Big Brother*. A mental image fills my head of a bunch of nerds sitting around watching me on a TV screen while eating popcorn as they all shush each other while trying to listen in and laugh at the pathetic life I was living.

'Okay, so does anybody know when and where my funeral is?' I ask, with probably the strangest question that's ever been asked by anyone in history.

'I've already checked, it's tomorrow at midday,' Tutti informs me.

'That's just gonna be weird,' I mutter. 'But if that's what it takes to find out what's happened, then I'm up for it.' Lara and I nod in agreement at each other.

I feel as though I'm beginning to come to grips with everything that's happened and I'm starting to fully come to grips with how things work around here. I know there's obviously still a lot I don't understand or know yet, but the basics are clear now. We're in a solar system which I never knew about, this planet has a forcefield around it which stops zombies from devouring everyone, and if it's removed, they're all toast. I now know that Sorceress Katarina is my sister, and I must kill her because she's possibly possessed by some evil dude that lived years ago, and I'm still as useless as I was before I got here.

'We'll just grab some breakfast and then head out if that's alright with you Tutti. We'll go to the museum first, and then make our way to the arena for the Wand Wars tournament. I've got you a front row seat with Caprice. I thought it'd be handy having someone with you seeing as you won't know what's going on. The rules are pretty complex,' Lara informs me.

'Cool,' I reply nonchalantly. I'm still unsure what Wand Wars is, but if it's as good as everyone is making out, hopefully it should take my mind off all this other business. Lara and I enter the living room to a mountain of freshly buttered toast and cups of tea scattered around the table. 'Thank god, I thought it was going to be biscuits for breakfast,' I retort cheekily and receive a nudge from Lara's elbow.

'We'll meet up here tomorrow morning so we can go through everything,' Tutti instructs us. 'I'll have to run through the basics with you before you use the drone.'

Scoffing down our breakfast greedily like gannets, we bid farewell to Tutti and make our way down via the elevator to walk out onto the street. I can still feel the heat from the blazing sun, but its brightness is somewhat diminished due to the forcefield above. The streets are surprisingly dead, and having no concept of what time it is, it's difficult to judge whether it's even morning.

Lara breaks the silence to say, 'I heard from Rex that we got you at just the right time. I hope you understand that I couldn't really do anything to get back. I tried, God knows I tried, but it just wasn't possible, I knew nothing about where I was, and...'

I interrupt her speech, grab her hand, and plant a kiss her on her lips.

'I forgot how much I missed your kisses,' she mutters romantically under her breath, her eyes still closed and her head inches from mine, revelling in the moment. Slowly, we separate from the embrace after the few moments of bliss, then hold hands as we make our way towards the side of the quiet road.

'So, where's this museum?' I ask, panning my head in both directions and wondering why we're standing stationary on the pavement. 'How long will it take to get there, and how do we get there? No doubt there's a magic bus or a flying carpet that we can take.'

'You watch too many movies Tristan.' She holds out her wrist and presses her left thumb against it. 'Just give it a few seconds and it should be here,' she says, smirking menacingly.

'What should be here?' She chooses to stand at the side of the road with her arms crossed and shoots a huge grin in my direction.

'I love this bit,' she says.

I gaze at her, slightly puzzled. 'What bi...'

A peculiar sight emerging from behind a large building in the distance catches my eye. The unicorn pelts towards us like a reindeer on Christmas Eve. With a fluttering of wings and a swoop like a barn owl, it slowly decelerates and stops gently in front us. The unicorn is beautiful beyond belief. A stump from a horn sits directly above its gorgeous, iridescently striking, pink eyes. Never have I seen a creature so wonderous.

Lara's wrist makes contact with the control panel located on the back of the unicorn's neck and she clambers up the stirrups to sit gallantly atop the stunning quadruped like a knight ready to joust. I follow suit, falling to the ground and landing on my backside after the first attempt, which causes Lara to guffaw loudly. As soon as I'm seated after my third attempt, the unicorn bursts forward, almost causing me to become unsaddled, only to be saved by the fact that my hands are wrapped tightly around Lara who sits in front.

'Isn't this amazing?!' Lara shouts excitedly at the top of her voice due to the tremendous force of the wind vetoing my ability to hear.

'Sure is!' I blatantly lie with a yelp, holding on for dear life and hating every second of it.

The view of the city from overhead is spectacular in its own special way. The jade green metropolis that is the city centre, comprised almost entirely of skyscrapers of all different shapes and sizes, glistens radiantly in the sunlight. The chromatic, ginormous, cube-shaped building I saw out of the window at HQ is also visible in the distance directly ahead. I'd ask Lara what that building is, but my inability to speak in the torrents of wind prevent any conversation. HQ looms above everything, floating in mid-air beneath the epicentre of the forcefield's projection.

As the unicorn begins its descent towards an official-looking building with flags raising from the top like antennae, it's clear that the streets are much busier than they were outside Tutti's apartment building. Almost nearing the ground, my eyes close, pre-emptively bracing me for impact, but as my eyes open just moments later, I become aware that we've landed softly without so much as a bump.

'Lara, your hair looks a bloody mess,' I tease her playfully as she disembarks onto the street below.

'And that's coming from you and that rat's nest you call hair?' she replies cheerfully with a smile.

I jump down to the side of the amazing creature and say my goodbyes to the amazing out-of-this-world animal before we make our way to the entrance of the building, up the marble-white stone steps. A member of the Doomguard blocks the entrance, keeping its eye out for potential wrongdoings from those who enter and exit the building.

I always expect museums to be completely jam-packed with tourists because for some odd reason, even though people say they're boring, they are always really busy. A giant title above the entrance reads *The Collective History Museum of Macro*.

'You can't make any noise in here, okay?' Lara informs me as the unicorn's wings flap loudly from behind as it takes to the sky.

'So can we not speak at all?' I ask, upset that I can't do my usual thing and ask a ridiculous number of questions.

'Here you go,' Lara says, pulling out two devices from her pocket that look like panes of glass, and hands one to me. She then pulls out two pairs of glasses and hands me a pair. 'Just write on the tablet with your finger and I'll be able to see what you've written and vice-versa. We've only got half an hour before we need to make our way to the match, so try and take in what you can. I think this would be a good place to start to learn about the history of Macro, especially seeing as you now know you're from here. How do you feel about it anyway, you know, knowing you're from Macro? Are you still not freaked out by it all?'

'Na, not really. I mean, it's weird and all, but it doesn't really change anything. Even knowing I'm Katarina's brother doesn't really do much for me either. In my head everything's still the same, and I'll do my best to keep it that way.'

'What if somebody told you they could return your memories to you?' she asks me.

'Really? They can do that?' I ask, intrigued by the notion. I ponder this for a few seconds wondering whether that would be a good idea. As much as I'd like to get my memories back and know who I was before I was sent to Earth, I'd be scared in case it changed me as a person. I know I sometimes act as if I don't, but I like who I am. I feel my heart is in the right place and I'm kind enough when I can be… I think.

'No doubt it would be difficult, but I'm sure Tutti could find a way. You ready to enter?' she asks, completely changing the topic of conversation.

CHAPTER 17

The Collective History Museum of Macro

The fascinating museum opens up into a huge circular room filled with glass chambers that contain a collection of various artefacts and curios. Scrolls and books also sit in the glass cabinets over to the left side of the room, and the ceiling above must by a hundred feet high, arching up into a space-rocket nose-cone shape. Two robotic curators on wheels roll around the room with various cleaning tools to polish everything on display.

I attempt to utter my musings audibly, but I'm reminded of my inability to speak. The place is deadly silent, it's eerie, there's not even the sounds of footsteps or people coughing; it's completely muted. A message appears in front of my eyes on the glasses lens unannounced. *'Anything you wanna look at first?'* it states.

Rather than use the tablet, I point my finger towards a large, enclosed glass display to my right and mouth the words, *'over here.'* Lara follows me over to the glass display, which contains multiple models; eight to be exact.

A sign on the floor below reads: *Macro Through the Ages*. The models appear to be in a timeline. They're all numbered from 1 to 8 and follow each other in order across the curious display. I approach the first model placed on the far left-hand side so I can move my way across in order, and I'm taken aback by how the models move holographically.

The sign reads: *Year – 17053, Population – 3 billion. Macro thrived and was the most magnificent planet in the solar system. People travelled from all over to visit Macro to witness its splendour and beauty.*

The people were healthy, and these were truly great times.

The model pulsates with a warmth that I find difficult to describe. The planet is blossoming in greenery, and it looks superb compared to how it looks now. The whole planet is occupied, and it has a certain brightness about it. Moving swiftly on, I shift my gaze right towards the next model.

Year – 17176, Population – 3.5 billion. A virus broke out on the planet, and health worsened with each passing day. The virus begun spreading rapidly and was turning inhabitants into mutations that were trying to pass the virus on by eating one another. Macro was surely heading for doom with the unprecedented speed that the virus was spreading.

Year – 17177, Population – 2.7 billion. The virus was destroying the planet slowly as it spread. Only one city, Xana, remained unaffected by the virus thanks to the magi, who tried their best to prevent the virus reaching the city. As the virus reached the city, the magi used their magic to ascend a magic stone up into the sky to project a forcefield down to cover the city; this stone was known as the Xanarock.

So, there's just a small stone up there? Why is there now a gigantic rock in the sky where the stone should be? I decide to read on to see if any of my questions are answered. The next model is completely different to its predecessors as the planet is mostly scorched, except for a small city which remains covered by a dome.

Year – 17179, Population – 20 million. With the virus eradicating almost the entire planet, it was inevitable that Macro was doomed. With a forcefield covering the entire city, there was no way to enter/exit the planet; this was especially devastating for trade. With no access to fresh water and no atmosphere, there didn't seem a viable way for the planet to survive. The magi planned to use the forcefield until the infected had died, but they wouldn't die. The infected would not perish and survived on the other side of the forcefield, meaning that the forcefield could not be disabled.

Year – 17180, Population – 21 million. A destruction sphere was used in a section of the forcefield to remove any matter from the surrounding area, this created a hole in the forcefield which could now be used to enter/exit the planet. The city of Xana was renamed Macro as it was the only habitable city left on the planet. Although this gap was made, planets were still wary of travelling to and from Macro because of the virus.

I read on with fascination, waiting to see what information each plaque tells me next. It's utterly enthralling reading the story about how the planet was formed and the history behind it all; it's even more fascinating as I read on knowing that I'm actually from here and this is part of my heritage. It could even be possible that my ancestors may have played a part in making all this happen. I approach the next model to continue reading on.

Year – 17200, Population – 27 million. The city is beginning to overflow as there is still no travelling allowed to and from Macro. In this year, the High Council of Neplio declared that travel and trade can resume to the city. Later that year, as more foreign beings arrive on the planet, thieves and terrorists attempt to steal or destroy the Xanarock. The Protectors of the Xanarock (POX), a group of mercenaries who vow to protect the rock at all costs, is formed.

Year – 17208, Population – 18 million. The POX continue to protect the Xanarock, and to fortify its defences, they order the magi to construct a fortification around the stone. Because of the magical matter surrounding the stone, the forcefield can project through as if it's not there. A series of caves and labyrinths are constructed inside the shell to ensure maximum difficulty to anybody who poses a threat.

It's difficult to believe that the huge rock up in the sky houses a tiny stone that projects the forcefield. This isn't what I was expecting at all; I assumed the rock was projecting the forcefield.

Year – 17303, Population – 20 million. After almost a hundred years of successfully protecting the stone, the POX built a structure in the sky directly underneath the Xanarock to use as their primary base, which was aptly named HQ. With HQ being so close to the rock, the POX could sufficiently monitor and protect the Xanarock. Only members of HQ know where the entrance is as you can't simply fly up there. HQ contains no visible entrances/exits, and a specific portal must be used to gain access.

This is truly fascinating. I glance at Lara who stands beside me, also inspecting the models. Her hand moves down to start scrawling hastily on the tablet. The words *'get a move on'* appear on the lens in front of my eyes. I take this as an obvious hint and make my way over to the final display. The planet sits exactly as it is now; the lone city, accompanied by the infected people outside the forcefield. The forcefield is projected with a small gap near the top to allow shuttles in and out. I thought the history of Earth was amazing with the different ages we've been through in the past, but this is on another level.

Today, Year – 19020, Population – 24 million. The planet imports and reuses anything it needs, including water. The city of Macro reigns as probably the most visited planet in the solar system due to its individuality and distinct ways of life. To this day, the Xanarock remains in place to protect the city from harm.

Lara begins striding off towards another section of the room with a swift gait, so I follow her, hoping to find out a lot more about this amazing world. We reach a wall of photographs, but there's nothing outer-spacey about them, they're just normal photos of various people. The title above the portraits reads, '*Past High Ministers of Macro*'.

All the individuals on display look like royalty of some sort because they hold various sceptres and wear peculiar crowns on their heads. As I make my way across the portraits, I take note of their names:

Simona Souargon – The First.

Julian Frelings – The Unicorn Whisperer.

Patton Lethbridge – The Jade Builder.

The strange names continue until I reach the final portrait, which jumps out at me because I recognise the person in the frame instantly.

Katarina Halfheart – The Heartbroken Beauty.

So that's Katarina? She's a lot more beautiful than I thought she was going to be, as I imagined an older lady with an evil look, crooked teeth, and dark scraggy hair; a witch basically. She's stunning, with charcoal-coloured hair, and eyes like green sparkling diamonds; the only thing that's missing is a smile. I bet she has amazing teeth as well. She looks completely different from when she was a child, as I recall from those dreams anyway. The accompanying text below reads:

When Katarina was just eight years old, her older brother, Salamander, was banished to Earth for his remaining life. Some say she never recovered from this, and her heart was completely broken. During the following years, her mother and father, who obviously couldn't live with the loss of their son, ended their lives tragically. Katarina was left alone and was placed in care until she came of age. Katarina excelled academically and went on to higher education, following in her father's footsteps to learn the justice system. At the age of twenty-three, she became the youngest ever High Justice Minister of Macro.

Lara watches me intently, but impatiently, tapping her foot on the floor silently with crossed arms. Personally, I could stay here all day learning about this spectacular world which I originated from.

The words, *'let's go, we're gonna be late,'* appear in front of my eyes and I take the hint.

We both stride hurriedly back towards the exit, Lara more reluctantly than me, and walk out into the now completely different atmosphere on the street outside. The streets are filled with all kinds of different people; it's like match day when there's an important football match on.

All the people seem to be walking in one particular direction, most of them wearing intriguing colourful garments and clothing of specific designs. Huge elephant-type creatures tower above the crowds, and I can just about make out the multiple trunks dangling down in front of their large, brown heads. People are mounted atop the creatures, covered in merchandise, which the trunks pass down to the customers below. With flags waving and chants filling the air, I get the feeling that this must be one hell of a game to these people.

CHAPTER 18

Ward Wars – Part 1

The walking hordes push and nudge me through the massing crowds and the sense of excitement and trepidation seems to be growing immensely. We pass food stalls that sell insurmountable amounts of foreign delicacies while entertainers use magic to amuse the passing folk, and there are obscure balloons of various colours that move and make noises as if they're alive.

'Fancy some Miso Sea Monster?' Lara asks me, pointing over to a small shack that sells food. She looks so excited. I don't think I've ever seen her like this before, even during our wedding. A band are stood on top of a giant plinth at the side of the street, belting out songs for the crowds to sing and dance along to, but it doesn't sound the slightest bit familiar.

'What's it taste like?' I ask, realising that I'm quite hungry now that foods been mentioned; I haven't had a proper meal in days.

'It's quite nice, it just puts you off the way it wriggles as you're eating it,' she declares.

'I think I'll pass,' I reply, almost balking at the thought of eating something that's still moving.

'So which team are you?' I ask, wondering whether Lara could be some sort of celebrity. 'Was that where that guy in the queue for the bar knew you from? Because you play Wand Wars?'

'Yeah, most people probably know me because of Wand Wars. Almost everyone in the solar system will be watching the match today. The tournament goes in stages, and today is the grand final of the *Katarina Gem*, which is a tournament held in Katarina's honour. The final four teams will battle it out to see who wins.'

'Wouldn't this be the semi-finals if there's four teams remaining? Are there multiple games being played to see who goes through to the final?'

She smirks at me cheekily. 'I don't want to spoil anything, but no, all four teams will play at the same time and whoever wins will win the ultimate prize.'

'And that is?'

'We don't know yet, you don't find out until you've won. It gives the teams more of an incentive in case you don't like the winning prize.'

The gigantic rectangular-shaped building begins to appear over the horizon of the oddly shaped skyline. The apex of the building stands hundreds of feet above everything else. I recall seeing this building a few times but never got around to asking what it was. Nearing the building, the sounds of commentators on speakers and chanting from fans becomes clearly audible. Crowds of what must be hundreds of thousands of people fill the streets leading up to the building. I've never seen this many people gathered in one place throughout my entire life and the celebrations remind me of the scenes of Chinese New Year, which I've only ever seen on TV.

An overly excited small group of people approach us. 'Lara! Oh my goodness it's really you, it's really you! Can I get your autograph? I am such a huge fan, you are amazing, I love you so much!' a tall pink-haired man blurts out to Lara in complete infatuation. He's dressed from head to toe in yellow with streaks of red running down the sides of his outfit.

'O… kay,' she replies to the man, who is now jumping up and down on the spot in excitement at this point and giggling hysterically. Lara takes the man's tablet from his extended hand and signs it with her finger, then kisses the screen romantically as the man looks like he's almost about to pass out in adoration. She hands it back and continues to walk with me through the crowd. His squealing is still audible as we get further away from them.

'Got to keep the fans happy, haven't you?' Lara chuckles and winks in my direction. A laugh escapes from me at the absurdity of it all. I never expected this, I never expected this at all. Back at home she was just a regular girl and hated crowds of people; the people she hated most were fanatics who devoted every second to a specific topic, i.e. sports fans.

Lara drags me to one side as we reach the barely navigable entrance to the colossal building. The place she leads me off to has a large archway with a sign that reads 'Contenders Entrance'.

'Here's where I leave you,' she says. 'Here's your tickets to enter. I got you and Caprice front row seats,' she informs me and passes me two metal objects that look a bit like credit cards.

'Where is Caprice?' I ask, looking around the crowds searchingly. 'How am I supposed to find her among all these people?'

'She should be here any second. She's been here with me plenty of times before, so she knows where she's going. You gonna be alright on your own until she gets here? Have a browse through a couple of the stalls over there while you're waiting.'

'Yeah, sure.'

'Okay, sorry I've got to go, I'm already running late. I'll meet up with you afterwards. Enjoy the show.' Lara kisses me on the cheek, offers me a huge smile, and then turns to make her way through the archway and out of sight around a corner.

Even though I can barely navigate my way to the stall with the hordes of strangely dressed people gathered around, I squeeze my way through to see what wares are on display. A tremendous array of memorabilia and sporting gear including wands, robes and other strange items of clothing, decorate all sides of the minuscule stall. A small plushie of Lara is sitting on one of the shelves. There's so much merchandise on display that I can barely see the two-headed person manning the counter. The heads speak simultaneously to the customers at the counter, with four arms reaching out to shelves to grab goods.

'What can I help you with sir? Got some lovely robes that would fit you here. Let me show you how they'd look,' one of the heads says in a gravelly, sinister tone.

Not feeling comfortable with the risk of buying colours that aren't for Lara's team, I turn the robes down. 'I'll have a hat though. One of those yellow and black ones please,' I request, spotting a strange hat that fastens under the chin with a strap.

'Gotcha,' one of the heads replies, and one of the hats suddenly appears magically on my head.

'Tristan!' I hear Caprice's familiar voice shout over the crowds.

'Gotta go!' I tell the man/men at the counter, putting my chip against the ruby-red shining platform which stands on the counter that is presumably for paying.

'Thanks for your business sir, we'll see you again sometime,' they say as I head in Caprice's direction.

Caprice looks me up and down suspiciously with her one visible eye. 'You know that hat is for one of the teams Lara's up against, don't you?'

'How was I supposed to know? He just made it appear on my head, and then you shouted over, and I was pressured. Gimme a break.'

We squeeze our way through the parade of fans towards one of the archways labelled *VIP*. There aren't as many people gathered around this entrance, and I'm guessing that's because there must only be a select few VIPs. It's probably full of rich people and family members of the players. Members of the *Doomguard* stand randomly around the entrances and you can't miss them due to their sheer size and ugliness. They interest me in a peculiar sort of way, they're like mutations that have been created in a lab and their sole purpose is to be police and security officials. After granting us access, we find ourselves in a tunnel that connects to the inside of the gigantic building.

'So how much do you know about Wand Wars?' Caprice asks curiously.

'Nothing, I just know it's some sort of sport, but Lara won't tell me bugger all because presumably, she wants me to see it in the flesh and not ruin whatever happens,' I reply. 'She hasn't shut up about it since I met up with her.'

'It's a first for me then, I can honestly say I've never been to a game with someone who doesn't know what Wand Wars is. This should be fun, I've heard you like asking questions,' Caprice smirks.

At the other side of the tunnel, the sun penetrates through a gigantic window-filled entranceway with elevators and desks. Giant walk-through scanners line the back wall of the room, and a queue of people line up to make their way through to the other side. I can't help but feel the excitement that radiates from every single fan in the room.

'That leads through to the arena. You've got nothing that'll set off the scanners, have you?' Caprice asks.

'All I've got is our two tickets and maybe a couple of liquins that Rex gave me.'

'Cool, let's go then,' she answers, beginning to make her way forward to join the queues of people.

'Where's Mogson?' I ask, more to make small talk than actually wanting to know where he is. Caprice really doesn't speak much, or maybe I just speak too much.

'He's with Rex back at HQ. You're not allowed pets in here. If I get into trouble, he'll come running because he can sense it through our interlinked chips. Lara said it's important that we're here as the Sorceress could attack with so many people being gathered in one place.'

Caprice walks through a large security scanner before me, and for the first time, I can hear the crowd roaring from inside as I get closer. I copy what Caprice does and tap my ticket against a scanner mounted on the wall, which flashes green. We walk forwards through another dark corridor labelled 'Arena Entrance'. A green light shines through the darkness to light up the corridor in a tinge of emerald. The roaring and exuberant cheering gets louder and louder with every step as we approach the end of the corridor. Holographic posters of famous players seem to smile back at me from the walls. The fans are squeezing through a gap in a curtain to enter the arena up ahead. I have to admit that I'm getting quite excited about all this; the hype and excitement from all the other fans seems to be contagious.

Caprice holds the curtain open surreptitiously to grant me access to the other side. She waves a hand to hint that I should go through and gives me a beaming smile. Even though it's just a curtain, once it's moved aside, the noise explodes like an atomic blast. Fans are screaming and singing, chanting and bawling; they're so animated. The arena must be the size of a small village and it causes me to stop open-mouthed, staring blankly at the view in front of me.

A gigantic, silver, translucent cube floats in the middle of the room. I'm not even sure this could be classed as a room as it's so vast; it's more like an oversized airport hangar. Hundreds of thousands of fans sit around the edges of the room, and even the floor has seats directly underneath the cube which look up. The tremendous array of colours and shades that cover the fans remind me of abstract art; it's as if everyone has been dipped in multicoloured paint before they entered. Inside the cube that sits in the centre of the arena, a labyrinth of corridors and rooms of different shapes and sizes fill the entirety of it, and the whole inside seems to be filled with a layer of frost or ice from what I can make out.

'Would you move out of the way please?!' A rude voice calls from behind, snapping me from my total awestruck examination of this impossible place. I turn around to a large queue of unimpressed faces forming behind us on the aisle leading down to the seats at the front of the arena nearest to the cube.

'Sorry!' I call out apologetically and swiftly begin to make my way forwards.

'Straight down to the front!' Caprice calls down to me through the overpowering noise of the crowd. I continue walking down the aisle, but I can't help looking around in wonder. The fans are throwing things, casting spells, climbing over each other, and absolutely going nuts. They're loving every second of it. In the row to my side, one person casts a spell on somebody else to make their hair light up with fire, then he puts it out instantly and starts laughing his head off, hyena-like. The scene resembles what you'd see in the monkey enclosures in a zoo, except the monkeys are probably more well behaved.

'There's our seats!' Caprice calls to me, then leans down into my ear and points to two empty seats on the front row. I take my seat next to an extremely obese woman with green skin and red spots that cover her entire body. A large yellow tongue hangs down from her slobbering mouth and I can't help but feel nauseous. I definitely got the short straw here as Caprice is sitting next to a tall skinny man wearing a pair of goggles who looks relatively normal.

'Are you a Thundercats fan?' The woman beside me spits into my ear. It was almost as bad as that shower I had yesterday.

Presumably, the hat I'm wearing must be for the support of a team called the Thundercats.

'Not really,' I reply. 'Just like the colours. Are you a fan of the weirdoes?' I ask and have a giggle to myself in my head for the witty remark.

'I've never heard of them, what planet are they from?' she replies seriously with a slobber that lands on my trousers.

'Never mind,' I reply to her still chuckling internally.

'So how do you play then? What's the rules?' I ask Caprice, turning back to her.

'We've only got a few minutes until it starts so I'll have to be quick, but here we go,' Caprice says, taking a deep breath to begin her thorough explanation.

'So, each team has five players, which can be from any planet or species. Only registered WW players can enter the arena and it's strictly forbidden to anyone else. Only wands supplied by the Committee of Wand Wars Specialists, or COWWS, are permitted to be used, which are only capable of casting freeze spells. The aim is to freeze all the other players out of the game or take their gem, which is located at each team's starting point, also known as their base. Throughout the match, the course will change, but the bases will stay in the same place, this is so players can't memorise the layout and adds a level of excitement and surprise. Every ten Earth minutes, the place goes completely black and the course changes, which is called the *switcheroo*. Each team usually goes for a formation that suits them; if they have an offensive team they'll go all out and try to freeze the other teams, and some teams may opt for a more defensive approach and try to protect their gem and freeze out the other team while they're on the attack. Players are banned from physically touching each other and anybody found deliberately making contact with another player will be automatically frozen out of the game. Erm, what else?' she muses, rubbing her head in deep thought.

'During the switcheroo, when the course changes, one player from each team will be unfrozen randomly. The players inside cannot see or hear anything from outside, and the fans outside can't hear anything inside the cube. Apart from the teams participating, there is only one person allowed inside the cube and that's the referee, who stands at the exit so if there's an issue, he can run inside and get a message to the players that there's something up. Once the match is over by either win condition, the cube turns completely green, and all the players are unfrozen to make their way to the exit.'

'Jesus, you alright there?' I ask Caprice, worrying as her face has now turned bright red with the lengthy explanation. I'm pretty sure she's never spoken so much in her entire life. 'What's that big circle thing up there?' I ask, pointing at a large wheel above the cube which resembles a giant clock face.

'At the start of each match, they spin a wheel to see what abilities each team will have throughout the duration of the match. You can get secondary wands that unfreeze teammates as often as you like, your team can get visors that protect them from spells that hit your head, footwear that makes you move faster, a silence spell cast on your team so they make no noise as they move around the arena, auto-blasting wands which fire multiple spells each second, and finally, the ability to teleport. The teleport ability can only be used once per match and the team captain can use this when the team are losing miserably and the whole team gets transported back to their base, all unfrozen. Because only the captain can use this, if they're frozen out, they're unable to use the ability.'

This game sounds fantastic! Nothing like I thought it was going to be, but with a name like Wand Wars could it have ever been rubbish?

'What do you think?' Caprice asks me, and I can see from her face she's waiting for me to praise this sport that they all think so highly of.

'It does sound amazing to be fair, what team is Lara on?'

'She's the team captain of the *Boisterous Bitches*,' she informs me, causing me to immediately burst out laughing due to the absurdity of the name. 'There are four teams playing today, and it's the grand final. Each team will have a base against each wall, and there can be a maximum of sixteen teams playing at once, but with this being one of the smaller arenas, its maximum occupancy is eight teams.'

'This is one of the smaller ones? Geez, the others must be

mahoosive,' I reply, trying to picture mentally how large these other arenas must be.

'Believe it or not, Wand Wars has only existed for around a hundred years. An explorer named Cabera Shabera was travelling through the ice caves on *Photon* when he was caught in an avalanche. As he was making his way back out to the exit, the entire cave looked different. On his way through the caves there were multiple frozen figures, who were obviously explorers who'd been out there before him. He came up with the idea of turning it into a sport, and now it's become the main source of entertainment throughout the entire solar system, with him becoming one of the richest people that ever lived.'

Suddenly, the crowd begin to calm down and the atmosphere completely changes. The lights dim and an announcer begins to speak:

'*Welcome to the finals of the Katarina Gem! We welcome you all to this major event. May we first say a thank you to our sponsor* Majestical Missionaries *who have helped to organise this tournament. Now let us welcome our four teams to this grand event! Everybody give a big hand and applause to our first team. Here they come… Please welcome The Tempest Stormbringers!*'

The announcer is standing on a platform near the entrance to the arena next to the single door that leads inside the cube. The referee Caprice mentioned earlier stands near the entrance door and holds it open for when the teams are ready to enter. The five teammates stand in a row making gestures to the crowd to rally them for support. Cries and cheers erupt in support of the team, and the players continue to wave and blow kisses to the masses. There is a small bald man, a man in goggles, a stunningly pretty girl who must only be in her late teens with silver hair wrapped around the back of her head and neck cobra-like, a dark-skinned man with a long grey beard and bright yellow eyes, and an overweight girl who must be the same species as the woman sitting next to me. The ugly woman next to me screams in support of who must be her daughter. The cheering ceases, and the place falls silent once again.

'*Thank you Stormbringers. They're led by their captain Taz Lovell. Zakk Donovan and Ezmae Everett are on the attack, and Gaia Ochoa* and Roseanna Ballard fill in the defence positions. Let's find out what the wheel has in store for you!'

The players, referee and announcer all look up to the heavens at the gigantic wheel above the cube. The referee points a wand at the wheel, causing it to spin rapidly. Once the wheel stops, it lands on a section of green containing an image of a feather.

That's the sonic boots for the Stormbringers! And remember, if you want to taste victory, you've got to make history!'

The referee opens the door, and the team captain leads his team through into the arena. Every one of them is smiling excitedly and pumping their fists.

I turn to Caprice after being completely engrossed for the last few minutes. She's nothing like any of the other fans in here; she stands completely still and almost expressionless.

'What's up?' I ask her with concern.

'Nothin', just not one for acting a tool,' she replies. 'I'm also keeping watch for anything suspicious.'

She does make me laugh at how nonchalant she is. She doesn't speak much and she's probably more laid-back than anyone I've ever met, even the short sentences add to the coolness she portrays.

'It's time to welcome our second team. Please give a round of applause and show your appreciation for the team in yellow and black, it's the Thunderous Thundercats! Leading the team out is Fionnuala Hick, beside her we have Krista Trejo and Efe Davila. In defence, right at the rear of the pack are Hollie Rayner and Jaxx Laing.'

The captain, Fionnuala, has purple and green hair evenly split down the sides of her head, which has to be probably the most astonishing hairdo I've ever come across. As she puts her tongue out to jeer the crowd, it splits into two sharp, pointed, pink prongs.

The most fascinating member of this team is the life-size teddy bear, which really does freak me out in a massive way. I wonder where these people even meet each other. What kind of world is this where a teddy bear can be friends with a demonic crazy-haired woman? How does that conversation even start? The announcer shows the crowd a gigantic smile of pearly white teeth and continues his speech.

'Excellent. Spin the wheel!' The announcer calls. The colourful wheel rotates and eventually lands on an image of a speech bubble

containing a single dot.

'*That's the silence ability for the Thundercats. You may now enter the arena. And remember, if you want to taste victory, you've got to make history!*' The crowd join in this time with what must be the announcer's slogan when welcoming each team to the cube.

After a sigh from getting an obviously unwanted ability, they enter the arena and the next team walk out from the darkness to be introduced. These are in red garbs with white trimmings around the edges and every one of them has their hood up over their head.

'*Welcome Dangerous Diamantes. They thrashed the semi-finalists with all five players still unfrozen when the game ended, it was quite something. We have Cali Sheriff as the team's captain at the front, River Merritt and Simra Maple in the middle, with Subhaan White and Charlie Canis at the rear.*'

Cali looks very similar to Tutti; they must be the same species. River is a Draqowl, the species that attacked me in the station. I just hope that stare they can use is banned, it'd seem a bit unfair to the other players if they could use that. Simra has three tails, one black, one white and one brown. She also has a pair of eyes that stick out of the top of her head like a snail. Subhaan is another of those teddy bears from the previous team but this one is black. The final player in the team is Charlie, who fascinates me more than the others because he's only a young boy around eight years old. I never thought in a million years that I'd be more shocked by a young man than a live teddy bear. What has my life become?

'*Welcome, welcome. Let's see what the wheel has in store for you. Cali, what ability would you go for if you could choose?*'

'Auto-blast, obviously,' she tells the announcer.

'That's the one that rapid-fires spells,' Caprice's voice reminds me.

The wheel spins and lands on the teleportation ability. The team look ultimately disappointed at this, meaning it must be one of the more rubbish abilities you can get based on their reaction. It does seem a tad unfair that you could potentially lose a match due to getting a worse ability, but who am I to question the rules?

'*Excellent. That's three of our teams. Diamantes, you may enter the arena. And remember, if you want to taste victory, you've got to make history!*'

Lara's team must be last to come out. I know she's going to be amazing at this game as she's always been nimble and fit as anything, she could whoop me at any sport.

'*Can we have silence for our final team?*' the announcer calls. The room does as it's told and goes completely silent; you could hear a wand drop. I can feel the tension building inside the arena, as if this moment is iconic and it's the thing that everyone's been waiting for. The announcer takes his time to continue speaking as if he's trying to build an atmosphere and get everyone in the arena excited. Finally, he proceeds:

'*Thank you for your patience. It is my honour to welcome to you, the Boisterous Bitches!*' he calls out at the top of his voice. The roars which fill the arena are deafening and the entire place trembles and shudders as if a bomb has just been detonated. The crowd roar and cheer, they dance and wave; it is truly astounding.

The first player I see exit from the tunnel on to the stand is Lara, except she looks different. Her teammates follow from behind and I finally understand what the cheering and applause was for. The five most impossibly beautiful woman I've ever laid my eyes on stand dressed in rainbow-coloured garments. I hate to say it, because I think Lara is beautiful anyway, but it's like she's been given an aura or a glow that radiates from her making her even more stunning. They all have varying bright colours for hair, Lara's is lime green, and the others are yellow, orange, pink and purple; you could probably spot them for miles. The males obviously cheer because they're beautiful, that's evident. The females must be cheering because they're supporting the only all-girl line up.

'*Welcome ladies!*' the announcer calls out. '*At the front of the team, their captain Lara Jones. Playing in the middle we have Lucille Okran and Chaya Avalos. In defence we have Liya Lovegod and Asa Legge. And may I also add that these are without doubt the most beautiful team to have ever graced the sport.*' The announcer approaches Lara and speaks to her directly. '*Are you prepared for this ladies? This one isn't going to be easy. There's some tough teams out there today.*'

'I'm sure we'll be fine,' Lara replies sweetly into the microphone, to which the announcer and most of the crowd reply with laughs.

'*If you're to win today, you'll be the first all-female team to ever win a major trophy. Are you ready for the wheel?*'

'Ready as we'll ever be,' Lara declares. The announcer points up to the wheel and it begins to spin ferociously. The crowd continue to cheer and chant something which I can't really understand, but my guess is it must be the name of one of the better abilities. Finally, the wheel comes to a stop and a rapturous applause sounds out as it lands on a depiction of a wand with flames ejecting from it.

'*My, my. It's your lucky day ladies. Auto-blast it is! If you weren't rooting for them beforehand, you sure as hell will be now,*' the announcer calls out. '*Good luck ladies, and don't forget...*' he holds his microphone up to the crowd for them to shout the next bit.

'*If you want to taste victory, you've got to make history!*' they bawl at the top of their voices and begin stamping feet and clapping fiercely. Before entering the arena, Lara makes eye contact with me and gives me a thumbs-up. I reply with my own thumbs-up, and then she's gone through the door and into the arena. It seems strange that we'll all be watching from out here and they won't be able to see or hear anything.

'Just give the teams a few minutes to get ready and you're about to have your socks blown clearly off,' Caprice says from my side. A few minutes pass, and I can see all the fans attracting the attention of the snack sellers that fly through the air around the arena dispensing goods from their packs before the match commences. The huge lady next to me must buy fifteen tubs of god knows what food and starts scoffing it down rapidly like she's never eaten before, with her oversized mouth, which makes me physically nauseous.

'*Ladies and gentlemen, let the wars commence!*' the announcer bellows, and the lights dim slightly to give an atmosphere of what will probably end up being one of the most memorable times of my life.

CHAPTER 19

Wand Wars – Part 2

What puzzles me about this arena is that none of the fans are segregated into which team they support, they're all intertwined. Usually, I'd be able to look around at the different sections of fans and determine which team they're supporting, but this just feels strange.

Once the announcer calls for the commencement of the match, the players begin to manoeuvre strategically around the cube. Some of them stay in groups and others split off from the pack to hunt down the other teams. It must be tedious work to come up with a strategy when you can't physically see what the other teams are doing and where they are. One player I'm watching peeks around a corner and blasts a freeze spell at an opponent to turn him to ice while his back is turned. A cheer emanates around the arena, and a scoreboard high up towards the ceiling listing the four team names and a number underneath changes. Three of the teams are set to zero, and the Dangerous Diamantes' score is now showing as one due to having a player frozen.

I follow Lara closely moving around with one of her teammates, and when they encounter an opposing player, they shoot machine-gun type blasts of pulsating blue ice at them to freeze them to the spot. Each team are using their abilities to their advantage; I can see the Stormbringers using their increased speed to both attack and flee from perilous situations. The Thundercats run about the arena knowing they can't be detected through sound, and they use this ability cleverly to sneak up on their opponents. Lara's team shoot rapid-fire spells to freeze out almost everyone they fire at with tremendous ease; it'd be difficult not to with the amount of ice being fired at them and I can see why that was the most favoured ability.

After around fifteen minutes of the most amazing, jaw-dropping display I've ever witnessed, the whole arena is plunged into darkness.

'What's going on?' I whimper to Caprice next to me, thinking that something's amiss.

'I told you before, it's the switcheroo. At the end of every round, the arena blacks out, and the course changes to make the game more interesting.'

'Oh yeah, course I remembered!' I reply and remove my hand from her arm which I instinctively planted on her in panic.

The arena lights up again as if the sun just emerged from behind the darkest clouds to commence the action, and the course has, in fact, completely changed. The players remain in their same positions as when the light diminished, but every wall and floor seem to be in a completely different place. As Caprice explained earlier, one frozen player from each team is unfrozen at the start of the next round. Lara's team still have all four players in the game, each other team only has three. It's utterly chaotic trying to keep an eye on everything that's going on at the same time. I want to watch Lara solely, but in the rest of the cube there's so much happening, it's like watching multiple TV screens simultaneously.

I watch as one player uses a frozen figure as a shield while shooting out from behind it to freeze an opponent meaning the Thundercats only have two players remaining now. My concentration doesn't falter from the awe-inspiring presentation occurring in front of my eyes as the highly skilled players use every trick they know to freeze out the other players, until the lights disappear for a second time. The entirety of the place falls silent once again, and I realise that this must be one of the traditions of the game to add tension for when it reboots, and the lights return.

The silence is eerie and if I had just woken up, I wouldn't know where I was because you can't so much as see a speck of light or hear a thing.

A deafening CRASH fills the entire arena, and this is followed by piercing screams of terror. Instantly, I know this isn't supposed to happen. A hole of light has appeared in the ceiling of the arena, but it's still too dark to make out what's happening. I can make out shadows moving across the hole, but I can't figure out what it is.

'Tristan!' Caprice shouts to me from less than a foot away. 'We need to get to Lara! Come in, Rex! Anybody in HQ, she's here, you have to get down to the arena asap!' Within seconds, the scene has turned from ecstatic fans cheering loudly, to wails and desperate screams of terror as though they're about to meet their end.

The screams get louder and louder and I can hear bodies stumbling over behind and beside me in the dimness. In the blink of an eye, the lights are reborn, and it feels like they've been missing forever. It takes my eyes a few moments to adjust to the sudden change in light, and the scene I'm welcomed to is chaotic. It's complete pandemonium to say the least. People are clambering over each other in panic, spells are flying around the arena in the hundreds, and bodies are flying through the air as the spells collide with them to launch them from their feet in one hit. Hundreds of small, purple, impish creatures are soaring through the arena like wasps around a honeypot. They expel spells from their fingers and laugh maniacally with giggles and hisses. The evil-looking Sorceress is floating in the centre of the arena underneath the gigantic hole which has been blown into the ceiling. Two small men dressed as court jesters float either side of her and make sure they're not missing out on the maniacal laughing; one is dressed in yellow and white, and one in green and white. The Sorceress is dressed all in black, has sallow, pale skin, and you can even see from this distance how crooked her teeth are as she laughs uncontrollably.

'Get to Lara! She's still inside the cube and they'll be oblivious to what's going on outside. You need to get in and warn her. If you head down there, you'll be able to reach the platform to get up to the entrance. The referee who guards the door is the only one who can enter, you either find him or you find another way to get in! Go, now!' Caprice screams in panic and points down towards the entrance to the arena where the platform is. 'I'll go after *her*, I need to make sure she doesn't get away before the others arrive.' Caprice runs through the chaotic crowd to disappear from my line of sight, and I have to give it to her, she is one bad-ass chick.

Attempting to get to the entrance to the cube, I have to clamber over multiple bodies, some who are still alive but writhing in agony. I push people out of the way and scream obscenities at those who block my path until I get nearer and nearer to the staircase leading up to the platform. A man next to me is thrown multiple feet into the air as he's pummelled by a spell from one of the evil-looking imps above us. The chaos doesn't seem to be receding and every step I take is felt with anticipation, not knowing if my life will end here or not.

The staircase stands in front of me like a path to heaven. Even if I get inside there, I can't see a way out, but the least I can do is get inside to warn her and if worse comes to worst, at least we can die together rather than out here among the other thousands of corpses. I climb what feels like the longest staircase in existence to reach the top and I'm immediately reminded how unfit I am when I realise that I'm panting like a dog who's just ran a marathon. The match continues to be played inside the cube and they are completely unaware of the current predicament.

The referee's unresponsive face leers back up at me from outside the doorway and a sole imp stands triumphantly over his still corpse; it must have only just killed him. Why wouldn't he have tried to enter the arena earlier before he died and lock himself in or warn the players?

The imp's glowing eyes flicker intently at me and it lets out a sinister laugh. A fireball shoots its way towards my direction from its crooked, purple fingertips. Taking cover behind a pillar, which is conveniently placed beside me, I let the fireball zoom past and explode on the wall behind. The cackling from the imp resounds around the corner, but rather than instil fear inside me, it fills me with an impetuous rage that makes me want to kick its bony backside. Remnants of the opposite side of the pillar fly past me and I can feel my skin almost scorching from the heat emanating from the fireballs.

As soon as the barrage ends abruptly, I peek my head around the corner to see why it's halted its onslaught. The unconscious referee has woken and is grabbing at its leg desperately. Almost instinctively and without any prior consideration, I break from the defence of the pillar and charge like a raging bull towards the imp, fury and rage filling my soul as I try one last-ditch attempt at getting to the woman I love. It spots me, kicks the dying man aside to once again point its elongated fingers at me and release a bolt of lightning. I jerk my head to the side to dodge the bolt and it flies past my ear with a deafening crack as I continue to rush forwards. My fist connects with its face before it can get another spell off, causing it to fly backwards, hitting the floor as if it's just been hit by a train. I didn't even know until know I was capable of this level of bravery and violence; is this what love and desperation can do to a man?

The imp lies unconscious on the ground with its limp tongue hanging over its cheek. I'm going to have to get a move on here before it wakes up.

'You still awake?' I ask the man who lies metres from the door and give him a small nudge with my foot attempting to wake him. He doesn't move, and I can tell just by looking at him that he's a goner. The red light blinking underneath the skin on his wrist glows faintly but still could be useable. Maybe I can use this to activate the door. He's the only one with access to enter the arena, so presumably I'll have to use his chip. A sudden sick thought of having to either remove the chip with something sharp or remove the guy's arm sends a wave of terror and total disgust through me. Reaching down, I grab the man's arm and drag his corpse over to the panel beside the door. It won't reach so I'll have to lift his whole body to reach the panel. Just as I attempt to grab the man from under his armpits to hoist him up, the imp starts to stir. Dropping the man, I send a left foot into the side of the imp's head causing it to jerk and drop back down. Hopefully it shouldn't wake until I get inside.

I touch the man's wrist against the panel, and it flashes green in confirmation. A wave of relief cuts its way through me. If his chip wouldn't have worked once he was dead, no doubt I'd be screwed. Spells and screams continue to emanate through the air to remind me of the current predicament I'm embroiled in. This is like a version of hell that I'd not want even my worst enemy to visit. I yank the handle of the door towards me and a gust of bitter cold air hits my skin as if I've just opened a freezer.

A noise from behind startles me and makes me whip my head around in alarm. An imp is gliding down through the air towards me hissing uncontrollably. The cold air constricts around me as I yank the surprisingly heavy door open. The door whacks against the dead man's boots as I try to close it and the door stays open.

The impact of the imp crashing into the door sends shivers down my spine, and I instinctively kick the foot out of the way to pull the door closed once again. The strength of the imp pulling on the door from the other side is too much for me; how can such a small creature have so much strength? Could it have something to do with the fact that it's a demonic evil creature from the depths of hell maybe? We continue to battle in our attempts to win control of the door's direction and when I think all my chances have finally gone, it reaches its hand in to grab me. Finding a last surge of strength which I never knew I was capable of through desperation and fear, I smash the door home into its rightful place and the bottom half of the imp's arm becomes my only companion in this ice-cold maze.

The imp's screams from the other side are immediately silenced once the door closes, which must have something to do with the fact that you can't hear or see anything outside when you're inside the cube. The imp's dismembered arm lies on the ground below and green slime oozes out over the snow-covered ground.

Before I can even realise it, I'm bent double, puking my guts out all over the icy floor. After finishing regurgitating everything I've probably eaten since leaving Earth, I use my sleeve to wipe my mouth and make my way into the depths of the arena.

A noise behind me from the doorway I just came through startles me and invites me to turn around. The dismembered arm is walking towards me using its fingers as feet. What the hell? This is probably one of the freakiest things I've ever seen. The hand causes me to be so freaked out, that I run like the wind into the cold icy tunnels of the arena. I zigzag through the labyrinth, and after running until my breath has expired, I keep going and must pass at least four people who are frozen from the game of Wand Wars. Not being able to run another step, I stop to regain my breath and hold my hands to my knees. My breath visibly fills the cold air as I exhale.

Because I was running like a headless chicken with no regard for remembering my route, I wouldn't be able to remember which way I've just come from. Maybe Lara will know a way out when I find her.

The lights disappear. Pitch black now surrounds me and I don't think I've ever felt more lost. Noises are coming from somewhere, but I can't place where they're emanating from or what the noises even are. When the lights are rebooted, the walls that previously surrounded me have changed. Where there was once a wall either side of me in the corridor, there's now a wall in front and a corridor to the side. How the hell am I supposed to know where I'm going? Maybe I didn't think this through. No, I can't think like that, I must keep moving and find Lara.

Eventually, I reach a large room. Two iced figures face each other with their spells pointing at one another. I'm pretty sure I recognise them from when I was watching from outside earlier, which seems like hours ago. A flash of blue light fills the room and it's suddenly evident that one of the players has just fired a spell at me. I take cover to dodge the shot behind a huge block of ice beside me.

'Who's that?!' I shout. 'It's chaos out there, the place is under attack, and they're all being slaughtered outside!' I shout urgently.

'Ha! I've seen these tactics used before. Tell me a bunch of lies and get me to come out in panic so you can take me out. I wasn't born yesterday!' the voice shouts back.

'No seriously, I know you can't hear anything that's going on outside but please just trust me, you have to get out of here and save yourself. Do you know where Lara is?' I ask, hoping he's taken the hint and finally believes me.

'Okay, I believe you, just come out and we'll decide what we're going to do,' the voice calls out. His voice sounds closer this time as if he's slowly sneaking towards me. He's going to try and freeze me with a spell because he thinks I'm one of the other players, I'm not that bloody stupid. I can't afford to be frozen, not now, any time but now.

Searching the ground around me, I look for something to use as a weapon, but nothing, unless I want to throw a snowball at him. The only thing I can see which I could possibly use is a wand that one of the players who got frozen have dropped. It's too far away, I'd have to break my cover to crawl out and reach it. I can't hear them sneaking up on me so it must be one of those players who had the silence ability; fantastic!

A movement from the doorway catches my eye, and I turn my head to see the dismembered imp's arm running towards me from the way I entered. Its fingers are moving faster than a stenographer's. The speed it uses to make its way towards me is horrifying and it gets closer and closer with each millisecond.

'I'm serious, tell me what's going on out there and just come out and talk to me,' the voice says from what must be mere feet away by now. The arm runs closer and uses its super-strength fingers to make it leap into the air towards my face.

My arm reaches out to grab the limb as it's only inches from my face and I swing out from behind my hiding place to wallop the man in the head with it. He stumbles back as it connects with his face, knocking him backwards and sliding across the ice. The arm stays firmly gripped around his face and he struggles with screams and spasms that look horrific from where I'm standing. His whole body writhes in agony and I can't help but feel guilty about what I just did to the man, but it was either this or get frozen and not get to Lara. I pick up the stray wand which he dropped and aim it at the arm, hoping my accuracy isn't so bad that I'll hit him. His struggling seems to become more wild with each attempt to get the arm off his face and both his hands claw ferociously to remove it.

I point the wand towards the arm, all my concentration going into firing a spell, which I've never done before. Nothing happens no matter how hard I try.

'How do I fire the damn thing?' I ask the struggling man in desperation. He replies with a sequence of sounds and muffled words that the hand distorts as it wraps around his face.

'Alli... gator,' the voice says muffled behind the hand.

'Alligator!' I shout, pointing the wand and try to fire. Nothing once again.

'I can't understand you properly! Can you give me a hand?' I know it's not the time for jokes, but even in the current circumstance,

I couldn't let a joke like that slip by without saying it.

In a last-ditch attempt to speak, the man gives it one last surge of strength to push the hand away and speak simultaneously. '*Salvo Glacier!*' he screams as if it's his last breath.

My hand points once again at the limb smothering his face. He's fidgeting so much as he fights for his life that I can't get a perfect shot on the arm. I haven't ever fired one of these things before; I hope they're accurate.

'*Salvo Glacier!*' I shout, unexpectedly loud and causing an echo from each wall. Something triggers inside my body, like it's been missing for a long time, and I've finally rediscovered something that's been absent. My whole body is covered with goosebumps as I feel the magic coursing through every single vein and fire through the wand to the tip and burst out of the end like a cannon. The blue blaze spurts out thunderously and a jet instantly freezes the arm, which spreads down onto the man's face and then the entirety of his body. He is now completely frozen with an imp's arm attached to his face, but how do I unfreeze him? I don't know any spells.

'Tristan?' Lara's confused voice calls from behind. 'What the hell are you doing here? Only participants are allowed in the cube.'

'The Sorceress is here. She's murdering everyone in the whole arena. It's chaos out there, we have to do something.'

'Oh my god!' she exclaims. 'Did Caprice make it out?'

'I'm not sure, she just ran off into the mayhem and told me to enter the cube to alert you on what's going on.'

Lara looks panicked by this, and rightly so. We're trapped inside this unescapable cube with god knows what surrounding us outside. The scariest thing about all this, which I'm only just realising now, is that they can see us in here. Once everyone else in the arena is taken care of, it'll only be a matter of time before they enter the cube and get to us.

'How do we get out?' I ask Lara. 'Is there any way out without going back out there?'

'Afraid not,' she replies with all hope drained from her now pale skin. For probably the first time in her life, she looks hopeless. After noticing this expression on her face, I know our chances of getting out of here alive are zero to none.

'How do I unfreeze him?' I ask, pointing to the man on the

floor. 'I cut off an imp's arm on the way into the arena and it was running around like it had a mind of its own, then latched onto his face. The only option was to freeze it. Can you do anything?'

'In the Wand Wars tournaments, only freeze spells are permitted, the wands are allocated by the committee, and we can only use these. Luckily though, I brought my own wand in case we ran into trouble. Nobody is going to question why I've got a make-up brush in my pocket; a girl's always got to look her best.' She nods at me and walks over to the frozen figure, breaks the arm free without shattering the man in any way, and discards it into the corner of the room.

'*Salvo Flare!*' Lara shouts as she points at the man.

Flames shoot from the make-up brush wand Lara aims at him and as it makes contact, the flames are devoured by the ice, causing an evaporating steam to rise and revive the man to his normal state. The man looks dazed and confused for the first few seconds that he's revived and asks us both, 'What's happening?'

'No time for talk, we've gotta fight our way out of here. Follow me,' Lara says and takes the leader role she loves so much. Before we can set off, a huge crashing noise reverberates its way through the meandering corridors and bounces with an echo from every single surface. 'They've broken inside. We have to find a way out now!' Lara bellows, and both me and the man run after her. It's like a slalom the way we run and strafe around each obstacle that blocks our path. I must admit, the fitness of the other two exceeds mine massively, to the point where it's kind of embarrassing. If I make it out of here alive, I'm making a conscious effort to improve my fitness levels.

The noises grow significantly louder from behind us and it's got to a point where the hysterical giggles and lunatic laughing are more overpowering than our panting and stomping as we run breathlessly. The man, who is metres ahead of me, looks back over his shoulder, then stumbles and falls as he attempts to leap over a block of ice which is inconveniently placed on the ground in front of us. I overtake him, then stop suddenly to turn back and help him. A horde of the freakish imp creatures come into view, filling the entire corridor with wickedness; there must be thousands of them. They clamber over each other and pounce off the walls and ceiling like they're in a race to see who can reach us first. I've got no chance of saving this guy, I'm going to have to stick with Lara.

I run my fastest to catch up, but as I arrive around a corner, she's staring blankly with an entirely wet, tear-strewn face.

'What's wrong, why have you stopped?' I ask in panic.

'It's a dead end. This is it, Tristan. I've always loved you,' she sobs. Her make-up brush wand falls from her limp hand to the floor, and her weeping continues until our ultimate end arrives in a few moments time. I retrieve her wand from the icy ground and accept the fact that we're not going to live more than a few minutes, so I hold her tightly and wait for the deathly horde to reach us.

'Do you not know any spells that could kill them all?' I ask her.

'Not on that scale, there's thousands of them,' she mutters under her breath.

I drag Lara around the corner we arrived from, to be faced by the sight of a tunnel filled with imps parading forwards like bloodthirsty hyenas ready to pounce on their prey. They're metres away from me and Lara now, and we hold each other tight knowing we're about to face certain death.

Without any kind of reasoning or knowledge, a cognitive, instinctive flicker of something unknown sparks inside. I'm not sure how I do it, or how I even know how to do it, but it's like I'm being possessed. I don't feel like me anymore, and I've been taken over by something. I raise Lara's make-up brush wand up in front of me, but I don't point it at the imps, I point it towards myself.

A switch has flicked in my brain. A few seconds ago, I was cowering in fear and dreading the death that was coming for me, but now I feel alive. As they're almost upon us, almost deafening us with the horrifying noises resounding from them, I scream the words 'Ultima Colossus Warp!' at the top of my lungs.

I'm not sure what those words mean, or where I know them from, but it's certainly me that says them. And I'm not sure if the darkness that follows is down to the end of another round in Wand Wars, or my consciousness has left me, but it's certainly darkness. Confusion seems to be a common occurrence at the minute.

CHAPTER 20

Rude Awakening

The pain searing through my head is unbearable. The numbness that spreads through every one of my limbs is torturous. The darkness is still here. My mind seems completely blank, but the blackness won't leave me. Where am I? I can't seem to remember anything that isn't completely blank. I try to recall my name, but nothing comes to mind. I can't even recall who I am, never mind what my name is.

My eyes eventually open to the sight of wooden panels that glare down at me and something does seem familiar about it. Swivelling my head from side to side to examine where I am, nothing else seems recognisable. There's a small door, a window on the opposite side of the room, and another bed over the other side of the minute room. I can hear the distinctive noise of clattering kitchen utensils from the other side of the door somewhere, but I'm not sure what it could be. I'd get up to go and investigate, but my body feels like it's been beaten to oblivion.

The small wooden door begins to open slowly with a creak and I'm not sure who or what to expect, I'm not even sure if I remember anyone who could be turning up. A small man enters with a snouted nose and round-rimmed glasses. He strokes his whiskers as he speaks to me in a soft tone.

'Tristan, you're finally awake. Don't try to move, you just get as much rest as you can. I've alerted Lara that you were coming round so she should be on her way. Do you remember who I am?' he asks me gently, obviously concerned.

I rummage around my memory banks, trying to figure out who this man is, and why he seems so recognisable when I can't remember a damn thing about anything. 'Fruity?' I ask confusedly.

'Not quite,' he replies. 'Care to try again?'

'Erm... Booty?'

The small man chuckles. 'It's Tutti. Your memory should return within the next few hours. You've been comatose for the last fifteen hours, but now your brain's active, it shouldn't take too long to refresh. Can you remember anything from before you blacked out? Anything at all?'

'Nope, don't even know my name.'

'Tristan,' he replies.

I glare at him disappointedly. 'Tristan? What a stupid name.'

'I'll get you a cup of tea. Things should start coming back to you shortly and we can discuss what's happened. No rush, you just make sure you get plenty of rest.'

Tutti leaves the room and returns a few minutes later with a steaming hot cup of tea and a plate of biscuits. Something about them seems familiar as well. He places the tea and biscuits down on the side table next to me, gives me an amiable nod, and leaves the room to let me rest. Over the next hour, as I lie in silence and attempt to make sense of reality, I do begin recollecting things. A beautiful woman seems definitely familiar. I hope she's with me, she's gorgeous. Thousands upon thousands of zombies, an evil bitch of a woman who wants to kill everyone, but there's a sad desperate loneliness that seems so familiar. Slowly but surely, the memories do start to return. Maybe I watched a movie before I blacked out because none of these thoughts seem possible.

The sound of a door opening outside alerts me that somebody has entered the building I'm in. Although some memories are returning, I'm still oblivious to where I am. The small door opens once again to introduce me to the beautiful woman from my recent thoughts.

'Tristan, you're okay! I've been so worried!' she hollers with great relief and drops to my lying position to hug my tightly.

'His memory is still hazy, I wouldn't start asking him about things, it'll just confuse him,' Tutti advises from behind her.

'Really? Do you know who I am?' she asks me.

'I think you might be my wife or girlfriend or something,' I say assumingly.

'Oh great. Do you know what my name is?' she asks.

'Erm, Laura? No, wait.' I think again for a few seconds, almost certain that the previous guess was wrong. 'Llama?' I ask. 'No wait. La… r… a?' I ask, pausing between each letter to receive confirmation from their gazes that each letter is correct.

'Spot on,' she says, and then glares back at Tutti. 'He's not that bad, the way you were talking about him I was expecting to turn up and he's mumbling nonsense or jumping around the room like a kangaroo.' She leers at me disconcertly. 'Tristan, today is important. You've got a few hours to rest and then we have to get to your funeral,' Lara informs me.

'My funeral?' I ask, majorly confused. 'How can we go to my funeral? I'm not dead, I'm sitting right here.' Lara's head drops and I can tell that she is livid that I'm unable to remember whatever it is she's referring to.

'How long's it gonna be Tutti?' We can't exactly rearrange the funeral, can we? If he isn't all here, I'm gonna have to go on my own.'

'Honestly, it shouldn't be long, I've done my research on this. He's ten times better than he was when he woke. Let's just give it a couple more hours and see how we get on. Tristan, drink your tea, it should help revitalise you. Let me read through some of my books and see if I can find a way of speeding this process up,'

'Do you mind me asking why I can't remember anything? Seems probably the first thing we should have talked about,' I ask.

'We'll go through that later. I'm giving you an hour and then we're getting prepped. Try and get some more sleep,' Lara says, then leaves the room swiftly.

I sit in silence for another hour, desperately trying to make more sense of my thoughts. Things are coming more into focus the harder I think, and I feel almost revitalised. My energy levels are returning, and my mind seems a lot less hazy. The only blank that seems to be a constant is what happened after I went into the Wand Wars cube. I remember the Sorceress showing up, I remember fighting the imps to gain entrance to the cube, I just can't really remember what happened when we were in there.

Tutti and Lara enter the room once again. 'Lara, I can remember everything now, all except what happened inside the cube. I remember going in there, but the rest is a blank.'

Lara sits down at the end of the bed and puts a warm hand on my leg sympathetically. 'We got surrounded by imps and we were cornered. Luckily, I had my wand with me. I dropped the wand and you picked it up, then you cast a spell I've never heard of before. We both woke up here, in Tutti's house. Surely, you must recall the spell from your time growing up as Salamander, but how would an eleven-year-old boy know a spell like that?'

Tutti stays in his standing position and leers down at the two of us with an intensity on his face that I can't fathom. 'Lara described this spell to me, and I've researched it profusely to figure out its origins. I can only find one reference to this spell in a history book from hundreds of years ago. This is really dark magic; there's no possible way Salamander could have known about a spell like this. The skill it requires is beyond the level of any adult, never mind a child. They'd be able to cast it fine, but unless you've got the spirit and knowledge required, it'd be instant death ninety-nine per cent of the time.'

'Could we have just got lucky then? Maybe I cast it because it was in the back of my mind somewhere, and I was part of the zero-point-one per cent that survive by sheer luck.'

'I very much doubt it. It's possible but extremely unlikely,' he assumes. 'From what I can gather, the spell, *Ultima Warp*, was used by the Oryx when he was around all those years ago. I'm not sure how this spell originated, but it must have been created by somebody with evil intentions. According to history, the Oryx would use this spell to transfer either victims, or his minions, by the millions. There are two different types of spells we can cast: single-target spells and colossus spells. A colossus spell is capable of targeting multiple subjects at the same time. In the cube, you've evidently have cast this on both you and Lara using the colossus form of the spell to transport you both out of the arena.'

'That's a valid point. We still haven't told you anything about spells, have we?' Lara says.

'Not a sausage,' I reply, unsure why this subject hasn't arisen already with the amount of irrelevant, less-important nonsense they've told me over the previous days.

'There are five different types of spells which can be cast, all dependent on the caster's skill level. We have *Salvo* spells, which are spells for casting elemental spells; fire, ice, lightning etcetera. Then there are *Fortify spells*, which are defensive spells that are used to creates shields and reflect opposing spells. We then have *Voodoo* spells, which are what is commonly known as hexes and are usually just cheap tricks. We then have *Nova* spells… look, I won't go through every single spell because I know it's a lot to take in, but this is just a bit of info for you so you know what you're dealing with. There are *Diruo* spells, but the only one I'm aware of is the one we use to banish people to Earth. The final type of spell is the *Ultima* spell, these spells are not to be used under any circumstance and are illegal throughout the entire universe. Ultima spells are exactly what they say on the tin, they're ultimate spells. Only the most experience casters in the universe could use these without dying, and I'm telling you now, there's not many out there.' Tutti finishes his explanation and then leans back against the wall twisting and stroking his whiskers.

'So, this spell that I cast, what did it do exactly?' I ask, rubbing my forehead with the information I'm trying to retain in such a state.

'*Ultima Warp* transports the caster to a place that they focus on in their mind. It has to be said, I do feel honoured that the first place you thought of was my house. *Ultima Colossus Warp*, which is the colossus version of the *Ultima Warp* spell, was able to transport both you and Lara simultaneously,' Tutti explains.

Lara gives me a thankful look and squeezes my hand as if she owes me her life. As she begins to explain what happened, a lone tear begins to flow down her left cheek, which she wipes away with her free hand. 'We were surrounded, facing certain death. You picked up my wand and transported us out with that spell. Before I knew what had happened, I woke up here and you were completely unresponsive. You saved my life Tristan. If we hadn't brought you here, or if you'd not come into the cube to save me, I'd be dead by now for sure. You were so brave coming in there to get me. You've changed so much already; the old Tristan wouldn't have been brave enough to do that.'

My whole face begins burning with a sensation like no other feeling I've ever experienced. The most beautiful woman I've ever laid eyes on is telling me I'm brave and I've just saved her life. What do you even answer to that?

'What happened with everyone at the arena after we got out? Was Caprice okay?' I ask, concerned.

'Yeah, she got out alright. The POX and the Doomguard turned up to fight her and she disappeared,' Lara replies. 'We're going to have to get a move on Tutti. We've got to get to the funeral for twelve, shall we go through the plan? Also, I want to try and get some training in with Tristan if that's okay.'

'Training?' I ask.

'I managed to get hold of a wand for you. I wanna go through a few spells so you know how to fight. After the arena fiasco, I'm sure she'll show up sooner than we think, and we're going to have to be prepared. Can we use the training facility Tutti?' Lara asks him.

'Sure can, I'll go and get everything ready, but we don't have a lot of time so please try to be quick,' Tutti urges impatiently and leaves the room.

'Okay, so here's the plan. We do your wand training first, then we go into the drone chamber in the other room. Once we're inside the drones on Earth, we'll go to your funeral, and while we're there we'll find Gregory. Once we've found Gregory, we'll question him to see what he knows about the night I disappeared,' Lara says.

'Does any of this even matter now?' I ask her. 'You ended up here and then you got me here, does it matter why we're here?'

Lara gives me a hardened stare and immediately I know that this must be important to her. Her disappearance from our home must be the single most important thing that's ever happened in her life, and she must want to know why it happened.

'We need to find out why the Sorceress went through the trouble of sending one of her minions to Earth and located us specifically. Although we know that she's your sister, we still don't know why she would have wanted you sent here, why not just leave you alone? She may want to kill you, she may even need your help, but all I know is that we have to find out. Did you get the impression from Gregory that he knew something like this was going to happen?'

I ponder this thought for a few seconds, and nothing seems to come to mind at first, but the more I think about it, the more something doesn't seem right. 'It does seem strange that he asked me to come over and set up his TV, there seemed to be urgency in his voice. One thing I do remember, is that when he was looking up at the stars, he was naming all the planets, but they were similar names to what these lot use out here.'

'Really? So he's not from Earth? I'm telling you Tristan, there's a lot more going on here than we initially thought, that's why we need to find him. I'm starting to think maybe he wanted you to visit his house for a specific reason, but why? Remember how I said it was one of Katarina's minions who came in, they could have mistaken who I was in the dark and cast the spell on me thinking it was you and it was Gregory's job to lure you over there.'

'It's possible I suppose,' I reply. 'But if he was in league with the Sorceress to transport me over there, couldn't he have just done it himself?'

'Are you two ready or not!' Tutti's voice shouts impatiently from one of the other rooms.

We decide to exit the room and go through another door to enter another of the rooms before Tutti gets a strop on. The room we find ourselves in has a huge flat screen on one wall. Reaching into her rear pocket, Lara pulls out what can only be described as a marker pen. 'Here you go,' she says, handing it over to me.

'What's this? You want me to write something?'

'That's your wand,' she says as I take it from her. I sense a slight tingle surge through my body at the touch of it. That feeling again of picking up a wand, it's strange to say the least.

'Couldn't have got me anything cooler? Why are they all household items? Why aren't they brown sticks like in the movies?' I ask, recalling that every wand I've ever seen in a movie is a stick of some sort.

'Because what contains the magic isn't the item itself, it's the stone that's embedded inside it. Wands are made from a variety of complex components, and all these components are combined to make a small magic stone. These magic stones can be inserted into whatever you want, the item you use is just a vessel which carries the stone. If it's the right shape and size, it should be compatible.

You'll notice that they're all the same shape; Rex's cigar, my make-up brush, your marker pen.'

'Can we please get a move on for the third time?' Tutti interrupts us in an attempt to hurry us up.

'Sorry Tutti,' we say simultaneously like schoolchildren who have just been scolded for loitering in the hallway.

'Now, the spells it's imperative that you know, are the *Salvo* spells, these will be the most useful in fighting your enemies. We have *Salvo Flare*, which is fire. *Salvo Glacier* is ice. *Salvo Storm* is lightning, and *Salvo Zephyr* is wind. Please point your wand at the target screen and use *Salvo Flare* if you could please Tristan,' Tutti instructs me.

'Sure,' I say, and raise the wand with both arms to point towards the screen. '*Salvo Flare!*' I shout with as much effort and concentration as I can. A lone spark shoots out of the wand and hits the floor before getting anywhere near the screen.

'Try again, more gusto this time!' Tutti barks.

'*Salvo Flare!*' I shout vehemently. A spark once again ejects from the end of the wand and lands softly on the ground, although slightly further than the previous one.

'Again! Show me some passion!' Tutti wails excitedly.

'*Salvo Flare!*' I scream, as if I'm trapped inside the depths of hell with no way to escape. A streaming jet of fire booms from the end of the wand and crashes into the screen. It's as if the screen becomes my arch enemy for a few moments, as if it's just murdered everyone I know and I want the sweetest of revenges. The fire streams continuously out the end of the wand, and I keep it going until I see Tutti raise his hand in a notion to stop me.

'Wow, impressive!' Lara says. 'Now try this one: *Fortify Somatic*, cast that one on yourself.'

'*Fortify Somatic!*' I shout, trying to match the passion I put into that last spell. I feel my bones tighten as if my body is preparing itself for a beating. An aura seems to be radiating around my body like a shield of light and I feel almost invincible.

Out of the blue, Lara's fist swings up from her side and connects with my face with a venom I never would have anticipated. Expecting the blow to knock me three feet across the room, her hand bounces off and I'm unscathed, I don't seem to move an inch. 'Cool, isn't it?' she says and chuckles loudly at my flinching, my hands reaching up to my head to parry the blow.

'Will you two stop messing about, we really need to hurry! It's almost eleven and we still have to prepare the drone chambers,' Tutti presses us impatiently and taps his wrist. There's no watch there, he just taps it for effect.

'I was having fun there, spoilsport,' Lara says to a now rather irate Tutti. 'If we must. What do you need us to do?' she sighs.

'I'll get the drone chambers ready, meet me in the other room in two minutes time so I can talk Tristan through everything.' Tutti exits the room huffing and puffing and leaves me and Lara alone.

After a few more attempts at casting spells, some successful and some failing miserably, Tutti calls furiously from the other room. 'Are you coming or not?!'

'I think we'd better go before he gets mad. Then again, I think we're past that now. I suppose we are going to have to leave though, we don't have much time until the funeral starts,' Lara hints, making her way into the other room.

'This is going to be weird; I haven't seen my family in weeks,' I mutter as I follow her out of the room.

CHAPTER 21

I See Dead People

Four chambers are stood against the wall like pillars that are made entirely of glass. Inside, a multitude of wires and gadgets hanging down from the ceiling are visible. Mounted on the adjacent wall are an array of monitors, all showing different views from many sets of eyes in real-time. The last thing I expected from Tutti was technology as he doesn't seem the type that would be into all this stuff.

'These are the drone chambers, just step inside and pop on the headset and I'll sort all the other connections out once you're hooked up.' Tutti says this with a hint of impatience, and I can feel him pushing me from behind to try and quicken the process. 'Once you're in control of the drone, if you need to get out, just clap three times and it'll set off an alarm in here so I can disconnect you. Failing that, just sit on the floor and tap the bottom of your feet together and it'll override the controls and disable the headset, got that?'

'Yeah, got it, clap three times or clap the soles of my feet together.' I give Tutti a thumbs-up with both hands once the headsets wires are dangling over my face.

'Can I have someone better this time?' Lara asks him. 'I ended up as a guy who had green hair last time. Green hair! I've got nothing against people who dye their hair green, but he was wearing a blue suit at the time. That's just not stylish.'

'Sorry Lara, I've had to use two drones who are close to where you're going, so you'll have to make do with what I've got. I've gathered them together a couple of miles from the church.' Tutti gives her a stern look but Lara doesn't seem impressed at all.

Tutti connects all the wires to my headset and other various parts of my body, while Lara connects herself up. She must have done this loads of times before as she knows exactly where everything connects.

'All ready?' he asks.

'So, we're going to wake up as two random people on Earth near the church where my funeral is taking place? Except it's not me who they'll be mourning the death of, it's actually that Wainwright guy. Couldn't be simpler!'

'It's St Anne's church; I'm guessing you know where you're going.' Tutti closes the glass doors on the chambers and a feeling of claustrophobia is undeniable as there's barely any room to move. Approaching a control terminal near the monitors on the opposite wall, he types something onto a keyboard which causes a strange distortion in my brain. My eyes can't focus properly, and my legs feel slightly numb.

A flash of light fills my vision, and when my eyes open, they're greeted by a strange-looking man looking back at me. As I spin around in awe, I realise exactly where we are. I've been here hundreds of times; we're in a village called Little Chesterton. It's a quaint village, but apart from the church, various newsagents and a pub, there's nothing else really going on.

'Who are you?' I ask the man, rather confused as I was expecting Lara to come here with me, but as I speak, I notice that I don't sound like me at all, I sound more like a young boy whose voice hasn't quite broken yet.

'It's me you idiot,' the man replies in a gruff voice. She doesn't look the happiest I've ever seen her for sure.

I laugh hysterically at the scruffy beard which now adorns Lara's face. As the laugh leaves my mouth, I stop within milliseconds as I grasp what must have happened; surely there's been some sort of mix up. I look down to eye a pair of breasts in a bright red, tight-fitting, summer dress. Lara's masculine booming laugh must be heard in the next village as she roars and points at me, almost falling to the floor in hysterics. After getting over the initial shock of the body I'm temporarily inhabiting, I too join in the mass hysteria which comes over Lara. People must think we're nuts; two random people in the middle of a deadly silent village pointing and laughing at each other for no reason.

'I think Tutti put us in the wrong chamber,' Lara blurts as she starts to calm down again from the fit of laughter.

'Yeah, I think he did,' I reply. 'Nice beard.'

'Nice dress. Although with them shoes and that dress, I think I'm going to have to call the fashion police because that's a disaster waiting to happen.'

'Alright, it's not like I chose it. The church is up here if you're quite finished,' I reply in my high-pitched voice. 'I don't think we've got a lot of time.'

Taking my first step towards the direction of the church, gravity seems to remind me that it's still a massive factor in my life as I begin to face-plant towards the floor. My foot twists as the high-heeled shoe hits the floor at an angle. Instinctively, Lara throws her/his hands out in front of me and catches me before I hit the concrete paving slabs below.

'How the hell do you walk in these?' I ask her, puzzled at the thought that people actually wear these. Why would you put yourself through this?

'You just get used to it. Take them off if you need to, I always do at the end of the night when I'm on my way home. I think we're gonna have to jog if you can.'

After undoing the shoes, I remove them from my feet. We both start jogging in the general direction of the church, it's probably only a ten-minute jog if we can keep a good speed. A few minutes in, I can't help but moan about every aspect of being a woman. 'How do you run with these things?' I ask Lara, pointing to my chest.

'You just get used to it,' she replies once again.

'And how am I supposed to keep up when the dress only lets my legs separate an inch at a time? Being a woman is harder than it looks!' I moan once again.

'You just get used to it,' she replies.

We jog down the beautiful tree-lined country lanes and finally turn onto the road that houses the church. I've pondered many times about who would attend my funeral and how many people would be there. I'm gobsmacked to see that there's actually lots of people attending, I thought there would only be a handful. I can't help but feel guilty about how I acted over the last year with the self-pitying and the suicidal thoughts. How selfish was that?

'Mr popular you, weren't you?' Lara says.

'I didn't even know I knew that many people, never mind been close enough to them to attend my funeral,' I reply. 'Are you sure Tutti hasn't got the wrong funeral?'

'Positive,' she replies. 'He may be a moaner, but he knows what he's doing.'

'Is that right?' I add, looking down at the body I'm now inhabiting.

The church is huge, an old light-bricked cathedral style church with a graveyard to the right-hand side. The low winter sun reflects off every inch of the large stain-glass windows causing me to squint profusely. Black limousines and a hearse sit outside the church gates and hordes of people squeeze their way through the entrance into the grounds of the church. The sea of black suits and dresses send a wave of guilt through me as I admit to myself that this is ultimately all my fault.

'This is all Rex's bloody fault Lara,' I say to her/him, hoping that I can successfully divert the blame away from me.

She looks at me with her bushy beard and dark blue eyes and says, 'I know, but it may prove to be useful. If Gregory's here, we'll be able to find out what happened to me. I suppose he did you a favour though; it gave us the opportunity to come here and maybe track Gregory down.'

Crossing the threshold of the church, we join the back of the crowd to gain entrance. I catch a glimpse of my Aunt Gladys from behind. It's difficult to recognise who any of the women are with all the oversized headwear, but she's easy to spot because she's so morbidly obese; she actually waddles like a penguin as she walks. The whole church is packed full of people, some I recognise, but some I've never seen before. It's not like I can walk over to them and ask 'Hey, how did you know me?'.

As we search around for a place to sit, it's evident that there's not one seat available. There's no way I knew this many people. Maybe some of these people knew me from my life on Macro before I was banished to Earth. They could have travelled to Earth to pay respects and attend my funeral; it doesn't seem likely, but it's still a valid theory. If this theory is correct, then lots of these people I don't recognise could even be family from Macro.

Without a seat, we choose to stand at the back of the church with all the others who were too late to find a place. After a few minutes of looking round trying to find any hint of Gregory, the ceremony begins. Everybody stands and the priest speaks gently about the passing of life and how I've moved on to a better place.

'Any sign of Gregory?' Lara whispers to me over the priest's speech.

'Nothing yet, there's some creepy guying sitting over there who keeps turning around and looking at me, is there something on my face?' I reply.

'That happens a lot, he probably just fancies you. It's something you just get used to as a woman. There's always creepy men staring at us.'

I've never really considered what it must be like to be a woman. There are so many things I'd never even thought of, can that guy really fancy me? That just seems unfathomable.

My dad climbs the few steps to stand atop the pulpit and say a speech. He mentions a few things about my upbringing, some of it being things I can't recall because it was before my accident. These things must be stories he's made up in his own head because I know they're not my real parents. He then goes on to talk about how I met Lara and I can sense the emotion pouring from her when he mentions that I'm probably up in heaven with her now. How would my parents have hidden the fact that I was adopted at eleven years old but make sure I never found out? It just seems odd, why not tell me? Wouldn't people have noticed when they had no kids and then miraculously had an eleven-year-old and question where I came from?

It's a lot more difficult than I'd have imagined watching people who love you suffering, and there's not a thing you can do about it. I just wanna run up to my dad and tell him it's all fine and I'm okay, but even I know that's impossible. Would he believe a woman he'd never met before who came up to him claiming to be his dead son? Somehow, I doubt it very much. It's a similar situation Lara found herself in when she wanted to send someone to tell me where she'd gone.

As I listen more intently to the stories about my teens and early twenties, tears begin to run uncontrollably down my face, and before I know it, the emotion has taken over and I'm sobbing like a child who's just dropped his ice cream. Lara puts her arms around me, hugging me tightly, her bushy beard tickling every inch of my shoulder and neck. The slight giggle at the tickly facial hair already starts to cheer me up. There she goes again, inadvertently making me laugh without even realising she's doing it.

The ceremony continues and I find myself searching through every face in the church trying to find Gregory. It makes the job a lot harder when you can only see the back of everyone's head. Finally, we reach the stage of the funeral where all the Catholic people visit the altar to receive communion. I'll have to use this opportunity to check everyone out and see if I can find him.

We queue up down the central aisle and I constantly pan my head left and right to look for that familiar face. Upon reaching the altar, I'm now close enough to examine the coffin. A photograph of me smiling sits proudly on top of it. It's one of the photographs from the dining room in my parents' house of me in secondary school.

After receiving communion from the priest, I have the perfect view of the entire place as I make my way slowly back down the central aisle towards the rear of the church. I scan each face with extraneous concentration, trying to pick Gregory out of the crowd, but I'm starting to think he mustn't be here. Have we really done all this for nothing?

Sitting at the far end of one of the pews near the centre of the church, I finally spot Gregory reading from a hymn book and crying. The stand-out feature was the hat he always wears. He's dressed in a black suit and appears to be alone from what I can make out. The urge to approach him is overwhelming, but how could I do that? It'll be too hard to speak with all these people around. Lara and I finally reach the back of the church and I can't tear my eyes away from the vicinity where Gregory was sitting.

'I just saw him,' I whisper loudly to Lara over the melodic hymns from the organ. 'He's down there near the middle, it should be over soon so we can catch him outside. We'll try to get out first and wait for him.'

As soon as the mass ends, the coffin is carried out by my dad, my two uncles, Stan and Eric, my two brothers, Jonathan and Levi, and my cousin, Steve. Everybody else who has attended follow the coffin to the paved area outside on the church grounds. I swear down dead, once this thing is over, I'm going to find a way to go home, even if it's just a couple of times a year. I can't put my parents and the rest of my family through this when I'm absolutely fine.

Lara and I are the first out of the church after rushing rudely out of the doors as soon as mass is finished, and we eagerly wait near the gates that leave the church grounds and onto the country lane. We examine each face, waiting for our target. It's taxing to process them all, but we do our best and hope we don't miss him.

'Once he passes us, we'll follow him so we're out of earshot and we can have a nice little chat,' Lara says, scanning the crowd with ultimate concentration. After almost each person has left, Gregory finally exits, trudging down the concrete steps of the church and making his way towards us.

'Almost everyone has left, let's just do it now,' I suggest to Lara as Gregory reaches just a few metres away. He stops randomly as he reaches us and stares blankly, his mouth then turns into a mischievous grin.

'Young Tristan, Lara, how have you been? I've been waiting for you two to show up, where have you been?' he says with a nod and leaves me and beardy dumbstruck.

'What?' we both reply, and look around as if he's talking nonsense. As my eyes meet Lara's, we concede unanimously that he knows our identity.

'How did you know it was us?' Lara asks the surprisingly cheerful old man.

'Isn't it obvious?' he replies.

'Look, I don't give a crap how you knew it was us, I want you to tell me what happened to Lara and why, right now!' I rasp vehemently. 'I went through twelve months of absolute hell and if you've got anything to do with it, it'll be your funeral we're going to next.'

'Keep your hair on young Tristan, I'll tell you everything. Where would you like me to start?' Gregory says.

'Well, we know that Sorceress Katarina was behind it, and that little jester guy who turned up at your house was one of her minions. Was it me or Lara they were after?' I ask the old man.

'It was you. She sent for you. I invited you over to my house to speak to you alone, to alert you that you should be on your guard because dangerous people may be after you. Lara came over instead and the plan was kind of ruined from there. My guess is that they were watching the house and got confused thinking you were there, and not Lara.'

'I know she's my sister and that must have something to do with why she wants me, but do you know why she might send someone to kidnap me?' I ask.

The smile fades from his mouth and a serious tone takes over. 'That's something I don't know, I'm sure once you meet her, you'll be able to ask the question. I've been watching over you for years; it wasn't just coincidence that I lived next door to you. A promise I made to your father, your biological father that is.'

'Really?' I ask. 'You knew my father?'

'Yes, we were like brothers. Couldn't leave his young lad to grow up with some hoodlum family once he died, could I?' he says.

'But how did you know who I was?' I ask. 'I thought it was impossible to find somebody once they'd been banished as they get new DNA and look completely different.'

'You just need to know where to look. I had the exact date and time you were banished all those years ago, so I accessed the hospital records to see who had been sent to hospital with amnesia around that time. One thing a lot of people don't know about banishment is that you can figure out where they're going to land based on Earth's rotation at the time. They will always land on the surface that's directly facing Macro and it is programmed to always avoid seas and oceans. It took a while but eventually I found you.'

'You've been watching over me ever since?' I ask, open-mouthed.

'Yes, of course, I even got my son to attend your wedding so he could keep an eye out for any dangers. I knew the Sorceress was going to try and take you, but I couldn't pinpoint which day it would be.'

'Was he the one we saw in the photographs?' I turn to Lara and ask.

'He must have been. We didn't spot him on the day, but we saw him afterwards on some of the photographs,' Lara adds.

'Unfortunately, the *Ocular Illusion Apparatus* doesn't work with photographs or mirrors.'

'Ocular Illusion?' I query.

'Yes, you won't know what that is, how stupid of me. It's a belt that can be worn to make you invisible to others,' he explains. 'It doesn't seem to work with photographic lenses or mirrors.'

'I've got a question,' Lara says, putting her hand up like she's in a classroom. 'Why couldn't you have just flown to Macro and found me? Or went and found Tristan?'

'It's not that simple dear. I ran into some trouble a few years back so I found a way to remove my chip and couldn't be tracked. Without my chip I had no passport. I'm stranded on Earth, unless somebody can come and smuggle me back out.' He says this with a melancholy tone. Why does everyone outside Earth hate it so much, it's not that bad. 'I tried to find Tristan, but he moved house after the incident and I didn't know where to look.'

'What happened to you then?' Lara asks. 'After the spell hit us, I woke up in a cell on Macro, somewhere underground, and didn't have a clue where I was. After a couple of days somebody came in and let me out, but I'm still not sure who it was.'

'I'm sure you'll find out soon enough. Look, there's something I need to ask both of you, and it's a matter of tremendous importance. It could be a matter of life and death. I was hoping you'd find me because I need you to do this for me.'

'Sure,' I say. Lara and I lean our heads in closely, waiting to hear what this important information could be.

Suddenly, out of nowhere, a bang reverberates through the atmosphere like a shockwave from the heavens. A blow with the force of a jackhammer knocks me forward towards Gregory, but I pass right through him. I can hear a voice shouting, but I'm not sure what direction it's from.

Another flash bangs loudly and my eyes blink for a

millisecond, opening to Tutti panicking frantically and running around befuddled. The chamber door is open for me to exit and I step out, grabbing him anxiously in an attempt to calm him down.

'Tutti, what's the matter?!' I yell, holding his shoulders to keep him still.

'She's here! She's destroyed HQ! We have to get down there now!' he squeals.

'Calm down, what are you talking about?!' Lara asks him.

'She turned up out of nowhere and destroyed HQ, it's smashed on the ground in ruins, I'd be surprised if anyone survived!'

Lara stares at me and Tutti open-mouthed in absolute shock. After a few seconds, she comes around. 'You got your wand Tristan?'

'Yeah,' I reply.

'Then let's get over there!' she screams passionately and pelts her way over to the door without a moment's hesitation.

CHAPTER 22

The Fall of HQ

The unicorn ride from Tutti's place doesn't take as long as I thought it would have. Below, all I can make out is chaos descending across the entire city. Plumes of ash and smoke fill the atmosphere from the ruins of HQ, which now lies in a million pieces on the surface. Everybody who was in there must surely be dead. Lara, Tutti and I have had to share a unicorn to fly there because we would have been forced to wait for another one, but with the current red-alert situation, it would have been hard to even find a second unicorn. Just by chance, we walked downstairs and once we reached outside, there was a unicorn literally going past.

During the journey, Tutti has been telling us about how he saw HQ go up in flames and start dropping from the sky while he was watching from the monitors in his house.

'Did you find anything out from Gregory?' he calls as we begin to swoop down into the clouds of smoke.

'Not as much as we thought!' Lara shouts back to him, her hair slapping against her face in the wind. 'He was about to tell us something, it sounded important, and then you extracted us!'

'Sorry about that!' he calls. 'I hope you can understand the importance of the situation!'

As we drop lower through the dense clouds of grey and black smoke, visibility becomes almost non-existent. HQ was massive, and the mile or so drop must have caused a tremendous amount of devastation. From what I can make out, we land smoothly without so much as a bump. Unicorns must have good eyesight to be able to see where they're going through all this smog. The three of us jump off the side of the unicorn and try to navigate our way through the rubble and debris to at least find somebody we recognise.

'Tristan, you check over that way, we'll check over here,' I hear Lara's voice call to me in panic as I waft a hand in front of my face to clear my line of vision. I follow her instruction and make my way blindly over to another section of the debris. How am I supposed to find anyone in all this? Everything looks the same, it's just piles upon piles of rubble. I search for a short time, lifting chunks of material out of the way and chucking them to one side, when I hear a voice call out to me faintly, somewhere to my left.

'Who's there?' I call out, and immediately endure a coughing fit after the smoke enters my lungs. A small creature's silhouette becomes faintly visible and my eyes instinctively squint to try and make out who has arrived at the scene.

'Hey Tristan! It's me, Mogson.' He too starts coughing outrageously. 'I only went to the shop to get some food and when I left the shop to return, I heard people screaming. I looked up to see the Sorceress and a load of those imps attacking HQ. I think she must be planning on taking the Xanarock, we're gonna have to do something. Caprice was inside when the place was attacked and I can tell how she feels through my chip because it's linked to hers, and the strange thing is, it's telling me that she's fine.'

'Maybe she wasn't in there,' I say encouragingly with my t-shirt now pulled up to cover my mouth and nose. 'What about Rex?'

'He was in there too.'

'Can you tell where she is through your chip or is that not a thing?' I ask.

'Usually, but for some reason I can't pick up where she is. The signal stopped before HQ was even taken down, it's weird,' Mogson replies. He sits still, closes his eyes, and fully concentrates. 'I got nothing!' He shrugs and then begins running in another direction. I follow him with extreme difficulty over the jagged debris beneath my feet until he stops. 'You hear that? Try checking under here,' he says hopefully.

Immediately, and without any hesitation, I clamber onto the pile of rubble and start launching rocks to one side. After excessive choking and coughing, I can make out sounds from underneath. I move a few more pieces of rubble and the noises become more audible. Then I notice the hair, then the face, and then one of the arms attempting to reach out.

'Tristan,' she murmurs under her breath with a wince. She looks in a lot of pain, I wish there was something I could do but it's way too late for that now. The sound of oncoming footsteps behind alert me to Lara and Tutti's presence.

'Caprice!' Lara shouts in desperation. Mogson begins licking Caprice's face wildly in despair, probably hoping that this will heal her somehow, or comfort her at least. Lara begins stroking her hair, giving constant reassurance that everything will be alright. I know she's a goner but she's still making slight groaning sounds. Something about her looks different. Her skin looks a slightly different shade, and her hair even looks a slightly different colour. Something about her just doesn't sit right with me.

'Does she seem different to you?' I ask Lara quietly.

'Yeah, I noticed it before when I was at HQ with her, but I think she may have just been a bit shook up after what happened at the arena.'

'Lara?' Caprice mutters under her breath, causing Mogson to stop licking and jump down from her face. 'Look after Mogson for me. I love you, little guy,' she says and frees her hand to stroke Mogson's furry little head.

'Course I will,' Lara replies. 'I won't have to though; you'll be able to do that once we get you out of here.'

'I won't be going anywhere; my legs are trapped. Just promise me you'll look after him,' she says. I can tell she's only got moments left before she's done for, and I suppose she did well to make it this far after falling all that way and being crushed.

'Mogson, do you know where Rex was at the time?' Lara asks. Mogson doesn't answer. Instead, he cries his eyes out and rubs his face against Caprice's while she gives one last attempt at a smile and her head begins drooping into unconsciousness.

'He said he was in HQ somewhere, Mogson nipped out and saw it all happen. He said the Sorceress appeared with all those imps and blew HQ up,' I inform the others.

'I'm gonna kill that bitch!' Lara exclaims venomously. 'I know she's your sister, but she's dead when I get hold of her.'

'Mogson seems to think she might be after the Xanarock,' I tell Lara.

'Sweet Lord!' Tutti wails. 'If she takes the Xanarock the forcefield will disappear and the whole planet will be overcome by the zombies outside!'

I can tell at that moment that the reality of the situation hits all of us collectively. This is way more serious than just the HQ being destroyed, the whole planet could be wiped out, including us.

'How are we supposed to get up there without HQ being intact? We've got no way of getting up to the Xanarock,' Lara says sternly. I can see the panic spreading across her face like a rash. Meanwhile, Mogson continues to weep uncontrollably as Caprice's last breath leaves her body. Lara leans down next to her and checks for a pulse, but upon finding nothing, she bows her head, which sends Mogson into a fit of hysterical whimpering. He bawls loudly, not attempting to hide the emotion he's feeling. When I first met them, it was obvious how they felt about each other. A bond that was stronger than steel, a pair of souls that had spent their whole lives intertwined. When her parents left her in the care of doctors all she had left to rely on was Mogson, they were like actual soulmates. According to Rex, the chip that they shared bonded them on a level no human could ever dream of.

The cries that emanate from Mogson seem to be getting more and more desperate, they get deeper and deeper in pitch the more he cries. He bellows more and more until I can physically feel the emotion radiating from him. The sounds get stranger, and his skin begins to turn bright red.

'Are you alright mate?' I ask him and plant a comforting palm on his back. 'Ow!' I yell, retracting my hand with lightning speed. 'He's boiling hot, what's happening to him?' I exclaim, in worry for the little guy.

'This is impossible, truly impossible, surely not!' Tutti remarks with his mouth gawping. 'I thought this was just a myth. He's transmogrified. A surge of emotion so powerful that it has...'

A roar that must be ten times louder than a lion's reverberates triumphantly through the vicinity. The smoke which covered the scene is now forced to retreat as the wave of air from Mogson's lungs moves it aside with tremendous ease. Lara, Tutti and I, all cover our faces with bent arms to shield from the force. As I lift my head back up to look, the most magnificent sight greets me.

Standing there in front of us, a gargantuan bright red dragon with black wings and black spines looks down at us. Steam ejects from its sharp-toothed mouth and nostrils, which are the size of doors I might add.

'Mogson?' Lara asks, completely stunned at what just happened. 'How did you do that?'

'I'm not sure, have you ever been filled with so much rage that you thought you were going to explode?' he booms out unintentionally, not knowing how to control the volume in his new voice.

'Truly remarkable,' Tutti says in astonishment.

With the smoke around us now cleared from Mogson's roars, there's a clear line of sight up to the rock in the sky. My mouth turns instantly arid at the sight of thousands of small purple imps filling the sky above that must be protecting the path up to the Xanarock.

'She must be planning on taking the Xanarock and those imps think they can stop us,' I say, pointing up towards the sky. The others follow my gaze and tilt their heads upwards. 'What do you think Mogson, you think you can get us up there?'

'I don't know, I haven't tried flying yet, but how hard can it be? Jump on and we can go save the world,' he says with excitement and determination to exact revenge for his soul mate.

Lara takes command of the situation instinctively. 'Tutti, you stay down here, you have to warn everyone and get an army together to keep the zombies out. Is that okay?'

'Of course, leave it to me,' he replies. 'You two take care. We're counting on you.' Tutti spins around and runs off as fast as his small mole-type legs can carry him; it's not that fast, but I can tell he's having a good go.

Lara turns to me and smiles gleefully. Her right hand once again strokes its way across the fringe to brush my hair aside. This time, rather than being utterly romantic, it comes across as more casual than anything else. As she whips her hand away, a sudden stabbing pain ignites where her hand was.

'Ow! What was that for, why would you rip my hair out?' I retort, rubbing my head and staring daggers at her.

'It was only one strand, chill out,' she replies with no expression. 'Just something to remember you by if anything happens.'

'Well, I could have given you one of my shoes or something, did you have to rip a hair off my head?'

'Oh stop, you are such a baby, you wouldn't last five minutes as a woman, we have to pull our hairs out all the time, but then again, we knew that already didn't we,' she sniggers.

Lara and I jump on Mogson's back cautiously, me near the tail end, and her near his neck. I'm hoping to god I don't get hurt by one of these spines on his tail, if they so much as touch me they could cut me into pieces.

'Got your wand?' Lara asks me as she pulls her make-up brush out from her back pocket. I take my new marker-pen-shaped wand out and give her a nod as if to confirm that I'm well up for this. This could look so much cooler if we had actual wands. I suppose it'll just make the stories more fascinating when people find out we saved a whole planet with a marker pen and a make-up brush. I'll omit the dragon part.

Lara gives Mogson a tap on the back of his neck as if she's riding a horse and he begins to flap his wings, elevating us towards the army above. It's difficult work trying to hang on, and even in the first few seconds I almost tumble off to my death. As we reach only a few feet in the air, I can hear the terrifying screams and laughs of the small demonic creatures above as they realise they're meeting a resistance. A fireball erupts from Mogson's mouth and hits one of the imps directly in the face, combusting into a heap of ash and causing it to fall to the surface like snow from the heavens.

'You remember the spells, don't you?!' Lara shouts.

'Yeah!' I confirm. *'Salvo Flare!'* I scream and aim the wand at a small group of imps heading straight towards us. With a combination of mine and Lara's spells, and the jets of fire that shoot from Mogson's mouth, we're destroying them rapidly by the dozens. We're completely surrounded within minutes and Mogson is hit by spell after spell, but he continues to fight as if he's armour plated. On top of the spells and spectacular flames, Mogson also whips them aside with his tail and his muscular arms. His arms are equipped with talons that swipe with razor-like claws that almost cut the imps in half. It's never-ending, and the barrage of imps only seem to be getting more intense, and as tough as Mogson is, I know he won't be able to last much longer taking this kind of beating.

Lara and I fight with all we've got. She uses a multitude of different spells and must kill four times as many as I do. Jets of flame, ice and thunder fly from her wand to eliminate our threat rapidly, but no matter how hard we fight, it doesn't seem to be making a dent in the quantity.

'We can't hold them off forever, there's too many!' Lara screams as she shouts, 'Salvo Zephyr!' Then blows a gust of wind, causing the imps to fly backwards.

'I've got a plan,' I shout. 'When I shout go I want you to hold on tight, point your wand up and cast. Mogson, do you remember how to do a barrel roll?'

'What for?' she asks me, now looking quite fatigued. Mogson doesn't answer but I hope he heard me. It's understandable though, his mouth is a bit occupied at the minute.

'Trust me, just give me a minute!' I scream back. Holding on for dear life, I shimmy my way down Mogson's tail towards the point, trying my best not to get cut by one of the spines running down his tail. I grip tightly to his tail, point my wand out and shout, 'GO!' as loudly as I can.

I feel the rotating motion instantly, and it sends tingles down my spine how much these two trust me; maybe I'd make a good leader one day. I hope this goes according to plan or we're toast, literal toast. 'Salvo Flare!' Lara and I both shout, which causes a continuous stream of fire to eject from our wands. The spin gathers more momentum with each rotation and before we know it, three separate streams of fire shoot out in each direction incinerating everything around us. Mogson shoots forwards with his mouth, I shoot out the back, and Lara spins wildly firing out from above her. I can't even make out if we're killing any of them, but one thing I do know is that I'm well and truly alive and this must look as cool as hell for anyone watching down below. All I've wanted to do up to now is get home and sit in front of the TV eating pizza and drinking beer, but this is what life's all about. I'm on a journey to fight the evil in the universe with a dragon and an amazingly beautiful woman. If it's my destiny to die here today, I'd gladly accept it and say it was worth every second.

With all three of us obviously dizzy, the rotations slow down and I'm starting to see the effects of what we just did. The number of imps has diminished drastically and the cave which houses the Xanarock is now within a few hundred metres. With the desperate fighting over, and my dizziness beginning to subside, one sight changes my mood from hopeful to devastated.

The yellow hue of the forcefield looks as though it's beginning to fade. The once bright yellow dome that covers the city looks a lot weaker than it has since I arrived here. 'She's already taken the Xanarock!' Lara shouts.

'How do we land on the rock?' I ask. 'It's just a big rock, how do we get in?'

'There's a platform that leads inside, Mogson knows where it is, he's been here many times before!' Lara's voice rips through the wind.

Mogson heads straight for a ledge attached to one side of the gigantic rock. We make easy work of the remaining imps that come in for the attack, and the ones that stay away get left alone for now; they must be too clever to go anywhere near us.

He flies vertically and swoops around onto the ledge, landing with a hard thump onto the surface. We both jump from Mogson's back to land on the hard, rocky ground.

I know Mogson took a beating during that battle, but it's a lot worse than I imagined upon further examination. He looks like he's about to pass out at any moment.

'You alright buddy?' I ask, approaching his lethargic head.

He grunts and hisses at the pain he's enduring. 'Not really, will you be alright from here?'

'You were amazing,' Lara says, patting his side in a congratulatory manner. 'We'll take it from here. You go fly down and keep an eye on Tutti for us. Get some rest, and once this is over, I'm gonna take you out for an all-you-can-eat buffet, whatever food you want.'

'That'd be amazing,' he whispers in his agony. He then puts

all of his effort into flapping his wings once again to take off and swoops down over the edge of the rock towards the city below.

'Thanks, Mogson!' I shout, but he's already departed by the time I speak.

'You think he's permanently like this then?' I ask Lara.

'I'm not sure, Tutti seems to think so. I'll ask him once we...' Lara is stopped mid-sentence as the blast of a spell levitates her into the air, causing her to be thrown from the side of the platform and she pummels head-first down towards the ground.

'Lara!' I scream in a combination of panic and rage, lunging towards the edge of the platform and sliding stomach-down onto the floor. My head peers over the side to watch her figure tumble down into the smoke-filled city below. I lose track of her once she hits the thick clouds of smoke and I pray with all my heart that Mogson is still on his way down and he's caught her somehow. I turn back to the rock to see where the spell was fired from, and my gaze is met by two small figures.

The two jesters, who are the Sorceress' right-hand men from all accounts, stand at the entrance to the cave within the rock.

'Which one of you fired that?' I ask the two figures.

'I did,' one of them says.

'No, I did,' the other says.

'Well in that case, I'll just kick both your arses if that's how you want to play it,' I remark confidently.

'Play what?' The one in green asks the other. 'Does he want to play a game?'

They both chuckle to each other with annoying laughs. I don't think I've wanted to inflict pain on anyone so much in my entire life. I've only been speaking to them for a minute or so and they're getting on my nerves already. That's nothing new these days though, everyone seems to annoy me in some way lately; maybe I'm just reaching that age.

'Where's Katarina?' I ask them both sternly.

'She's waiting for you inside; do you still want to play a game?' the one in green asks.

'The only game I want to play is the one where I grab both of your heads and bash them together,' I rasp.

They both turn to look at each other simultaneously. 'That's not very nice, is it?' the one in green says. 'Maybe we have to teach him some manners.' They both snigger at this and I know I'll have to prepare myself for when they try something funny.

'No fancy wands or liquins will help you against our magic. If you leave now, maybe we'll let you live!' the one in green snorts.

The sentence he just said sends a brainwave through every synapse in my head. I've been so caught up in using magic I forgot about liquins. I wonder if I still have it. My left hand reaches down into my pocket as the two jesters hop on the spot excitedly. There's nothing there. I swap my wand to the other hand and reach into my right pocket. I can feel it; a small round sticker the size of a postage stamp clings to the inside wall of my trouser pocket.

'Have you decided yet, life or death?' the one dressed in green asks with the farcical tone dropping from his voice. Even I know this isn't going to end with me alive whichever I choose.

'I'll choose live,' I say with a smirk.

'Good, good,' says the one in green. 'And how do you expect to get back down without your pet, need some help with it?'

'I don't plan on going back down, I'm staying right here and finishing this,' I reply.

The two figures begin howling with laughter and clutch their stomachs as they drop to the floor in hysterics. Meanwhile, I take the invisibility liquin from my pocket and put it on the side of my neck. Waiting a few moments, I look down at my body, but nothing's happened. Please don't say this is faulty, from what I can remember Rex said they work almost instantly.

'Where has he gone?!' one of the jesters shouts. 'Go and find him!' he calls to the other. 'I wasn't looking, were you looking?'

'No, were you looking?' the other one replies, utterly confused.

'I just said I wasn't looking!' the other replies.

As both of them search the small rocky platform for any sign of me, I take the hint that I must only be visible to myself and nobody else can see me. I sneak straight past the baffled idiots as quiet as I can and enter into the pitch-black cave.

CHAPTER 23

Sibling Rivalry

I can't see a thing in here. Since leaving the entrance to the cave, the light seems to have almost vanished. What was that spell Lara used in the sewers again? Nova something wasn't it? I can't remember for the life of me. I don't have time for this, the zombies could be inside the city now and I don't even know if Lara is alive or dead from the fall. How am I supposed to make it through this darkness without a light? I need some kind of guide to get me through. My hand slaps against my head as I recall what the word was. I hold my wand up and call *'Nova Guide'*.

A shining ball of light expels from the end of my wand and hovers around me like a firefly. The cave becomes fully lit all around as the ball of light illuminates the way for my certain death. All I've been concentrating on is getting to the Sorceress and restoring the Xanarock, but the more I think about it, the less confident I am. I don't even know what the Xanarock looks like. If I can get it back, I don't know where to restore it to if I can retrieve it, and on top of all that, there's my evil sister blocking the way who apparently has spells that I can only dream of. Uphill battle or what?

Reaching the end of each corridor, I find my path blocked by cavernous walls and I keep backtracking to find another way. I always loved mazes when we used to have days out as a teenager, but they were a million miles away from what this is. A noise rebounding off the walls from down the corridor ahead causes me to stop in my tracks. Cackles and overly loud voices inform me that I'm at least heading in the right direction. I creep forward cautiously, hoping that she's close by and keep my wand held up at the ready.

The cavern tunnel seems to be widening as I get further, and the voices seem to be getting louder. A light from up ahead casts a faint shadow on the walls beside me. I need to get this light to go out somehow, but I don't even remember Lara casting a spell to make it go away when she used it. Maybe I just need to cast the spell again and it'll cancel it out. As I might have guessed, I was completely wrong. 'Nova Guide,' I whisper, but nothing happens. Maybe I'm not saying it loud enough. 'Nova Guide,' I say louder, and another ball of light pops out to join its mate and slowly orbit around me like a satellite. I am such an idiot; I've made myself less difficult to spot.

I reach my hand out to touch the light that's spinning around me, wondering if I can just throw it away, and as my hand touches it, it jumps back into the end of my wand. I do the same with the other one and I'm returned to darkness. All that remains is the faint light from the room ahead to guide me. Dim lights are emitting from hanging lanterns on the walls as I sneak my way stealthily into the room. Large rocks, stalagmites and stalactites fill the room like an underground cavern, and a bunch of small demon creatures are huddled around the Sorceress chanting and cheering. What am I going to do? I can't exactly run in, all wands blazing, but I don't exactly have time to think of something.

As if instinct grabs hold of me and desperation that a whole planet is at stake, I lean around the corner and shout 'Salvo Flare!'. My attempt to kill the evil woman in the middle of them fails miserably, and my second successive shot hits one of the imps and explodes it into ash.

Ducking back behind a large rock, I regret my decision to jump out and fire like a maniac.

'Who's there?' the evil voice asks coyly. Even the voice sounds sinister. If I hadn't seen her before and only heard the voice, I probably wouldn't be far off guessing a similar description. 'Is that who I think it is?'

'And who do you think it is?' I call, shaking like a leaf.

'Well, I only have one brother, who else could it be? You're the reason I'm here. I'm glad you came to see me. It saves hunting you down,' she says. Although her voice sounds sinister and evil to the core, I can't help but pick up a sense of respect in her tone, like she's speaking to her subordinate and not just some nobody.

'Why did you want to find me?' I call. 'Put the Xanarock back so none of them die!' My shouts echo from each wall as if there's four of me in here.

'And why would I do that? I'll tell you what, you seem very desperate to have this puny rock put back in its place, so how about we make a deal?'

I can hear the gulp like it's a cannon firing inside my throat. 'Go on, I'm listening,' I say. Something doesn't seem right, why would she be playing games with me when she could just kill me now and not have to try and strike a deal?

'I'll put this rock back in exchange for your soul. I want you at the front of my army ready to take on the entire universe. Imagine that; the brother and sister who conquered life and ruled the universe under the Oryx's control. I could replace those two incompetent imbeciles with you.'

My head drops and I know what I must do. I can't let any more people die. The thing that worries me, more than being a puppet in an army which is going to conquer the universe, is that she could take my soul, and then just remove the Xanarock again. I don't have a choice; she'll kill me anyway.

'Fine, I'll do it, just put the rock back first.' I know I'm not in a position to demand, but I've got to try and get the forcefield back online before they all die. For all I know, the forcefield has already faded and there's a full-blown massacre on the surface. I pop my head out from behind the rock and she's standing mere feet away, arms crossed and not looking impressed. Why is she playing games?

'Done!' she calls. 'Your precious little stone is back in its place. Now come out, I fancy a little chat.'

I have no choice but to hold my hands up as if I'm being commanded by the police to emerge from my hiding place. I know she's going to kill me now, but even if I've bought them a bit more time, it's got to be better than letting her just kill me outright.

A pedestal is visible on the wall behind her that houses a glimmering bright red orb, which must be the Xanarock. As I take a step towards her, her features become more and more clear. She is without doubt the most hideous woman I've ever seen, and I've been to some dodgy nightclubs in the past. Her grey hair is thin and scraggy, which hangs down to her shoulder, but it looks as if someone has pulled huge clumps out of it. Her teeth are razor sharp and look a dark shade of brown in the dim light. She adorns a black veil over her head which spreads out to wrap around her entire body. Her pale skin makes it look like she hasn't seen the sun in years, and she is holding a bright white wand in her grasp that looks oddly familiar.

'Hang on, is that the...' I stop talking because my mouth stops working temporarily as I gawp in awe.

'Recognise it do you? It took me a while to find, but I found it in the end. I can't believe they used this as a bit of cheap voodoo for banishing idiots when its potential is almost impossible. This *Banishing Wand* was created for so much more. Can you believe I only found it yesterday after all this time? Hidden inside the arena.'

'What? Is that why you attacked the arena?!' I rasp viciously.

'Not just that my dear brother. It was a bonus collecting so many souls for my master,' she says.

'So, what does the wand even do?' I ask.

'This wand belonged to the Oryx. It was found many years after he disappeared and was modified so that these pathetic troglodytes could banish people to Earth, have you ever heard such nonsense? To use the Oryx's wand, the most amazing being that ever graced this universe, and use it for complete rubbish like that.'

'Go and guard the entrance!' she calls out to the imps that accompany her. 'I don't want anybody interrupting our little family reunion.' The imps do as they're told and fly their way toward the entrance which I came through. Their footsteps resound from the walls as they scramble away following their master's command.

'Now, where were we?' she squawks. She says something I don't understand, in a dialect which sounds completely alien to me and binds shoot out from her free hand to blanket me and wrap me like a present with my arms down to my side.

'Do you remember when dear old mum and dad died? Of course you don't, you were long gone by then, you selfish cretin. I was taken into care. Can you imagine? The High Justice Minister's child taken into care. What must people have thought? That destroyed me inside. Do you know about the history of the Oryx, or do I have to tell you?' She gesticulates, with her sharp teeth grinning at my face.

'No, I couldn't give a crap to be honest,' I retort back to her in retaliation.

She points her finger toward me and my lips seal indefinitely. No matter how hard I try to speak, my mouth won't open.

'The Oryx lived on Earth originally, a long time ago, back when it was part of the solar system. One day he fell into a trap. This trap was a portal that transported him to another place in the universe. Little did he know, the person who set the trap was a sick and twisted man. This man tortured, abused and experimented on him to the point of near death. He suffered pain and agony that you wouldn't believe was even possible. During his experimentation, the man gave him unimaginable powers; it's thought he wanted to turn him into an evil killing machine for his own benefit. Finally, after many years, he escaped, but the damage was done; he was on an evil path to oblivion. The sick and twisted things he endured left him wanting to cause pain and misery to every molecule in the universe. What people don't understand, is what he went through. If you'd been through the same thing, you'd want to kill everyone who ever lived too. Add to the fact that he was modified so much that he will live until the end of time, I can see why he did what he did.

Is this true? What sick person would do such a thing? More so, why is she following him now?

'The man who tortured him, had a wand created for him; the most powerful wand ever made. This wand right here,' she says and holds the wand up in front of her, pointed directly at my face. 'Say nothing if you'd like to hear more... I'll take that as a yes then. This wand had allowed him to absorb the souls out of his victims once they were dead, which could then be turned into these imps you see roaming around. The more souls he collected, the larger his army became. Full of revenge on what life had done to him, he aimed to collect as many souls as he could to increase the size of his army and destroy the universe inch by inch. The plan came to a tragic end when some clever, puny man came up with a plan to trap him on a magnetar. They used a pulsar to fire a beam of electromagnetic radiation at him. Not being able to die due to what the man did to him, he lives forever, sucked in by a magnetar. If anybody attempts to rescue him, they'll get sucked in too. The millions of imps which followed him on his path to destruction were obliterated, and the Oryx was stranded in a torturous abyss of loneliness and despair until the end of time. If only there was a way to release him.'

A clambering noise from behind her in the large, cavernous room causes her to turn around. A shadow in a dimly lit corner is making its way over to us slowly.

'You bitch, you absolute bitch. I'm going to make sure you burn in hell!' the voice shouts vigorously. The shadow is getting closer now and I can see some sort of long stick in its grasp clutched with both hands. Thank goodness, this person must be here to save me. They'll be able to cast a spell with their wand, free me, and we can get the hell out of here. Talk about timing!

The Sorceress laughs evilly as the figure steps closer, becoming more visible with each step. 'What do you expect to do with that, little man?' she says to him.

Eventually, they get close enough to give me a clear view of their face. 'Tristan, are you alright?' Ralph asks, visibly shaking. The small nerdy-looking man from the Tech Team in HQ stands a few feet in front of us with a baseball bat held out ready to swing. Well, isn't this just great? I thought this was going to be a big daring rescue attempt and my hero ends up being a nerdy middle-aged man armed with a baseball bat. Without moving, the Sorceress uses some sort of telekinetic power to launch him up to the ceiling and impale him on a stalactite. The baseball bat drops to the ground below with a sickening clunk which echoes around the cavern. His screams can probably be heard from Earth, and I'm forced to listen to all of it seeing as my hands have been bound in a cocoon around me and I'm unable to cover my ears.

'Was that your big rescue attempt? I think I'll have that one,' she says with a chuckle, then points the wand upward toward the ceiling to suck a beam of light from his corpse.

'Now, where were we?' she says nonchalantly. 'I know what you're thinking; why is she telling me all this? I suppose I just want you to know the truth before I take you to the Oryx and we turn you into the king of the living dead army who is going to be responsible for the demise of the entire universe.' She cackles once again and all I can do is watch and take it on the chin. 'While I was High Justice Minister of Macro, me and a few of the other ministers went on an expedition to see if we could find where he was. There were no evil intentions, just an instinctive curiosity. As we got close, which nobody is advised to do, his voice appeared in my mind. He ordered me to kill the others who accompanied me and build up an army to set him free. My appearance changed, any thoughts of good escaped from my mind, and ever since, I've been building an army of millions and trying to figure out a way to set him free.'

'Any questions?' she asks, then frees my mouth again to speak.

'Why did you listen. Are you being controlled by him?' I ask under harsh breaths.

'You could say that, or maybe I was just in a similar position. I had everything taken away from me, including my family. I was put into care, and nobody in the entire universe cared that I even existed. You know what the worst part about all of this is?'

'What?' I ask sternly.

'It was all your fault!' she booms, showing me every one of her crooked teeth and drenching me with sputum. 'If you hadn't stolen father's wand and got yourself banished, we would have grown up a happy family. You chose this route, not me. You will be ultimately responsible for the destruction of everything that exists. You need to take this like a man and accept that you're no better than me.'

'But I don't remember any of this. It wasn't me. It was who I was in the past, Salamander doesn't exist anymore.'

'Do you think that's true, maybe I can help you with that? I did say this was the most powerful wand in the universe, didn't I? It has the ability to banish, but it also has the ability to reverse it. Come back to me brother!' she yells. The wand is held out and pointed at my face. She roars something else that I can't make out and blasts a beam of light right between my eyes. The pain in my head is worse than any pain imaginable. It's like someone taking a hammer to my cranium and bashing it as hard as they can.

My eyes open to an evil woman staring back at me. Who is she? We seem to be in a cave, and I'm encumbered. Who... who are you?' I ask the woman. 'Why can't I move? Where are we? The last thing I remember was being banished.' I look down to see my body isn't mine and it's been replaced by an older man's. 'Whose body is this? Why am I in a man's body?' I ask her. I begin crying uncontrollably. 'Where's my mum and dad gone, and where's Kat?'

'Who are you?' she asks me.

'I'm Sal,' I say, between snorts and sobs that I can't prevent. 'I want my mum!' I bawl.

'I'm bored of this already,' the evil woman says and points her white wand towards me. That's my dad's wand, the one I used on Theo, the same wand that I hid, and they couldn't find. A beam of light shoots out of the end and hits me square in the face.

Opening my eyes, the Sorceress is staring back at me; she looks like she's enjoying every second of this. 'What did you just do?' I ask desperately and start to weep as the pain seems to intensify.

'So, you don't remember what I just did?' she asks curiously. 'How intriguing. I think I'll keep you with me so I can talk to my brother whenever I want; we could talk about the good old days and reminisce about mum and dad. Are you ready to become the Oryx's plaything?'

'Screw you!' I scream, with a rage consuming me from within.

She laughs at this and replies, 'I'm bored now, let's get going, we've got a universe to conquer.' The Sorceress lifts her long, wrinkly fingers that wrap around the Banishing Wand, and she points it at me once again. 'Any last words? I'll be able to pass them on to your pathetic little girlfriend.'

'Just one. Duck.' I say, with what energy I can muster, lifting my head pathetically.

'What is that supposed to mean?' she asks.

'It means duck,' I repeat. The wand flies out of her hand to skim across the floor like a stone in the ocean. Her head lurches to the side as her body goes along with it to crash against the floor as Rex connects the baseball bat with her skull. In the corner of my eye, I saw him moving slowly towards her, but even glancing at him for a second would have given the game away.

'Rex, how the hell did you get here?!' I ask, completely overcome with relief and excitement bursting from my voice.

'I was in HQ, and I saw her attacking from out of the window. There was no way out and all the exits were disabled. I ran to the Tech Team and me and Ralph escaped through the matter transporter by putting in the coordinates for the Xanarock and we've hid in here since, waiting for a moment to strike. I tried to hold him back earlier, but he was furious. I'm gutted actually, he was a lovely guy,' he says respectfully, turning to look up at his corpse stapled to the ceiling. 'I was just waiting for the perfect moment. How did you get up here? I thought I was going to have to tackle this on my own.'

'Look, it's a long story. Will the forcefield have faded even though it was placed back?' I ask hurriedly. 'And can you free me from this bloody cocoon?'

Rex casts the *Salvo Flare* spell, and the cocoon is lit with fire, scalding almost every part of me.

'What was that for?' I shout and jump up and down on the spot trying to calm the heat down.

'Look, I haven't got time to sit here and think of the most appropriate spell to use, have I? I just cast the first one that came to mind. Regarding your earlier question about the Xanarock, I'm not sure, we've never tried to remove it. My guess is that once it was removed, it disappeared, and once it was put back, it reappeared, but it's anyone's guess really. What do we do with her? She'll wake up any second,' he asks, looking down at the unconscious Sorceress splayed out on the ground.

I ponder the predicament I'm in at the minute with my unconscious sister on the floor. She's not my sister though, she was Salamander's sister, but I'm Salamander, aren't I? At least I used to be. Even if I had a way to kill her now would I really want to? She's the only living biological relative I know of that's still alive in some way. I can't kill her, but I also can't let her continue terrorising, and probably eventually destroying, the universe. I can't have both, or can I?

'I've got a plan,' I inform him. 'We can't kill her, and she'll always come back, right?'

'Yeah, we've tried killing her loads of times, but she can't die, that's why we were using the destruction sphere, it'll send her into a void that'll trap her forever, lost in a spiral of nothingness. I haven't got it on me, it was back in HQ when I got outta there. Is it a quick plan or we gonna be here for days? There could be all hell breaking loose on the surface.' Rex is starting to look impatient and worried now.

'I'll be two minutes. Let me just get this,' I say, bending down to pick up the Banishing Wand.

'Where the hell did she get that?' Rex asks in complete shock. 'It's been missing for years, if it's the real one of course.'

'She said it was hidden inside the arena. Look, let me just do this and we can get out of here.' I point the wand down at Katarina, and with all the concentration I can muster, I shout *'Diruo Eternal!'*. A large bubble appears around her, followed a few seconds later by a deafening noise that radiates around the cavern, and a bright light that flashes like a lightning strike. Dropping my arm, which was held up to cover my eyes, I look down to now see that she's vanished. Hopefully, she'll wake up on Earth, not knowing who she was and looking like a different person, then she can go and live happily ever after; maybe even start a family and get a job.

I'm ecstatic that I didn't need help with casting that spell and feel like I'm finally starting to pick things up. I've heard that one a few times now and it's hard to forget once you've witnessed it on multiple occasions.

'Hey, brilliant idea!' Rex says, sniffing the bubblegum-scented air. 'I never would have thought of that. Maybe Lara was right bringing you here.'

'Cheers. Now let's get down there. Lara fell from the rock down into the city, but I'm not sure if she survived or not. I'm just hoping Mogson caught her,' I say hopefully.

'How is Mogson gonna be able to catch her? He's just a small pet, she'd crush him like a pancake,' Rex replies, and I realise that he doesn't know about the whole dragon business. Still, I'm relieved that he knows what a pancake is.

'You'll see,' I say, then begin to jog with Rex back through the cave.

CHAPTER 24

The Great Escape

We make our way to the exit through the meandering tunnels of the cave to the entrance. Rex seems to know the route perfectly as if he's etched it into his mind; he must have been here tonnes of times. The light makes me squint harshly with the transition from dark to brightness and my arm covers my eyes before I can check on the status of the forcefield. After giving them time to adjust, a deep breath leaves my body as I notice that the forcefield is still intact.

Rex and I peer over the ledge like Olympic divers to examine the city below. Smoke clouds still cover the surface meaning it's impossible to tell whether there's been any zombies running around murdering people or not.

'You know any spells that can make us float down?' I ask.

'Na. I've got a better idea. You like slides?' he asks with a mischievous look on his face.

'Slides?' I ask. Is he talking about the same thing I think he is, or is a slide a completely different thing out here?

Rex takes his cigar-wand out of his suit pocket, takes a pull on it, and exhales a cloud of smoke which gives out small sparks like fireworks that pop in front of his face. With his wand then held out in front of him, he says, '*Salvo Glacier.*' A continuous beam of ice ejects from his wand and his hands swirl and swoosh to create a maelstrom of icy blue matter. His hand moves in all directions with intense concentration as he forms a swirling slide that looks like the biggest helter-skelter I've ever seen. I can't even see the bottom seeing as it's a mile down to the ground.

'Wanna go first?' Rex asks me. 'Love a good slide me.' Rex then pulls his jacket sleeves up to his elbows and gets himself ready to jog as I watch in fascination at what he just did. 'Fine then, if you're not gonna answer I'm going first, your loss,' he shrugs. He runs towards the icy slide and launches himself forward head-first to fly down the slide rapidly like an excited child. This guy is something else, he's like a child stuck in a grown-up's body. His exuberant, exhilarated, enigmatic screams echo through the air to eloquently entice my eagerness.

Do I have a choice but to follow him? I'm terrified at the thought of going down a mile-long slide, but thinking there's a bigger picture here, I copy Rex and take the leap of faith; either way I'm going down, might as well get on now rather than wait.

The slide twists and turns for what feels like an hour and a nauseous feeling begins to stir inside me. Every time I reach a bend where it swirls, I feel like I'm going to fly up the sides and be thrown off to splat on the ground. The way he's designed it, with high walls like a toboggan track, makes sure I stay on course.

I try to get a glimpse from the sides down below, checking to see if the zombies have attacked or the forcefield did its job and stayed in place, but the speed I'm travelling keeps my line of sight near enough glued to the sky above. The first clue I get that something's gone horribly wrong, is when I turn a bend, so I'm forced to face right, and I see a dragon flying across the skyline shooting a blaze of fire down below.

Before I'm even aware that I'm close to the ground, I'm thrown off to land on what feels at first like a giant pillow. I struggle with great difficulty as I attempt to make my way off the thing that cushioned my blow. I must look like someone who's trapped behind a car's airbag after it's gone off as I fight with the material to get a foothold. Scrambling across, I fall off the side and land face-first on the ground below. Looking back at what I landed on, I now notice that it was a huge half-inflated bouncy castle.

Rex looks down at me as I lay sprawled across the floor. 'You like bouncy castles?' he asks seriously. 'I couldn't get it fully inflated in time for ya but suppose it's better than smashing into the ground.'

'Not really. I fell off one when I was younger and sprained my arm,' I reply. Rex reaches his hand out and pulls me to my feet.

'Have you got any idea why there's a dragon flying around Macro setting everything on fire? I could swear I never noticed that before,' Rex says as if he's asking me an everyday mundane question.

'That's Mogson, he transmug... transma... he changed into a dragon!' I shout.

'Cool. As long as he knows he can't sit in my lap anymore that's fine by me.'

The forcefield stands proudly in place, but my main worry is how long it was removed for, and how long it was completely faded. How many zombies made their way into the city?

'Where do you think they'll be Rex? Do you all have some meeting place that you go to when it hits the fan?' I ask.

'We usually just go to HQ if there's an issue. Do you know if Caprice escaped by any chance? I've tried calling about a million times but can't get hold of her.'

I've been dreading him asking me this. I think I've just been hoping he wouldn't. Do I play it safe and tell him I don't know, or do I tell him she's dead?

'I don't know mate, we got to HQ and there was nobody there, it was just mountains of rubble,' I say, before my mind can decide what to tell him.

'Okay, how about we try Tutti's house? He's got all his fancy gadgets and things. Maybe he might be able to do something.'

'Good suggestion,' I reply.

We jog through the deserted streets, which are still filled with smoke and debris after the fall of HQ, until evidence of a fight begins to become apparent. There are bodies strewn across the ground, which I can instantly recognise as both dead and zombified. This can't be good.

With my fitness levels being as bad as they are, I do struggle to keep up, but Rex deliberately slows down without letting me know so I can catch up. What I originally thought about this guy is beginning to change. I thought he was a complete nutter at first, but I'm starting to realise that he's just a tad eccentric, but he's a good guy. Does being a bit weird really make a person bad or unlikable?

'His house is only a few minutes away now and I haven't seen any zombies, so I think we should be alright,' Rex assumes.

Maybe Tutti managed to get enough people together to fight them off, or maybe the forcefield only disappeared for a short time and not that many got through. Something inside tells me Lara is okay, I'm not sure what it is, just one of those feelings you get in your gut that reassures you that everything's fine. If anything happened to her, I don't know what I do as I've previously proven to myself.

As we near Tutti's house, so do loud noises of obvious battle. The groaning of the zombies is mixed with the screams of living people. Upon turning a corner next to a gigantic building, thousands of zombies can be seen trying to breach one specific building. Not just any building, the building with Tutti's house on top.

'Holy hell, would you look at how many there are; it looks like closing time at the Galactica,' Rex says, looking a tad concerned.

I've seen this so many times in zombie movies on TV when the good guys are trapped, and the hordes gather around their location to try and break through and eat their brains. It usually ends with either the good guys disguising themselves as zombies and walking through the mob so they can't be detected, or something else ends up distracting them so the horde turn away and decide to chase something else. Somehow, I doubt that either of these options are possible as this isn't a TV show or a movie; this is reality.

'Why are they all gathered around Tutti's building, what's so special about it?' I ask Rex.

'Dunno. What if whoever is in there are the only people left in the city and they're trying to have them for dessert?' he replies.

Something doesn't seem right about this. I'm not even sure what these zombies are, but why would they all be trying to get into Tutti's place? Does he have a magic wand in there that can turn them all back to normal? Maybe he knows a cure for it and they're all trying to get in to get the information from him. Who knows? I just know that there's a high possibility that Lara's in there with Tutti and we're probably going to have to fight our way through.

'Hey, maybe we can act like zombies and walk through them,' Rex says as he rubs his chin searching his brain for ideas.

'I'd rather die before I stoop that low Rex,' I reply, clearly offended by the idea.

We stand still staring at the thousands of zombies and try to think of a way to bypass them or annihilate them. It's as if all our prayers are answered when Mogson swoops around a building and starts igniting the poor beings with jets of flames and fireballs. At one point he actually lands on a roof, rips a stone gargoyle from the decoration, and launches it down at the crowd.

'Let's not just stand here watching, let's give him a hand,' I suggest. These words send shivers down my spine at the realisation of how much I've evolved through this ordeal. I've only been aware of this existence for less than a week, and I've found a bravery and gall which I never knew I had. Deep down inside, I wasn't the coward I always thought I was. I've found that I'm not scared of death anymore and I'll fight tooth and nail to protect both Lara and me and these fascinating people around us. Even when Katarina was asking me to give my life for the rest of Macro and I agreed, there's no way in the past I would have been brave enough to make a stand like that; I'd have cowered and ran away. The first time I noticed myself making a stand against anyone was back at the police station when Wainwright was trying to interrogate me and send me to a mental facility. I suppose injustice and unfairness have made me realise that bad things only really happen to good people: i.e. me. What's the point of letting people walk all over you when you haven't done anything wrong in the first place? Alright, I locked a woman in a storage cupboard in the hospital and broke a couple of traffic laws, stole a granny's car, and fled from the police, but there was no malice involved.

We charge into the crowd with screams of fury and rage. Spells blast from our wands at a distance in order to either draw them away from the people that are making a stand or diminish their numbers.

I've never seen Rex cast spells except for when he's doing something other than fighting; he's unreal. As he advances forward, he pulls out another wand and uses two simultaneously to cast multiple spells each second. With a cigar in one hand blasting away, and some sort of flute in the other, the spells diminish the crowds rapidly. At one point, he puts the two wands together in his right hand and casts some kind of super spell, but it's all happening so fast I can't pick up a word of what he's saying. No wonder the Xanarock was so safe and nobody's ever succeeded in taking it with this guy around.

The zombies gain ground as he walks forward firing all sorts of spells rapidly. What is he doing? He's going too deep into the crowd and he's going to be surrounded within seconds.

'Run now, get up to Tutti's flat, see who's up there!' Rex bawls as they begin to gain even more ground on him. He then takes his sunglasses out of his pocket and puts them over his eyes.

'No!' I scream in a frenzied and confused rage. 'Just turn and run away, we can retreat and come back for a second attack!'

'That's not my style, trust me, just run and I'll take care of these!' he screams furiously. They're within feet of him now.

Suddenly, I have a brainwave. They're rare and not usually useful, but I do have them sometimes. I try to recall the defensive spell Lara cast on me that made me immune to being hit. Maybe if I can cast it on Rex, they won't be able to attack him and he can get away unscathed. Wasn't it one of those *fortify* spells? I can't remember for the life of me.

'Rex, what's that *fortify* spell that shields you?!' I shout over as he makes one of the zombie's heads explode with a spell I can't make out because of the sound of groans and bodies hitting the floor.

'Good idea!' he calls. Rex turns one of the wands on himself and shouts, '*Fortify Somatic,*' which changes his aura and gives him an invulnerable glow.

I fire spells at the crowd, not wanting to leave Rex on his own, but there's not much point really; Rex is probably annihilating twenty of them for each one I'm killing.

'Just go you idiot!' he exclaims, refusing to take his eye off his targets.

Without hesitation, I run towards the building as every one of the zombies are busy either dying or trying to lunge at Rex. Mogson continues to rain hell on them from above and my body sticks close to the walls so that I don't get caught in the crossfire.

There are so many corpses scattered across the ground that I need to literally climb over them to reach the front doors to the building. The door is completely barricaded as there's some kind of spell obstructing the way in. An ethereal barrier of glowing white blocks the entrance. There's no way I'm going to be able to get inside without finding another entrance. This must be the work of whoever is in there; it's got to be Tutti and Lara trying to keep them out.

How did we get in the first time I went to his house? Of course, through the sewers!

My head pans around the street looking for one of those circular grates in the asphalt that I can climb down and make my way in through the cellar. With so many bodies lying around, it's hard to make out where it could even be and eventually, I spot one, right in the middle of the street. Glancing back to where Rex was further down the road, it's impossible to make out what's happening as there are thousands of figures massed together, and for all I know he could be dead.

My attempt to lift the grate is feeble at most and it doesn't so much as budge when I yank on the handle. I point my wand at it and use the *Salvo Flare* spell, but it doesn't have any effect. If I can find a tool to use to loop through the handle and pull it up, I should be able to get a good enough grip with just my hands. Nothing seems useable, but maybe I can just tie something through it and pull it up. Approaching one of the nearby corpses, I remove their belt, slot it through the hoop, fasten it as tight as I can, and then with all my strength, wrench the grate open.

To my surprise, once it's opened, every single pair of undead eyes on the whole street stop what they're doing and turn in my direction in one spine-chilling motion; it's as if they've realised that there's a way into the building that isn't the front door.

'See ya suckers!' I shout, and then wish I were dead because I made myself cringe with the cheesy remark.

Jumping down into the sewer, not waiting to see if they head my way, I plunge into the darkness with a soft landing into the foot-high water below. Using the *Nova Guide* spell, I summon a light to guide me through the tunnel towards the entrance to the cellar. To my knowledge these zombies don't use spells so, hopefully, they can't see a thing down here. The journey up to the roof is arduous and tiresome without the elevator in working condition, but eventually, I get to the top unscathed. Everything seems to be as it was when I was last here; at least it seems that way from the outside. Entering the building, I'm completely gobsmacked by what I walk into.

'Okay, this was the last thing I expected, what the hell's going on, where are the others?' I ask the old lady in front of me, more confused than ever.

'My master has chosen me now that Katarina has gone. He has requested that I collect his wand. Thank you very much,' she says, then reaches at my trouser pocket to take the Banishing Wand.

'Doris, what are you talking about? How come you're not cursed anymore?' I exclaim, slapping her hand away from getting anywhere near the wand.

'My master was biding his time. He kept me dormant under his curse. Now she's gone, he has awoken me!' she says with a harrowing announcement, then gives me a stern, eerie glance as she reaches for the wand once again.

I've never hit a woman, never mind an old woman, but I suppose you can't really class her as a woman if she's being controlled by something evil. My fist shoots up to connect with her wrinkly old face and she staggers backwards towards the wall with the wand in her grasp, knocking books from the shelves on her way down. If she had any real teeth, they'd probably be flying across the room.

I lunge forward to pounce on her with a rage that she's just awoken inside me, but before I can reach her, as I'm flying through mid-air, she's too quick for me. Her body spins around with speed that should be way too fast for an old lady. Her wrist flips towards me with the Banishing Wand in hand and a spell bursts its way towards me as she shouts *Diruo Eternal* at the top of her lungs.

A bubble becomes visible around me as I float in mid-air suspended by an invisible force. I can see outside the bubble, but it's as if time has come to a complete standstill outside. A boom and a flash give me a quick reminder of what this wand is capable of. My reality seems to vanish from existence as the flash ends my life as I know it. My last thought before the eternal blackness is a proudness that I went out fighting. I'd rather have gone through all this and died at twenty-nine than lived to ninety back on Earth; what a ride it's been. I can only hope and pray to whatever supernatural force is out there, that I just end up as a nice person when I wake up on Earth. Even though I won't remember any of this, I don't suit being an idiot.

CHAPTER 25

Aftermath

My senses kick into action abruptly. My first breath is a gasp, followed by rhythmic, fast, puffs. My first conscious thought arrives in my mind, but it's hard to decipher its meaning.

Where am I? Who am I? I know I live on a planet called Earth, and I know I'm a human being. I know I'm lying in a hospital of some sort because I remember what a hospital is. Was I in some sort of accident? Have I been in a coma? Nothing relevant seems to come to mind; absolutely nothing. I'm struggling to even recall my own name.

My hand reaches for my head as the pain sears from one side to the other. My whole body is aching tremendously from head to toe.

Using every ounce of energy that my body will permit, I lift my head and look around the small private room. A small window looks out at a single, swaying tree on the opposite side. A singular birch-coloured door stands against the opposite wall.

I reach for the small plastic cup beside a jug of water on the side table, pour the water in, and gulp it down as if I haven't had a drink for weeks. Maybe I haven't had a drink in weeks; I could have been in a coma for ten years for all I know. I take another drink of water and place the cup back on the side table.

Why is everything so blurry? Do I wear glasses and I've lost them? My hands pat the surface of the bed, but there are no glasses here. What if I've been in an accident and it's damaged my eyesight? There doesn't seem to be an emergency button to call the nurses on the wall.

'Hello!' I call, but my shout falls upon deaf ears.

'Anyone there?!' I yell, but once again, there's no response.

I lie still for the next few minutes: not by choice, but because all my energy has been sapped from me. A noise from outside makes me hold my breath to ensure I definitely did hear something, and it wasn't me just imagining the whole thing. Another noise, but closer this time. The noises get nearer until the door swings open rapidly. A beautiful woman and a small man who looks a bit mole-like enter the room and look delighted to see me. They must know who I am!

'Do you know who I am?' I ask urgently.

The beautiful woman laughs, and the man just fiddles with his whiskers. Why does he have whiskers? Is it possible that everything I know about Earth is just made up in my head and I'm actually not from there? What if Earth is just something I've dreamt about and it's not even real.

'We've been looking for you for weeks! We've had to process some pretty difficult calculations to find out where you are, but eventually we found you. I'll have to thank Gregory for tipping us off on how to find someone who has been banished when I see him,' the lady says. 'It's crazy seeing you looking completely different, but we might be able to fix that.'

The man reaches into one of his pockets and hands me a small mirror. I examine myself, smiling and frowning and brushing my hair to the side. I'm not even sure if I look like me, because I'm not sure who I am. I do know that I've got long ginger hair, hundreds of freckles, teeth that look too large for my mouth, and piercing green eyes. It could be worse I suppose. I don't think I'm ugly by any means; I could live with this.

'So who am I?' I ask the pair.

'Your name's Tristan. You saved an entire solar system with bravery and courage that I didn't even think were possible. Not only that, you're also the love of my life,' the lady says, holding my hand with a stern grip.

Is she joking with me? This must be a prank. No way could I pull a woman like that.

'Come on then, let's get up, we've got a universe to save,' she says, grinning from ear to ear as she pulls at my hand to get me out of the bed.

Future works

The next novel in the Astral Revelations series is The Chrono-Trigger where we can dig deeper into the universe and get to expand on the current story so far. I can promise that any future works will live up to expectations and the content will only get more interesting and entertaining.

Printed in Great Britain
by Amazon